WESTERN

Rugged men looking for love...

The Maverick Makes The Grade
Stella Bagwell

The Heart Of A Rancher
Trish Milburn

T0362985

MILLS & BOON

Stella Bagwell is acknowledged as the author of this work
THE MAVERICK MAKES THE GRADE
© 2024 by Harlequin Enterprises ULC
Philippine Copyright 2024
Australian Copyright 2024
New Zealand Copyright 2024

First Published 2024
First Australian Paperback Edition 2024
ISBN 978 1 038 91777 5

THE HEART OF A RANCHER
© 2024 by Trish Milburn
Philippine Copyright 2024
Australian Copyright 2024
New Zealand Copyright 2024

First Published 2024
First Australian Paperback Edition 2024
ISBN 978 1 038 91777 5

This is a work of fiction. Names, characters, places, and incidents are either the
product of the author's imagination or are used fictitiously, and any resemblance to
actual persons, living or dead, business establishments, events, or locales is entirely
coincidental.

MIX
Paper | Supporting
responsible forestry
FSC® C001695

Published by
Harlequin Mills & Boon
An imprint of Harlequin Enterprises (Australia) Pty Limited
(ABN 47 001 180 918), a subsidiary of HarperCollins
Publishers Australia Pty Limited
(ABN 36 009 913 517)
Level 19, 201 Elizabeth Street
SYDNEY NSW 2000 AUSTRALIA

Cover art used by arrangement with Harlequin Books S.A.. All rights reserved.

Printed and bound in Australia by McPherson's Printing Group

The Maverick Makes The Grade
Stella Bagwell

MILLS & BOON

Dear Reader,

Fall is coming to Bronco, Montana. Leaves are beginning to turn red and gold, fireplaces are crackling and, even better, school is starting. And that makes Stacy Abernathy declare fall her favourite time of the year. As a teacher at Bronco Elementary School, she's eager to get back into the classroom after the long summer break. Dealing with her little students doesn't give her time to dwell on the fact that she's still single with not even one steady boyfriend to call her own.

Widower Win Jackson has moved himself and his two sons, Joshua and Oliver, to Bronco to start a new life. With his sons to raise, a ranch to build and his job as the new agribusiness teacher at Bronco High School, Win is a busy man. He doesn't need or want a relationship. And he certainly doesn't need his talkative young son trying to hook him up with a pretty blonde teacher. But after Win takes one look at Stacy, he can't forget her. And soon he begins to wonder if a man can truly love again.

It's always such fun for me to visit the world of the Montana Mavericks, and I hope you enjoy strolling the streets of Bronco again and reading how two lonely teachers finally realise that together they make the perfect family.

Stella Bagwell

DEDICATION

To all the wonderful teachers who dedicate their lives
to helping young students be the best they can be.

CHAPTER ONE

STACY ABERNATHY WAS pinning red and gold paper leaves to the edge of a bulletin board when a movement beyond the open door of her classroom caught the corner of her eye. The last bell of the school day had rung a while ago and the students had already exited the Bronco Elementary School building, so when she looked over her shoulder for a closer look, she expected to see a janitor or a fellow teacher. Instead, she spotted a fairly tall boy with a shock of dark blond hair and an olive-green pack resting against his back. He was clearly too old for her second-grade class, which would make him a student in Dante Sanchez's third-grade group or Reginald Porter's fourth-grade class.

Placing the remaining decorations aside, Stacy walked over to where the boy continued to stand just beyond the doorway.

"Hi!" he greeted her. "Are you a teacher?"

"I'm Ms. Abernathy," she informed him. "What's your name?"

"I'm Oliver Jackson," he said with a grin. "I'm in fourth grade. Mr. Porter is my teacher."

He was a cute kid, Stacy thought, with long, lanky limbs and bangs that fell over one eye. A spattering of freckles dotted the bridge of his nose while dimples dented both rounded cheeks. Because the school wasn't all that large, she usually recognized all the students and could call them by name. This one was obviously a newcomer and with school only having started a few days ago, she'd not had a chance to acquaint herself with the new students.

"I see. So have you lost your way around the building?" she asked then gestured down the empty corridor. "The exit door to the parking area is at the opposite end of this hallway and around the corner."

Shaking his head, he gave her another confident grin. "I'm not lost. I'm waiting on my dad and brother to come pick me up."

Stacy discreetly glanced at the watch on her wrist. Apparently, something had happened to cause the child's father to be late.

"Your father must be running late. Everyone will be leaving the building pretty soon and I wouldn't want you to have to stand outside alone," she told him.

The boy didn't appear to be the least bit concerned over the prospect.

He said, "Oh, it's not unusual for Dad to be late. See, he's the new agribusiness teacher at Bronco High School and that makes him super busy. 'Cause ag teachers have all kinds of extra things they gotta do. He'll be here any minute. I'm not worried."

She'd not heard about the school district hiring a new agribusiness teacher. But that was hardly surprising. With Stacy working at the elementary school there were plenty of matters regarding the high school that she never heard about.

"Most teachers are very busy and I'm sure your father has plenty to do," she replied while wondering about Oliver's mother. Apparently, the woman's schedule made it impossible for her to pick up her son from school.

"My dad's name is Winston Jackson, but everybody calls him Win. And my brother's name is Joshua. He's fifteen and in ninth grade." A smirk twisted his young features. "Joshua thinks he's cool now because he's in high school. But I can't see he's any different than he was this summer."

Stacy kept her smile to herself. She knew firsthand what it was like to have older siblings. Being petite in stature and the baby of the family, she'd often been referred to as the runt. Most of the time the teasing hadn't bothered her, but there had been occasions it had hurt.

"You know something, Oliver? Being a fourth grader is just as important as being a ninth grader. I imagine you're about ten now. Right?"

Clearly impressed that she'd guessed his age, he said, "Yeah. How did you know?"

"Well, usually fourth graders are ten or somewhere close to it," she explained.

He shifted his weight from one foot to the other and Stacy noticed the boy was wearing a pair of brown cowboy boots. The heels were the Western-slanted kind and the snub toes were scuffed. Oliver clearly wasn't the athletic shoe type, she mused silently.

"Are you married?" he asked frankly.

Accustomed to young children asking personal questions, she gave him an indulgent smile. "No. I'm single."

Surprise widened his green eyes. "What about kids? I bet you have kids."

"I don't have children of my own, but I consider my students as my children," she told him.

"That's not the same," he pointed out then swiped at the hank of hair pestering his eye. "My mother died when I was only three. I don't remember her. But I've seen pictures of her."

Several scenarios had already gone through Stacy's head about the mother of the Jackson family, but none had included the woman being deceased. The information caught her completely off guard. "I'm very sorry to hear that, Oliver. Then it's only you and your brother and father living at home?"

"Yeah. Just us three," he answered and then promptly asked, "Do you have a mother and dad?"

"Yes. They own the Bonnie B Ranch. That's where I live—on the ranch in a cabin of my own."

The word *ranch* caused his eyes to suddenly sparkle. "I live on a ranch, too! Dad's named it the J Barb. He bought the place when we moved here a few months back. It's not all built yet, but it's gonna be good. We already have cattle and horses. But Dad is planning on buying lots more. He says you gotta have plenty of livestock to make money."

So apparently the Jackson family hadn't always lived in the Bronco area, she thought. But investing in ranching property implied the new agribusiness teacher was planning on staying permanently.

"That's true," she said, asking, "Do you like living on a ranch?"

A look of comical confusion swept over his face. "Gee, doesn't everybody? It's great. We've always lived on a ranch. Living in town wouldn't be fun. Back in Whitehorn, I had friends who lived in town and they had to follow rules that were just awful. When we played in the yard we couldn't yell 'cause the neighbor didn't like kids yelling. And they couldn't let their dogs out of the backyard. That was sad. 'Cause dogs like to run and explore."

"Town life is different," she agreed. "But not everyone is fortunate enough to live on a ranch."

"That's what Dad says. And he says land costs too darn much. That's why we have to take care of it."

Sounded as though Winston Jackson was teaching his boys to be good stewards of the land, she reasoned. That meant he was probably a wonderful agriculture teacher.

Oliver glanced down the hallway at the same time Stacy caught the sound of footsteps thumping against the tiled floor.

She followed the boy's gaze and instantly caught sight of a tall man wearing a gray cowboy hat and black boots. His long legs were taking purposeful strides straight toward them and just as Stacy was thinking he had to be Winston Jackson, Oliver declared, "There's Dad! Come on, Ms. Abernathy! I want you to meet him!"

Oliver scurried off and, not wanting to appear unfriendly, Stacy followed at a sedate pace until the three of them met in the middle of the wide corridor.

Standing proudly at his father's side, Oliver quickly made introductions. "Dad, this is Ms. Abernathy. She teaches second grade. We've been ranch talking. She lives on a ranch, too. The Bonnie B."

The moment Oliver's father had walked up to them, Stacy had felt herself gawking at the man and now, as he extended his hand to greet her, she felt a wash of heat sting her cheeks.

"Nice to meet you, Ms. Abernathy. I'm Winston Jackson—just call me Win. I hope Oliver hasn't been talking your ear off. In case you haven't already guessed, talking is his best subject."

The man was a dream in the form of a cowboy. Well over six feet with broad, muscular shoulders and dirty-blond hair that waved around his ears and slightly onto the back of his neck. He was wearing dark trousers, a pale blue Western shirt and a bolo tie with a slide fashioned from a malachite stone. The green color matched his eyes, she thought and then immediately wondered why in the world she'd be noticing something so insignificant about Win Jackson.

"It's nice to meet you, Win. And please, call me Stacy—everyone does—except for the students, of course."

Those deep green eyes met hers and Stacy felt certain her heart skipped a beat or two. The strong reaction caught her by surprise. She was accustomed to seeing good-looking cowboys around town. After all, Bronco was full of them. But she'd never met one that struck her as hard as this one. Or could it be her erratic pulse was simply trying to tell her she'd gone without a date for far too long?

Thankfully, Oliver suddenly spoke up and interrupted her silly thoughts.

"Aww, shoot. Guess that means I have to keep calling you Ms. Abernathy," he said.

Stacy gave the boy an indulgent smile. "I'm afraid so, Oliver. If the other students heard you calling me Stacy, it would cause problems. Because here at school I'm Ms. Abernathy, the teacher. Do you understand?"

She looked over to see Win was running a quick gaze over her face and Stacy decided it wasn't the sort of look a man gave a woman when he was romantically interested. Instead, he appeared to be summing her up as a teacher and nothing more.

"Since I'm a teacher, Oliver gets to thinking he can get personal with other teachers. I'll make sure he remembers you're Ms. Abernathy," he said.

"I won't forget and slip," Oliver told her, then looked up at his father and added, "Ms. Abernathy isn't married. She doesn't have any kids, either."

Win scowled at his son. "Oliver, how many times have I told you not to be asking people personal questions? All of those things are Ms. Abernathy's private business, not yours."

Seeing a dejected look come over the boy's face, Stacy quickly spoke up with a little laugh, "Oh, it's okay, Win.

I've lived in Bronco all my life. Everyone around here knows everything there is to know about me. Half of them could probably tell you what I ate for lunch."

Her attempt to joke didn't produce a chuckle from Win, but it did put a faint smile on his face.

"Thanks for being understanding about my son's nosiness," he said.

A nervous tickle suddenly struck her throat but she refused to clear it away. The last thing she wanted was for this rugged man to get the idea he was making her feel like an awkward teenaged girl.

"Oliver tells me you're teaching agribusiness at the high school. How's your new job going for you?" she asked politely.

"I've taught agribusiness for sixteen years; it's old hat with me. But being at Bronco High School is a new experience. So far, I've not had any problems. Most of the students are obedient and attentive and the school administration has been great."

It was sinful for a man to look as good as him, Stacy thought. He probably had a list of girlfriends as long as his arm.

Pushing that thought aside, she said, "Well, I hope you enjoy living in Bronco, Win. Naturally, I'm biased, but it truly is a great town."

"It's beginning to feel like home to the boys and me," he said, placing a big hand on Oliver's shoulder. "Come along, son. Joshua is waiting and we have lots of chores to do before supper."

Oliver gave her a little wave. "Bye, Ms. Abernathy. Maybe I'll see you here in the hallway tomorrow."

Stacy gave the boy a nod. "You certainly might."

"Good meeting you." Win tossed the pleasantry at her before hurriedly bustling Oliver down the hallway.

Stacy watched the father and son until they reached the end of the corridor and disappeared around the corner. As she turned to walk back to her room, she couldn't help thinking Win Jackson was certainly a hot hunk of cowboy, but he hadn't seemed overly sociable.

And why would he be extra sociable with you, Stacy? You're not exactly a glamour girl and, from the looks of the man, he can have his pick of women.

The mocking voice bouncing around in her head was suddenly interrupted by two female voices directly behind her. Turning, she saw Emma Garner, the first-grade teacher and teacher's aide, Carrie Waters.

"Stacy! Who the heck was that?" Emma asked.

"I think I need to turn on the air conditioner!" Carrie exclaimed as she used one hand to fan her face. "It's way too hot in here!"

Trying her best to appear cool and casual, Stacy said, "That was Win Jackson. He's the new agribusiness teacher over at Bronco High."

Carrie, a redhead who was all for having a night of fun, released a wistful sigh. "Oh my. He's a dream in cowboy boots! But I'll bet he's married. The ones who look that good always are."

Emma rolled her eyes. "The ones who look that good are always trouble—whether they're married or not."

Stacy said, "Win is a widower. That was his son, Oliver, with him. He also has an older son in high school."

"A widower," Carrie repeated soberly. "That's terrible. Those poor boys."

"I'd say poor Win, too," Emma added thoughtfully. "To be a widower so young—I can't imagine going through that kind of pain."

"I can't imagine it, either," Stacy replied. "Losing his wife and the mother of his children had to be heartbreaking."

"Wonder how long he's been a widower?" Carrie thoughtfully voiced the question then looked to Stacy for an answer.

Stacy's first instinct was to tell Carrie she had no idea how long it had been since Mrs. Jackson had passed away. The information was Win's personal and private business. On the other hand, it was hardly a secret. Not with a talkative son like Oliver.

"From what Oliver told me, his mother has been gone seven years. Since he was three years old. He says he doesn't remember her."

"Heartbreaking," Emma murmured. "I wonder if Mr. Jackson ever thinks his boys might need a mother in their lives?"

Stacy had been wondering the same thing, but she wasn't going to admit it to her coworkers. Both women were often suggesting that she needed to date more. She didn't want either of them to latch onto the idea that she might be interested in Win Jackson.

"Possibly," she answered Emma's question. "But he's been single for a long time. It doesn't look like he wants another wife or a stepmother for his sons."

"What a waste," Carrie replied.

"Everyone deals with loss differently," Emma said with a rueful grimace. "And some people only have it in them to love once in a lifetime."

Was Win Jackson in that category? Stacy wondered. Had he already used up all his romantic love on his late wife? The idea was disturbing. She would think a man like him would be full of needs and passion. But then, what did she know about a hot romance? Her limited encounters with men could be labeled lukewarm to cold, she rationalized ruefully.

Deciding it was time to change the subject, Stacy pointedly checked her watch. "Oh my, it's getting late. I need to collect my things and head home."

Minutes later, as Stacy drove away from the school parking lot and steered her little sedan in the direction of the Bonnie B, she tried not to think about Win Jackson. She even turned up the radio volume in hopes the blasting music would push his image from her mind. But it didn't work. She kept seeing his rugged features with his faint crook of a smile and the calloused feel of his big hand as it had wrapped around hers. Oh, he was all man and then some. Just looking at him had filled her stomach with butterflies.

Yet the image of his sexy good looks wasn't the only thing about Win going through her mind. She kept picturing him and his boys going home to an empty house, with only the three of them sharing dinner. In comparison, it almost made her feel guilty to be heading home to eat dinner with her parents and most likely a sibling or two.

But did that make her more fortunate than Win? At least, he'd been deeply in love once. He'd experienced marriage and, most of all, he had two sons. She didn't even have a steady boyfriend. Maybe she should worry about her own love life instead of Win Jackson's.

Two days later, Win stood in front of his desk as he presented questions to the class of twenty-two sophomores. It was the last hour of the school day and usually by now most of the students were too busy thinking about the bell ringing and what they were planning to do later that night than to focus on learning. That often created a challenge for Win to hold their attention throughout the hour. But this particular group was actually showing interest and he was making the most of the last few minutes.

"Okay, here is your next question. If a cattle rancher

is hit by a drought that wipes out his hay crop, would it be more profitable for him to sell his herd and wait for his hay meadows to grow again before he restocks, or to purchase high-priced hay from another source and try to hang on to his cattle?"

Sitting at the back of the room, a girl with short brown hair was the first to thrust her arm in the air.

Win quickly acknowledged her. "Okay, Bethann, tell us how you'd handle this situation in the most profitable way."

The girl said, "Well, Mr. Jackson, the answer will depend on the market price for cattle at the time of the drought. If the market is flooded and the rancher takes a huge loss at the sale barn, then purchasing the high-priced hay would be the best way to go. That's the way I see it."

"You are correct," Win told her. "It all comes down to market prices. Not only for the cattle but also for the hay."

A tall blond boy seated two desks away from Bethann let out a loud groan. "Aww, Bethann knew the answer 'cause her dad works on a ranch. How's the rest of us supposed to know these things?"

"I knew the answer because I use my brain to think, Ralphy," Bethann shot back at her classmate.

Win held up his hand to ward off the chuckles erupting around the room. "The answers were all right there in the two chapters you were assigned to read last night," Win told the boy. "You don't have to have a friend or relative in the ranching business to learn about ranch management. That's why I'm here. To teach you."

"Yes, sir," Ralphy meekly replied. "I understand."

Win glanced down at the notes he was holding, but not before he saw Ralphy send Bethann a sheepish grin that turned her cheeks a shade of pink. The exchange had Win remembering his days in high school and the juvenile attempts he'd made at flirting with the girls. That time in his life was long past and since Yvette's death, he'd had no desire to flirt with any woman.

Until last night, he reminded himself. Until he'd walked upon Stacy Abernathy.

Nearly two days had passed since he'd met the second-grade teacher, yet her image was still far too fresh in his mind. Sparkling blue eyes, smooth ivory skin surrounded by golden-blond hair, lips the color of crushed strawberries. She'd been lovely and, for the first time in a long time, he'd noticed.

Damn it! He wasn't in the market for romance. Other than her being pretty, he didn't know why he was still thinking about the woman. Hadn't he learned his lesson back in Whitehorn?

Purposely shaking that mocking question aside, he focused on the notes in his hand and was about to present another question to the class when the loud buzz of the bell interrupted his plans and he quickly dismissed the class.

As the students gathered up books and supplies and hurriedly filed out of the room, Win rounded his desk and began shoving a stack of test papers to be graded into a brown canvas duffel bag.

"Hey, Win. You haven't forgotten about the meeting tonight, have you?"

Win glanced over at the open doorway to see Anthony Landers, Bronco High's phys ed teacher and baseball coach. In his late twenties, with a head full of curly black hair and a constant grin, he was a likable guy, plus a hard worker. He had quickly grown into Win's best friend in Bronco.

"Meeting? I guess I have. What sort of meeting?"

Entering the room Anthony pulled a folded paper from his back pocket and handed it to Win. "Didn't you get an email about the meeting? I made a print of mine."

Win quickly scanned the message then cursed under his breath. The meeting started at six tonight. That would hardly give him enough time to collect the boys, drive out to the J Barb, do the evening chores and then drive back into Bronco.

Handing the note back to Anthony, he shook his head. "If I did, I don't remember it. Now I've got to figure out what to do with the boys while I'm at the meeting."

"Oh, that's easy enough. I'm leaving the gym open so any of the teachers' kids can play basketball or volleyball while we're at the meeting."

Win let out a mocking laugh. "And who's going to keep the kids from cutting the nets off the goals or scarring up the floor with hard shoes? Teachers' kids aren't always angels, you know. My two boys included."

Anthony laughed. "Your boys are well mannered. No worries, though. A couple of teacher's aides have volunteered to oversee things until the meeting is finished."

"Thanks for letting me know, Anthony. I'll send the boys to the gym. Do you have any idea how long these meetings last?"

"Usually not more than an hour or so. Just long enough to make you good and starved by the time you get home."

"Yeah," Win said wryly. "Joshua and Oliver will be complaining that they're about to collapse from starvation."

Anthony chuckled. "You'd probably have time to take them out for a quick bite to eat before the meeting. I'd go with you, but I have some extra things to do in the gym."

Win shook his head. "I let them eat fast food last night. I don't want them to have it two nights in a row."

"Oh, to be a father. I'm glad I'm not there yet," Anthony joked before turning to start out of the room. "I'll see you at the meeting."

The young man was about to disappear through the door when Win called to him. "Do you have another minute, Anthony?"

"Sure. You need a favor?"

Win walked over to where the other man stood. "Thanks, but no. I just have a question for you. Are you acquainted with the Abernathy family?"

Anthony chuckled. "That's a mighty broad question, Win. The Abernathys are one of the oldest and richest families in the area. There are dozens of them around here, but I'm only slightly acquainted with them. They're sort of out of my league, if you get my drift."

"You mean because they're rich? Are they snobby?" Win arched a brow at him while thinking Stacy Abernathy hardly came across as a woman with her nose stuck up in the air.

"Not the ones I've been around. Actually they're all pretty down to earth. But—" He paused and shrugged. "I guess being around wealth reminds me of my own meager bank account. Anyway, why are you asking about the Abernathys? Do you have one as a student?"

Win felt like an idiot. "No. I met a teacher over at Oliver's school by the name of Stacy Abernathy. I was just wondering about her—'cause Oliver seems to be overly taken with her."

Anthony frowned thoughtfully then nodded. "Yeah. I've seen her at a few school events. She's from the Bonnie B bunch of Abernathys. The youngest of the family, I think. She always came across as the quiet type to me. But then, I only know her casually. Mostly through school events. I'm more acquainted with her brothers since I run into them at Doug's bar and other places around town. They're all good guys."

It didn't sound as though the Abernathys put themselves

above everyone else. But that didn't mean he should be daydreaming about the pretty blonde teacher, Win told himself. "Well, you know Oliver, he can make anyone talk," he said jokingly.

"Uh, is Oliver in Stacy's class this school year?"

Win glanced over to see Anthony eyeing him with a curious look. "No. She teaches second grade."

"Oh. Well, Oliver probably won't have much contact with her then," Anthony replied. "If that's what's worrying you—him getting too attached to a teacher as a mother figure."

Grimacing, Win turned toward his desk and picked up his duffel bag. Oliver often asked if he'd ever have a mother, and Joshua, when he wasn't trying to be cool, admitted he missed his mother and wished she was with them. Win understood it was a tough situation for both boys, but he couldn't bring Yvette back. And he sure as heck wasn't going to marry just to give his sons a stepmom.

Holding back a heavy sigh, Win said, "I'm not worried. But sometimes I wish he'd be more like Joshua."

"And steer clear of females completely?" Anthony asked then laughed. "Sorry, Win. But I figure both your boys will make the most of their dating years."

Win groaned at the thought. "You're probably right. I might as well get ready for my sons to have their hearts broken a few times."

"It's a part of a young man's growing pains," Anthony replied. "At least, that's what my dad always told me."

Yeah, Win thought grimly. A man learned about falling in love. Then he had to learn all about losing it. As far as he was concerned, he'd had all the love lessons he could stand in a lifetime.

"So how does it feel having Joshua in your freshman ag class? I can't imagine having my own child as a student."

Win flashed him a pointed grin. "It's not always easy trying to walk the fine line between teacher and father. But so far things have been going okay," he said, then deliberately glanced at his wristwatch. "We'd better get going."

"Right. Or I'll be late for the meeting."

The two men left the room together and, after parting company in the hallway, Win hurried out to his truck. With any luck, he could get to the elementary school and collect Oliver without running into Ms. Stacy Abernathy a second time.

The pretty blond teacher had made him uncomfortable in a way he'd not felt in years. He didn't need that kind of temptation. Or the reminder that the days of him having a woman in his life were long over.

CHAPTER TWO

AS STACY ENTERED the Bronco High School building and found her way to the conference room, she was feeling a bit of nerves about attending the district meeting. And that was a ridiculous reaction. She'd been to these workshop-type meetings dozens of times. Mostly, she'd ended up being bored with hearing the same old motivational talks about keeping the students focused on their lessons and eager to learn.

But she needed to be honest with herself. Nothing about the meeting was causing her stomach to flutter and her palms to grow damp. What was really on her mind was the idea of seeing Win Jackson again. Would he notice her? And if he did, would he bother to acknowledge her?

Pausing in the hallway, outside the closed door of the conference room, Stacy took a moment to glance down at the brown suede midi skirt and waist-length pumpkin-colored sweater she'd changed into before she'd driven here to the high school. The pieces weren't exactly glamour-girl attire, but if Win did glance her way, he might think she looked nice.

Nice. Is that the best you can do, Stacy? If you want to catch the eye of that hunky cowboy, then you're going to have to do better than nice!

Shaking away the annoying voice in her head, Stacy entered the meeting room to find most of the teachers had arrived, with many of them already taking up seats at the rows of long utility tables. The administrative staff was gathered at a table near the podium at the head of the room. She spotted the principal of Bronco Elementary along with the assistant superintendent, comparing notes, while near the podium an older man was setting up a projector screen.

She was casting her gaze around the room, searching for an empty chair, when she spotted Emma waving to catch her attention. Stacy made her way over to her friend and sank into the folding chair next to her.

Emma leaned her head close to Stacy's and spoke in a lowered voice. "I was beginning to wonder if you were going to get here. It's almost time for the meeting to start."

Stacy blew out a weary breath. "I had to go home to change clothes because my dress got streaked with mud during recess. Seven-year-olds forget about putting dirty hands where they don't belong. Anyway, I think I broke the speed limit on the way back to town. Thankfully, I didn't get pulled over."

"You speeding? I'd never believe you'd do anything that…reckless. Especially for a change of clothes." Emma rolled her eyes and chuckled. "But you do look pretty to-night."

"Thanks. I was afraid you were going to say I look nice."

Emma's brows lifted. "What's wrong with looking nice?"

Because being a step above ordinary would never catch Win Jackson's attention, Stacy thought, immediately wishing she could kick herself. This sudden infatuation she'd developed over a man she'd spoken to for less than three minutes was ridiculous and she needed to stop it. Now!

"Not a thing," Stacy replied. "Nice is better than homely."

Emma grunted with humor. "You, homely? You can be so funny at times, Stacy. And speaking of looking good, I see the hunky ag teacher just walked into the room. Too bad there's not an empty chair at our table. He might've joined us."

"I doubt it." Stacy steeled herself not to turn her head and stare, but found it impossible to keep from slanting a look from the corner of her eye.

Taller than she remembered and dressed in black Western-cut slacks and a gray shirt, Win Jackson carried his black Stetson in one hand as he made his way to a table where several male teachers were seated. He sank into an empty chair next to Anthony Landers and, from the way the two men greeted each other, it was clear they'd become friends. The notion had her wondering who else the man might've made friends with since moving to Bronco. Some of the young female teachers at Bronco High? Or some of the women he'd encountered around town?

Her thoughts about the man were on the verge of spinning out of control when he suddenly looked up and straight at her. He didn't smile or nod or acknowledge her in any way, yet when their gazes clashed, Stacy was certain she'd seen a flash of recognition in his eyes.

"Looks like things are finally going to get started," Emma mumbled under her breath. "It's about time, don't you think?"

Stacy jerked her gaze away from Win Jackson to stare blankly at Emma. "About time? For what?"

Emma rolled her eyes. "Stacy, that hurried trip you made to the Bonnie B to change clothes must have scattered your senses. I'm talking about the meeting getting started. What else?"

Feeling like a complete fool, Stacy blew out a long breath. "Oh—yes. The meeting. Sorry, Emma, my day has been hectic from the moment I got up, and I have a dozen different things on my mind."

Like one tall cowboy with wavy blond hair and green eyes. Right, Stacy?

Thankfully, the mocking voice in Stacy's head was

drowned out as Leonard Mangrum, superintendent of the school district, suddenly spoke into the microphone.

"Good evening, everyone. I'm happy to see all you dedicated teachers here tonight. I hope…"

The rest of the man's words were lost on Stacy as she glanced discreetly over at Win's table. Expecting him to be focused on Leonard, she was shocked to see he was looking straight at her. Again. Was it possible he might be interested? Maybe, just maybe, after the meeting ended, he'd come over to say hello.

AFTER LONG YEARS of teaching, Win would rather count the horn flies on a bull's back than sit through a workshop. But it was a part of the job and, frankly, he loved teaching. The profession was rarely easy, but it was always rewarding to see his students grow into productive adults. Still, he wished tonight he was sitting anywhere but directly across the room from Stacy Abernathy. Fate was definitely trying to tempt or torment him, he lamented. Each time he glanced over at her, he was struck with a strange sense of connection. He barely knew the woman. How could that be?

Win was deep in thought, attempting to answer the self-imposed question when Anthony's elbow gouged into his rib cage.

"Hey, Win. Wake up. The meeting has ended."

Anthony's voice jarred him back to the present and he looked around to see most of the crowd heading toward the door. Embarrassed that he'd been caught daydreaming, he snatched up his hat and crammed it onto his head.

"I knew the meeting was over. I was…thinking about something."

"Ha! Don't try to fool me. You were about to fall asleep."

Relieved that his friend hadn't noticed he was actually woolgathering, he joked, "After that last motivational talk, can you blame me? Come on, let's go see if the gym has been demolished."

Five minutes later, after Win collected Oliver and Joshua from the gymnasium, the three of them walked to the designated teachers section of the parking lot. Win's black four-door truck was parked in the middle of the back row and as soon as it came into view, the boys took off in a trot toward the waiting vehicle.

Win punched the key fob to unlock the doors and by the time he climbed in the driver's seat, the boys were already strapped securely inside their seat belts.

"I'm starving, Dad," Joshua said. "Are we going by the burger place before we go home?"

"No! Let's get fried chicken and gravy!" Oliver spoke up. "We have burgers all the time!"

"That's because burgers are better than chicken," Joshua argued. "Especially with cheese fries."

"Sorry, boys, we're not going to eat fast food tonight." He clicked in his own seat belt before glancing over his shoulder. Both his sons looked disappointed. "I'll fix something when we get home. There's plenty of leftover stew. How does that sound?"

Joshua groaned out a protest while Oliver clapped in agreement.

"I'm all for stew. I like it," he said, leaning forward to be closer to his father's seat. "Dad, did you see Ms. Abernathy at the meeting tonight?"

Win frowned as he stuck the key into the ignition. He should've expected Oliver to question him about the pretty blonde. He'd brought her name up several times in the past couple of days and Win was beginning to wonder if Anthony might've touched on something when he'd suggested Oliver might be getting attached to Stacy as a mother figure.

"Yes," Win answered. "I saw her sitting across the room."

"Gosh, I'll bet she looked pretty," Oliver said in an excited rush. "Did you get to talk to her?"

Win had thought long and hard about talking to her. He'd even considered going over to her after the meeting and inviting her out for a cup of coffee. With the boys accompanying them, it would've been a harmless enough outing. But then he'd remembered how he'd thought one casual outing with Tara wouldn't hurt anything. Instead, she'd turned into a villain from a badly written horror movie.

"No. The meeting was long and everyone was in a rush to leave," Win told him, thinking he wasn't really stretching the truth. Once the workshop had ended, almost everyone in the room had darted toward the exit.

Oliver said, "Well, you should've talked to her, Dad. She's really nice. You'd like her."

From his side of the seat, Joshua let out a derisive snort. "Oliver, you're so goofy. Dad doesn't need a woman. They're nothing but trouble."

Oliver glared at his big brother. "How do you know? You're just a kid like me!"

Win started the engine. "That's enough, boys."

Ignoring his father's warning, Joshua blasted back at his little brother. "I'm not a kid! I'm fifteen!"

"That's still a kid, too! And I know women aren't bad. You're the one who's goofy! You—"

The contentious bickering between the boys was suddenly lost on Win as he started to back out of the parking space and spotted a woman at the far end of the parking lot lifting the hood of her car.

"Oliver? Do you know what kind of car Ms. Abernathy drives? That looks like her over there."

Win's question quickly put a stop to his sons' argument

and Oliver peered out the passenger window to follow his father's gaze.

"Yeah! That's Ms. Abernathy's car. It's little and white. And that's her! She must be having trouble, Dad. You'd better go help her."

Just when he'd been telling himself that he should avoid her and temptation, this happens, he thought wryly.

Reaching for the door latch, he said, "You're right, son. We can't leave Ms. Abernathy stranded."

"Why not?" Joshua mumbled. "The lady must have a cell phone. She can call a garage. And I'm hungry."

Win slanted his son a look of warning. "Right now, I'm going to pretend I didn't hear you say what you just said. But when we get home, you and I are going to have a talk."

Joshua grimaced then dropped his head and mumbled, "Okay. I guess I wasn't being very nice."

Oliver turned a sneer on his brother. "You don't know how to be nice, Joshua!"

This was not the way Win wanted to spend the evening—with two quarreling kids and a woman who made him itch in all the wrong places.

"Dad, Oliver is being a brat and—"

Win quickly interrupted. "No more arguing out of either of you."

Oliver turned a pleading look at his father. "I don't want to stay here with Joshua. Can I go with you, Dad?"

Win realized Oliver's request was more about seeing Stacy Abernathy rather than getting away from his wise-cracking brother.

"All right," Win told him. "As long as you stay out of the way."

STACY HAD NEVER considered herself a mechanic, however her father and brothers had taught her a few basics about the workings of a vehicle, just in case she had trouble on the road. And unfortunately tonight she was having trouble. She wasn't exactly sure why her car was refusing to start, but before she called one of her brothers for help, she'd make an effort to fix the problem herself.

Pulling on her jacket, she exited the car and lifted the hood. After a quick glance to make sure no wires were hanging lose, she turned her attention to the battery. She was checking the cables to make sure they were secure and making contact when a male voice called to her.

"Need some help?"

Turning, she was totally surprised to see Win and Oliver striding up to her. After the way he'd hurriedly left the conference room without a word to anyone, she wouldn't have expected him to still be on the school grounds.

Stepping away from the car, she met the pair on the middle of the concrete walkway that ran adjacent to the parking spaces. "I'm not sure if my battery is dead or if there's some other problem going on, but the car refuses to start," she explained to Win. "The car was fine when I parked it here before the meeting. Now, it's not making a sound. Not even a click. The gas tank is nearly full, so it didn't run out of fuel."

"I'll have a look." He stepped over to the car and peered beneath the hood.

Stacy and Oliver stood to one side while they waited for Win to finish his inspection.

Turning his back to the vehicle, he asked, "Has the car done this before?"

"No. It's never given me any trouble," she told him. Then, not wanting Oliver to feel ignored, she gave the boy a smile. "How are you, Oliver?"

"I'm good, Ms. Abernathy," Oliver spoke up. "And don't

worry. Dad knows how to fix all sorts of things. Even trac-
tors. He'll get you going."

"I wouldn't start making promises, Oliver," Win told
his son. "The problem might be something that will require a new part from the auto supply store."

Stacy watched him jiggle a pair of wires then lift the
cover on the battery and peer into the three holes on top
of the square apparatus.

After putting the cover back in place, he said, "Try to
start the car again so I can hear what's going on."

She hurried around to the driver's side of the vehicle
and slipped beneath the wheel. When she turned the key
in the ignition, there wasn't a sound to be heard.

Climbing out of the car, she went to stand next to him.
"Usually when a battery goes dead it will, at least, make
a clicking noise. It's not even making that sound."

With an understanding nod, he said, "You're right. But
nowadays most batteries don't give you any warning that
they're going bad. It just happens all at once without so
much as a click. I have jumper cables in my truck. We
might be able to jump-start it."

"Are you sure you have time?" she asked. "I imagine
you and the boys need to get home."

He slanted her a wry look. "I'm sure you need to get
home, too."

"Shoot, Ms. Abernathy, we never know when we're
gonna get home," Oliver assured her. "Sometimes it's way
past my bedtime."

Win let out a good-natured groan. "Oliver, you're going
to have Stacy thinking I'm not a good parent. You know
you're usually in bed on time."

Grinning, Oliver scuffed the toe of his boot against
the concrete sidewalk. "Yeah, mostly I'm in bed on time."

Stacy smiled at the child then looked at Win. "You need

to remember I teach elementary school, Win. I'm used to my students saying anything and everything. Usually how they describe something is far different than how it actually is."

He let out a short laugh. "You're telling me. I never know what's going to come out of Oliver's mouth. Joshua's, either, for that matter," he said, adding, "I'll go get my truck. Hopefully, a jump will get you going."

Five minutes later, with Stacy's battery hooked to Win's, he tried starting the car, but it refused.

"It's determined not to start." Stacy stated the obvious.

"No. I'm afraid you're going to have to call a garage and have a new battery installed."

Even though she wanted to let out a groan of disappointment, she choked it back. Not for anything would she do a bunch of complaining in front of Win. She hardly wanted him to view her as a woman who had childish meltdowns over a minor problem.

"Well, Bronco probably does have a twenty-four-hour garage, but Dad has a certain mechanic he always uses. I'll call him tomorrow and ask him to come do the repairs."

He began unclipping the jumper cables from both batteries. "You'll need a lift home," he said.

"No problem," she assured him. "I'll call my parents, or siblings. One of them will come and pick me up. I can wait right here in the car."

His brows pulled together in a frown. "The night is already getting chilly and you obviously can't run the car heater. I can drive you out to the Bonnie B."

He didn't sound annoyed with the situation. On the other hand, he didn't appear to be all that thrilled about the prospect, either, Stacy thought. That was understandable. He had children to care for and most likely ranching chores to deal with before he retired for the evening.

Still, it would've been nice of him to smile when he'd made the offer.

Instinctively raising her chin, she said, "Thanks, but I'll be fine waiting here. This is a safe neighborhood. Besides, I've interrupted your evening enough already."

He glanced at her. "You said that, I didn't."

Oliver suddenly piped up. "Dad, we really should drive Ms. Abernathy home. That's the way guys are supposed to treat ladies. Right?"

"Right, son," he told Oliver then cast a wry smile at Stacy. "If you'll fetch your things from the car and lock it up, we'll be on our way."

To argue further would only make her look ungrateful. Besides, who was she kidding? Spending a few more minutes in Win's company was the most exciting thing that had happened to her since last year when her students had presented her a cake on her twenty-seventh birthday.

"Thank you, Win. I really do appreciate this."

"Forget it," he said. "If I ever get stranded, you can give me a lift."

While Win put the jumper cables away and shut both hoods on the vehicles, Stacy gathered a tote bag filled with books and school papers she was planning to go over later tonight, along with her jacket and handbag.

"I'll carry those things for you, Ms. Abernathy," Oliver offered.

Smiling at the sweet boy, she handed him the tote bag. "Thanks, Oliver. It's not too heavy for you, is it?"

"Gosh no! I can carry a whole bucket of feed easy. Dad says toting feed buckets will build my muscles. Do you help do the chores on the Bonnie B, Ms. Abernathy?" he asked as the two of them made their way around to the front passenger door of the truck.

"Not very often. My brothers do most of the ranch chores."

Her answer put a disappointed look on his face. She supposed Oliver was like most of the folks around Bronco who'd known her since she was a child. Because she'd been born and raised on a ranch, everyone thought she should want to be a cowgirl. However, dealing with livestock had never been her thing. Not that she disliked animals; she loved them. But books and teaching had always been her main passion and she was very thankful her family had understood she'd needed to take a different direction with her life.

Oliver said, "Oh. Well, I guess you being a girl and all, you probably don't want to build muscles."

She wanted to laugh but held the reaction back in fear it might hurt Oliver's feelings. He was such a friendly child and it was obvious he wanted to impress her. Just like most boys wanted to impress their mothers. Except that Oliver and his brother didn't have a mother, she recalled sadly.

"Girls want to have a few muscles and be strong, too," she told the boy.

Oliver looked curiously up at her. "Did you ever play baseball?"

She said, "No. But I've played a little softball."

He appeared to be impressed that she was able to do more than teach school and read books. "That's good. I play Little League. But it's over for the summer."

Oliver placed her tote bag on the floor in front of the passenger seat and Stacy was about to climb into the truck when Win appeared at her side and quickly slipped a hand beneath her elbow.

"I'll help you," he said. "It's a tall step up."

Although it was an innocent touch, the feel of his warm fingers against her arm was enough to send her pulse into a wild gallop.

"Thank you, Win."

"Sure," he replied. "Can you find the seat belt? It's rarely ever used. The boys always sit in the back, so the belt might have slipped between the cracks of the seat."

He was standing so near, she could feel the heat radiating from his body, smell the faint earthy scent emanating from his shirt. She'd never had a man make her hands tremble before, but as she dug around for the seat belt, she realized hers were shaking. Hopefully, the semidarkness of the parking lot made it impossible for him to see her fumbling fingers.

"Uh, here it is. I have it."

Satisfied that she was all set, he shut the door and promptly instructed Oliver to join Joshua, who'd been waiting in the back seat all this time.

When Win slid behind the wheel and started the engine, Stacy felt as if the interior of the truck had shrunk to half its size. The man's masculine presence was overwhelming and even though she wasn't looking at him directly, she was totally aware of his long, lean body, the scent of his skin, and the flex of his shoulders as he steered the vehicle out of the parking lot.

"Stacy, I don't think you've met my older son yet," he said, glancing back over his shoulder to the teenager. "Joshua, say hello to Ms. Abernathy. She teaches second grade at the elementary school."

Twisting around in the seat, Stacy looked around the headrest to greet the older boy. "Hello, Joshua. It's nice to meet you."

"Hi."

The one word was all he said, and Stacy wondered if the teenager was usually this quiet or if he was shy.

"We're going to take Ms. Abernathy home. She lives on the Bonnie B Ranch," Win explained to his older son.

"Oh. Where is that?" Joshua asked.

"About ten miles from our ranch," Win answered.

Joshua didn't say anything after that and Stacy got the feeling the boy was pouting about something. His dad helping a woman? Or her making them late getting home?

"Don't pay any attention to Joshua being so quiet, Ms. Abernathy," Oliver told her. "He doesn't know how to talk to women. Not like I do."

"Shut up, you little jerk," Joshua barked at his brother.

"Then why ain't you talkin'?" Oliver taunted back at him.

"Don't say *ain't*. You know what Dad says about saying *ain't*!"

"You two also know what I say about arguing," Win told the boys. "Especially in front of company. Now, pipe down back there."

Silence ensued and, after a moment, Stacy awkwardly cleared her throat. "Oliver tells me you're in the process of building your ranch. How's that going?"

"I wish I had more hours in the day to do more. But now that school has started—well, as a teacher, you know how limited our time gets. And once it gets dark, there's not much work you can do out of doors. Still, I'm pleased with how it's all going so far. I have a small herd of Black Baldy and a few horses."

"We have cats and dogs, too, Ms. Abernathy," Oliver added. "And a pair of burros to guard the cattle."

"Oh, I imagine they're cute little things," she said.

"They're mean." Joshua spoke up. "They'll bite you if you don't watch them. We've had them for a long time. Even when we lived in Whitehorn. Dad says they're family, so they moved here with us."

"I see," she murmured and then glanced over at Win's dark profile. He appeared to be focused on the highway and the intermittent traffic, but she wondered if he might be thinking back to Whitehorn and the life he'd had there with his late wife. Was his heart still wrapped up in her memory? Was that the reason he'd remained single for so long? If so, he might never want another wife. "What made you decide to move to Bronco?" she asked. "Did you hear it was a good ranching area?"

He shrugged one shoulder. "I was ready for a change and when I researched Bronco, it seemed like a good place to build a ranch and teach school."

"And Dad wanted to leave Whitehorn because of Tara," Oliver added tersely.

"Shut up, Oliver!" Joshua muttered under his breath.

"You're the one who needs to shut up!" Oliver practically shouted.

Win turned a look of warning on the two boys before glancing at Stacy. "I apologize for my sons' behavior, Stacy. It's probably hard to believe, but they're usually not this unruly. I hope you don't think my students are this disruptive."

At the moment, Stacy wasn't thinking about his sons or his students, she was wondering about Tara and what had happened with her and Win. But he clearly wasn't going to explain Oliver's remark and Stacy wasn't about to ask.

CHAPTER THREE

OLIVER HAD HIS nose pressed to the passenger window as Win drove through the ranch yard and on to the big ranch house.

"Wow! This place is really big!" the boy exclaimed. "Look at that gigantic barn, Joshua!"

"Yeah. It's bigger than ours," Joshua replied. "Is that log mansion where you live, Ms. Abernathy?"

"That's my parents' home. I have a smaller cabin of my own about a half-mile behind this one. But I stay here with my parents fairly often, too."

"Why?" Oliver wanted to know. "Because this place is big and fancy?"

She answered, "It's a big house, but I wouldn't call it a mansion, Oliver. It's not overly fancy—just nice and comfortable. Ever since I was born twenty-eight years ago, this has been my home. And even though I have a place of my own, I stay here often because—well, my parents enjoy my company and I enjoy theirs."

To her, it probably wasn't a mansion, Win thought. But to him and the boys, it was fancy. In fact, from what Win could see about the Bonnie B, everything was bigger and more impressive than most of the places he'd seen around Bronco. That didn't surprise him. Anthony had already told him how the Abernathys were some of the most affluent of families in and around Bronco. And from the looks of this place, he doubted Stacy had ever had to want for anything.

Just one more reason Win needed to keep his distance from the woman, he told himself. Not that he was poor by any means, but his financial status could hardly stand up to that of Stacy's family. And he figured she'd never be the type to lower her standards. Even for love.

Love! Hell, he must've gone too long without eating today, Win wryly chided himself. Otherwise, that word would've never popped into his head.

"Well, here we are," she announced as he pulled the truck to a stop in front of a yard fence made of split rails. "I'd be happy if you'd all come in and have some of Mom's homemade cookies. At least it would be a little repayment for all your trouble."

Win didn't allow himself the time to consider her invitation. No matter how nice she was being and how innocent her offer, he needed to put some distance between the two of them. "Thanks. It sounds very nice, Stacy. But we really should head on to the J Barb."

Oliver immediately let out a loud wail. "Oh, Dad, can't we go in just for a few minutes? We don't ever get to eat homemade cookies! Unless we visit Grandma and Grandpa!"

"I wouldn't mind a few cookies myself," Joshua added.

Seeing both boys were on board for the treat, Win could hardly refuse. Besides, turning down her offer would probably make her see him as an unfriendly jerk. "All right," he conceded. "But we can't stay for very long. Ms. Abernathy has things she needs to do and so do we."

"Yeah! Homemade cookies!" Oliver exclaimed. "This will be good!"

They departed the truck and, with Win carrying Stacy's tote, she walked along beside him as the two boys followed a few steps behind the adults.

The night was cool with a breeze gently ruffling the

leaves that were still clinging to a couple of Aspen trees growing in the far corner of the yard. A multitude of stars dotted the inky sky while a crescent moon was rising on the eastern horizon. In the distance, beyond a group of barns and corrals, he could hear a pair of dogs bark and the sound of bawling cows and calves.

"Sounds like it's weaning time on the Bonnie B," he commented.

She sighed. "Yes. I hate weaning time on the ranch."

Her remark disappointed him. In spite of her not being an outdoor, cowgirl type, he wanted to believe she respected the ranching profession. "Why?" he asked. "The noise gets on your nerves?"

Smiling, sheepishly, she said, "No. It's not that at all. It's because I'm too softhearted, I guess. It's sad to hear the mothers and babies calling so desperately to each other. But Dad says it's a part of life—like kids growing up and leaving the nest, so to speak." She glanced at him. "Do you have calves on the J Barb to wean this fall?"

"I finished separating the cows and calves a couple of weeks ago. I wanted to have it done before school started."

"Do you have hired hands to help on your ranch?" she asked.

Even though her question was a reasonable one, it very nearly made Win laugh. "Yeah. These two guys behind me. They're my helpers." Seeing the faint look of surprise on her face, he went on to explain, "My ranch isn't big enough to support hired help. Especially on a full-time basis. I basically take care of everything that needs to be done, and the boys have been learning how to do things around the ranch since they were very small. They're good help."

"I see. Sounds like my dad and brothers," she said. "Mom says he put them in the saddle when they were toddlers."

They stepped up on a wide-planked porch that ran the

entire width of the enormous house. To the left and right of the entrance, there were groups of cushioned furniture, and porch swings were located at both ends. In several spots, pots of yellow, copper and white chrysanthemums grew in huge clay plots. The flowers made it clear there was a woman's touch on the Bonnie B, Win thought. Something that he'd missed since losing his wife.

"My dad was the same way with me and my brother," he said. "And my boys have been riding since they were very small."

"Like father, like son. Right?" she said with a knowing grin.

"Right."

She stepped up to open the door, but before she could reach for the handle, the glass-and-wood panel swung wide to reveal a tall woman with light-colored hair peering at them.

"Oh, Stacy, it's you! I thought I heard a vehicle pull up." Her brows arched with curiosity as she glanced over her daughter's shoulder at Win and the two boys. "I see you brought company home with you."

"Yes. Or I should say, they brought me home. I had car trouble and had to leave it in the parking lot at the high school. So Win kindly offered to bring me home," Stacy quickly explained then gestured to Win. "Mom, this is Win Jackson. He's the new agribusiness teacher at Bronco High School and these are his two sons. Joshua is fifteen and Oliver is ten. You guys, this is my mother, Bonnie Abernathy."

Stacy's mother quickly stepped onto the porch and, with a wide smile, reached for Win's hand. "A pleasure to meet you, Mr. Jackson. It's certainly nice of you to bring Stacy all the way out here to the Bonnie B."

Bonnie's handshake was as strong and confident as the

look in her eye, and Win immediately liked her straightforward demeanor. "The pleasure is all mine, Mrs. Abernathy. And just call me Win. I hear Mr. Jackson all day at school."

She chuckled. "I'm sure you do. So, Win it will be."

Gathering his sons in the curve of one arm, he urged them toward the ranching matriarch. "Boys, say hello to Mrs. Abernathy."

"Hello, Mrs. Abernathy," they repeated in perfect unison.

Laughing, she grabbed both children by the hand and pulled them toward the door she'd left standing open. "No need to call me that, boys. Just call me Bonnie. Now, come on in and make yourselves at home. I'll bet you two would like some cookies, wouldn't you?"

Oliver looked totally puzzled. "How did you know that Ms. Abernathy said we could come in and eat cookies?"

Laughing, Bonnie looked back at Stacy and Win and winked. "Oh, I just sort of guessed," she told Oliver. "Baking cookies is something I do pretty often. In fact, I just took some cowboy cookies out of the oven and they're still warm."

"What's a cowboy cookie?" Joshua wanted to know.

Bonnie's indulgent smile encompassed both boys. "Oh my goodness, a cowboy cookie is just stuffed with yummy things like chocolate chips and nuts and coconut, and a few more things. I think you'll like them."

"I know I will!" Oliver exclaimed.

Curving an arm around both boys' shoulders, her mother ushered them into the house, leaving Stacy and Win to follow the trio into a short foyer.

"You guys come along with me to the kitchen," Bonnie said to the children and then darted a glance at Win and her daughter. "Stacy, why don't you show Win to the den where he can relax while the boys have their cookies.

And, don't worry, Win, I won't let them spoil their appetites. After all, I'm expecting the three of you to stay for dinner. I promise I've cooked enough to feed an army. Or have you three already had your dinner?"

The woman's sudden invitation took Win by surprise and he glanced uncertainly at Stacy. But she merely smiled at him as though to say she wasn't going to argue his case for him.

To Bonnie, he said, "No. We've not eaten yet. And it's very thoughtful of you invite us to stay. But I wouldn't want to intrude. I'll fix Joshua and Oliver something when we get home."

"Nonsense! Even with three extra mouths to feed, I'll have leftovers to deal with. I won't hear of you leaving without dinner. Especially after the trouble you've taken to help Stacy get home."

The woman was being especially warm and welcoming and Win certainly appreciated her kindness. Yet he was barely acquainted with Stacy and had never met any of the Abernathys. To be thrust into a family situation like this, especially without any warning, was making him darned uncomfortable.

"Bonnie, I honestly don't need any sort of repayment for helping Stacy and—"

"No arguments," she firmly interrupted. "You and your sons have to eat. You might as well do it here with us. Stacy, fix him a nice drink. Dinner should be ready in about thirty minutes."

She hurried away with the boys and Stacy gave him an apologetic smile. "Look, Win, I can see you aren't keen on staying for dinner. But you'd be making my parents happy. And my family is fairly easygoing. We usually don't have loud arguments at the dinner table. Plus, Mom is a wonderful cook. Everything she makes is mouthwatering."

"I'm not worried about your mother's cooking skills. I—" He broke off as it struck him that any excuse he made to skip dinner would make him sound as though he was desperate to hightail it out of this log mansion, which he was. But he didn't want to hurt Stacy's feelings. Even if it meant him being miserable for an hour or so. "I appreciate Bonnie inviting us."

A tiny smile tilted the corners of her plush lips and Win suddenly wondered if she'd ever kissed a man with heedless abandon or experienced real passion in a man's arms. From what little time he'd spent in her company, he'd gotten the impression that she was reserved, not anything close to reckless. Yet, at the same time, she had a sweet sexiness about her that made every male cell in his body hum with pleasure.

"I'm glad," she said. "I'd very much appreciate your company."

Her words alone were not that suggestive, but the soft tone in which she'd said them rippled down his spine like the seductive trail of a fingertip. How the heck was he supposed to reply? Out of politeness, he could say it was a nice opportunity for him to get to know her better. But damn it, she might end up being just like Tara—reading more into his words than he'd meant.

Clearing an awkward lump from his throat, he said, "You're probably going to find my company boring, Stacy. My life is mundane."

With a soft chuckle, she stepped closer and motioned him forward. "A teacher's life is never boring or mundane. If it is, then he or she isn't doing their job," she said as they moved out of the foyer. "Come on, I'll show you to the den."

They entered a grand-sized room with high ceilings, polished wood floors and a row of windows facing the north. Win missed most of the details about the formal living area. He was too busy focused on her soft scent swirling around him and the way the folds of her brown skirt were brushing against his leg.

Several months had passed since a woman's body had been close enough to touch his, even in the most innocuous way. And for the most part, he could easily say he'd not missed the stress of dating and trying to dodge the marriage traps that had been constantly thrown in his direction. In fact, he'd pretty much convinced himself that he could do without a woman's charms indefinitely. But being this close to Stacy was making him rethink his plans to remain celibate the rest of his life.

"This is a huge house," he commented as they walked down a long hallway. "You must have several siblings or your parents simply like plenty of living space."

She smiled at him. "I have four siblings. Three brothers and a sister. I'm the youngest of the bunch and the only one who often stays here in the big house. My sister lives with her husband nearby on the Broken Road Ranch. All the others have cabins of their own on the Bonnie B, which gives them privacy while still remaining close."

He glanced at her. "Guess your frequent stays here in the main house means you don't need extra privacy."

She shrugged. "Well, I'm not married or engaged, like my siblings," she explained. "And besides, my parents don't hover over me. I'm busy. They're busy. We all stay out of each other's way. Unless we want to be together, of course."

They reached an open doorway where she guided him into a long, rectangular-shaped room furnished with three couches and several armchairs all done in various shades of green and brown leather. At the far end of the room, a small fire was burning in a wide, native-rock fireplace.

Other than the crackle of the burning logs, the room was quiet, but Win had a feeling it wouldn't be staying that way for long.

"Here we are," she announced once they reached the center of the room. "Sit wherever you'd like. You might find it more pleasant down by the fire. This room can get drafty at times. Especially when it's breezy outside."

He crossed the room to where a couch was angled toward the fireplace but still far enough away to keep from being roasted. After sinking onto an end cushion, he pulled off his hat and hung it over one knee.

A few feet away, she went behind a short bar and pulled out a yellow-and-green-enameled tray. "What would you like to drink?" she asked. "Something with alcohol? I don't fancy myself as a bartender, but I can mix a few simple drinks."

"Uh, no thanks. I'll be driving myself and the kids home in a bit."

"Good thinking," she said. "So, how about a soda? Ginger ale? Or juice?"

"I'm not choosy. I'll have whatever you're having," he told her.

"Coming right up," she said.

Short minutes later, she appeared in front of him carrying a tray with two glasses filled with crushed ice and some sort of yellow-orange liquid, garnished with a slice of lime.

"Looks good. Thanks," he told her as he picked up one of the glasses.

She placed the tray on an end table then carried her glass over to the middle of the couch and took a seat a couple of cushions down from him.

After she'd watched him take a sip of his drink, she said, "Don't ask me what you're drinking. Some sort of fizzy fruit juice. Mom special orders it. She and Dad went on vacation to Spain several years ago and she says this drink reminds her of their time there."

"It's nice. I like it," he said then slanted a curious glance at her. "You didn't go to Spain with them?"

She licked the moisture of the drink from her lips and Win purposely turned his gaze away from her and onto the pile of burning logs. He had enough thoughts about kissing her without adding such tempting images to his mind.

She said, "At that time, I was still in college trying to finish out my teaching degree. Anyway, they were celebrating one of their anniversaries. They didn't need any of us kids along."

He turned his eyes back to her face. "So you have four siblings," he commented. "Are any of them teachers, like you?"

She chuckled as though the idea of her brothers or sister teaching school was definitely amusing. "No. They all think I'm a glutton for punishment to be a teacher. I mean, don't get me wrong, they admire the profession and they've always supported my desire to teach. But in their opinion, they could find plenty of jobs with less stress."

He chuckled wryly. "The way I see it, every job carries some sort of stress with it. What do your siblings do for a living?"

"Billy, the oldest, is a rancher and helps Dad take care of the Bonnie B. He's married to Charlotte Taylor and she's currently pregnant. They also have three teenagers, Branson, Nicky and Jill. My other brothers, Theo and Jace, help work the family ranch, too. On the side, Theo does a podcast called *This Ranching Life* and Jace is a volunteer firefighter for the Bronco area. My sister, Robin, who's three years older than me, is married to Dylan Sanchez, and she has a horse therapeutics line that's doing well for her. They don't have any kids. Not yet, that is."

"What about Theo and Jace?" he asked. "Are they married?"

"Theo is engaged to Bethany McCreery. She's six months pregnant, so they'll soon be parents. And Jace is engaged to Tamara Hanson. She's a nurse and they have a fourteen-month-old son, Frankie."

She'd given him a load of information to digest and keep straight, but one thing stuck out clearly to Win. Each of Stacy's three brothers had families and a sister who was married, but with no children yet. So why was Stacy still single? True, she was only twenty-eight, which was still very young. But, to Win, she seemed like a woman who'd put a husband and children high on her lists of life goals. Just guessing, he'd bet she didn't even have a special boyfriend. Otherwise, when her car had failed to start earlier tonight, she would've called the guy for help.

Casually sipping his drink, he glanced at her from the corner of his eye. "Sounds like your siblings are busy expanding the Abernathy family. I'm surprised you're not yet married or engaged."

Her lips formed a smile, as though to imply his question hadn't bothered her, yet he could see a rosy-pink color staining her cheeks. He'd thought women had quit blushing long ago. Tara had certainly never expressed any kind of embarrassment with pink cheeks. He couldn't remember his late wife blushing, either. Yvette hadn't been a reserved type like Stacy. She'd been more of a rough-and-tumble girl who'd worked hard all of her life.

"If you're wondering if I have something against love or marriage, I don't," she said. "It's just that I…haven't met the right man yet."

"Particular, eh?"

"Not necessarily particular," she retorted. "I happen to think a person needs to be careful when they're choosing a lifelong mate. It's not like you're trying to decide if you want apple pie or cherry for dessert, you know."

His question had certainly ignited a spark in her and as his gaze slipped over her face, he decided he liked the way it made her blue eyes glimmer and her lips pucker into a perfect little bow. A very kissable bow, at that, he thought.

Forcing his eyes off her lips, he said, "Well, sometimes a person takes so long trying to decide which flavor he wants that the pie ends up spoiling. And that's a real waste."

A frown puckered the middle of her forehead. "What I consider a waste is devoting yourself to someone who, in the end, doesn't give a darn about your feelings."

The hard edge to her voice surprised him and he shifted around on the cushion to study her more closely. "Has that happened to you?"

She looked over at him and Win noticed a hollowness to her expression that implied she was carrying an empty spot inside her. Why? he wondered.

She sighed. "No. Not really. Oh, I've had a few relationships that fizzled, but I wasn't really that invested in any of them."

His lips twisted. "Did you ever think that might have been the reason they fizzled?"

"Sure. But you can't force yourself to feel something that isn't there. You know?"

Oh yes, he definitely knew how boring and tedious and even depressing it had been dating Tara. The woman had tried so hard to make him fall in love and propose marriage to her. But he'd not been interested in either of those things and the more she'd pushed and demanded, the more Win had withdrawn. He'd lost his one true soulmate. He wasn't looking to find another. Could it be that Stacy was a bit like Win and had given up on finding a lifelong partner?

He said, "Yeah. I'm an expert on losing interest."

Her brows rose slightly, but thankfully she didn't pursue his remark. Still, he couldn't help but wonder what she was thinking about him now. That he expected too much from a woman?

Telling himself her opinion didn't matter, he drained the last of his drink and was placing the empty glass on an end table next to his right elbow when a young man wearing faded jeans and flannel shirt, and a blond woman in a flowered maxi-dress strolled into the room. The man's arm was snugged affectionately around the woman's pregnant waist and the two were exchanging warm glances, making it obvious they were a couple.

"Mom told us we had company," the man said to Stacy as he glanced at Win. "We thought we'd come say hello."

"Hi, you two." Stacy immediately rose to her feet, gave the couple a brief hug, then gestured for Win to join them. "Meet Win Jackson. He's the new agribusiness teacher at Bronco High School. And, Win, this is my brother Billy and his wife, Charlotte."

Win stood and walked over to the young rancher and his wife. "A pleasure to meet you both," he said as he shook hands with Billy and then Charlotte.

"The pleasure is ours," Billy said. "It's always nice to have company. And we're especially glad Stacy had enough sense to invite you out to the Bonnie B for dinner."

Win noticed Stacy's cheeks once again turned pink. Obviously, it was making her feel awkward to have Billy linking the two of them together.

"Uh, I didn't exactly invite him," Stacy quickly corrected. "I had car trouble and Win was kind enough to bring me home."

"And your mother insisted I stay for dinner," Win added to her explanation.

"Sounds like Bonnie," Charlotte said with a wide smile. "Are those your sons we saw in the kitchen?"

Win nodded. "Joshua and Oliver. I hope they weren't trying to eat all of Bonnie's cookies."

Billy chuckled. "She'd never allow that. She's actually put them and our kids to work setting the table. We have three teenagers. Branson, Nicky and Jill."

"Seventeen, fifteen and fourteen," Charlotte told him. "Billy says they're the reason he's starting to gray at the temples."

Billy's grin was full of pride. "They're basically good kids. We love 'em lots, don't we, honey?"

"More than anything," she agreed then patted her rotund belly. "And we already love this little one, too."

Billy reached over and placed a hand on the growing child and Charlotte cast her husband a look that caused Win to remember back when his wife had once looked at him with deep, genuine love. But that part of his life was over and finished, he thought dully.

Stacy lightly cleared her throat. "Would you two like something to drink? We just had some of Mom's fizzy fruit juice."

Billy said, "Actually, I think dinner is just about ready. Dad just came in and has gone to wash up. And Robin and Dylan are supposed to be here any minute."

"Oh. They're coming tonight?" Stacy asked.

"That's what Bonnie told us," Charlotte said.

Hearing more people would be arriving caused Win to cast a concerned look at Stacy. "I'm thinking I should take the boys on home. Your mother has plenty of dinner guests without us causing more work for her."

Billy let out an easy laugh. "Forget it, Win. Most every

night of the week, some of us are here to eat. If we didn't show up, Mom would think something was wrong. She's used to her kids popping in and out, so she always cooks plenty."

"That's right, Win," Charlotte added. "The more, the merrier. Bonnie could never have too many mouths to feed."

"Yes, but we're not family," he pointed out. "We're only here by happenstance."

"Listen, Win," Billy said, "you helped my sister. That makes you a friend of the family."

Family. Each time he heard the word, it was like a punch in the gut. He didn't need these reminders of all he'd lost—of everything his boys had lost when their mother died. But he couldn't just walk out. Stacy would view him as an ungrateful creep.

And why should that matter, Win? You didn't care what Tara thought when you walked out on her.

"Hey, Dad, Grandma says dinner is ready."

The announcement interrupted Win's dour thoughts and he glanced over to see a tall boy with dark blond hair wearing jeans and a graphic T-shirt. Obviously, he was one of Billy's sons.

"Thanks, Branson. We'll be right there," Billy told him.

The teenager quickly disappeared and the four adults slowly migrated from the room. Out in the hallway, Stacy once again walked close to Win's side and he was surprised at how nice and natural it felt to have her next to him.

As the group moved down the hallway, Stacy said, "Billy, you might be interested to know that Win has a ranch not far from here—the J Barb."

"So that place belongs to you now," Billy stated. "I'd heard someone had purchased the property, but I didn't know who. It used to be a profitable ranch at one time, but when the owner got too old to take care of things, it began to get run down. He had a couple of kids, but they never cared to help him."

"His children were the ones who sold the property," Win replied. "I got the impression they wanted to get it off their hands."

"Yeah, so much for leaving your kids a legacy," Billy said somewhat sorrowfully.

"Not everyone has a desire to be a rancher," Stacy told her brother.

Billy laughed. "You would say that."

When they reached the dining room, Stacy quickly introduced Win to her father, Asa, a vibrant man with a strong handshake and an affable smile. Her sister Robin and husband, Dylan Sanchez, had also arrived and they greeted Win as though it wasn't unusual to have extra company at the Abernathy dinner table.

Once everyone was seated and the bowls of food began to make their way around the table, Asa asked, "So, what do you think of Bronco, Win?"

"So far, I'm glad I made the move," Win replied. He ladled a serving of macaroni and cheese onto his plate then handed the bowl to Stacy, who was seated next to him. "The town is a lot tighter knit than I thought it would be."

Bonnie laughed. "You have to be careful what you say and who you say it to, Win. Otherwise, you might offend someone's friend or relative."

"I'm definitely learning to watch what I say around Bronco," Win told her.

Oliver spoke up. "Dad says gossiping about people is mean, so I don't gossip about anyone."

Joshua grunted and rolled his eyes, causing Billy's three teenagers to snicker with amusement. At the same time, Win noticed Stacy smiling with approval at Oliver.

It was no wonder his young son viewed her as an angel, he thought. She seemed to want to shield him from the banter of his older brother.

"I think that's very admirable of you, Oliver," she said. "If everyone made an effort not to gossip, we'd all be better off."

"True," Robin agreed then added jokingly, "but what would that leave us to talk about? The weather?"

"I've heard enough about the weather." Charlotte spoke up. "I want to know if anyone has heard any news about Winona."

Stacy glanced over at Win. "Have you ever met Winona Cobbs?"

"No. I can't say that I've heard that name," Win told her. "Is she a relative?"

Asa cleared his throat and Billy chuckled under his breath.

Win glanced around the table while wondering if his innocent question had opened a can of worms.

"Uh, when she was very young, she had a romance with an Abernathy ancestor that produced a child," Stacy explained. "It's a very long story. But to simplify things, that child made Winona connected to the Abernathys, but she isn't actually related to the family. Anyway, she's ninety-seven years old now, and she's gone missing."

"She's also Bronco's resident psychic," Billy added. "Don't forget that part."

"Plus, she's engaged to be married to Dylan's uncle, Stanley Sanchez," Robin said. "He's a young eighty-seven."

Win frowned with bewilderment. "I want to make sure I'm getting this straight. A ninety-seven-year-old psychic, who's engaged to be married to a man ten years her junior, has gone missing?"

"I realize this all probably sounds strange to you, Win,"

Bonnie said, "but if you knew Winona, you'd understand. You'd never guess she's in her nineties. And she actually is a psychic. Many of her premonitions have come true."

Robin cast her husband a look of concern. "Tell Win the rest of the story."

"There isn't a whole lot to tell," Dylan said with a helpless shrug. "When Uncle Stanley first met Winona, it was love at first sight for him and she seemed madly in love with him. Two years ago, they got engaged and he put a beautiful amethyst ring on her finger."

"Which she proudly showed off to everyone." Robin emphasized. "And their wedding was going to be a big romantic affair."

Nodding, Dylan said, "Which was going to take place a few weeks ago. But the day of the wedding, Winona just suddenly vanished without a trace. Everyone searched, but she couldn't be found, and a lot of folks around town believe she simply ran off because she got cold feet."

Win glanced around the table. "I'm assuming you folks don't believe that's the case."

"No!" Robin exclaimed while Dylan shook his head. "We don't know what to believe! All of us who are close to Winona think she might have been kidnapped. Stanley is convinced that something bad has happened to her. But then, her daughter Daisy received a note from Winona stating everything was well with her and she left because she needed to be free. Winona ended by apologizing for leaving without a word, but she thought it would be easier that way—without painful goodbyes."

Win frowned. "Just when I thought this story about Winona couldn't get any stranger, it does," he remarked and glanced questioningly at Dylan. "Did the letter look as though Winona actually wrote it?"

Dylan answered. "Well, at ninety-seven, her handwriting is a bit shaky, but Uncle Stanley believes she wrote it."

"What does your uncle think about her explanation?" Win asked.

"Stanley doesn't believe a word of it," Dylan told him. "And as you might guess, he's totally despondent. He can't believe that Winona jilted him. He's afraid that something bad must have happened to her, otherwise, he believes she would come back to him. This ordeal has been especially hard on Uncle Stanley because his beloved wife died about a year before he moved to Bronco in 2022. So he hadn't been a widower for very long when he met and fell in love with Winona."

"I'm sorry your uncle is going through this. Losing a loved one…isn't easy." As soon as Win said the words, everyone except Joshua and Oliver looked curiously at him and he realized the Abernathys were all waiting for an explanation. "I'm a widower. That's, uh, how I can relate to Stanley's sorrow."

Bonnie cast him an empathetic look. "Oh. We didn't know, Win. But we're glad you told us."

A moment of awkward silence passed and Win was wondering how he'd ever gotten into this uncomfortable situation in the first place, when he suddenly felt Stacy's hand give his knee a comforting pat. The notion that she seemed to understand how he was feeling touched him in a way he would've never expected.

"Sometimes people ask me if I have a mom and I tell them no. 'Cause, I don't," Oliver said glumly.

Even though the rib roast he'd been eating was delicious, Win felt a little sick at the lost look on his son's face. It was one thing to have Oliver lamenting to Win in private over the fact that he was motherless, but hearing him say it in front of a group of people he'd only just met was a whole other matter.

Billy's daughter Jill glanced down the table at Oliver and gave him an encouraging smile. "But you might get another mother, Oliver. Me and my brothers did and she's super!"

Another mother. Apparently, Charlotte wasn't the biological mother to these three teenagers, but from the glowing expression on the woman's face, he could see none of that mattered. She considered them her children, too. Win had to wonder if Billy realized how very lucky he was to have a whole family.

"Thank you, Jill. That's a super nice compliment," Charlotte told her.

"Well, I'm just fine without a mom," Joshua retorted.

Joshua's sulky tone didn't surprise Win, but he was a bit stunned that his son had spouted such a thing in front of the Abernathys. But he supposed Joshua didn't want these kids, who were his own age, thinking he was hurting and vulnerable. Putting on a cool and tough front seemed especially important to him now.

"Gosh, I wouldn't want to be without mine," Branson remarked.

Joshua's expression turned sheepish and he quickly turned his attention to the food on his plate. After that, the conversation around the table moved on to other things. Asa and Billy both wanted to hear about the J Barb and Bonnie talked about the Bronco Harvest Festival, an event that took place every October at the Bronco Fairgrounds. The mere mention of carnival rides and a midway got the kids all excited and Billy's teenagers eagerly explained to Joshua and Oliver what the festival usually entailed. Then Asa was quick to remind everyone that the festival wouldn't be the only big event to be held next month in

Bronco. The Golden Buckle Rodeo was going to be taking place at the Bronco Convention Center and, supposedly, Brooks Langtree, the first Black rodeo rider to be awarded the Golden Buckle thirty years ago, was returning to Bronco for the big celebration.

Win was glad his sons had been given something fun to think about and he was especially glad to see them making friends with Billy's three kids. But as for him, he'd definitely had more than enough family unity for one night. He simply wanted to go home and forget about the soft, pretty blonde sitting next to him. He wanted to forget the pleasure he'd felt when she'd given his knee an encouraging pat and the smiles she'd slanted him throughout the meal. Oh yes, he had to forget all those things, or he was going to be in a far worse mess than he'd found himself in with marriage-minded Tara.

Yet, to be fair, Stacy wasn't anything like Tara. Not in looks or personality. The tall brunette had been overly outgoing with a taste for the flamboyant. She'd also been the take-charge kind, who'd go to great lengths to get whatever she wanted. In the beginning, she'd been a fun date and just what Win had needed at the time to get his mind off losing the most important person in his life. Unfortunately, Tara had viewed every date as one step closer to the marriage altar. When he'd finally made it clear he wasn't interested in matrimony, she'd unsheathed her claws and proceeded to do a hatchet job on his reputation. And because she'd worked as a receptionist at the same school in Whitehorn where he'd taught agribusiness, she'd made his life and his job so miserable he'd sold his home and moved to Bronco to escape.

No. Even if a man broke Stacy's heart, he couldn't see her being vengeful. Frankly, Win couldn't even picture her being romantically interested in him. She was particular.

She'd said so herself. She was probably looking to start a life with a young man with a clean slate. Not one who was twelve years older than she, plus a widower with two boys to raise.

Still, each time he glanced at her lovely face, he could easily picture himself falling for her in a head-over-heels kind of way. And where his heart was concerned, that made her a dangerous woman.

CHAPTER FOUR

THROUGHOUT THE MEAL, there had been moments when Stacy had sensed Win was uncomfortable dealing with her big family. But there had also been occasions when she'd caught him looking at her with something like interest in his eyes. She was hardly an expert on men, but she had to believe he found her attractive. She just didn't know if the attraction would ever be deep enough to draw him to her.

By the time everyone had finished eating the main meal, Stacy half expected Win to forgo coffee and dessert and quickly say his goodbyes. But he surprised her by staying for the cherry cobbler and even waiting until Joshua and Oliver finished a second helping before he announced they had to be heading home.

Stacy followed them out to the foyer where the boys retrieved their jackets from the hall tree. While they pulled on the garments, Stacy reached for a plaid shawl her mother kept hanging by the door.

"I'll walk you out," she said to Win.

He glanced at her. "That isn't necessary. But it's nice of you."

Smiling faintly, she draped the knit fabric around her shoulders. "You're my guests. Of course, I want to see you off."

Outside, the boys trotted off the porch and on to the truck, leaving Stacy and Win to follow at their own pace. As they walked, she wondered how it would feel to be on a date with this man and have him reach for hand. How would it feel to have his strong fingers wrapped tightly around hers?

The fantasy was pointless, she thought. Win wasn't her boyfriend and this evening was anything but a date. Still, having his company, even as a friend, had been very special to her. And she couldn't stop herself from having a spark of hope that something deeper might develop between them.

"I'm afraid my dead battery has wrecked your evening," she said. "But you did get a fairly good meal out of the deal."

"The meal was delicious, Stacy. I've not eaten so much in ages."

At least her mother's cooking had impressed him, Stacy thought, even if she hadn't. "I'm glad you enjoyed the food," she told him.

Side by side, they started down the steps and once again Stacy's mind began to wander. There were plenty of shadows along the walk to the truck. How would it feel to have him draw her into the darkness and kiss her? She'd kissed men before, but she had a feeling that the experience would be totally different with Win.

And what if he did kiss you, Stacy? You think a kiss from a man like Win would mean anything? He's not looking for a woman. Not on a permanent basis.

Shutting her mind against the scoffing voice in her head, she said, "The night is beautiful. Fall is my favorite time of the year. Lots of pumpkin treats, hot chocolate and roasting marshmallows. And the weather is perfect. Not too hot or cold."

"It's also a busy time with a new school year starting. But I do enjoy the mild weather."

She looked up at his profile etched against the glow of

a yard lamp. "I imagine spring is probably your favorite time of the year."

"Hmm. Why would you think so?"

She laughed softly. "Because you're a rancher like my father and brothers. They're always happiest when they see green grass sprouting and knowing the days of spreading hay will soon be over."

He chuckled. "Smart deduction. Spring is a good time for ranchers. Green pastures and baby calves. Ranchers view those things as profit."

"Yes. Most every vocation boils down to money. But I have a feeling you're like my family—you don't just ranch to make money. You do it because you love the job."

He nodded. "Yeah. Like teaching."

"I was going to ask you earlier before dinner, but I didn't get a chance," she said. "What did you think about the school meeting tonight?"

"I had to keep pinching myself to stay awake," he admitted with a wry chuckle. "What about you?"

Instead of pinching herself, she'd been staring across the conference room at him and the few times she'd seen him staring back at her had given her the impression he might be interested enough to speak to her after the meeting. She'd been disappointed when he'd made a beeline for the door without even glancing her way. She'd even scolded herself for wasting such thoughts on the man.

"I hate to admit it, but most of the district meetings are pretty stale. At the elementary school, we teachers kind of get together on our own and try to come up with new and innovative ideas to keep the students interested in learning." She eyed him. "I have an idea that it's much easier keeping seven-year-olds involved in their lessons than it is teenagers. I imagine they try your patience."

His grunt was full of amusement. "You know how a

rubber band grows thin just before it snaps? Well, there are times that my patience stretches that thin. But, on a whole, I enjoy the kids."

"So do I," she murmured. "I can't imagine being anything else but a teacher."

"What about being a mother?"

The unexpected question very nearly caused her to stumble and his hand slipped under her elbow to steady her balance as they covered the last few feet to the truck.

"I'm hoping the children will come," she told him. "Whenever I find the right man."

"Ah, yes, the one who can hold your interest."

He was teasing and she was glad. It was far, far too early for Win to learn just how quickly she was becoming infatuated with him. And keeping things light between them for now was probably for the best. Still, she couldn't help thinking how one little innocent kiss from him would've made her whole week.

The foolish thought made her silently groan. She wasn't being herself tonight, she thought. It wasn't like her to lose her head over a good looking man. Especially one who didn't appear to be the least bit interested in her.

Shoving that thought aside, she forced out a soft laugh. "He'll come along. Sooner or later."

They reached the driver's door of the truck and he caught her completely by surprise by reaching out and enveloping her hand between both of his. His palm was a bit rough and callused, and the warmth of his skin pressed against hers sent a streak of sizzling heat all the way up her arm.

"Thank you for the dinner, Stacy."

A blush was burning her cheeks, but with any luck, her face was partially hidden from him by the shadows. She drew in a long breath then slowly eased it past her lips.

"You already thanked Mom, and she's the one who deserves your appreciation. Not me."

He continued to hold her hand and Stacy desperately wished she knew what he was actually thinking. Throughout this whole evening, he'd been giving her all kinds of mixed signals. At times, she'd gotten the impression he'd wanted to jump to his feet and run for his life. But now, as they stood close together in the semi-darkness, she was getting the odd feeling that he was reluctant to say goodbye.

"It was gracious of your family to have us. And it was good for Joshua and Oliver to have a sit-down dinner with someone other than their father."

What about him? Stacy wanted to ask. Had any part of the evening been good for him? More importantly, was there a chance she'd ever spend time with him again?

Deciding she didn't know him well enough to voice her questions out loud, she merely said, "I'm glad you think so."

He dropped her hand and opened the truck door. Stacy used the moment to stick her head inside the cab to tell Joshua and Oliver good night.

"You have to come eat with us next time," Oliver told her.

"Thank you for the invitation, Oliver. I'll think about it."

She moved aside and Win climbed into the driver's seat.

"Good night, Stacy," he said. "Maybe we'll run into each other again sometime."

Only by happenstance, she thought dully. Because he obviously wasn't going to repeat Oliver's invitation or ask her for her phone number. "Well, you and the boys should stop by the ranch again. We all enjoyed your company."

He started the engine. "Nice of you to offer, Stacy. But

I rarely have time for much of anything except school and taking care of things at home."

No time for dating? She was still wondering about Tara back in Whitehorn. Oliver had implied they'd moved from there to get away from the woman. Had she been Win's steady girlfriend? A mistress, who'd grown too clingy? Stacy was shocked at just how much she wanted to learn about Win's life.

"Well, just so you know you're welcome," she said.

He nodded then shut the door, ending any opportunity for her to say more, and as the truck pulled away, Stacy lifted a hand in farewell.

Win Jackson was an enigma, she thought as she watched the taillights of the truck fade into the distance. If she had any sense, she'd put him on her *don't bother* list. But where men were concerned, she'd spent the past few years playing it safe. Maybe that made her a coward, but she'd not always been so cautious. No, as a teenager, she'd done her fair share of dating and in spite of the normal drama associated with boys of that age, she'd survived without a broken heart.

By the time she'd entered college she'd thought she was ready for a serious relationship and when she'd met Spence she'd believed he was truly her dream man. Good looking, smart and ambitious, he'd checked all the right boxes on her list. They'd dated steadily for nearly a year and he'd begun talking about the two of them having a future together. He'd even visited the Bonnie B to meet her parents. But then suddenly, without any warning, he'd called it quits and started dating someone else. His desertion had been humiliating and heartbreaking. And had left her leery to trust her happiness to any man.

Nearly eight years had passed since then and though Stacy had gotten over losing Spense long ago, she'd not

forgotten the hard lesson learned about trusting her heart
to someone. Yet something about Win made her want to
throw caution to the wind. He made her wonder if the time
had come for her to take a few risks. Suffering through a
broken heart couldn't be any worse than being alone and
wondering when, or if, the right man would ever come
along.

THE FOLLOWING SATURDAY dawned clear and just warm
enough to not have to deal with a jacket. It was the sort
of day Win loved to use working around the ranch. Especially doing some needed repairs to a cross fence, along
with exercising the horses. Instead, he and his sons were
headed to the annual back-to-school picnic being held at
Bronco City Park.

Actually, it wasn't mandatory that all teachers attend
the social function, but because Win was new to Bronco
High School, he felt it was important for the parents and
students to see him making an effort to be a part of the
community and the school.

"Dad, do you think we'll see Ms. Abernathy at the picnic?" Oliver asked as Win searched for a spot to park the
truck.

"I don't know, son. We might."

"Why do you care if she's at the picnic?" Joshua asked
with a heavy dose of sarcasm. "She's just a teacher. That's
all. And you see plenty of teachers at school."

"Stacy is more than a teacher," Oliver shot back at his
brother. "She's my friend, too. And I like her a whole lot.
So does Dad."

Even though Win was concentrating on spotting an
empty parking space, he didn't miss his sons' conversation. Nothing much had changed since the night they'd had
dinner with the Abernathys. Oliver was still infatuated

with Stacy, while Joshua wanted to cut her and all women down whenever he was given the opportunity.

"Do you, Dad?"

Joshua's question was more like a challenge than a desire to know the truth, and Win had to bite back a weary sigh. Once they'd gotten home from the Abernathys' the other night, Win had taken his elder son aside and talked to him about the snide remarks he'd made about not needing a mother. Even though it had been seven years since Yvette had died, Win realized Joshua still missed her terribly. He also understood that, at fifteen, Joshua was trying to appear cool and indifferent. But Joshua needed to learn the difference between being cool and being rude.

"Yes, I like Stacy. She's a very nice woman," Win answered his question.

"Does that mean we can go back to the Bonnie B real soon?" Oliver asked eagerly.

Win stifled a groan. Three days had passed since he and his sons had sat at the Abernathy dinner table, and the time had done little to get Stacy out of his mind. Frankly, he didn't understand why he was having these obsessive thoughts about her. It wasn't like she was a dazzling beauty, or a provocative siren attempting to seduce him. She was simply kind and pretty and sweet.

"We haven't been invited," he told Oliver.

He braked the truck to a halt in the nearest parking slot he could find, which was more than a block away from the park. Apparently, the picnic was a big deal for the Bronco folks, he mused.

Oliver was quick to correct Win. "We sure have been invited," he said. "Stacy said for us to come visit anytime. Remember?"

"Yes, I do," Win replied.

He also remembered vividly how it had felt to hold her

soft little hand and watch shadows flicker furtively across her lovely face. The thought of bending his head and kissing her had burned in his brain. But knowing his sons had been sitting in the back seat of the truck had put a damper on the urge. That had probably been for the best, because something told him that one kiss from her wouldn't have been enough.

They made the short walk to the park in less than two minutes and as they merged onto a grassy area near the picnic tables, where a crowd of people had already gathered for the back-to-school event. Children were running and playing, and excited shrieks and happy laughter filled the air. Because it was still a little early for lunch, he didn't see anyone eating yet, but some folks had already taken seats at the picnic tables and spread blankets on the ground.

"Gosh, this place is running over with people!" Joshua exclaimed as they worked their way into the edge of the crowd. "Do you see anybody you know, Dad?"

Joshua had barely gotten the question out when Win spotted Anthony, along with a history teacher who doubled as an assistant baseball coach.

"Yes, I do. There's Anthony and Raymond. Let's go say hello."

Win talked to his colleagues for a few minutes before he noticed Joshua and Oliver practically jumping up and down to move on and hunt for their friends.

Once they left the two coaches and headed deeper into the crowd, Joshua found a group of his high school friends and, a short distance away, Oliver ran into his best buddy, Artie, who'd brought his collie dog to the picnic. Win was content to stand in the shade of an evergreen tree and watch the youngsters keep the dog busy fetching a Frisbee.

"Hello, Win."

The soft familiar voice caused his pulse to quicken

and he couldn't stop himself from smiling as he turned to see Stacy striding up to him. Wearing a pair of dark blue jeans and a black cotton sweater with long sleeves, she had pulled her hair up into a wavy ponytail and gold hoops dangled from her ears. She looked incredibly sexy and very different from the prim teacher attending the district meeting.

"Hello, Stacy. Nice to see you."

She smiled back at him. "I wondered if you'd come today."

He chuckled. "You sound as though you expected me to skip this picnic."

She laughed. "You don't exactly seem like the picnic type. More like the chuckwagon-and-eating-around-the-campfire kind of guy."

"Yeah, with a herd of bawling cattle in the background," he added with a wry grin. "To be honest, that's the best kind of outdoor eating. But I don't have much opportunity to do it. Did you come to the picnic alone?"

She nodded. "Yes. But I've already run into several colleagues and friends."

"Am I included in the friends group?" he asked.

The impish smile on her lips was enough to lift his spirits.

"Of course, you're included," she said then darted a quick glance around her. "Where are the boys?"

He gestured to a spot beyond his right shoulder where a group of young people had gathered around a picnic table. "Joshua is over there with his friends. And Oliver is on the playground with Artie and his dog."

She glanced over to her right just in time to see Oliver toss the Frisbee. The dog jumped and caught the piece of plastic long before it hit the ground and both boys shouted in triumph.

"Looks like those two are having a blast," she said.

"Artie is Oliver's best friend, so I'm glad he's here and the two can spend some time together away from school."

"I taught Artie when he was in second grade. He's a good kid. At that time, his mother was concerned about the boy's learning skills, but he turned out to be an A student."

"Hmm. Sometimes parents expect too much from their kids. Or maybe I should say, demand too much. I often have to remind myself that my sons aren't adults and I can't expect them to behave as such."

She nodded. "I think all adults are guilty of expecting too much from children. Including me. I just hope that whenever I have children of my own I won't treat them as little students. I want to believe I'll forget I'm a teacher and discipline them as a loving mother with a firm hand."

He scanned the soft expression on her face. "You'd like to have children?"

"Ever since I was a young girl I've dreamed about having a house full of children." She glanced at him and shrugged. "Obviously I've not started on a family yet. But I hope to—as soon as I find the right man."

As Win watched a wan smile tilt her lips, he found himself thinking she would eventually make a great mother for some man's children. He imagined she'd be loving but firm when necessary. Most of all, she would put her children's happiness and well-being before her own. Yes, she'd be very maternal and nurturing, he imagined. And a woman like her deserved to have a family of her own. But the idea of her getting that close to some other man bothered him in a way that he never expected.

"What kind of man would be right for you?" he asked.

"Well, I want him to be honest and trustworthy. Compassionate toward others, but strong enough to stand up for himself and his beliefs. He'd need to be a man who loves children and wants plenty of his own. And, of course, I want him to love me, just for being me. See, my ideal man is nothing out of the ordinary," she said with a wide smile.

"Sounds good. But you left out a major detail. You want to be in love with him, don't you?"

Pink color seeped into her cheeks before her gaze darted away from his. "Absolutely. Loving him would be my first requirement."

He shook his head as he tried to shake away the image of her wrapped in a passionate embrace with a man she'd vowed to love until death parted them.

She cleared her throat. "Now back to being a parent, from what I see, you do a great job with your sons."

"I, uh, don't know about great. I try. I feel like I should apologize to you and your family for Joshua's rude remarks at the dinner table the other night. I'm sure Billy's kids thought he sounded like a creep."

"I'm pretty sure they understand that Joshua is still hurting because he lost his mother."

He sighed. "I hope so. I had a talk with him once we got home that night. Whether it will make a difference is anybody's guess."

Her expression was full of empathy as she looked at him. "It can't have been easy raising your sons alone after your wife died. But you must be very glad that you have them."

She seemed to understand his situation far better than Tara ever had. Moreover, Stacy didn't resent the fact that he had two sons; she actually cared about their welfare.

Watch it, Win. Right now, all you're seeing in Stacy is her good qualities. She's still a woman. Especially a woman who's the marrying kind. Just what you don't want.

Shutting out the mocking voice, he said, "You're right. I'm very blessed to have my boys."

"Tell me about your wife. Was she a strict mother?"

Not many people asked him about Yvette. Probably because they thought bringing up her memory would upset him. But Stacy's question didn't bother him. In fact, it felt good not to have to skirt around the subject of his late wife.

"Yvette was actually stricter with the boys than I've ever been. She wanted them to grow up strong. Both morally and physically and though they were very young when she died, I think she'd managed to start them out in life on a solid foundation."

"Did the four of you do many family things together?"

He looked out across the grassy slope of lawn as memories of his life with Yvette paraded through the back of his mind. "As much as we could. We were like most couples. Busy with our jobs and we had the ranch to care for. But we did take the boys to family type events and always a camping trip in the summer."

She let out a soft sigh. "I'm sure you miss her. And I'm sorry you lost her. Sometimes life is very unfair."

Win could see she truly was sorry about Yvette's passing and the fact drew him to her in a way he'd never expected.

After a stretch of silence passed between them, she cleared her throat and spoke. "I see some of my colleagues have gathered at the picnic table near the cottonwood tree. Would you like to walk over and meet them?"

"Sure," he said. "Just let me tell Oliver where I'll be in case he starts looking for me."

She nodded. "I'll come with you and say hello."

They talked to Oliver a moment then left him playing with Artie and the dog.

"I understand this back-to-school picnic happens every year," Win said as the two of them walked together across a grassy slope. "Do you attend every year?"

"Always. This event has been going on for as long as I can remember. I think the kids would be in an uproar if we didn't have it."

She smelled like sunshine and wind and something else that was sweet and soft. The scent was evocative, almost as much as the feel of her hand resting gently on his forearm. Why hadn't he noticed these things about other women? he wondered. What was it about Stacy that made him think about such feminine nuances? He didn't know. He only knew that when he was with her, he felt more alive than he had in years.

ONCE THEY REACHED the table near the cottonwood, Stacy introduced Win to Emma Garner and Reginald Porter, along with Carrie Waters and Amelia Holsten.

"Emma teaches first grade, Reggie teaches fourth, Carrie is an aide and Amelia handles the kindergarten class," she explained to Win.

"Nice to meet all of you," Win said as he shook hands with each one. "And good to see you again, Reggie. I hope Oliver hasn't been giving you a bad time so far."

Stacy laughed with embarrassment. "What was I thinking? I forgot that Reggie was Oliver's teacher, so you two have obviously already met."

The middle-aged man with thinning hair and droopy features smiled and shook his head. "Oliver is polite and very attentive. I only wish I had more students like him."

"I'm relieved to hear it," Win told Reggie.

"Oh, here comes Dante and Eloise and little Merry," Emma announced. "Dante teaches third grade at Bronco Elementary."

Win turned to see a couple, both with dark brown hair and in their early thirties. The man was holding a little girl that Win would guess to be somewhere around a year old. Presently, the baby was squirming and wriggling in an effort to stand on the ground.

"Merry sees the girls on the playground across the way playing soccer and thinks she's big enough to join them," Eloise said with indulgent smile for the toddler.

"She'll be their age before you know it," Stacy told her. Then placing a hand on Win's arm, she quickly introduced him to the married couple, while adding, "Dante and Eloise are newlyweds. They had a lovely little backyard ceremony a few weeks ago."

"Congratulations," Win told the beaming couple.

"Thanks," Dante told him. "We were going to have a big wedding but with all the trauma going on with Uncle Stanley and Winona's disappearance we thought it best to keep everything low-key."

"Yes, Stacy has told me about the situation with your uncle and Winona. I hope everything turns out well."

"Thanks for your concern," Dante told him.

"Dylan, whom you met during dinner at the Bonnie B is Dante's brother," Stacy told Win.

"I see the resemblance," Win told him, adding with a chuckle, "I also see why the Abernathys warned me about saying anything about anyone around town, unless you're saying something nice, that is. Everyone seems to be related or best friends."

Dante laughed. "The rule of living in a town like Bronco," he said. "So, you're the new agribusiness teacher I've been hearing about. Welcome."

"Thanks," Win replied. "I hope what you've been hearing isn't too bad."

"On the contrary. Everyone who's mentioned you has great things to say. This area of the state thrives on agriculture, so we need teachers like you to educate the next generation of ranchers and farmers."

"Are you a rancher, along with being a teacher?" Win asked him.

"Dante helps his brother Dylan run a car dealership," Eloise answered for her husband. "You wouldn't happen to be looking to purchase a new vehicle, would you?"

Everyone laughed at Eloise's playful sales pitch and, for the next few minutes, the group talked about everything from school events to the latest local news.

Eventually, Oliver arrived to inform his father he was getting hungry, and a quick glance at his watch told Win he'd already been at the park much longer than he'd planned.

"Okay, son," he told Oliver. "We'll go find Joshua."

He'd said his goodbyes to the group and was walking away with Oliver at his side when Stacy quickly caught up with them.

"I don't mean to pry, Win, but did you bring lunch for you and the boys?"

He paused to answer her. "No. I had several chores to take care of at the ranch before we left the J Barb to come here. I didn't really have time to make anything, so I promised the kids I'd let them eat takeout."

"Oh. Well, fast food is fun, but you'd have to leave the park to eat." She encompassed Win and Oliver with an eager smile. "I brought a picnic basket with enough food for several people. I'd love to share it with you three. That is, if you like fried chicken and a few other things to go with it."

Oliver began to jump excitedly on his toes. "Fried chicken! Mmm! Can we eat with Ms. Abernathy, Dad? I love fried chicken!"

Win looked at her. Had she extended the invitation because she felt sorry for him and wanted to be polite? Or did she really want his company? He hoped it was the latter but then promptly wondered about his own motives. Why did he want to spend time with this woman when he knew there could never be anything serious between them?

He didn't want serious. He didn't want a relationship where he might risk opening his heart and having it crushed all over again. He couldn't live through that again, he thought bleakly. And yet, something about Stacy made him want to be close to her. To pretend, just for a little while, that he could have a whole family again. Maybe that made him a fool. Or maybe he was finally finding the courage he'd lost seven years ago.

"It sounds delicious. But we'd be imposing on you," Win told her. "Especially after we've already had one Abernathy dinner."

She laughed lightly. "I promise you, Win, two or even three Abernathy dinners wouldn't be an imposition. And I'd hate to eat alone."

Oliver said, "Yeah, Dad, it would be sad if Ms. Abernathy had to eat at a picnic all by herself."

"You are so right, Oliver." Smiling, she gave the boy's shoulders an affectionate squeeze then glanced hopefully at Win. "My basket is in my car. It's parked not far from here."

Win couldn't stop a smile from spreading across his face any more than he could dampen the joy he was suddenly feeling. "Okay. There's no way I can refuse your offer. Oliver would never forgive me. And I'm getting fairly hungry myself."

"Great," she said. "I'll let you guys do all the toting."

"It's the least we can do," Win told her.

The three of them started walking to the far side of the park where her car was located and, along the way, Win reached for her hand. She didn't hesitate to wrap her fingers around his.

The sweet connection caused his chest to swell with an emotion he couldn't quite describe. He only knew that the feeling was nice and warm and he wasn't sure he wanted it to go away.

CHAPTER FIVE

EARLIER THIS MORNING, while Stacy had been getting ready to drive into town for the picnic, she'd wondered if Win would be taking part in the school event. It wasn't mandatory for teachers to attend the picnic and she figured he'd much rather use his Saturday to work on his ranch. Still, she'd hoped he might feel obligated to take his sons and she could accidently-on-purpose run into him.

She'd been chatting with Emma and Carrie when she'd spotted him standing in the shade of the cottonwood. Dressed all in denim with his black hat and cowboy boots, he'd stood out from the crowd and his tall, sexy image had sent her pulse pounding. And now that he and his sons were sitting with her on a blanket spread on a patch of grassy ground, eating the lunch she'd provided, she felt sure the sky had grown bluer and the sun a bit brighter.

"Joshua, you could have invited your friend to join us," Stacy told the teenager. "We have plenty of food for her, too."

"That's okay, Ms. Abernathy. Katrina had already told me she'd have to eat with her parents and little sister Gena."

A few minutes ago, when the three of them had returned with the picnic basket and located Joshua, he'd been sitting beneath a tree with a young, dark-haired girl who appeared to be around his age. He'd introduced her as Katrina Wymore and she'd informed them that she and her family had only moved to Bronco a year ago. Stacy hadn't missed the furtive looks Joshua had been sending the girl and the shy smiles she'd been giving him.

"Gena is my age," Oliver interjected as he dug a chicken leg from a plastic container sitting in the middle of the blanket. "She sits at a desk next to me."

"Is she cute?" Win asked him then winked conspiringly at Stacy.

Oliver wrinkled his nose as he thoughtfully considered his father's question. "Yeah. I guess so. She has brown hair and freckles."

"Nothing wrong with freckles," Win told him. "You have a few of your own."

Oliver squinched up his nose even tighter. "No. But she talks. A whole lot."

Win chuckled. "Kind of like someone else I know. I feel sorry for Mr. Porter. He probably has to constantly quiet you two down."

Oliver cleared his mouth of chicken before he spoke. "We don't talk in class, Dad. We don't want to get in trouble."

Joshua released a scoffing grunt while Stacy and Win exchanged amused looks.

"Katrina says Gena never shuts up," Joshua said. "And I told her that Oliver was the same way."

"Why don't you shut up, Joshua?" Oliver snapped at his brother. "All you ever say is something mean."

Stacy hadn't been around Win's sons all that much, but enough to notice that if one boy fired off a cutting remark, the other one was quick to utter a sharp response. But in this case, Joshua wasn't shooting a string of sarcastic words back at his brother. Instead, he was studying Oliver in a bewildered way.

"Dad, do I always sound mean to Oliver?"

"Most generally," Win told his elder son.

Joshua's expression turned sheepish and Stacy wondered what was coming over the teenager. Win had told her that he'd had a talk with Joshua the other night. Perhaps some of what he'd said to the boy had sunk in.

"Gosh. I don't want to sound like a creep all the time," Joshua admitted in a plaintive voice.

The plastic fork in Oliver's hand hovered over the food on his plate as he looked at his brother. "It's okay, Joshua. I still like you anyway. You're my brother."

Grinning now, Joshua reached over and gave the top of Oliver's head a playful scruff.

"Yeah. You're a pretty good one, too."

Seemingly at peace, the boys went back to eating and, as Stacy watched them devouring the chicken, potato salad and baked beans, she thought how blessed Win was to have two sons. When he'd asked her if she wanted children, she'd not been able to express to him just how much she yearned to have babies and a family of her own. Each year that passed without so much as a special boyfriend in her life, the more she wondered if having a family wasn't meant for her. And the more she feared that the ideal man she'd described to Win would never walk into her life.

As for Win, it was tragic that he'd lost his wife, but Yvette lived on through Joshua and Oliver. He had to be thankful for his children, she thought. But did their constant presence make it impossible for Win to put his late wife behind him? She wanted to ask him. But she didn't want him to think she was prying into his private life.

"Did you cook all this food?" Win asked as he ladled more beans onto his paper plate. "It's delicious."

She cast him a guilty little smile. "Only the beans and dessert. I love to cook, but to tell you the truth, my teaching job doesn't leave me much extra time to do the things I enjoy. Thankfully, Mom took pity on me and made the chicken and potato salad when she saw I was so short on time."

He nodded with understanding. "Same with me. In fact, this morning I was thinking about how many things I needed to do on the ranch. But that's the way it is when you have a weekday job and another on the side."

"You must really like ranching because I imagine it, along with your teaching position, surely has you stretched."

A half grin quirked one corner of his lips. "I'm not complaining. I do love ranching and I want the boys to grow up learning about the vocation, even if they eventually decide to do something else with their lives. It's a good foundation. You know, going out in subzero temperatures and spreading hay or cleaning horse stalls. That kind of work has a way of keeping a person grounded."

She smiled. "Literally."

"So do you have something other than teaching that keeps you busy?" he asked.

Shrugging, she said, "I used to do all kinds of volunteer work for the library and getting hot meals to the elderly, but that was before teaching second grade took over my life. Now, the only extra work I do is to stay late at school on certain evenings to tutor adults who are trying to obtain their GEDs."

"That's an admirable job."

"I like to help people learn," Stacy said. "Especially when I know it's going to improve the quality of their life."

He nodded. "That's the same reason that keeps me in the classroom. This might sound corny, but I like to think I'm helping give young people a better start on their future."

"If that's corny, then we're both old hat," she told him then cast him a curious glance. "You mentioned having a brother. What sort of job does he have?"

"Shawn is thirty-eight. Two years younger than me. He helps our dad run the family ranch near Whitehorn. Being a rancher is all he's ever wanted to do."

"Hmm. So, as far as ranching goes, you two are alike," she commented. "Is he married?"

"He was when he was in his late twenties. It didn't work out," he said with a grimace. "Thankfully the union didn't produce any children."

"What do you mean? Shawn wouldn't make a good father?"

Win shook his head. "No. Because the marriage didn't last but about two years. It's not easy to raise kids on your own and, if they'd had children, I figure Shawn would've had to take on the major load of parenting. Anyway, I don't think he cares if he ever marries again."

And what about him? Had he decided he didn't want to be a husband for a second time? Even though she wanted to ask the questions, Stacy realized it was far too soon for her to pry into such a private subject. Besides, the boys were sitting close enough to hear every word that was said.

"I'm sorry for your brother. I remember what an awful time my brother Billy and his kids went through when he and his first wife got a divorce," she said soberly then purposely gave him a cheerful smile. "But as you might've noticed the other night, he and Charlotte are incredibly happy now. So, your brother shouldn't give up on finding happiness. And neither should you."

And what about herself? Was she truly happy? Stacy hadn't really asked herself that question until recently—until she'd met Win. Before their paths had crossed, she'd mostly focused on her teaching job and pushed the personal side of her life to the back of her mind. When she did allow herself to think of becoming a wife and mother, she told herself to be patient and it would happen. But this past year she had to admit her hopes had dimmed.

She noticed his eyes had narrowed as he continued to study her face and Stacy got the impression he resented her remark.

"What makes you think I'm not happy?"

He didn't appear to be all that annoyed with her, but the clipped tone of his words said otherwise. Still, she wasn't about to apologize.

"I didn't mean you weren't happy," she said. "I only meant that you...well, you're still a very young man and have a lot to look forward to."

His lips twisted. "Very young? I'm twelve years older than you."

"That doesn't change the fact that you're still a very young man," she told him.

The twist to his lips changed from mocking to amused. "You're not wearing glasses, so you must be wearing rose-colored contacts."

She laughed. "Hardly. My vision is perfect."

"Hey, Dad, I'm finished eating." Joshua spoke up. "Is it okay if I go now? Katrina might be looking for me."

"Sure," Win told him. "We'll hang around the park for a little longer. I'll look you up when I'm ready to go."

Stacy reached inside the picnic basket and pulled out a flat plastic container with a lid. "Here, Joshua. Take a brownie with you. Or take two. Katrina might like one."

The teenagers face lit up. "Oh, brownies! Thanks, Ms. Abernathy!"

She wrapped two of the desserts in a napkin and after she handed them to Joshua, he took off in a trot to the other side of the park.

His face a picture of bewilderment, Oliver stared after

his brother. "He sure is acting weird today. You think he's getting sick, Dad?"

Win and Stacy exchanged knowing smiles.

"He's not sick," Win assured the boy. "He's just growing up a little today."

Oliver drew back his shoulders in an effort to appear taller. "Am I growing today?"

Stacy wanted to laugh but managed to hold her reaction to a broad smile while Win gave her a conspiring wink.

He said, "You're growing every day, Oliver. And you'll keep on growing until you become a man."

His expression skeptical, Oliver asked, "Do you think I'll get to be as tall as you are, Dad?"

Win gave his son an indulgent smile. "Probably taller. Especially after the way you've eaten so much of Stacy's food. I think you and Joshua have eaten everything she had in the basket."

"Gosh, Dad, that's why she brought the food. So we could eat it."

Win slanted Stacy a wry look. "It's a good thing you showed up or my boys would've starved," he joked.

"I came prepared," she said simply. He didn't need to know she'd purposely asked her mother to prepare extra food just in case she had a chance to invite him to share her lunch. Win wasn't a man who'd appreciate being chased by a woman and she hardly wanted to give him the impression that she was running after him.

Oliver stood and rubbed a hand over his stomach. "I still have room for a brownie," he said to Stacy. "Could I take one to Artie, too?" he asked.

"I think it's very nice of you to think of Artie." Stacy reached for the container and, after wrapping two more brownies, she handed them to Oliver.

"Thanks! This is great!" He took off in a run then put

on the brakes and looked back at Win. "Me and Artie will be over on the playground with Leo."

"Who's Leo?" Win wanted to know.

"His dog! Bye!"

Oliver raced away and Win took off his hat and ran a weary hand through his hair. "I imagine your head is spinning."

Stacy laughed softly. "Are you kidding? I hear kids chattering all day long. And I'm glad to see your sons enjoying themselves. But there is something I'm curious about, Win. Do you not allow your sons to have cell phones? Nearly every child I see has one. Even some of my second graders have dragged them out of their backpacks while in class and then, of course, I have to confiscate them. It's a difficult thing for parents to deal with."

"When Joshua turned thirteen, I let him get a phone. But it's only to use for calls to his family or friends at the appropriate time. It's not equipped for surfing the web. I'm not going to allow that sort of thing until he gets somewhat older. At times, he gripes that I'm an old fogey but, for the most part, I don't hear much complaining. As for Oliver, he couldn't care less about a phone. He'd rather be outside playing with the dogs or cats."

"Sounds like you're being fair and wise," she said with an approving nod. "I should've known."

He let out a low, mocking grunt. "My sons wouldn't always agree to the fair part. But it's nice to hear you say it. To be honest, both boys expected this picnic to be boring. They thought it was going to be a bunch of teachers sitting around talking shop. They didn't think any of their friends would be here. In fact, they made me promise I wouldn't keep them here at the picnic for very long." He let out a short laugh. "If I tried to take them home now, I'd hear all kinds of squawking."

His hand was resting on his knee and she couldn't stop herself from reaching over and touching her fingers to his. The warmth of his skin matched the glimmer in his eyes and, as their gazes locked, a strange flutter struck the pit of her stomach.

She inhaled a deep breath and slowly released it. "I'm glad," she murmured. "It's nice to have your company."

"That goes both ways, Stacy. It's nice to be with you."

His voice had lowered to a rough murmur and the sexy sound caused a nervous lump to enter her throat. She swallowed then swallowed again before she ventured to speak. "Uh...after I put away this food, would you like to walk around the park? It might actually be a little quieter on the far end—away from the picnic tables."

"Sounds good," he said. "I'll help you pack up these things."

AT STACY'S CAR, Win placed the picnic basket filled with the remnants of their lunch onto the back floorboard and, after she tossed the blanket onto the seat, she punched a button on the door to relock the vehicle.

"Now that we've cleaned the kitchen," she said with an impish grin, "we can explore some of the park. Have you ever been here before today?"

"I've driven by a few times, but never stopped," he admitted.

"Good. Then maybe you won't be too bored."

"I doubt that will happen." Not with her company, he thought.

They moved away from the parking area and, as they began walking across a wide expanse of lawn, Win instinctively reached for her hand and tugged her closer to his side. She didn't resist his touch. In fact, the smile she flashed up at him said she enjoyed being close to him and Win wondered if he was losing his senses.

He didn't want to get involved with this woman. Sure, she was sweet and pretty. And judging by the beans and brownies she'd cooked for the picnic, she could cook. But he didn't need a cook. After all these years without a wife, he was fairly adept at putting a meal together. Besides, Stacy was the marrying kind of woman, not the casual affair sort. And he didn't need her, or any woman, putting a rope around him and tugging him down the marriage aisle.

What about needing her in your bed, Win? Have you forgotten how long and empty your nights have been? Wouldn't having her warm arms around you be worth putting a ring on her finger?

The taunting questions traipsing through his head should've been enough to make him release his hold on her hand and put a cool and sensible distance between them. But having her close to him was like hot coffee on a cold night. He didn't want to give up the pleasure before the cup was empty.

"Mmm. The breeze is just right. It's a perfect day." She looked up at the sky where a few clouds were scudding from north to south. "What I love about the park at this time of the year is the trees. The bright-colored leaves of the hardwoods look so beautiful next to the evergreens."

His gaze drifted away from the tempting line of her neck to where her attention was cast on a row of trees outlining the far end of the park.

"The leaves are starting to turn on the J Barb, too. The cottonwood in front of the house is a bright yellow now. I have to admit it's beautiful." It was on the tip of his tongue to suggest she come over and see the tree for herself, but he stopped the words from slipping past his lips. Why get entangled in a relationship that could never work? He'd be asking for trouble. And yet the empty holes in him were crying for him to reach for any kind of happiness she might give him. No matter how short-lived.

She sighed. "Sounds lovely."

Not nearly as lovely as her, Win thought as his gaze swept over her sun-kissed face. He couldn't ever remember seeing skin like hers. It was so fine and smooth, he couldn't spot one single pore. No doubt it would feel like silk against his cheek, beneath his lips.

He cleared his throat. "Yes, but the beauty doesn't last long. Then we're staring at bare limbs for several months."

A faint smile tilted the corners of her lips and Win wondered what she might do if he suddenly pulled her into his arms and kissed her. Would she curtly remind him that they were both teachers at a public function and had to behave with decorum?

He was still imagining the kiss when she said, "I'll tell you something else that looks beautiful at this time of the year. The huge pumpkin patch at the Bronco Harvest Festival. It's especially beautiful at night with the moon shining on everything."

Had she ever visited the pumpkin patch in the moonlight with a man at her side? With her looks and social status in the community, Win figured there'd been plenty of guys lined up at her door, but she never mentioned dating. And when Anthony had found out about Win having dinner at the Bonnie B, his coworker had remarked that he couldn't recall Stacy ever having a serious boyfriend. She'd told Win she'd not yet married because she was going to be particular, yet he couldn't help but wonder if there was another reason for her remaining single. A broken heart? A love that was never returned? He wanted to ask her about her past dating life, but if he did, she might get the idea he was getting seriously interested. And that would be misleading. He wasn't about to wander down that path again.

Pushing aside the rambling thoughts, he said, "It sounds as though I'm going to have to take the boys to the festival and the Gold Buckle Rodeo. I'm sure they'd enjoy both of them, plus I want them to feel like they're a part of Bronco's culture."

Her expression curious, she asked, "Did Joshua and Oliver like the idea of moving here to Bronco? Or would they rather have remained in Whitehorn?"

Win shrugged and hoped she wouldn't notice how uncomfortable her question had made him. Not that he had anything to hide from her or anyone. It was just that the ordeal he'd gone through with Tara still had enough sting to embarrass him. And he wasn't at all sure how Stacy would view the situation. There'd been friends and family who'd called him a coward for moving away from the only place he'd ever lived. And maybe a part of him had been a coward, he thought. Maybe, if he'd been a stronger man, he would've stood up and defended himself against Tara's trash talk. But, ultimately, he'd decided moving far away would fix the problem.

"At first, they weren't too keen on the idea. Especially moving away from their grandparents. But, thankfully, both boys started to view the move as an adventure and now I'm happy to say they love it here. In the end, I think it's best that they're not living in the same house as they lived with their mother. Reminders of her were all around the place and they kept her death fresh in Joshua's mind especially. And mine, too," he admitted.

"Had you and Yvette lived all your married life on the ranch?" she asked.

"Yes. I'd purchased the place before I asked Yvette to

marry me. At that time, it wasn't much more than a piece of land with a house on it. So we built it into a ranch together."

"Oh my. No wonder the place held so many memories." A pained looked crossed her face as she gently squeezed his fingers. "I hope living in Bronco helps dim the loss for all of you."

The tenderness he saw in her eyes caused his chest to swell with an emotion he didn't quite understand. He tried to tell himself it was simply gratitude, but he knew the feeling was more than gratefulness.

"Hey, Stacy! Win!"

A female voice calling out their names caused them to pause and look around to see Robin and Dylan hurrying forward.

"Hi, you two!" Stacy said when the pair finally reached them.

Robin gave Stacy a brief hug as Dylan shook hands with Win.

Robin patted the picnic basket Dylan was carrying. "We're going to have lunch with Dante and Eloise. They should be around here somewhere."

Stacy said, "We ran into them earlier when we were chatting with the other elementary teachers."

"They're probably chasing after Merry. She loves being outdoors," Dylan said. "Would you two like to join us for lunch?"

Win groaned and rubbed his midsection. "I'm stuffed. Stacy shared her lunch with me and the boys."

Robin's brows lifted ever so slightly as she turned a smug sort of smile on her husband.

Win figured the woman was thinking there was something brewing between him and Stacy, which wouldn't exactly be wrong. From the moment she'd first walked up to him here in the park, he'd felt undercurrents of electricity flowing between them. But if he had any sense at all, he wouldn't allow the sparks to ignite a fire.

"We would've been here earlier," Dylan explained. "But Uncle Stanley asked me to make a few phones calls for him this morning—to see if anyone had any new news about Winona."

"Has anyone heard anything new?" Stacy asked.

Robin sadly shook her head while Dylan frowned.

"Unfortunately, no," Dylan answered. "And I'm getting extremely worried about Uncle Stanley. If Winona doesn't show up soon, or we don't get some kind of word from her, I'm afraid he's going to have a mental breakdown."

"I'm worried, too." Robin added to her husband's concern. "If he isn't pacing, he's staring off into space, imagining the worst. I feel so sorry for him. But there isn't much anybody can do. Every lead has been exhausted and there are no new clues to her whereabouts."

"Stanley must be wildly in love with Winona," Win said.

Robin said, "Their relationship was deep and genuine. That's why no one can believe Winona simply ran away with cold feet."

"I have to believe Winona will be found safe," Stacy replied. "Bronco isn't the same without her. Just think of all the couples she helped to get engaged and married."

Win shot her a puzzled look and Dylan snickered.

"Is Winona some sort of matchmaker?" Win asked. "I thought she was supposed to be a psychic."

Robin said, "Winona can see things about people that normal folks can't see. She just intuitively seemed to know who should be matched together."

Win didn't bother to hide his skepticism. "Don't tell me she sprinkled some sort of magic love dust over these couples. I won't believe it."

Both Robin and Stacy laughed while Dylan shook his head with amusement.

"Nothing so obvious," Dylan told him. "She planted ideas and gave little nudges. That's all."

"And that's one of the many reasons we need for her to come home," Robin added. "So she can plant more ideas and nudge more folks toward happiness."

"Well, tell Stanley not to worry," Stacy said. "And that we're all praying for Winona's safe return."

Dylan assured Stacy he'd pass on the message and, after talking for a couple more minutes, the husband and wife said goodbye and headed to the opposite end of the park to search for Dante and Eloise.

Stacy and Win continued on their walk toward a grove of trees. As they strolled over the dormant grass, Win returned to the subject of Winona.

"Do you really believe Winona makes a man and woman fall in love?" he asked.

"Not at all."

Her unexpected answer caused him to pause and stare at her in wonder. "I don't get it. Not more than five minutes ago, you were saying she helped couples get engaged and married."

"That's true. She did. I could probably name you several couples that would thank Winona for nudging them in the right direction. But she doesn't *make* people fall in love. They do that on their own. At least that's how I imagine it will be for me."

His lips took on a wry slant. "Are you saying you've never been in love? That's hard to believe."

"Oh, there were times when I was younger that I thought I was in love. But later I realized it wasn't the deep feelings that truly defines love and all it means." She looked at him. "Did you know when you fell in love with Yvette?"

A few days ago, her question would have irked the hell out of him. He'd always considered his feelings for Yvette as private and, after she'd died, he especially hadn't wanted people digging into something that was none of their business. But something had apparently changed in him since he'd met Stacy. Now, he didn't resent her question. In fact, he understood her curiosity.

"It wasn't like a bolt out of the blue struck me. Our feelings grew gradually," he said gently.

Her eyes softened to a dreamy blue. "Instant or gradual it has to be magic."

He breathed deeply then urged her forward. "Yeah. Something like magic."

She didn't make any sort of reply and they continued to walk with their hands entwined. When they finally reached the grove, the sounds of the milling crowd were too far away to be heard and the branches of the evergreens created a screen of privacy.

"This is nice," Win said as he glanced around the cozy stand of trees. "I wonder why we're the only ones here at this end of the park."

Laughing lightly, she joked, "Because we're the only antisocial people here today." Her expression turned serious as she lifted her gaze up to his face. "Or maybe we're the only ones who appreciate being alone. At least, I enjoy being alone with you."

The glint in her eyes and breathless rush in her voice tugged on his senses and before he could stop himself, Win placed a hand on her shoulder and urged her deeper into the hanging branches of a huge fir.

Once he was certain they were hidden from view, he lowered his head until his face was mere inches away from hers. "Stacy, you're so lovely," he whispered. "And I've wanted to kiss you for so long."

She angled her face up to his. "And I've wanted you to kiss me, too."

His lips settled onto hers and a helpless groan rattled in his throat as lights flashed behind his closed eyes and his mind went momentarily blank. It wasn't until he felt her lips part and her palms flatten against the middle of his chest that he became fully aware of what he was doing. By then her soft, sweet lips were moving eagerly against his, inviting him to deepen the kiss.

Hot desire rushed from his loins to his brain and, without thinking, he pulled her into the tight circle of his arms. At the same time, he felt her body pressing itself closer, burning him with a need he'd long forgot.

Whether the kiss went on for long minutes or just a few seconds, Win couldn't say. He was only sure that he didn't want the contact of their lips to end. He didn't want to give up the heat flowing from her body and spreading through every cold, empty spot inside him.

When their lips finally eased apart, Win was so starved for oxygen, he turned his head aside and gulped in huge breaths of air. But replenishing his lungs did little to clear his senses. Everything around them was a spinning blur.

"Win," she whispered, "I didn't know it would be like this. So good."

His vision cleared just enough to see she was gazing up at him and the desire he saw flickering in the blue depths was enough to draw his mouth back down to hers.

Brushing his lips back and forth over hers, he whispered, "Too good."

This time when he kissed her, he wasn't expecting to find the same sizzle. But if anything, the connection was even hotter. In only a matter of seconds, he was totally lost in the softness of her lips and the sweet, mysterious taste of her. When his tongue pushed past her teeth and into the warm, moist cavity of her mouth, she reacted by curling her arms tightly around his neck. The shift in her body position caused her breasts to press against his chest and suddenly the need to make love to her was the only thought left in his brain.

It wasn't until a gust of wind caused one of the fir branches to lash against his shoulder that he managed to find the will to put an end to the fiery kiss and put some distance between their bodies.

Her expression dazed, she asked, "Win, I— Did I do something wrong?"

Stunned and embarrassed that he'd completely lost his control, he quickly turned his back to her and wiped a hand over his face.

"No. You did everything right," he said hoarsely. "That's why—well, for a minute there, I sort of forgot we were in a public park with a group of people not far away. I hope no one happened to walk by and see us."

Her hand came to rest in the middle of his back and, for one wild second, Win considered saying to hell with it all and pulling her back into his arms. But now was not the time or the place to let his sexual urges get out of hand. Where Stacy was concerned, there wouldn't be a right time or place for sex.

Sex? Who was he kidding? What he'd just shared with Stacy went far beyond physical pleasure. Kissing her had taken him on a magical journey and he'd felt things that he'd never experienced with Yvette or any woman. What did it mean? What *could* it mean?

"Don't worry. No one can see us where we're standing. Anyway, what if they did? We're both single adults. There's nothing wrong with us kissing."

She called that kissing? He'd thought they'd been on the verge of making love!

Straightening his shoulders, he said, "No. I suppose not. But I—" He broke off as he turned and reached for her arm. "I think we'd better head back. I need to find the boys and get home to the J Barb."

With a hand beneath her elbow, he started to guide her out of the stand of evergreens, but she stuck her heels in the ground and refused to budge.

"Just a minute, Win. I want to ask you something, and I expect you to be honest with me."

The stubborn set to her jaw told him she wasn't all that happy about his abrupt announcement. But he couldn't very well admit that having her in his arms and kissing her sweet lips had shaken him to the very core of his being. Or that he'd never felt so much searing intensity in any kiss before.

"All right," he said. "What's your question?"

Her gaze flickered but never left his face. "Are you sorry you kissed me?"

He stared at her in stunned fascination. "Did I behave like a man under duress?"

Her lips flattened to a thin line. "You didn't answer me. You asked a question."

A strange mix of emotions suddenly balled in his throat. This woman was doing things to him he didn't understand and it scared the hell out of him.

He sighed heavily. "Okay, since you want to know, then no. I'm not sorry. Why would you think that?"

"Maybe it has something to do with the look of sick regret on your face," she said glumly then instantly shook her head. "Forget I said that. Forget I even asked the question. It doesn't matter."

He didn't know why, but suddenly her feelings meant far more to him than any concerns he had over making a fool of himself.

Cupping his hand against the side of her face, he said, "Oh, Stacy. It does matter. And I think…well, you should know that kissing you was—it couldn't have been any better. I just think it would be best for both of us if we… slowed down a bit."

She closed her eyes as her lips tilted into a wry smile. "Yes. I understand."

"Do you really?"

Her blue eyes opened and looked directly into his. "Yes. You're not an impulsive person and neither am I. Slow and steady is the way we need to handle things between us. That's what you're saying. Right?"

"Yeah. Right."

Everything she'd just said was dead-on right. So why did he want to pull her back into the shadows of the trees and make love to her? Because he was lonely? Because living without a woman for all these years had left him feeling like only half a man?

Shutting his mind to those nagging questions, he placed a soft kiss in the center of her forehead and then ushered her out of the grove of the trees.

As they walked toward the busy picnic area, Stacy glanced up at the darkening sky. "Oh my, those clouds rolling in look ominous."

From the first moment he'd walked up to this woman in the hallway of the elementary school, he'd felt threatening clouds gathering over his head. Now he could only wonder how long he had before the storm actually hit.

"Yeah. Looks like it's time for us to go home," he replied.

And try to forget the brief passion they'd shared in the grove of evergreens.

CHAPTER SIX

THE FOLLOWING MONDAY, during afternoon recess, Stacy and
Emma sat together on a cement bench located at one end
of the playground, while the students from first and second grades released energy by swinging on several gym
sets and playing tag on a wide expanse of grassy lawn.

"That was quite a rainstorm that hit the back-to-school
picnic," Emma commented. "I'm just glad most everyone
had eaten before scrambling for shelter. I got drenched.
Did you?"

"No. I left before the rain started."

Curious, Emma looked at her. "Oh. I'd thought you
might come back by our table to chat a while. But after you
went to say hello to Win, I never saw you again."

Win. Even though two days had passed since she'd told
him goodbye at the park, her mind was still obsessing
over the man. The more time they'd spent together, the
more she'd been drawn to him. By the time he'd pulled
her into the thick grove of evergreens, all she'd wanted
was to hold him close to her, to kiss every hard angle of
his mouth and to show him how much he was beginning
to mean to her. And for those short moments she'd spent
in his arms, she'd believed he was feeling the same way
about her. But, obviously, she'd misjudged the hot kisses
he'd placed upon her lips.

When they'd parted at the picnic, she been practically
holding her breath, hoping he would say he wanted to see

her again, perhaps even ask her on a real date. But he'd not even offered to give her a call. So much for holding his interest, she thought glumly.

Sighing, she said, "I tell you, Emma, I honestly can't figure what Win is thinking."

Emma's expression turned wry. "I presume you're talking about what he's thinking about you."

"Yes," she mumbled, giving her head a hopeless shake. "At times, he seems like he's interested in me and then, just when I begin to feel hopeful, he goes all cool and distant. I might as well face it, when it comes to men, I'm a loser."

Instead of sympathizing with her, Emma laughed out loud. "Stacy, you must be half blind. What do you see when you look at yourself in the mirror? If you're not seeing a beautiful woman, then something is terribly wrong with you."

Frowning, Stacy looked away from her friend and out to the running and shrieking kids. Thankfully, the group continued to play without any arguments or skinned elbows or knees.

"Emma, it takes more than a nice appearance to hold a man. Especially one like Win. I think the way a person looks is secondary to him. He's more about personality, and mine must be boring as heck."

"So, what you're really saying is that you thought he'd ask to see you again and he hasn't. Right?"

Nodding, Stacy said, "Go ahead. Tell me I set my sights too high. I mean you know what the guy looks like. He could have most any woman he wanted."

Emma grimaced. "Have you stopped to think the man has been a widower for several years? Could be he doesn't want a woman in his life. Not a steady one, at least."

But when Win had kissed her, she could've sworn she'd felt desire on his lips. He was definitely capable of wanting a woman, she thought. But apparently he'd not wanted Stacy. Not enough to enter a relationship with her.

Still, she'd give her friend the benefit of the doubt. "You could be right, Emma. Besides, I shouldn't be asking for miracles."

Emma reached over and gave the back of Stacy's hand a motherly pat. "Look, Stacy, Win had dinner with you and your family on the Bonnie B. And the two of you shared lunch at the school picnic. That hardly sounds like a man who's disinterested. Anyway, he might be waiting on you to ask him out."

Stacy's jaw dropped and just as she was about to tell Emma she wasn't the man-chasing kind, the sound of the bell announced the end of the recess period.

Both women rose to their feet and began lining up the young students for an orderly march back inside the building. But even as Stacy dealt with her lively second graders, she was thinking about Win and wondering if Emma could be right. Maybe he was waiting on Stacy to make the next move. And if he was, did she have the courage to make it?

"REMEMBER, STUDENTS, TOMORROW afternoon is the field trip to the farm and ranch supply store," Win told his last class of the day. "For those of you who are planning to go, be sure to bring the permission slip your parent signed. For those of you who don't choose to go, I'll have something for you to study on the subject of budgeting and utilizing supplies for farming and ranching."

"I already have my permission note, Mr. Jackson. Can I give it to you now?"

Win looked toward the back of the room, where a tall, male student with carrot-colored hair was waving a small slip of paper in the air.

"Yes, I'll take it, Clete. Is there anyone else who wants to turn in their permissions slips today?" he asked.

Several students immediately held up their slips and Win walked around the room collecting them. He'd just taken the last one from a cheeky boy with a face full of freckles when the final bell rang to dismiss school for the day.

While backpacks were retrieved from beneath desks and kids called to each other as they quickly shuffled out the door, Win returned to his desk and began to gather the papers he intended to work on later tonight.

"Excuse me, Mr. Jackson. Can I ask you a question?"

He glanced up to see the last student in the room had paused at the corner of his desk. Julie was a petite girl with dark hair and a shy demeanor. So far, she'd been an excellent pupil, but Win had the feeling her life away from school was a struggle.

"Sure," he said. "What's your question?"

She nodded. "I was wondering if you're going to mark down grades for the students who don't go on the field trip tomorrow."

He studied her solemn face. "No. I won't be doing anything like that. I'll allow those students to make up their studies in some other way. Is there a special reason you're asking?"

Her gaze dropped to the floor as she fidgeted nervously with the shoulder strap of her handbag. "Well, I don't want to get a poor grade."

"You don't plan on joining us for the field trip tomorrow?"

"No," she mumbled. "I want to go—really bad. But my dad won't let me. He says I don't have any business leaving the school grounds."

Dealing with overprotective parents was hardly anything new for Win. Over the years he'd been teaching, he'd encountered plenty. But he had the feeling that Julie's home situation was more than an obsessive parent, and the idea bothered him greatly.

"Did you assure him that there would be plenty of chaperones with the group?"

She looked glumly up at him and shrugged both shoulders. "I tried. But he didn't care to hear about that."

Win thought for a moment before he suggested, "I'd be glad to call and talk to him if you think that would help."

A look of pure distress pinched the girl's features. "Oh no! Please don't! He, uh, isn't well. And he doesn't want to talk on the phone."

Because the man drank and wanted to hide it, Win wondered. Or was her father actually too sick to feel like holding a conversation? As Julie's teacher, it would be helpful to know the situation, but Win didn't want to embarrass the girl by asking her outright. "I see," he said and then carefully asked, "Does your mother live with you, or in town? I'd be happy to call her if you think it would help."

"She lives far away in Nevada. I don't see her very often."

Looking at this subdued child, Win had to wonder what his life would've been like if one of his children had been a daughter. Without Yvette to help him with parenting a little girl, he would've been lost.

"Well, it's okay, Julie. You're one of my best students. Don't worry about the field trip or anything else. However, if you need to talk to me for any reason, all you have to do is ask. Will you remember that?"

She gave him a timid smile. "Yes. I'll remember. Thank you, Mr. Jackson."

Win watched her leave the classroom while wishing there was more he could do for her. But, sadly, Julie wasn't the only student in Bronco High School whose home life was far from ideal. Win couldn't fix everything for those children. All he could do was teach the ones in his agriculture classes to the best of his ability and hope the lessons they learned would eventually help to give each of them a better life.

Picking up the canvas duffel bag he'd loaded with test papers and lesson plans, he left the room and walked down a long hallway until he reached an exit leading out of the building. As usual, he was running late and, as he headed to the teachers' parking lot, he expected to find Joshua already in the truck and waiting.

As he rounded a row of hedge and started down a long sidewalk to the parking area, he glanced toward his truck parked several yards away, then stopped in his tracks. His son was definitely waiting at the truck, but he wasn't alone. Katrina, the girl Joshua had introduced to him and Stacy at the school picnic, was standing next to him. And judging from the wide smile on his face, she must have been saying all the right things.

How had this little romance happened so quickly? Win wondered. Ever since Joshua's girlfriend in Whitehorn had dropped him, the boy had sworn off girls. Obviously, Katrina had managed to change his mind.

Like Stacy is changing yours?

The nagging question was rattling around in Win's head when he heard a familiar voice behind him.

"Hey, Win, wait up a minute."

Turning, he saw Anthony striding up the sidewalk. Dressed in gray gym clothes and a baseball cap, he'd clearly just come from a PE class.

Win waited until his friend was standing next to him before he said, "I've not seen you around the past couple of days. Where have you been?"

"Busy. I guess you haven't heard. I'm assisting the basketball coach now. Ronnie, his regular assistant, is laid up with a broken leg, so I had to take his place."

"No. I hadn't heard about Ronnie. What about your PE classes?"

"I'm doing those, too. And I'm dog-tired, that's what," Anthony told him. "And today has been one of those days best forgotten. I figure I deserve to take myself out for pizza tonight and I thought you and the boys might like to join me. My treat."

"Thanks for asking, Anthony. But I need to get home. I've been having trouble with an automatic valve on one of my watering troughs. I need to work on it before dark."

"Darn. Well, we'll make it another night then. That is, unless you're too busy seeing Stacy," he added slyly.

Win frowned at the younger man. "What are you talking about? I'm not seeing Stacy."

A smug grin crossed Anthony's face. "Could've fooled me. I saw you two walking everywhere together at the park last Saturday. And you looked pretty chummy. I imagined you would've already asked her out on a date by now."

Win came close to muttering a curse. For the past three days, Oliver had been hounding him about seeing Stacy. Now, Anthony had joined in. It was too much. Especially when he'd been trying like hell to get her and those hot kisses out of his mind.

"You figured wrong," he said stiffly.

Anthony looked puzzled. "Why? She's nice, and pretty. What's the matter? Is she too chatty for you?"

Talk wasn't the problem, Win thought as he stifled a helpless groan. Kissing was the crux of the matter. She made him feel and want things he'd not thought about for a long time. She made him dream and wish for all the things he'd lost when his wife had died. It wasn't right. It wasn't good. Yvette was the one love of his life. Why try to have another one?

Exhaling a weighted breath, he said, "No. I like Stacy. A lot. I just don't think now is the time to get involved with a woman."

Anthony's eyebrow arched. "You sound like a damned fool. When would be the right time? When you get old and the boys are grown and gone from home?" he asked with a heavy dose of sarcasm. "I'd call that wasting some good years."

"Look, Anthony, I know you mean well, but you don't understand. I told you all about the misery Tara caused me when I called it quits with her. I don't want to go through that kind of headache again."

Anthony leveled a pointed look at him. "You're right. I can't understand completely because I've not lost a wife like you have. Hell, I've not even had a wife to lose. But if you're worried that Stacy could be another Tara, you're delusional. You really want to know what I think?"

Rolling his eyes, Win glanced at his watch. "I think you're making me later than I already am."

He took off walking in the direction of his truck, but instead of being put off, Anthony stuck to his side. "You're going to hear what I think anyway. I don't believe you're a bit worried about Stacy behaving like Tara. What you're really worried about is loving her and losing her."

Win's boots practically skidded on the graveled surface as he stopped abruptly and turned to face Anthony. "Hell, yes, that worries me! Wouldn't it worry you?"

Anthony shook his head. "Life is too short to live in fear. If I had the opportunity you have with a woman like Stacy, I wouldn't be wasting it cowering at home, chewing on my nails."

"You're a real friend, Anthony." Win sneered.

The other man chuckled. "Why do you think I'm giving you a lecture? Because you're my friend and I want you to be happy."

Win swiped a hand over his face then glanced over to where Joshua and Katrina were still talking. His son was now holding the girl's hand and the sight of their young and tender relationship caused a pang of bittersweet emotion to slice through his chest. Win was glad Joshua had found a special someone. But how would his son handle things if his heart was broken a second time?

Forget about a second broken heart, Win. Think about the miserable life your son would have if he was afraid to love. Like you.

The little voice came from out of the blue and struck Win like a thunderbolt. He was being a coward. His own teenaged son had more courage than he did.

He let out a heavy sigh. "Yeah. I know you want me to be happy, Anthony. And I understand a person has to take chances in life if he's ever going to get the most out of it. So I'm...going to try."

Anthony gave Win's shoulder a friendly slap. "Now you're talking, buddy."

Giving his friend a lopsided grin, Win asked, "Why don't you come out to the ranch tonight? I have some frozen pizza I can bake. I might even find a beer to go with it. The boys would enjoy your company."

"I don't even have to think about an offer like that. I'll be there. What time?"

"Come early. You can help me with the water float."

Anthony chuckled. "I knew there must be a catch in there somewhere. Okay. I'll drive over after I go home and change."

The two men parted and Win waited long enough for

Joshua to give Katrina a quick goodbye before he drove the two of them away from the school building.

"Wow, Dad, you're late! Oliver might be locked out of the building!" Joshua exclaimed.

Win pressed down on the accelerator while keeping a cautious eye on the speedometer. Getting a speeding ticket would only make things worse. "I'm not that late. There's usually a teacher or two who stay after the last bell."

"Like Ms. Abernathy?" Joshua asked.

Win silently groaned. Ever since the three of them had shared Stacy's picnic lunch last Saturday, his sons had been making sly innuendos regarding the pretty teacher and their dad. As far as Oliver was concerned, he'd be thrilled if Win took Stacy on a date. As for Joshua, his older son appeared to be softening his opinion about women. But he wasn't sure how the teenager would view his father going on a date. Not that Win was planning such a thing, or that Stacy would agree to go out with him. No, as much as he'd been blown away by Stacy's kisses, he needed to keep a cool head and remember the reason he'd moved to Bronco in the first place.

"You and Oliver don't miss anything, do you?"

"We can tell that you like her," Joshua answered.

"I do like Stacy," Win said frankly. "Probably as much as you like Katrina."

A glance in the rearview mirror showed Joshua scooting as far up in the seat as the shoulder harness would allow. "Gosh, Dad, I really like Katrina. I even kissed her at the school picnic. And you know what?"

Win tried not to appear shocked, even though his head was spinning at the thought that he'd not been the only Jackson male to do some kissing at the school picnic.

"No. What?" Win asked.

"She kissed me back. And it was awesome!"

Another glance in the mirror revealed a big grin on Joshua's face. "That's the way it is, son, when you're with a girl you really like."

"Yeah, Katrina is a lot nicer than Monica back in Whitehorn," Joshua said, letting out a contented sigh. "Dad, I'm really glad we moved here to Bronco. Aren't you?"

In the beginning, when they'd first arrived in Bronco, there had been days that Win had questioned himself over the move. He'd wondered if he'd done the right thing by uprooting himself and the boys. And wondered, too, if they would fit in with the locals. Nowadays, he didn't wonder any more. He just thanked God that he'd made the move.

"Yes, I am," he told Joshua. "It feels like home."

Joshua leaned up closer to Win's shoulder. "You know, Dad, if you really like Stacy—I mean, Ms. Abernathy, you ought to kiss her. I bet you'd like it."

Win's foot very nearly slipped off the accelerator. He'd liked it, all right. So much so that he still couldn't get her or the kisses they'd shared out of his mind.

Clearing his throat, he said, "I imagine kissing Stacy would be nice. But a grown man doesn't go around kissing a woman just because he'd like to. Older women have different ideas about such things."

"Aww, shoot. If that's the way it is, then I'd rather just stay fifteen and not have to worry about all those other things."

Yes, things had been a lot simpler when Win had been fifteen. He'd not known then that he'd be raising two sons without his wife at his side. He'd not imagined that the idea of loving a second time would fill him with cold dread. When he thought about Stacy, he wished he could be young and innocent again. He wished he could start over with a heart full of love and trust.

Five minutes later, when he parked in front of the elementary school, Oliver and three other children were waiting on the steps at the front entrance of the building. Carrie Waters was there to make sure each one left with their authorized ride.

As soon as he'd hustled Oliver into the truck and pulled away from the school parking lot, his son let out a disappointed groan.

"You shouldn't have been so late, Dad. Ms. Abernathy had been waiting out on the steps with Carrie for a long time before she finally got in her car and drove off. You could've talked to her. I know she wanted to see you."

Joshua thought his father ought to be kissing Stacy while Oliver thought he should be talking with her. What was going on with his sons anyway?

"What makes you think she wanted to see me?" Win asked him. "Did she tell you that?"

"Well, no. Not exactly. But she did ask how you were doing. I told her I'd tell you to call her."

Win wearily pinched the bridge of his nose and tried not to groan out loud. "Okay, you've told me. Now, that's enough about Stacy. We're going to have company tonight. Anthony is coming over to eat pizza with us. And I want the both of you to be on your best behavior."

A glance in the mirror showed Joshua making a triumphant fist pump; which was hardly surprising. Anthony was one of the first people they'd met when they'd moved to Bronco back in the early summer and since then both boys had grown very fond of the young athletic coach.

"Great!" he exclaimed. "Does that mean we get to stay up late?"

"No. It means you're going to wash all the dirty dishes tonight," Win informed the teenager.

When Joshua groaned in protest, Oliver began to giggle.

Glancing in the rearview mirror at the pair, Win said, "Don't be so quick to laugh, Oliver. You're going to help him."

LATER THAT EVENING at the main ranch house, after the Abernathys had finished dinner, Stacy and Robin shooed their mother out of the kitchen and went to work loading the dishwasher and putting away the leftovers.

"I was planning to stay home and work on lesson plans, but when Mom called and told me you and Dylan would be here, I couldn't refuse the invite to join all of you," Stacy said as she placed a container of scalloped potatoes into the refrigerator. "I need to hear my sister tell me I'm making a fool of myself and then I might be able to do something about it."

Chuckling, Robin dunked a small copper stewing pot into a sink of sudsy water. "You've never made a fool of yourself. Why would you start now?"

Stacy shut the door on the refrigerator and walked over to stand next to her sister. "I've been asking myself that same question," she said. Then, shaking her head, she asked, "Wouldn't you say I'm usually a sensible person? That I'm not delusional trying to shoot for an impossible star?"

Robin rinsed the pot then handed it to Stacy for her to dry.

"I'd say you're one of the most levelheaded persons I know—even if you are my sister," she added impishly. "What's wrong, anyway? Did something happen at school to upset you?"

Corralling a room full of seven-year-olds while trying to teach them was a snap compared to dealing with the uncertainty she was feeling over Win, Stacy thought.

Sighing, Stacy opened a lower cabinet and placed the dried pot on a shelf. "This isn't about school. It's Win. I can't get him out of my mind. I'm worried that I'm falling for the man."

"Why should that worry you?" Robin asked with a quizzical frown. "Falling for a guy is nothing abnormal—it's actually wonderful. And let's be honest, Stacy. For you, this has been a long time coming."

Stacy bit down on her bottom lip as she glanced uncertainly at her sister. "If you're thinking I've been purposely avoiding falling in love because of Spence, you're wrong."

Robin grimaced. "I wasn't going to bring Spence into the conversation, because I know the memory of him makes you cringe."

"Of course it makes me cringe," Stacy said flatly. "He was the biggest mistake of my life. And after Spence all I've ever known is boring dates and men who leave me disinterested. How can I know what I'm feeling? The only thing I'm certain about is that I can't get Win out of my mind. And that can't be good."

Robin chuckled. "Stacy, you need to relax. Falling in love is a little like being obsessed. But it's a glorious sort of obsession. Especially when your partner is equally moonstruck."

Try as she might, Stacy couldn't imagine Win losing his head over her, or any woman. "Win isn't the dreamy sort. At least, not with me," she said dully.

Robin pulled the strainer from the sink and reached for a dishtowel. "What makes you think he isn't? I saw the way he was holding your hand at the picnic."

Rolling her eyes, Stacy said, "You sound like Emma now. Today, during recess, she suggested Win might be waiting on me to make the first move and ask him out. Can you imagine me asking a man like him for a date?"

"No. Because you'd be too afraid he'd turn you down and then you'd be terribly embarrassed. Right?"

"It would be humiliating," Stacy admitted, tilting her head to one side as she continued to consider the idea. "You remember that guy who caught my eye in college? The one before I started dating Spence?"

"Vaguely. Nothing ever happened with the two of you."

Stacy grimaced. "Exactly my point. I was infatuated with him. And when I finally got up enough nerve to ask him to join me for coffee, he acted as though I'd insulted him. I wanted to crawl in a hole. But that humiliation wasn't enough to make me think twice about dating. It wasn't long after that experience that I met Spence and— well, we all know how that turned out. When it comes to men my judgement is definitely shaky."

Robin shook her head. "From what I see, Win isn't a bit like those guys. He's settled and responsible."

"Yes," Stacy agreed. "But I'm not at all sure he'd appreciate me inviting him on a date. Still, if I did ask Win and he turned me down, I don't suppose I'd be losing anything—other than my pride. Nothing ventured, nothing gained. Right?"

"Right." With a smile of encouragement, Robin gave her a hug then stepped back and leveled a serious look at her. "I'm just wondering, though, if you've carefully thought through getting involved with Win. He's somewhat older than you. And he has two sons, who are at the age where parenting starts to get difficult. The other night at the dinner table, I recall how the older boy flatly stated he didn't need or want a mother. Talk about a challenge. I'd really have to love the man in order to deal with that sort of resentment from his child."

Stacy sighed. "Trust me, Robin. I've thought about all those things. Especially the fact that Win is a widower and Joshua is still clinging to his mother's memory. But

I— When I'm with Win, I feel like I want to take a risk and see if the two of us could have something special."

Robin's smile was understanding. "If that's the way you feel, then you should try to see him again. Then if the two of you click in the right way, everything else will fall into place."

If was a mighty big word and Robin had just used it twice, Stacy noted. Still, she wasn't ready to mark Win off as a lost cause. But were the two of them actually meant to be together? The answer to that question was something she had to find out for herself.

CHAPTER SEVEN

THE NEXT DAY, Win was even busier than usual with the afternoon field trip to the Bronco Farm and Ranch Supply store. But the outing turned out well and the students learned firsthand about the many common expenditures farmers and ranchers dealt with on a daily basis. That had been Win's main objective for the trip.

Just before the class had loaded onto the bus to leave for the trip, Win had handed out worksheets for the students who were staying behind in study hall. Julie had been one of them and when Win paused at the side of her desk, she'd stared soulfully in front of her rather than look up at him. He'd not questioned the girl again about her father. Rather than help the situation, he realized bringing up the issue a second time would only make her feel worse. He also realized Julie needed a mother in her life.

Oliver and Joshua need a mother, too. You can't do anything to help Julie, but you can damned well give your sons a mother.

The nagging voice in Win's head was a constant thing. So were his thoughts of Stacy. The time he'd spent with her at the school picnic had turned him into a daydreaming fool. No matter how hard he fought to push her out of his mind, he couldn't quit thinking about her kisses. He couldn't stop himself from wanting to hold and kiss her again.

"Dad, did you want me to give the horses the same amount of alfalfa tonight?"

Joshua's question interrupted Win's wandering thoughts and he glanced up to see the teenager had paused at the open doorway of the barn. Only a few minutes ago, he and the boys had arrived home from school and now the three of them were at the barn, taking care of the evening chores.

"Give them half a block extra this evening," Win told him. "The weather is getting colder and I don't see much grass left in the pasture for them to graze on."

"Okay. I got it," Joshua told him.

Off to the left of Win, two border collies were yipping with excitement as they ran tight circles around Oliver's legs. The task of feeding the dogs was something his younger son enjoyed, which explained Oliver's loud giggles as the pups playfully nipped at his heels.

"Oliver, be sure and fill the dogs' water tub," Win called to him. "I don't want them trying to jump up on the edge of the horses' water trough to get a drink. If one of them fell in, I'm not sure he could climb out."

Oliver gave his father an assuring wave. "Don't worry, Dad. I never forget the dogs' water."

Win gave the boy a thumbs-up then went on inside the barn where he had a sick cow and her calf penned in a stall. He'd just given the cow an injection of antibiotic and was pouring her a helping of feed into a rubber tub, when the cell phone in his pocket buzzed with an incoming call.

His first thought was to ignore it. He had a few more things around the ranch yard that needed his attention before dark. He didn't have time for a phone chat. But the possibility that the caller might be one of his parents, or his brother back in Whitehorn with important news, had him reaching for the phone.

The sight of Stacy's name and number on the ID momentarily stunned Win. Even though the two of them had exchanged phone numbers at the picnic, he'd not expected her to call any time soon. As for Win calling her, there had been several times during the past three days that he'd almost tapped her number. However, each time he'd told himself he'd be a fool to invite problems and had put the phone away.

Now his heart was suddenly racing as he clicked the accept button and held the phone to his ear. "Hi, Stacy. How are you?"

"I'm great," she said cheerfully. "Did I catch you at a bad time?"

"I'm just doing some chores at the barn. No big deal." The idea that he was trying to sound cool and casual caused him to silently curse. Since when did a forty-year-old man need to appear cool? After he'd let a woman turn him into a fool?

"Oh. I apologize for the interruption. I won't keep you long," she promised. "Uh, the reason I'm calling is… I wanted to invite you and the boys over to the Bonnie B tonight. That is, if you're able to finish your chores before too late. We've had a happy event take place over here and I wanted to share it with you. And have you three stay for dinner, of course."

After the family dinner he and the boys had shared with the Abernathys several days ago, Win had sworn it was the first and last. But things had changed drastically since then, he mentally argued. He and Stacy had gotten more acquainted. They'd also gotten close enough to exchange several hot kisses. And, anyway, he couldn't deny he'd been longing to see her again.

Smiling in spite of himself, he stepped out of the small pen holding the cow and calf and carefully latched the gate behind him. "A little happy news is always welcome. What's happened?"

"One of Dad's mares has foaled twins and they are absolutely adorable. I thought you and the boys would enjoy seeing them."

"Twins. That is a happy event. And rare," Win said. "I've heard of mares having twins, but never actually seen a set of them."

"Dad says he's never had a mare have twins before this one. You can imagine he's over the moon. Mom practically had to drag him away from the barn last night. The babies were born around nine and he wouldn't leave them until the vet arrived and declared the mare and foals to be healthy. And that ended up being around two this morning."

Win's mind was suddenly spinning. Not with the news of the twin foals, but with the fact that Stacy wanted to see him again. Still, going over to the Bonnie B might give her all the wrong signals. She might start thinking he was romantically interested in her.

And she'd be right, Win. You want like hell to see her again, too. Don't hem and haw and hide from the truth.

The taunting reprimand caused him to swipe a weary hand over his face. "Short night for your father. But I don't imagine he minded the loss of sleep."

She laughed softly. "Dad doesn't realize he's lost any sleep."

The joy he heard in her laughter had him thinking back to the school picnic and how happiness had showed on her face and twinkled in her blue eyes. He'd wanted to bottle up all her joy and use it later when the empty side of his bed caused an ache in his chest.

"Win? Are you still there?"

Giving himself a hard mental shake, he said. "I'm here. Uh, I guess you're waiting on an answer?"

"Well, yes. I need to let Mom know if she's having guests for dinner."

In spite of all the doubts and self-admonitions that had been going through Win's mind since he'd kissed her so wantonly, he couldn't stop a wave of eager excitement from rushing through him.

"Okay, Stacy. If you're certain you want us, we'll be over after we wrap up the chores."

He could hear a breath of air rush out of her. Had she been worried he'd turn her down?

"I'm so glad, Win. I— It will be good to see you again. And the boys, too."

The gentleness he heard in in her voice was genuine and it caused something in his chest to burgeon with unexplained emotions.

"It will be just as good for me, Stacy," he said huskily. "See you in a bit."

"I'll be watching for you," she said and promptly ended the call.

Win slipped the phone back into his shirt pocket just as Joshua walked up to him.

"Who was on the phone, Dad? You're smiling."

Yeah, he was smiling, Win thought. And it felt good.

"That was Stacy. She's invited us over to the Bonnie B tonight. One of Asa's mares had twins. She thought we might like to see them and have dinner. How does that sound to you?"

Walking up on the tail end of the conversation, Oliver reacted by making a few fist pumps. "Yay, Dad! Going to the Bonnie B would be awesome!"

Win directed a questioning look at Joshua. "What about you, Joshua? Do you want to go?"

Joshua shrugged both shoulders. "Would it make any difference if I didn't?"

"If you're asking if I'd call Stacy back and tell her we weren't coming, then my answer is no. But I'd like for you to want to go."

Joshua paused for a moment then grinned and nodded. "I'm with Oliver. Seeing twin baby horses would be cool. And I'm kinda starting to like Ms. Abernathy."

Win was beginning to like her, too, he thought. Whether that was good or bad remained to be seen.

AN HOUR LATER, Stacy was standing on the porch of the ranch house when she spotted Win's black truck coming up the gravel road that ran in front of the house and farther on to the ranch yard.

Unable to contain her excitement, she quickly bound down the steps and across the yard, then passed through the gate to wait for him to bring the truck to a stop.

"Hi, Win!" she called as he stepped down from the cab. "Welcome to the Bonnie B again. I'm so happy you could make it."

"Hi, Stacy!" he greeted. "Thanks for inviting us."

While he reached back into the vehicle for his jacket, Joshua and Oliver climbed from the back seat. Stacy said hello to them both before she turned to see Win shrugging the denim garment over his plaid flannel shirt.

"We hurried to get over here before dark, but I'd forgotten just how far it is from the J Barb to the Bonnie B," he told her. "I hope we're not holding up dinner."

"Not at all. In fact, we still have plenty of time to go see the foals. And no worries about it getting dark. There's plenty of lights in and around the barn," she assured him then turned her attention to the boys. "Are you guys ready to see the new babies?"

"Oh yeah!" Oliver exclaimed. "We've never had a baby horse on our ranch before. I can't wait to see them."

"I'm excited to see them, too," Joshua admitted. "Dad says twin foals are rare."

"He's right. They don't come along very often." She gestured toward a barn to the right of a large hay shed. "They're over in the big barn."

The four of them made their way across a wide expanse of graveled ground until they reached one end of the barn where a door with a wooden latch was located.

"This is actually the back entrance of the barn," she told Win as she lifted the wood handle and opened the door. "But this end of the building is where most of the horses are kept. That is, the horses that Dad wants stalled. The rest of the remuda runs loose in a pasture on the far east end of the ranch yard."

"We only have two horses on the J Barb," Oliver told her. "But Dad says he's gonna get two more pretty soon. That way all three of us will have a horse to ride and one extra in case we need it."

"Sounds like a good plan," Stacy said to him.

Win chuckled. "Especially for a kid who's crazy about horses," he said as he gave Oliver's head an affectionate scrub.

"Me and Oliver can ride good," Joshua told her. "Can you?"

Surprised and pleased that the teenager was making conversation with her, she looked at him and smiled. "Actually, I'm not all that good at horseback riding. I can stay aboard, but I do a lot of bouncing around. My brothers say I'm hopeless as a cowgirl. But my sister, Robin, is good at riding. She knows all about horses."

"My mom could ride good," Joshua said. "Couldn't she, Dad?"

Darting a glance at Win, Stacy expected to see a dark expression on his face. Instead, he gave her a wry smile that said his late wife would always be a part of their lives. The idea would probably discourage some women from trying to have a relationship with Win, but Stacy was trying not to let it daunt her. After all, it wouldn't be normal or respectful for any man to dismiss memories of his late wife, she thought.

"Yes. She was an excellent horsewoman," Win answered his son.

"I bet Ms. Abernathy could be excellent, too," Oliver spoke up. "If she tried hard."

The fact that Oliver wanted to defend her was so sweet, it brought a mist of tears to her eyes. After blinking the moisture away, she looked up at Win and smiled.

"I'd have to quit shaking in my boots first," she joked.

All four of them entered the barn and Stacy carefully latched the door behind them before they started walking down a wide alleyway with horse stalls situated on both sides. Fluorescent lights hung from the rafters and cast a soft glow over the entire interior of the building. Down the center of the high, open ceiling, heaters fastened to an iron I-beam were currently blowing warm air down into the stalls. At the far end of the building, a radio was playing soft music and the sound intermingled with the rustle of hay and the exchange of soft nickers between the horses.

"This is quite a setup," Win said as he gazed curiously around him. "I'd say the Bonnie B has some pampered horses."

"Dad loves his animals and his children." She slanted him an impish grin. "And you're probably thinking he spoils all of us."

He arched a quizzical brow at her. "Not really. You and your siblings don't appear to be spoiled."

Her grin turned into an all-out smile as she stepped

closer to his side and slipped her arm through his. "Thank you, Win. That's one of the nicest things you've said to me."

"Well, it's obvious you and everyone in your family all work for what you have. Besides, money and what it can buy isn't the only way a person can be spoiled."

"You're right. I see it every day with some of my little students."

Joshua and Oliver had walked on ahead of the adults and were now peering into each stall they passed. When they reached the one with the mare and her foals, they both dropped to their knees and peered through the bottom slats of the enclosure to get a better view.

"I told them not to be yelling, so they wouldn't scare the foals or the other horses," Win told her, adding with a chuckle, "I'm actually surprised they're following my orders. I guess they're too enthralled to start shouting."

Smiling up at him, she squeezed his arm. "I'm glad they're excited to see the foals. I wanted them to enjoy this evening. I want you to enjoy it, too."

"You needn't worry about that." He placed a hand over the one she had resting on his arm. "I'm glad you invited us. And the boys will be telling all their friends about this."

They reached the stall where Joshua and Oliver were still engrossed with the matching chestnut-colored foals and, for the next few minutes, all attention was on the mare and her babies.

"Dad named the one with the white star on its forehead Star," Stacy said with a little laugh. "Not very original, but it fits the little fellow. And the one with the white lightning bolt on its forehead has been named Comet. He's the feisty one."

"Star and Comet! Boy, I sure wish we had a pair of baby horses like this," Joshua exclaimed. "They're going to be awesome when they grow up."

"Look how tiny their feet are, Dad!" Oliver noted excitedly. "And they have white on their legs, too."

"Those are called stockings," Joshua informed his brother. "Right, Dad?"

"That's right, son."

A footstep sounded behind them and Stacy turned to see Rueben, one of the Bonnie B's long-time ranch hands, had walked up to them. As soon as Stacy began to introduce the rail-thin man to Win and his sons, he set down the bucket of water he was toting and pushed a battered brown hat back off his forehead to reveal a thick swathe of iron-gray hair.

"Nice to meet you folks," he said, shaking each of their hands.

"Looks like you're bringing fresh water to Lizzy," she said to the older man.

Rueben nodded. "She needs to drink plenty. It's going to take lots of milk to feed these two."

"What if she doesn't have enough milk?" Joshua asked worriedly.

Rueben gave the teenager a toothy grin. "Oh, if that was to happen, we'd bring out the bottle and feed them by hand. Don't you worry, son, these little hosses won't ever go hungry."

"What kind of milk would go in the bottle?" Oliver wanted to know. "Horse milk?"

Chuckling, Rueben winked at Stacy and Win, then began to explain to the boys all about milk formula and the nutrients needed to feed a foal. As they listened intently, Stacy pulled Win to one side.

"Would you like to go for a walk around the ranch yard?" she asked. "I'll tell Rueben to keep an eye on the boys and show them the rest of the stalled horses."

His hand came to rest against the middle of her back as

he gave her a clever little smile. "How did you know that was exactly what I wanted to do?"

Her heart beating fast, she flashed him a pointed grin. "Oh, it was just a guess."

After Stacy instructed Rueben to keep a watch on the boys, she and Win walked to the far end of the barn where another door opened out to a long loafing shed.

"When the weather is cold and wet, some of the cattle bunch under here for shelter," she explained. "And there's two more longer loafing sheds than this one out beyond that barn you can see in the distance. Right now, most of our cattle are still on the ranges grazing on what's left of the summer grass. What about yours?"

"I'm going to have to start buying hay soon. But that's to be expected."

He snugged his arm tighter around the back of her waist and urged her away from the barn door. As they walked over to the overhang of the tin roof, she took in a deep breath and said, "I'm going to make a confession, Win. I thought long and hard before I called you. I was afraid you'd think I was being forward and trying to twist your arm just so I—uh, could see you again."

His warm chuckle reassured her that she'd not made a mess of things with him.

"Stacy, you're hardly the forward type. And you're sure not big enough to twist my arm," he teased and then his voice lowered to a husky tone. "I'm glad you called and I'm glad I'm here. And in case you didn't know, you look beautiful tonight."

Laughing softly, she glanced down at her old jeans, simple brown ranch jacket and the yellow muffler she'd tied loosely around her neck. "Not like this. But thank you, anyway."

With his hands on both sides of her waist, he turned her

so that she was facing him. "Stacy, I don't think you invited me out here to talk about cattle or hay. And I didn't come out here to talk agriculture or ranching."

Even though they were standing in the shadows, there was just enough light for her to see stark need on his face. The sight of it put a lump in her throat and turned her voice into little more than a whisper.

"No. I guess I need to make a second confession," she said. "I wanted to be alone with you. After the picnic, I—"

The remainder of her words were lost as he let out a low groan and tugged her body forward until it was pressed to his.

"I can't get you and that day out of my mind, Stacy. I've tried. But I keep thinking about you and this."

Even as he said the words, his face was drawing down to hers, making it clear what he meant by *this*.

Closing her eyes, she breathed his name and tilted her lips up to his. The contact of his hard lips was just as magical as she remembered and as he quickly deepened the kiss, a rush of hot pleasure swept over her.

With a tiny moan, she wrapped her arms around his waist and leaned in against his hard, lean body. Her lips couldn't deny how much she wanted and needed him and she tried to let her kiss convey all the warm and wonderful feelings he evoked in her.

When he finally raised his head enough for them to drag in deep breaths, he reached up and stroked his fingers through the long strands of hair waving away from her forehead. The touch of his big hand was incredibly gentle and she found herself wishing and wanting his hands to touch more than her face or hair. She wanted to have them moving over every part of her body. She wanted to feel his rough palms sliding against her bare skin.

"I don't understand this, Stacy," he mouthed against her cheek. "No matter how much I kiss you, I still want more."

"Yes. Oh yes. I want more, too." She leaned her head back and met his gaze in the semidarkness. "That's why I wanted to see you again—to see if your kisses still turned my senses upside down."

His hands slipped to the middle of her back and tugged her upper body even tighter to his. "Do they?"

A little breathless laugh rushed past her lips and, in the back of her mind, Stacy wondered if she was morphing into a different woman right there in Win's arms. She'd never felt like this with any man. She'd never said such words to any man. And yet, with Win, it all felt natural and right.

"I think you've given them an even harder shake tonight," she murmured.

A lopsided grin twisted his lips. "I can't tell you what you've done to mine. I'm too addled to think."

She reached up and cupped her hand to the side of his face. "I'm a boring little school teacher, Win. I don't know the first thing about addling a man's senses. At least, not a man like you."

The grin on his lips deepened. "What does that mean? A man like me?"

Her cheeks were hot, but she didn't care if he could see she was blushing. The longer she was in his arms, the more her inhibitions slipped off into the darkness.

"You're not a geek, like most of my dates have been. And I'm not a sexy siren."

One of his hands moved to the back of her head and, as his fingers meshed in her hair, she felt certain she was going to melt right there in his arms.

"You underestimate yourself, Stacy. You're sexy as hell to me."

He didn't wait for her to respond with words. He lowered his head back to hers and this time when his lips fastened roughly over hers, she opened her mouth and invited his tongue to plunge inside.

Somewhere beyond the loud roar in her ears, she heard his needy groan, and somewhere in the far distance, a cow answered the bawl of her calf. Closer to the house, the engine of a vehicle fired to life, while just beyond the loafing shed where they stood, she could hear the wind rattling the leaves on the cottonwood tree. Strange that all those sounds could penetrate her senses even while she was enraptured by the taste of him, the warmth of his body enveloping hers, and the fire igniting each kiss.

A glorious obsession.

Yes, she thought. That described her feelings for Win perfectly.

Their embrace must have gone on for much longer than Stacy knew. By the time he finally pulled away from her, she was practically limp with the need for oxygen and she had to clutch his forearms to steady herself.

"Stacy, I—*we* need to get back to the barn. Before the boys come looking for us."

Gulping in a deep breath, she nodded. "You're right. We, uh, have probably been out here longer than I thought."

"We didn't get very far on our tour of the ranch yard," he said.

Her short laugh was more like a cough. "No. We sort of got sidetracked. Next time you're here, I'll show you the ranch yard for real."

His hand came to rest on her shoulder and she glanced up to see an uncertain expression on his face. She didn't know what he was thinking, but whatever was on his mind, she was bound and determined to deal with it.

"Next time? Is there going to be a next time?" he asked.

"Certainly. Why wouldn't there be?"

He took a moment, as if considering his response. "I don't know, Stacy. I—I'm not sure I'm ready for this. Something happens when the two of us get together. It's…"

"Deep? And a little scary?" she finished for him.

With a helpless groan, he buried his face in the side of her hair. "To me, it's a whole lot scary."

She turned her head just enough to rub her cheek against his. "This is all new for me, Win. Since I met you, my life has started to change, and I guess that's a little frightening. But it's a wonderful kind of frightening. Kind of like an adventure you've always wanted to take into the wilderness, but you're not sure what's waiting for you once you get to your destination. You just have to trust everything will be good."

He pulled his head back and she could see an anguished frown twisting his features. "That sounds very optimistic, Stacy. Or maybe I should say courageous."

She didn't let his doubtful expression get her down. He'd just made love to her with his kisses and, for now, that was enough to lend her all the hope she needed.

"That's better than being a doom and gloom person. Something I'm guilty of being too many times. I don't want to view myself or the future in that way. I want to be optimistic and I want the same thing for you."

His features softened and, for a moment, Stacy thought he might kiss her again, but then his arm came around her shoulders and turned her toward the barn door.

"We'd better go in," he said. "Before the boys start missing us. And I decide to kiss you again."

CHAPTER EIGHT

A FEW MINUTES LATER, when Bonnie announced dinner was ready, Win was surprised that more of the Abernathy family hadn't showed up to partake of the evening meal. This time, with only Stacy and her parents, and Win and his boys seated at the table, the meal felt much more intimate. Especially with Stacy sitting at his side.

Win couldn't deny the closeness he felt to Stacy, or the warm pleasure her presence gave him. He even caught himself wondering if their lives would always be this idyllic if they were to deepen their relationship and become man and wife. He'd have a whole family again and his sons would have a mother. But nothing remained perfect and blissful. Yvette's sudden death had opened his eyes to that dismal fact. And yet, when Stacy looked at him with her soft blue eyes or touched her hand to his, he wanted to believe things could be different with her. He wanted to think he had the right to have as much happiness as the next person.

"Grandpa Doyle has eight horses on the Jackson Ranch. But he doesn't have any baby horses."

Oliver's comment pulled Win out of his wandering thoughts and he glanced across the table to see Asa listening intently to the boy's conversation.

"Do you ride your grandfather's horses when you visit your grandparents' ranch?" Asa asked him.

"Oh yeah, me and Joshua ride with him to check on the

cows. He has a great big herd of Black Baldies like ours," Oliver told him.

"Does your grandmother help with the ranch work?" Bonnie asked, her smile encompassing both boys. "Or is she more like me—the cook of the crew?"

"Oh, Grandma Audrey does chores around the ranch yard. Like feeding the dogs and cats and sometimes the horses. And she cooks, too," Oliver answered. "Mostly things like stew or beans."

"She makes blueberry pies all the time," Joshua added. "Because that's Grandpa's favorite. That and apple. My mom made huckleberry pies. 'Cause we had a ton of huckleberry bushes on our ranch, didn't we, Dad?"

Win glanced down the table to where Joshua was sitting next to his younger brother. He was somewhat surprised at how much his sons appeared to be enjoying their talk with Stacy's parents. But with the older couple having five kids of their own, plus grandchildren, they seemed to know exactly how to communicate with Joshua and Oliver.

"Yes. Until a mountain fire swept through and burned most of them," Win replied. "After that, the berries were few and far between."

Joshua nodded as he swallowed a bite of enchilada. "Yeah. I remember Mom cried about the berries burning up."

Oliver looked wistfully at his brother. "I wish I could remember her like you do. I only get to look at her picture. She was real pretty. She had brown hair and a smile like she was happy."

Joshua frowned at him. "That's because Mom was happy. And Dad was happy. And so was I. But then she died." He turned a bleak expression on Asa and Bonnie. "Back then, I didn't know anyone as young as Mom could die. I thought that only happened to old people. But I guess it can happen to anybody. Even me or Oliver."

Asa and Bonnie were giving both boys empathetic looks while, beneath the table, Stacy reached over and gently rested her hand on Win's thigh as if to tell him she understood how hard it was for him to hear his sons talk about their mother's sudden death. The fact that Stacy was so sensitive to his and his sons feelings, and how genuinely empathetic she was to the whole situation, touched Win deeply.

Asa said, "That much is true, Joshua. But dying isn't something a person should dwell on. Otherwise, he'll ruin the time he's living. Do you understand what I'm trying to say?"

After giving the man's words a long thought, Joshua nodded. "Yeah. It means we shouldn't worry about what happened a long time ago. We should think about now and all the fun we're gonna have later on."

Asa gave the teenager a nod of approval. "You're right on target, Joshua."

Oliver looked around the table at the adults. "I used to get really scared when Joshua talked about our mom dying," he admitted. "I thought if it happened to her, it might happen to me. I told Grandpa Doyle what I was thinking and he told me that's not the way things worked. After that, I'm not a scaredy-cat anymore."

Bonnie looked over at Win and winked. "You have two very smart sons, Win. You should be proud."

I'm not a scaredy-cat anymore. Oh, God, Win hadn't known his little Oliver had been so afraid because his mother had died. He'd not really understood the confusion Joshua had felt over Yvette's sudden death. They'd never really talked about their fears to Win and he'd thought they were coping okay with the loss. Now, listening to them express their feelings to the Abernathys, he hated himself for not digging deeper into his sons' thoughts, because clearly Yvette's death had taken a psychological toll on his sons. Oh, he'd understood it wasn't easy for them to be without their mother. But he'd told himself that as long as they weren't crying or moping about, they were dealing with the void in their lives.

Win reached for his water glass and took a drink before he replied, "I am, Bonnie. Very proud."

"I think Win's sons aren't just smart, they're hungry, too," Asa told his wife. "Pass those boys some more enchiladas. I'll bet they can eat a second plateful."

"Can I have rice and beans, too?" Oliver asked Asa.

Win let out a good-natured groan, while everyone else at the table laughed.

"Sure, you can," Bonnie told Oliver. "But you need to save room for dessert. We're having tres leches cake."

"What's that?"

The question was spoken in unison by both boys, and as Bonnie began to describe the milk-soaked cake, Win leaned his head toward Stacy and spoke in a low voice. "My sons are enjoying the heck out of this meal, but what is it doing to your parents?" he asked.

She slanted him a coy smile. "Trust me. They're loving every minute of it. And in case you're wondering, so am I."

Win didn't want to be thrilled by her words. He didn't want to remember the delicious heat of her kisses or to think about making love to her. But he was. And there didn't seem to be a thing he could do about it.

Once dinner was over, Win stayed long enough to have coffee in the den with Stacy and her parents before he announced it was time for him and the boys to head home to the J Barb.

As Joshua and Oliver fetched their coats from a hall

closet, Stacy joined Win on the front porch while he waited for the children.

"I wish it wasn't a school night," she said. "Joshua and Oliver would've enjoyed making another trip to the barn to see Comet and Star before you left."

Win would've enjoyed another trip himself. That was exactly why it was a good thing it was time for him and the boys to go home. Otherwise, he'd be greatly tempted to carry her off to some shadowy spot and make love to her.

"They would definitely like seeing the babies again. But by the time I get them home and to bed, it's going to be getting late."

She reached for his hand and he gladly wrapped his fingers around hers.

"You're right," she said. "It's just that I wish we had more time together. This evening has been so nice."

Nice was too meek a word to describe what this night had been for him. He'd had his eyes opened to his children and to Stacy. She wasn't just a pretty girl with a warm smile. She was a woman who fit perfectly in his arms and, with each minute that passed, she was growing ever dearer to him.

His fingers gently smoothed over the back of her hand. "Yes, it has."

Her gaze on his, Win could see doubt flickering in her eyes. The sight of it surprised him. Hadn't his kisses told her how much he'd enjoyed being with her?

"Do you really mean that?" she asked.

"Yes, I do. Why would you think otherwise?"

She shrugged and glanced away from him. "Oh. Sometimes it feels like you're somewhere far away and not with me."

Sometimes he was far away, Win realized. He was revisiting that place and time in his mind and heart when he'd been happy and a moment later his world had gone dark.

"I'm not far away from you. I'm just thinking." He gave her a rueful smile. "My mother used to say I lived in my head too much. I guess I'm still guilty of that."

She started to reply but at that moment the front door of the house opened and Joshua and Oliver stepped onto the porch.

"Look, Dad! Bonnie gave us a box of cowboy cookies to take home with us!" Oliver held up the small cardboard box for his father to see. "Wasn't that nice of her?"

"I hope you thanked her for the gift," Win said.

"We both thanked her, Dad." Joshua spoke up. "And she said to tell you that she put a couple of extra cookies in there for you."

Stacy laughed at the helpless look on Win's face. "Mom doesn't limit her spoiling to only children. You might as well get used to it."

Oh yes, Win mused. He could get used to all of this family togetherness and having thoughtful things done for him. But would he ever get past the fear of losing it? And her?

Shoving the troubling thought out of his mind, he motioned for the boys to go to the truck and, as they bounded down the steps and trotted across the yard, Win and Stacy followed in a slow walk.

Throughout the short trek to the truck, neither of them spoke one word. However, when they reached the driver's door, Win felt compelled to bring up the subject of seeing her again.

"I'd like for us to get together sometime soon," he said. "Would you?"

"I'd like that very much."

The soft smile on her face caused his stomach to take a funny little tumble. "Well, my schedule is always changing. I promised three different students I'd stop by their homes after school to look over their show animals. And Joshua has decided to go out for basketball, so I'll be staying over late in the evenings to pick him up from practice."

Her smile deepened as if to say she wasn't a bit deterred. "I understand. You're not only a teacher, you're also a father. That makes you have double duty," she told him. "Well, maybe we can get together on the weekend. I'll certainly be free."

"Okay. I— Uh, I'll call you." Bending his head, he pressed a kiss to her cheek. "Good night, Stacy."

"Good night," she murmured.

Win quickly climbed into the truck and as he put the vehicle into forward motion, she stepped back and gave him a little wave.

Win waved back then, pressing on the accelerator, he determinedly focused on the dark road ahead of him.

"Dad, did I see you kiss Ms. Abernathy on the cheek?" Joshua asked.

"Yes. You did."

"Wow!" Oliver exclaimed. "Does that mean you like her a whole lot?"

A strange fullness suddenly settled in the middle of Win's chest.

"Yes. I like her a whole lot."

Win expected to hear some loud responses to his answer. Instead, long moments passed with both boys being unusually quiet. It wasn't until he'd turned off the gravel road on the Bonnie B and onto the highway that he heard his sons whispering back and forth to each other.

No doubt the boys were discussing their father's interest in a woman and wondering if this relationship would cause as much upheaval as the one he'd had with Tara.

"Don't worry, boys. Nothing is going to make us move from Bronco. I can promise you that," he said firmly.

Oliver leaned forward. "Oh, we're not worried, Dad. Are we, Joshua?"

"We're not worried about that or anything," Joshua declared.

Great, Win sheepishly muttered to himself. His ten- and fifteen-year-old sons had more confidence about the future than he did.

WHEN THE WEEKEND ARRIVED, Stacy was definitely expecting to hear from Win and she spent both days eagerly waiting for her phone to ring with his call, or at the very least, to signal her with a text message. Surely, he wanted to keep in touch and let her know about his schedule. But Saturday and Sunday both passed without a word from him and, by the middle of the following week with still no call or message, she had to face the fact that he'd changed his mind about seeing her again. Or perhaps he'd never intended to call her in the first place.

The idea hurt her more than she wanted to admit and, for the past couple of days, she'd begun to ask herself if she was making a mistake in trying to have a relationship with the guy. He'd been single for more than seven years. He didn't want a woman in his life on a permanent basis. That much was clear. And yet she'd felt more than just desire in his kiss. She'd felt loneliness and need and a reluctance to let her go.

"You're not eating your lunch, Stacy. Are you sick?"

The question came from Emma, who was sitting next to Stacy at a table near the back of the school cafeteria.

Stacy looked down to see she'd eaten only a small portion of the grilled chicken and vegetables on her plate. "I'm not very hungry today. I should've just gotten a carton of milk and left off the food."

Emma snorted. "You can't go all day on a carton of milk. And you don't have an extra pound to lose."

She deliberately stabbed her fork into a chunk of chicken and popped it into her mouth, but for all she knew, it could have been a lump of wet cardboard. "I'm not trying to lose weight," she said more crossly than she intended. "I just don't have an appetite today."

"Sorry. I wasn't scolding you," Emma said. "I'm concerned about you, that's all."

Stacy looked out over the rows of tables where the first- and second-grade students were busy eating. Up to this point of the lunch break, the children had been behaved, which was a relief. Normally, it didn't ruffle her nerves if she had to deal with loud arguments or rowdiness during the midday meal, but today she was rattled.

Sighing, she looked regrettably at her friend and co-worker. "No, I'm the one who's sorry, Emma. I didn't mean to sound sharp. I'm…well, I'm having a hard time today."

Emma shook her head. "I think you've been having a hard time all week. I didn't want to mention it to you, but you've not been yourself."

Groaning, Stacy placed her fork on the side of her plate. "I feel worse than stupid, Emma. I think I've made a big fool of myself and it hurts."

Emma's expression turned grim. "Does this have anything to do with Win Jackson?"

Heaving out a heavy breath, Stacy nodded. "I mistakenly thought he was becoming interested in me. Seriously interested. I couldn't have been more wrong."

"What happened? He told you to keep your distance? That he had other fish to fry?"

Stacy glanced down at her wrap dress. With bright orange and yellow swirls running through the fabric, it was one of her favorite fall garments and she'd purposely worn the dress today in the hope it would boost her spirits. Instead, she was wondering why she'd bothered.

"No. Nothing like that. He and the boys visited the ranch last week and had dinner with us. The evening was... well, very nice. He even said so himself."

"That all sounds great to me. So what's making the corners of your mouth droop?" Emma wanted to know.

Feeling a bit juvenile, Stacy picked up her fork and stabbed another chunk of chicken. "He promised to call— to let me know when we could get together again. And he hasn't. That was a week ago. It's obvious that what little interest he had in me has fizzled completely."

Emma dipped a spoon into a chocolate pudding cup. "Maybe his phone is broken. Or he's been too busy."

Stacy snorted. "Joshua has a phone he could borrow. As for being busy, how long does it take to send a short text message?" She rolled her eyes helplessly toward the ceiling. "I guess it's pretty obvious that, where men are concerned, I'm naive. But I truly thought Win was different."

"Hmm. He is different, Stacy. He's a widower and he's been single for a long time. If you want my honest opinion, he's probably having second thoughts about getting involved with you. But that's not to say he's writing you off. He just needs time."

Stacy frowned. "Seven years isn't enough?"

"Grief can't be measured with time, Stacy." She leveled a pointed look at her. "But forget all of that. If you're that concerned, call him."

Stacy didn't want to admit that the only reason Win'd had dinner on the Bonnie B last Wednesday night was that she'd taken it upon herself to invite him. But she had no intentions of doing the inviting a second time. She might be a fool, but she wasn't a man chaser.

"I get what you're saying, Emma. But for now, I don't think that's the right thing for me to do."

Emma shook her head and sighed. "Well, it's your life and your business. And considering my track record with love and marriage, I'm hardly one to be handing out advice."

Realizing the bright sunshine that had been slanting across their table had disappeared, Stacy glanced over at the row of windows that overlooked the playground. Rain had started to fall and she thought how much the weather matched her somber mood.

"Look, Emma. We can forget about having outside recess this afternoon."

Emma glanced at the rain beating against the windowpanes and chuckled. "All in a day's work, my dear," she said then reached over and gave Stacy's forearm an encouraging pat. "Cheer up. You're going to see sunshine again. Probably sooner than you think."

Stacy wasn't one to give up. Especially on something she believed to be worthwhile. But it was becoming more and more difficult to think Win could ever fall in love with her.

LATER THAT NIGHT as Win sat at the kitchen table, grading a stack of test papers, he wondered if it was the rain making the house seem unusually dark and chilly. The lights were burning over the table and the stove located a few feet away. The furnace was blowing warm air through the vents on floor. Why did he feel like he was sitting in a cold tomb?

Don't play ignorant, Win. The house has nothing to

do with the chill you're feeling and everything to do with Stacy. You need her. You just don't want to admit it.

Tossing his red pencil onto the pile of papers, he scrubbed his face with both hands. He felt awful about not calling her. Especially when he'd told her he would. But not following through on his word was only one of the reasons he was feeling miserable. No matter how hard he tried to ignore it or to deny it, he was aching to see her again.

For a week now, he'd fought with himself over this emotional tangle he'd gotten into with Stacy. She brought so many wonderful things to his life, yet the wounded part of him couldn't forget all the things that could go wrong.

Muttering a frustrated oath, he left his chair to pour a cup of coffee from the carafe sitting on the cabinet. Once he'd stirred in a spoonful of sugar, he glanced at the clock above the refrigerator.

It was late enough for the boys to already be in bed, but not so late that his brother back in Whitehorn would be asleep. Maybe if he could hear Shawn's voice, he could lift himself out of this dismal pit he'd fallen into.

Back at the table, he picked up his cell phone and carried it and his coffee out to the living room to take a seat in an armchair that overlooked a large picture window. At the moment, the only thing he could see in the glow of the yard lamp was sheets of rain pounding against the west end of the barn.

Shawn answered on the third ring and Win could tell by the groggy sound of his voice that he'd been dozing.

"Sorry, brother. Have you already gone to bed?"

"No. I've been watching something very exciting on TV. Can't you tell?"

Win smiled in spite of himself. "Yeah. So exciting, you dozed off."

"I'm guilty." He paused long enough to yawn then said, "But I have a good excuse. The episode was a rerun."

"Okay. So you're not entering old age yet."

"Not yet. What are you doing up this late anyway?" Shawn asked. "Has something happened?"

"No. I'm grading test papers," Win told him. "Your nephews are snug in bed. It's pouring rain here, and cold, and I was just sort of feeling lonely."

The was a silent pause and then Shawn asked, "Are you wishing you were back in Whitehorn?"

Was he? Funny how these past few days that thought had never entered his mind. "Hell no!"

"That was plain enough."

Win grimaced. "Don't get me wrong. I love seeing you and Mom and Dad. But otherwise, I don't miss it. Bronco is suiting me and the boys just fine."

"I'm glad to hear it. So why are you feeling lonely?"

Win closed his eyes and pressed his fingers against the burning lids. "I shouldn't have said lonely, Shawn. That's not really how I'm feeling. I'm messed up—in my head or my heart—I don't know which. Except that I'm miserable."

"Don't tell me. You've met a woman. Not only met her, but you've fallen for her."

Shawn was so close to the truth that Win's eyes popped open and he sat straight up in the chair. "Sometimes you make me sick."

Shawn laughed. "Why? Because I'm clairvoyant? Or because I'm your annoying little brother?"

With a good-natured groan, Win said, "Both, I suppose. But you're right, as usual. I have met a woman and I… I'm not ready to say I've fallen for her, but I—"

"You're so close to falling that you're on the verge of teetering off the cliff," Shawn finished for him.

"Yeah. And I'm scared to death."

"Why? You believe if you don't give her an engagement ring, she'll set off on a vendetta to ruin you? Like Tara went after you?" He snorted in Win's ear. "I can't imagine any woman being as vengeful as her. Unless it was my ex."

Win sipped his coffee before he answered. "Actually, I'm not thinking anything like that. Stacy is not that kind of a person. She looks at things reasonably and open-mindedly. She wouldn't hurt a fly. Unless it was biting her and, even then, she'd probably gently brush it away instead of smashing it with a swatter."

"The soft, gentle kind, huh? Nothing wrong with that. I always thought I wanted the strong, independent type. You know, a woman who could take care of herself instead of smothering me. Look how wrong I was."

"Vicki wasn't strong and independent. She was a cheater and a liar. There's a huge difference."

Shawn let out a heavy sigh. "I believe I'm supposed to live my life as a single man, Win. But not you. You were a great husband to Yvette and you're the best of fathers. It's in the cards for you to find love again."

Love. Ever since Win had met Stacy, he'd been shying away from that word. He'd not wanted to consider how it would be to love her. He'd not wanted to imagine how his life would be to have her by his side, loving him, supporting him. But now he could think of little else.

"You don't have a crystal ball, little brother. And neither do I, but I am certain about one thing. The more I'm with Stacy, the more I want to be with her. And—"

Shawn interjected, "Just how well do you know this woman? Stacy is her name?"

"Yes, Stacy Abernathy. There are several branches of the Abernathys around Bronco. From what I understand, it's an old, monied name—at the top tier of Bronco society. As for Stacy's branch of the family, they are definitely well off. One look at their ranch, the Bonnie B, and you know they're not hurting financially. But I can truly say they're not snobs."

"Hmm. So Stacy is an heiress. That's interesting."

Win grunted as he leaned over and placed his cup on a low table positioned next to his chair. "Being an heiress is the least interesting thing about her. She teaches second grade at Bronco Elementary, where Oliver goes to school. Besides being a dedicated teacher, she's beautiful and sweet, and is very good with children. I should probably also mention she's twenty-eight and never been engaged or married."

After a short pause, Shawn said, "I'm really curious now, Win. With this kind of résumé, why are you second-guessing getting involved with the woman? She sounds perfect for you."

Groaning, Win wearily pinched the bridge of his nose. "That's just it, Shawn. Perfection doesn't last. I…uh, don't think I could survive having my family shattered a second time."

Silence stretched again before Shawn finally spoke. "Hmm. You're thinking she won't stick with you? Or you have the morbid idea that she'll die from some medical problem or get killed in an accident?"

Hearing Shawn speaking Win's fears out loud made it all sound ridiculous. Even worse, it made Win appear as a coward.

Which you are, Win. Don't ever take your shirt off in front of Stacy. Unless you want her to see the giant yellow streak down your back.

Silently cursing at the taunting voice in his head, he said to Shawn, "Okay, I'll admit it. When I think of getting into a serious relationship with Stacy, all kinds of tragedies enter my mind. Call me stupid, but I just can't help it."

"All I can say is, you'd better give yourself a hard mental slap, brother. Otherwise, you're going to be worse than lonely. You're going to be downright miserable. I—"

Win interrupted his brother before he could say more. "Shawn, all of this is easy for you to say when it was *my* wife that died! You don't know what it feels like, or what it's done to me!"

"You're right, I can't understand what it feels like to have a spouse die. But I can plainly see what Yvette's death has done to you, and it's not good. When are you going to open your eyes and realize that you're not the only widower in this world? That you can't hang on to her ghost forever?"

Was he hanging on to Yvette's ghost? He'd never imagined himself doing such a thing. The only photos of Yvette that were sitting out in clear view were in Joshua's and Oliver's bedrooms. He'd purposely kept all reminders of her from the remaining rooms of the house. And he could truthfully say there were days that his late wife never entered his mind.

"You don't know what you're talking about, Shawn," he said flatly. "I'm not hanging on to Yvette's ghost."

"Maybe not her exactly, but you're hanging on to losing her. That's just as debilitating."

Win wanted to argue the point but deep down he realized that Shawn was right. He just didn't want to admit the truth, or to face it.

Closing his eyes, Win rested his head against the back of the armchair. "Okay. So what you're saying is that I need to get a backbone."

"More or less. And I'm saying if you feel anything at all for Stacy, then you need to make yourself clear to her. Instead of sitting back and worrying about all the bad things that could happen. 'Cause life isn't all bad, Win."

"You're right, Shawn. I'm my own worst enemy," Win

told him. "Actually, a friend of mine here in Bronco, a coach at the high school, in fact, has basically told me the same thing as you. But hearing it from you has hit me harder."

"Good. I hope everything I've said has hit you over the head," Shawn said with a chuckle. "Remember when we were kids and were always wrestling and punching each other? Back then, I could knock some sense into you. Nowadays I have to do it with words."

Win chuckled along with his brother. "Good thing. I'd hate to have to explain to my students why I had two black eyes."

Shawn laughed and then Win inquired about their parents.

"They're both fine. They miss you and their grandsons. But they're glad you're happy there in Bronco. I won't tell them you've been sitting in a dark room moping over what to do about a woman. There are some things they don't need to know."

No, Win thought. Their parents didn't need to hear that he was still stuck in the same old rut he'd been in since Yvette had died. He wanted his mother and father to think of him as an emotionally strong man.

Wiping a hand over his face, he muttered, "How do you know I'm sitting in a dark room? This isn't a FaceTime call."

Shawn's grunt held a bit of humor. "Remember, I see things even when I don't see them with my eyes. And I'll tell you what I'm seeing right now. You hanging up and calling your pretty teacher."

Call Stacy? He'd let a whole week slip by without saying a word to her. He'd been behaving like a jerk and whatever she was thinking about him now couldn't be good.

"I'm not sure she'd want to hear from me," Win mumbled.

"You won't know unless you try."

In spite of the pouring rain, Win felt his spirits suddenly lift. "You're right, Shawn. So, good night. I'll talk to you later."

He could hear Shawn's smug guffaw as he ended the phone connection.

ALREADY DRESSED IN her pajamas, Stacy was sitting on the side of the bed, running a brush through her long hair, when the cellphone lying on the nightstand rang.

Thinking it was probably a spam call or a wrong number, she took her time laying the brush aside and reaching for the phone. By the time she picked it up, the fourth ring had stopped and she expected to find the caller had hung up.

And then she saw *his* name. She'd given up on hearing from Win and now for him to be calling at such a late hour, she could only think something had happened to him or one of the boys.

Her hand shook as she punched the accept button and moved the phone to her ear. "Hello, Win."

"Hello, Stacy. I realize it's late. Have I caught you at a bad time?"

She frowned as all kinds of anxious thoughts raced through her mind. "No. I can talk. Is anything wrong? Has something happened to Oliver or Joshua?"

"No. They're fine. They were both in bed an hour ago." He dragged in a deep breath then blew it out. "I—uh, I'm sorry I haven't called sooner. Every day I picked up the phone, but—"

Her lips pressed together. "You got cold feet. Is that what you're trying to say?"

There was a pause and then he said, "Yes. Something like that. I— I've been trying to convince myself that you need someone else in your life. A man who doesn't have all the baggage I'm carrying around. One that can give you all the things you've hoped and planned for."

Her heart winced and she gripped the phone as though it was a lifeline. "Have you managed to convince yourself that you're wrong for me?"

"No. I've come to realize that I need to see you. And I hope you'd like to see me. That is…if you aren't too angry with me."

She was probably being a fool, but Stacy's heart was suddenly singing like a bird in springtime. "I've not been angry with you, Win. Disappointed, but not angry."

He responded with a sound crossed between a groan and a gurgle.

"I don't deserve you, Stacy. In fact, I don't know why you put up with me at all."

Even though she was yet to learn why he'd called, the fact that he hadn't given up on her completely had her heart thumping with hope. "Probably because I think you're worth the trouble," she said, trying to inject a teasing note into her voice.

There was a long pause before he spoke and when he finally did, a pent-up breath rushed out of her.

"Well, I'm hoping you think I'm worth going out to dinner with."

Stunned, she stared at the toes of her fuzzy house shoes without really seeing them. "You mean, like a real date?"

He chuckled, and so did she, and suddenly the cold, rainy night felt like a tropical paradise to Stacy.

"Yes. A real date," he said. "No trips to the barn or stepping around cow chips."

Lowering her voice to a provocative murmur, she said, "For your information, I don't have anything against a trip to the barn—with you."

He chuckled again. "I'll remember that," he said huskily before clearing his throat. "Is there a special restaurant you like? It doesn't have to be in Bronco. If you prefer, we can drive somewhere out of town."

"I'm not particular, Win. You choose and surprise me."

"Okay. Are you free Saturday night? I'd say Friday, but Anthony has a ballgame that evening and he'll be watching the boys for me."

Stacy felt as if she was going to float off the bed and fly around the room. But she did her best to hide the rush of excitement from her voice. She feared if he guessed how giddy he was making her, it might put him off the date completely.

"Saturday night is perfect. I can meet you in town, if it would make things easier for you."

"No way. This is going to be a real date. I'll pick you up at your parents' house on the Bonnie B at six thirty. Is that time okay with you?"

"I'll be ready," she told him. "And, Win, I'm very glad you called."

"I'm very glad I called, too. Good night, Stacy. See you Saturday."

"Yes. Good night."

Once the connection ended, Stacy placed the phone back on the nightstand, then smiled to herself.

Win had asked her on a date! A real date! She didn't know what had motivated him to call or why he'd decided he wanted to see her again. And tonight, she didn't care. Win wanted to be with her and that was the only thing that mattered.

CHAPTER NINE

ON SATURDAY EVENING, shortly after six o'clock, Stacy stood in front of the floor-length mirror on her closet door and peered critically at her image. This morning when Win had called to confirm their date, he'd not told her exactly where they'd be dining, he'd only said it was upscale, where they could drink wine in a cozy little corner.

The news that he'd be taking her to a fancy restaurant hadn't surprised her. He'd already hinted he wanted them to go somewhere nice. What had surprised her was the mention of the wine and the cozy corner. For as long as she'd known Win, he hadn't exactly come across as a man who was particularly romantic. Desirable, wildly handsome and very sexy. Yes, yes and yes, he was definitely all those things. But a flower-giving, gaze-at-the-moon type of man? No. But just in case he surprised her, she wanted to look the romantic part.

Now as she studied her midnight-blue dress, she wondered if she'd gone a bit too far with the romantic image. The velvet fabric made the dress look ultra-expensive and the sweetheart neckline was just low enough to show a shadow of cleavage. Teardrop-shaped pearls accented with blue sapphires dangled from her ears, while a matching necklace nestled in the hollow at the base of her throat. She'd swept the top half of her blond hair up and fastened it with a pearl-adorned clasp to allow the deep waves to cascade down to her back. Her feet were probably going to get cold in the strappy black high heels she'd chosen, but surely she could bear the discomfort for one evening.

Satisfied that she didn't look like she was going to teach a class of second graders, she turned away from the mirror and walked over to the dresser where her hairbrush was lying next to a digital alarm clock. As she picked up the brush, she glanced at the glaring red numbers. Six-fifty. Win was already twenty minutes late, but that was hardly enough to worry her. With two kids and a barn full of animals to see after, he had reason to run behind schedule. And she'd already learned he was usually late in picking up Oliver from school. It had to be an ag teacher thing, she thought.

While she was waiting, she brushed through her hair a second time, tidied up her room and laid out her coat and handbag. By the time she finished those tasks, another ten minutes had passed without a sign of Win.

When the clock eventually rolled to a quarter past seven with still no word from Win, she was beginning to fear he might be going to stand her up completely. But why would he? This morning when he'd called, he'd sounded enthused about their plans.

Deciding it was stupid to keep worrying and wondering, she picked up her phone to call him. However, before she could tap in his number, her phone dinged with an incoming text message.

I've had trouble. Be there in a few minutes.

He'd not bothered to explain the kind of trouble he'd encountered, but that scarcely mattered to Stacy. Win was on his way.

After dropping her phone into her handbag, she snatched it and her coat from the bed and hurried out of her bedroom. She was walking through the living room on her way to the porch when she met Robin entering the front door.

"Oooeee! Look at my little sister!" She hurried over to Stacy and holding on to both her hands, stood back and gave her appearance a keen perusal. "Where are you off to? Someone's wedding? Why wasn't I invited?"

Stacy laughed. "No wedding. And you weren't invited because I'm going on a date—with Win."

Robin's jaw dropped. "Win? Really? When did this happen?"

"He phoned me Wednesday night. I was going to tell you about it, but you've been busy and I have, too." She gave her sister a dreamy smile. "I don't want to...well, put too much into this, but I'm sure you can tell I'm feeling on top of the world."

Gently patting her cheek, Robin said, "Your smile tells me how happy you are. I'm glad, sissy. I hope this is the beginning of everything you've ever wanted."

"I hope so, too." Stacy gave her sister a grateful hug and glanced toward the door as the sound of a vehicle caught her attention. "That's probably him. He's running late, so I'm going out to meet him."

Robin kissed her cheek. "Have a good time."

"I plan to," Stacy said as she hurried through the door.

WIN WAS OUT of his truck and halfway to the yard gate when he spotted Stacy walking down the porch steps to meet him. Even in the dim light of the yard lamp, he could see she was wearing a lovely dress and a pair of high heels, all of which shouted she was expecting their dinner to be special. He could also see that she looked incredibly beautiful and, the closer she got to him, the faster his heart thumped.

"Hi, Win. I'm so happy to see you finally made it."

For once Win didn't care if any of her family was watching, he pulled her into his arms and placed a brief kiss on her lips. "Stacy, I'm so sorry about being late. I've had a heck of a time getting here."

"What happened?"

Taking her by the hand, he urged her toward the truck. "I'll tell you about it as soon as we get on our way."

After helping her into the cab, he took his place in the driver's seat and quickly steered the truck back in the direction of town.

"I was beginning to think you'd changed your mind and weren't coming." She removed her coat and placed it across her lap before she buckled her seatbelt.

Sighing, he shook his head. "Not a chance. I had tire trouble. After I dropped off the boys at Anthony's house, I'd gotten about five miles out of town when my tire went instantly flat."

"Oh no. A blowout?"

He shook his head. "No. I think I ran over some sort of debris. Anyway, it cut a huge hole in the tire."

"But you had a spare, surely."

Chuckling at her practical remark, he slanted a wry look in her direction. "Yes. I never go anywhere without a spare. But something went haywire with the jack. It wouldn't lift the truck. I worked on the jack for at least twenty minutes and still couldn't get it to work. Finally, I gave up and called Anthony and had him bring his jack out to where I was stranded on the side of the highway."

"You mean no one stopped to offer help?" she asked with dismay. "Usually, a good Samaritan will show up to lend a hand."

"No such luck tonight." He shook his head. "Anyway, I finally got the tire replaced, but by then I was so dirty and greasy I had to turn around and go back to the J Barb to change clothes." He shot her an apologetic look. "I really hate that all this happened, Stacy. I wanted this date to be special."

A relieved breath rushed out of her. He hadn't called to cancel their outing and that was all that mattered. "Don't worry about it, Win," she told him. "Just being with you will make it special."

His groan was full of misgivings. "I'm glad you think so, because it's an hour's drive from Bronco to the restaurant where I had made reservations and there's no way we can make it on time. I had to call and cancel, so I hope you won't mind eating elsewhere. We could try to get reservations at DJ's Deluxe, but it's Saturday night. At this hour I doubt we'd have much luck."

"Right. And I'm too hungry to sit around and wait for a table to become empty there or anywhere else." She flashed him a cheery smile. "Let's find a place where we can just walk in and sit down."

Win allowed his gaze to leave the road long enough to take a brief survey of the dark blue dress clinging to her curves and the way the top part of her hair was pulled up to cascade in shiny waves against her back. This wasn't the same woman he'd first met at the elementary school, or the one who'd escorted him through the horse barn on the Bonnie B. This Stacy looked so alluring and sexy; she was making every masculine cell in his body stand at attention.

Turning his focus back on his driving, he said, "Fine with me. But you look so beautiful tonight, Stacy. You're fit for a queen's ballroom and I've messed up everything."

"Nonsense. I rarely have a reason to dress up and you gave me one. I'm thankful to you for that much."

He glanced ruefully down at his jeans and dark green shirt. "You probably won't believe this, but I did dress up more than usual this evening. But rolling around beneath the truck trying to fix that damned tire left me looking like a mechanic. But don't worry, at least I have a jacket in the back seat and can cover up most of this wrinkled shirt."

She shook her head. "You look fine, Win. You look better than fine. You look exactly like the man I want to be with. And as for our dinner, I'm sure we'll find something yummy."

"Thanks for being so patient," he told her.

She slanted him a wry smile. "You have to remember I'm a second-grade teacher. My middle name is Patience."

He cocked a curious brow at her. "Is it really Patience?"

"No. But it should be," she said with a soft laugh. "Anyway, I'm sure teaching teenagers all these years has taught you to be laid-back and easygoing."

A short laugh burst out of him. "I'm glad you weren't with me earlier this evening when the jack wouldn't work."

She chuckled. "Well, you are human. And we all have our moments."

"What did Joshua and Oliver think about you going on a date?" she asked. "Or did you tell them you were taking me to dinner?"

He glanced over to see she'd crossed her legs and the sight of her bare calf made him want to reach out and glide his hand over the smooth skin.

"I did tell them," he said. "Oliver was thrilled and Joshua seemed okay with it."

"The night you three came out to see Comet and Star, I felt like Joshua was warming up to me a bit. But I get the feeling he's not ready for his father to be...dating. Me— or any woman."

Win shrugged. "He's a teenager. He's moody. One minute he's happy and easygoing and the next he thinks the sky is falling in on him. But you shouldn't worry about Joshua not liking you. I'm fairly certain he does."

She smiled at him. "I can't ask for more than that."

"So what's been going on with your family since we visited the Bonnie B? Has your brother-in-law heard any news about Winona Cobbs?"

"Sadly, no." She shook her head with disbelief. "How does a ninety-seven-year-old woman just vanish without someone seeing her? And if she's been kidnapped, there's been no request for ransom. It's a real mystery. And each day that goes by, the more Stanley grieves and worries."

"Hmm. Could be she truly did get cold feet about walking down the aisle."

Frowning, she said, "I'll never believe that happened. Winona was crazy about Stanley. And I feel so sorry for him. He and Winona attended many of the special events in Bronco. If she wasn't missing, the two of them would be planning to go to the Gold Buckle Rodeo next month, and last year they were showing off Winona's engagement ring at the Bronco Harvest Festival. Now, without her, I doubt Stanley will want to attend either function."

"Well, let's keep our fingers crossed that she'll show up or someone will find her," Win replied. "I'd honestly like to meet the woman."

She laughed softly and Win realized he'd missed the warm sound as much as he'd missed hearing her voice and feeling the touch of her hand.

"You don't actually believe that psychic stuff, do you?" she asked.

"No. But I think some people have strong intuitions that happen to come true." He looked at her and grinned. "When I was a kid, there was a woman who lived alone in a cabin just beyond the north boundary of our ranch. Everyone called her a gypsy and, supposedly, she could read your palm or look at the cards and foretell your future. I didn't much go for any of that, but I sure thought she was beautiful. She had waist-length black hair and black eyes, and she wore layers of beads around her neck and wrists. I was in love."

"What happened to this woman?" she asked curiously. "Is she still there?"

"No. She moved away. No one seemed to know where she went or why she left. I guess you could say she was like Winona and just disappeared."

"Aww, that's kind of sad." She cast him an impish smile. "So when did you decide you liked women without the long black hair and layers of beads?"

"When I met a blond-haired teacher with tiny gold birds hanging from her earlobes," he said with a husky chuckle.

Frowning slightly, she touched a finger to her earlobe. "Was I wearing my little gold bird earrings when I met you?"

He nodded. "They dangled when you moved your head. Very pretty."

She reached over and clasped her hand around his. "It's nice of you to remember. To be honest, I never thought you noticed things like…well, my earrings."

With a wry laugh, he said, "In other words, I don't come across as a romantic type of guy." He glanced over to see a sheepish expression on her face.

"Not exactly," she answered. "But that's okay. I hardly come across as a glamour girl. We are who we are and that should be enough."

Squeezing her fingers, he said, "You look beautiful tonight. And I don't need or want a glamour girl."

A faint smile touched her lips as she looked at him. "I don't expect you to be the flower-and-poetry kind, either. As long as you want my company, that's enough."

He wanted more than her company. He wanted all of her. But he wasn't sure she was ready to take their relationship to an intimate level.

Shouldn't you be asking yourself if you're ready, Win? Are you ready to share more than talk and kisses with Stacy?

The questions waltzing through the back of his mind were annoying, but tonight Win was determined to push them aside. He was so weary of weighing every step he took. He was tired of trying to decide what was good or bad for him and his sons. For tonight, he simply wanted to be a man enjoying a warm and beautiful woman.

WHEN THEY REACHED the outskirts of town, Win pulled into a parking lot and stopped the truck beneath the glow of a streetlamp. With the slim hope they could still make a reservation somewhere, he called several local restaurants, but after a few minutes, he put down the phone and slanted her a dismal look.

"No vacant tables. No cancellations," he said ruefully. "I'm really sorry, Stacy. It's too late for us to have a fancy dinner where we could have wine and a little secluded table with a linen tablecloth. Man, I've really turned this date into a fiasco. This will be one you won't forget."

She reached over and curled her fingers gently around his forearm. "You're right. I won't forget it. And not because we're going to settle for something less than fancy. But because this is our first date and I'm with you. That's enough for me. So please quit beating yourself up over this."

With a helpless twist to his lips, he leaned across the console and pressed a kiss to her cheek. "I'll make this up to you. I promise."

"You just did, Win."

His green eyes were soft as they slowly scanned her face, and she held her breath, certain he was going to give her a full-fledged kiss on the lips, but after a moment, he cleared his throat and straightened back in his seat.

"We'd better go find something to eat. You're starving and so am I."

For the next twenty minutes, Win drove through town, passing all the restaurants they were both familiar with, but most of them appeared to be filled to the brim with evening diners.

Finally, Stacy said, "Look, Win, why don't we just do fast food? I'm almost to the point of settling for raw macaroni!"

He shot her an amused look. "That might be a little too crunchy for my taste. And think about it, Stacy. We deal with kids all day long. Any fast-food joint tonight will be running over with kids. I doubt we could hear ourselves think much less be able to talk to each other in a normal tone."

"You're right," she said glumly and then suddenly snapped her fingers as a thought struck her. "I know where we can eat, Win. The Gemstone Diner. Are you familiar with the place?"

His expression brightened as he nodded. "On Commercial Street down in Bronco Valley? That's a great idea! We should have thought about the diner earlier. It's not fancy, but the food is good." He grinned. "And I'm pretty sure the macaroni there will be cooked."

Stacy chuckled. "I can't wait."

Minutes later, when they entered the diner, they found the place busy but not so packed they couldn't find a booth at the back of the room. As they walked through the crowd of diners, Stacy noticed several people glancing at them. No doubt they were wondering what she was doing wearing velvet and pearls to a diner. Especially with her date wearing jeans and a denim jacket.

"It's not a linen tablecloth," he joked, "but it's clean."

The vinyl bench-type seats were big enough to seat four with two on each side of the table. When Stacy slid onto one of the benches, she expected Win to take a seat across from her. Instead, he chose to sit beside her, and the closeness of his body next to hers was enough to make her heart flutter.

Smiling at him, she murmured, "This is nice."

"What? The country music playing in the background? Or the rattling dishes behind the bar?"

She placed her hand over his. "Neither. I'm talking about us sitting close together."

His lips took on a wry slant as his gaze traveled over her face. "It's about time we had a chance to sit close together. Don't you think?"

"Definitely. And this booth is just as cozy as one of those ritzy tables you wanted."

"Only we don't have the wine," he pointed out.

"We'll get that later."

He arched a questioning look at her just as the waitress appeared with glasses of iced water and plastic-coated menus. After that, the mention of wine was forgotten as they studied the list of meals offered by the diner.

Both of them ended up ordering hamburgers, fries and milkshakes, and they shared a laugh when the platters of food and shakes were finally sitting in front of them.

"This is not a two-fork dinner," he said.

"No, this is good ol' finger food. And it's delicious. Especially when you're hungry."

Actually, Stacy could've been eating charred wood and she probably wouldn't have known it. And even if they had that bottle of wine he'd talked about, her spirits couldn't have soared any higher. No, she was happy because Win was sitting so close to her that their thighs were pressed together and the sides of their arms brushed with each bite they lifted to their mouths. And he was smiling at her. A real smile that said he was just as happy to be with her.

Ever since Win had called and invited her to dinner, Stacy had tried not to put too much meaning into his motivation. Taking her on a date didn't mean he'd had a sudden change of heart about the two of them having a deeper relationship. But now, as they sat close together and chatted about anything and everything, she couldn't help but hope he was finally seeing them as a real couple.

"There was a diner back in Whitehorn that had great food. Until the management changed. After that, it was terrible," he said as he dipped a fry into a mound of ketchup. "But I didn't eat out all that much when I lived there. Mom and Dad were always inviting me and the boys over to eat with them. Just like your siblings drop in at the Bonnie B to eat dinner."

She took a sip of her soda. "Hmm. I imagine they miss you and their grandsons. Did they try to talk you out of moving to Bronco? I think if I decided to move away, my parents would do plenty of talking. Not that they try to tell us kids how to live our lives. It's just that they're accustomed to me being nearby and often staying over in the ranch house with them."

"The ranch house on the Bonnie B is a huge nest. I get the idea your parents aren't the sort to hover over you. As for my parents, they kept advising me to think long and hard before I sold my ranch in Whitehorn and quit my teaching job there. But I finally managed to convince them it was the right thing for me to do." His gaze met hers as he reached for his soft drink. "Do you remember when I drove you home that night your car was on the blink? And during Oliver's chatter about our move from Whitehorn, he brought up a woman named Tara?"

Trying not to appear surprised, she nodded. "I do. I didn't ask who she was because…well, it wasn't any of my business."

He grimaced. "I told you then that I moved because I needed a change, and that much was true enough. But Oliver was right. We also left Whitehorn because of Tara. She was my girlfriend—for a while."

"I suspected something like that," Stacy admitted. "What happened? She ended things and broke your heart?"

"Hell no! Nothing like that," he said then quickly apologized. "Sorry, Stacy. I didn't mean to curse. It's just that… well, I was never emotionally close enough to Tara to get my heart broken. But she sure damaged my life."

"If you weren't in love with her, then how did she damage your life?"

His expression grim, he said, "It's a long story. You see, when I first started dating her, she was fun to be around and not fussy or demanding. Which made her a fit for me because all I wanted was someone to spend time with."

"Was she the first girl you dated after your wife passed away?"

"Yes. It took years for me to finally decide I needed to socialize and try to date again. But when I asked Tara out, dating was all I had in mind. I wasn't ready for anything serious with the woman. But she and everyone else in Whitehorn, it seems, had the idea that widowers are always itching to get married again. I think she believed that if we continued to date, I would eventually ask her to marry me."

"But you didn't."

"No way. I had no intention of marrying her. She was fun as dates go, but even if I'd wanted a wife, she wasn't what I considered wife material."

Frowning, Stacy took another sip of her soda. "I don't

understand, Win. You broke up with her. I can't see why that forced you to leave Whitehorn. Was the experience with Tara that bad?"

He released a heavy breath. "You're probably thinking I'm some sort of helpless wimp. But you see, Tara was hard to ignore. She worked as the receptionist in the principal's office at the high school where I taught agribusiness. We had many mutual friends and acquaintances, so the word *bad* doesn't begin to describe the hell she put me through."

She looked at him in wonder as the French fry she was about to pop into her mouth paused in midair. "You make the ordeal sound terrible."

He twisted around on the seat to face her. "I need to start at the beginning so you'll understand. Tara and I dated about three months and, during that time, I suppose she started thinking that was more than enough time for me to pop the question. By the time Thanksgiving arrived, she and her parents were expecting me to show up with an engagement ring. When that didn't happen, Tara was furious. She threw a walleyed fit."

"And showed her true colors," Stacy replied while trying to imagine Win dealing with such a woman.

"I'd never seen that side of Tara and I didn't hesitate to tell her I wanted her out of my life. Things should've ended right then and there, but she refused to forgive and forget. She was out for blood. Her main goal in life turned into ruining mine."

Frowning, Stacy asked, "What did she do? Begin stalking you?"

"No. She was more insidious than that. She started telling our friends and colleagues at school that I had been stringing her along, playing her for a fool for my own entertainment. According to her, I had purposely and ruthlessly broken her heart. To put it simply, she painted me as a no-good jerk who had no business teaching a group of impressionable teenagers."

She stared at him in disbelief. "Win, I can't imagine any woman being so vindictive. More than that, I can't imagine your friends and coworkers believed such garbage."

Grimacing, he said, "You'd have to know Tara to understand. She had a charming way of making people like and trust her. Anyway, after weeks of her spreading lies, only a few of my closest friends took my side of things. The rest turned their back on me. People I'd worked with for years looked at me like I was a creep. Eventually, it became unbearable to go to work and try to avoid being shunned as though I had a contagious disease."

"Oh my. You must have felt so hurt and betrayed."

"It was very hurtful losing friends that I believed were loyal to me. It also made me angry. But eventually, after I took the time to think the matter through, I decided I'd not really lost anything because they obviously weren't true friends in the first place."

She nodded. "I'd see it the same way. A true friend doesn't desert you. They stand by you no matter what."

He shrugged his muscular shoulder. "Sometimes I wonder, Stacy, if I mishandled the whole incident. For sure, I should've never gotten involved with Tara. But to my friends and coworkers, I should've stood up and defended myself. Instead, I kept quiet, thinking it would all blow over."

As her gaze slipped over his rugged features, she could only imagine the hurt and frustration he must have gone through. "And when it didn't blow over, you decided moving away was the best thing to do."

He nodded. "I suppose plenty of folks would call that the coward's way out. But, ultimately, I was thinking of my sons. My hide was tough enough to deal with a slashed reputation, but my boys are still very young and impressionable. I want them to be proud of their father and be able to respect the man I am."

Smiling, she reached to fold her fingers around his hand. "You want to know what I think?"

His gaze locked with hers and, at that moment, Stacy was hardly aware of the people sitting nearby or the sounds of conversation and laughter in the background. Her entire focus was on him and what he could possibly be thinking. Not only about his escape from Whitehorn, but what this night might come to mean to the two of them.

"I do want to hear your thoughts," he murmured.

She breathed deeply. There were so many things about his life back in Whitehorn she'd like to hear about. And so many questions she'd like to ask him about his late wife. But now wasn't the right time, she thought. The last thing she wanted to do was come across to him as intrusive or pushy. "Okay. On one hand, I hate that you went through such a horrible ordeal. But, on the other, I'm really glad that you decided you had to move away from Whitehorn. And you chose Bronco for your new home. Otherwise, we would've never met. And that's too sad to think about."

She could see a smile in his eyes long before it ever reached his lips, and the sight was like sunshine peeking through a storm cloud.

Lowering his lips close to her ear, he said, "Okay. Once we finish eating, what would you like to do? I hope you're going to say you want to go somewhere nice and quiet and private."

Her pulse was suddenly thudding with eager anticipation. "I couldn't agree more. And I know just the place," she told him. "My parents have a guest cabin on the ranch. Nothing fancy. Just a little two-room log house with a great view of the mountains."

"No one is using it now?" he asked.

She shook her head. "About the only time it's ever used is when Mom wants to get Dad away from ranch work for one night."

"Sounds perfect," he said with a sly grin. "We'll pick up a bottle of wine on our way."

And once they were at the cabin would she end up in his arms? The mere thought made her inwardly shiver with anticipation.

CHAPTER TEN

THIRTY MINUTES LATER, Win steered the truck over one of
the several graveled roads on the Bonnie B, while Stacy
navigated him to the cabin.

"I didn't realize this little guest lodge was going to be
so close to the big house," he said as he noticed the lights
of the ranch house glittering through a grove of evergreen
trees.

"Well, the cabin is a guest house and you don't want to
put your guests way out in the boonies," she teased. "But
don't worry. My parents won't know we're at the cabin.
And even if they did, they wouldn't care. I am a grown
woman, after all."

He glanced over at her while his stomach made a funny
little flip. "Yes, I have noticed," he said in a husky voice.
"I've more than noticed."

She leveled a pointed look at him. "I wonder. If I hadn't
kissed you that day in the park, I might still be waiting for
you to take notice."

He chuckled. "You kissed me? I thought it was the other
way around."

She laughed along with him and instead of feeling the
bumps in the road, Win felt sure they were floating on air.

"Well, maybe it was a mutual thing," she said then
pointed to a dim road leading off to their right. "Turn
here. The cabin is at the end of this short lane."

Two minutes later, he stopped the truck near a small

log structure with a tin roof and a tiny porch that sheltered the front door. Stepping stones led up to the porch, while a giant blue spruce stood on the east side of the house and a grove of a mixture of evergreens shrouded the west side. As they made their way to the house, a cool brisk wind blew through the tree branches and filled the air with the pungent scent of juniper.

Shivering slightly, she snuggled closer to his side and Win tightened his arm around her waist to keep her anchored there.

"It's a bit chilly tonight," she said. "We'll have to build a fire."

He very nearly groaned out loud. She'd built a fire in him from the moment her lips had first touched his and since then he'd tried, but miserably failed, to cool his thoughts of making love to her.

"I see a chimney so there must be a fireplace," he commented. "Is there firewood stored around the place?"

"Always," she answered. "Dad makes sure the hands never let the woodbox get empty."

As soon as they stepped into the cabin, Stacy flipped on a lamp then closed the heavy, wood-plank door behind them. Win glanced around the room that was furnished with two armchairs and a long couch. All of which were covered in nubby rust-colored fabric.

Spotting a low wooden table jammed between the chairs, he walked over and set down the bottle of wine he'd purchased before they'd left town.

"Mom comes up here fairly often and keeps the place dusted and swept." Stacy bent at the waist to open the screen on a small fireplace built into the east wall of the room. Once she straightened, she gestured to a woodbox sitting in a far corner.

He grabbed an armload of wood and brought it over.

"Why don't you let me take care of it? I'm an old hand at building fires," he told her.

"Thanks for the offer, but I can start the fire. It's all ready with paper and kindling. All I need to do is tee-pee the logs and stick a match to it. I'll do that while you open the wine." She pointed to a short row of cabinets in the back corner of the room. "If you need an opener, there should be one over there in that drawer, and glasses are in the cabinet."

While she dealt with the fireplace, Win hung his jacket on a peg on the wall then opened the bottle of chilled wine. After searching through one of the cabinets, he found two squatty goblets and poured a generous amount in each one.

"Someone must enjoy wine when they visit this cabin," he said. "I found a pair of goblets."

"My parents. They think of this place as a romantic get-away without the travel expense," she said with a chuckle.

"I'd say you have smart parents."

"You've probably already noticed how much they adore each other. In some ways, they've treated each day of their married life as a honeymoon. That kind of devotion doesn't come along every day." She turned away from the fire-place and glanced in his direction. "It doesn't take long for the fire to warm up this small room. Unless it's sub-zero or blizzard weather. But the cabin is rarely used in such bad weather."

Marriage. Devotion. Win was glad she'd moved on from those subjects. Or was he? Maybe he needed to know if she was considering their relationship in those terms.

And what would you do if she was? Tell her you never want to see her again? Face it, Win. You've reached the point of no return.

Shoving the heckling voice out of his head, he carried both glasses over to where she stood.

When he offered her one of them, she said, "Let me get out of this coat first."

He waited for her to slip off the garment and, while she placed it on the back of one of the chairs, he used the moment to take in her slender silhouette. Unlike his late wife and Tara, who'd both had tall, sturdy builds, Stacy was petite, her curves delicate. And he found everything about her figure incredibly alluring.

"There. That's better," she said.

She reached for one of the glasses and he handed it over.

"Should we make a toast?" he asked impishly.

She flashed him a coy smile. "We should definitely make a toast. To this special night."

He touched his glass to hers. "It started out on rough footing, but it's ending nicely."

She said, "I'll drink to that."

She tilted the glass to her lips and as Win watched her sip the dark liquid, he realized he didn't really want the wine. All he wanted was her.

Lowering her glass, she asked, "Why aren't you drinking with me?"

"Uh... I— I'm too busy looking at you."

She laughed softly and he could see she was taking his compliment lightly. That was hardly a surprise. Since he'd gotten to know her, he'd learned that she didn't think of herself as beautiful or sexy. And that was a shame because she was both those things and more. Much more.

"You kept insisting you wanted us to have wine on this date," she said. "Now you're totally disinterested."

He purposely tilted the glass to his lips and, after taking a short drink, set the glass on the table between the chairs. As he walked over to a window looking out the front of the cabin, she followed and something inside him quivered as her soft, flowery scent drifted up to him.

"It's quiet here," he remarked. "All I hear is the wind in the trees."

"The solitude is one of the things I love about the place. Sometimes, after I've had a really hectic day at school with the kids shrieking and shouting more than usual, I come up here and soak up the quietness. It recharges me."

A crescent moon had risen since they'd entered the cabin and the silvery light illuminated the stretch of ground leading to a patch of thick woods. It was an eerie but beautiful sight and Win thought how it somehow matched the unfamiliar feelings swirling inside him.

"I know what you mean. Teenagers can be mean and sarcastic even when they don't know they're being mean and sarcastic. It gets hard to deal with at times. But then I think about how they need to learn and how an education will help to build their lives, and I'm able to push the stress of teaching aside." He looked thoughtfully down at her as an image of his student Julie flashed in his mind. "Is there ever a child, or multiple children in your class, you worry about?"

"You mean about their ability to learn? Or worry about their home life?"

"Home life."

Her sigh was a sound of regret. "Oh yes. There have been times I've discussed a child's physical condition with the school nurse and, once, I reported a disturbing incident to the principal about a child being left home alone. I don't know how you feel about such things, but I want to step in and make a fuss—to make sure every child is loved and cared for. But in the end, Win, we can't always do that because they're not our children. So we merely have to do the best we can."

Her words touched him far more than she could ever

guess and, without thinking, he curved his arm around her shoulders and turned her so that she was facing him.

"You just said everything I feel, Stacy. And I… I don't know how to say it, except that I think we're kindred spirits."

Her palms came up to rest against his chest while her lashes lowered to hide most of her blue eyes. "It's hard for me to believe you think that, Win. I mean yes, we're both teachers and we both choose to work in the classroom for the same reasons. But I'm not a typical ranch girl."

"What's that got to do with anything?"

"Ranching is your life," she said quietly. "I heard Joshua talking about how well his mother could ride a horse and I imagine Yvette was capable of doing other things around the ranch."

"I don't want a ranch hand, Stacy. I want a woman," he told her.

Her lips twisted to a rueful slant as she glanced at him. "When we were first getting to know each other, you told me you didn't want a woman. Period."

His hands wrapped both her shoulders and the warmth of her flesh seeping into his fingers made him want to move them over the rest of her body, to have her curves filling his palms.

"That's what I thought," he said huskily. "But you're beginning to change my mind."

She released a shaky breath and Win slid his right hand downward until he reached the spot just above her left breast. He could feel her heart thumping at a rapid pace, but it wasn't racing nearly as fast as his.

"I don't know what to say to that," she said in a voice just above a whisper. "Or what to think."

Positioning his hands at the small of her back, he pulled her against him and her head lolled back as she looked up at him. He could see questions marching across her face and in her eyes. Questions that he wasn't ready to answer. Not to her or himself.

"I don't know what to think about it, either," he said. "But I can tell you what I'm feeling right now. I want you very much. If that isn't enough, I—"

His words paused as her forefinger reached up to touch the middle of his bottom lip.

"It's more than enough, Win." Rising on the tips of her toes, she tilted her face to his. "Can't you see how much I want you? Can't you feel it when you touch me?"

Groaning, he lowered his mouth close to hers. "When I touch you, I feel fire and pleasure, and all kinds of things that are too good to describe."

"Mmm. All I feel is desire," she confessed. "The desire to be closer to you, to give all of myself to you. It's like nothing I've ever felt before."

"Stacy. Stacy."

Breathing her name was all he could manage before he closed the tiny space between their lips, and once he began to kiss her, he realized no more words were necessary. There were plenty of other ways he could convey the desire coursing through his body.

His lips searched hers until the connection turned to hungry need and his tongue was delving into her mouth, his teeth nipping at her lips. She responded with a fervor that shocked him and sent his desire skyrocketing to an even higher level.

If it hadn't been for the need of oxygen, he would've kept on kissing her, but his burning lungs demanded that he lift his head. When he finally eased back from her, he saw that her eyes were closed and her lips were swollen. The pink lipstick she'd been wearing was now only a memory, but there was plenty of rosy color glowing on her cheeks and Win could only think he'd never seen a more beautiful woman in his life.

Her eyes fluttered open at the same time her fingers reached out to gently touch his cheek. "Win, I think it's time I showed you the bedroom."

A ball of emotion suddenly formed in the middle of his chest and spread upward to his throat. "Stacy, are you sure about this? Me?"

His voice sounded like he'd been eating gravel and his hands trembled as they moved against her back. Something was happening to him, he thought. Something strange and wild and wonderful.

"I realize if you count the days we've known each other, it wouldn't be all that many. And some people might say we've not been together nearly long enough to make love. But I feel like I've known you forever. I feel like I've been waiting for years for you to come into my life. Now that you have, I don't want to wait any longer."

As his gaze roamed her lovely face, he told himself he wasn't going to think about what she might be expecting from him. Or even what he expected from himself. The only thought he was going to allow into his brain was this moment, this night, and her.

"Neither do I."

His words barely made it past his tight throat, but she managed to hear them and she responded by folding her hand around his and leading him away from the window.

They passed through a door located behind the kitchen area and into a bedroom just big enough to hold a double bed and one chest of drawers. Two windows were on the east wall, allowing fingers of moonlight to slant across the quilt covering the bed.

"I hope you weren't expecting a fancy suite," she said with a husky laugh. "Because this is only basic comfort."

Laughing with her, he snaked an arm around her waist and pulled her tight against him. "Funny girl. As if I have comfort on my mind." Raising a hand, he smoothed his fingers over the wave of blond hair at her temple. "You know, before we met, I had practically forgotten how to laugh."

Her hands slid up to the ridges of his shoulders. "I must be having a positive effect on you."

"Hmm. You're having all kinds of effects on me, my beautiful lady." As soon as he whispered the last word, he covered her lips with his and the sweet contact sent a flash of fire straight to his brain.

Stacy reacted by quickly deepening the kiss and, in a matter of seconds, Win's senses were flying around the room, making it impossible to think about anything but getting her undressed and into his arms.

When their lips finally parted, she looked up at him with smoky-blue eyes that struck something deep within him.

"You can't know how much I want you, Win," she whispered. "It's scandalous, and I should be embarrassed to admit it to you. But my desire for you isn't something I want to hide. I want to show it to you. Over and over."

She was saying things to him he'd never expected to hear. Touching him in ways that shattered the barrier he'd long erected around his heart. Each time their lips met, every time she touched him, he felt a part of himself breaking. The feeling was both thrilling and frightening. It was also something he couldn't stop. Even if he wanted to.

"My Stacy. My sweet, sweet Stacy."

He placed another long kiss on her lips before urging her over to the side of the bed. When he reached for the tied sash on the side of her waist, she smiled and pushed his hands aside.

"This dress is complicated to get in and out of," she

explained. "It might be better if I do mine and you do yours. Okay?"

He chuckled under his breath as he began to shed his shirt and jeans. "You think I'm going to complain about that? As long as we're lying together on that bed in the next two minutes, I'll be a happy man."

"Two minutes, huh? I'll bet I'll be there before you are."

As soon as her dare was out, clothes, boots and high heels began flying. Eventually, Stacy hit the mattress a few seconds before Win and, as he stretched out beside her, she made a triumphant fist pump.

"I'm the winner," she announced.

Rolling onto his side, he reached out and touched a hand to one small perky breast. The pink nipple instantly hardened against his callused palm.

"You look even more beautiful without your clothes," he murmured. "Beautiful and perfect."

"So do you."

He closed his eyes as she trailed her fingers along his arm then onto his chest and down to his navel. Rivulets of fire followed in the wake of her touch and he wondered how he was supposed to survive the heat and the sheer need that was quickly beginning to consume him.

"No. Nothing about me is perfect, Stacy. But if you want me, the rest doesn't matter."

Her hands cupped his jaw then slid upward until her fingers were thrust into his hair. "Everyone has flaws. That's why we need each other. That's why we can be so good for each other."

"Good, yes." He leaned his head forward and, with his eyes still closed, placed a kiss on her forehead, the tip of her nose and the bottom of her chin. "So very, very good."

She sighed and her soft breath fanned the side of his face. The sensation was just as erotic as the touch of her hand and, with a needy groan, he buried a hand in the hair at the back of her head and drew her mouth to his.

The kiss went on and on until her slender body arched into his and her fingers began to dig into the flesh on his back. When he finally pulled his head from hers, they were both panting for air.

Sliding one leg over his hips, she said, "If you kiss me like that again, I'm going to break apart."

The glow he saw on her face was more radiant than the flames in the fireplace and he was mesmerized by the sparkle in her eyes, the pink color on her cheeks and lips. How had he not noticed before that she was so stunning, so utterly desirable? Had he deliberately been keeping his eyes shut because he'd been afraid of her? Of this?

No. He wasn't going to question himself now. He wasn't going to think. He was only going to feel.

"You won't break apart because you're going to be right here in my arms and I'll hold you together."

His hand slipped between the juncture of her thighs and when he touched the moist folds of her womanhood, he thought he might be wrong. He might be the one breaking into helpless pieces.

"Oh, Win. Win. Make love to me."

"It'll be my pleasure. My deepest pleasure," he whispered against her lips. Then suddenly his head came up and he stared at her in astonishment. "I think— Oh, Stacy. I wasn't thinking about you and me like this. I don't have a condom with me and I doubt your father has any extra laying around the cabin."

She chuckled. "If he does, my mother might think it a little suspicious. Anyway, there's no need for you to worry about a condom. I'm on oral contraceptives."

He arched a brow at her. "For real?"

The naughty grin she gave him was another surprise.

"Yes. But not for the obvious reason. I take them for other reasons—medical purposes—but I'm protected just the same."

Groaning with relief, he eased his head down next to hers. "Guess it's easy for you to figure out why I don't carry a condom in my wallet. I don't have a need for one," he said wryly.

"I don't think either one of us needs to apologize or feel embarrassed for not having an active sex life. Do you?"

With a hand in her hair, he tugged her close enough to place a kiss on her forehead. "Like I said, we're kindred spirits."

Her arm slipped around his neck. "And we're together."

Together. For how long? How long would he be allowed to feel this much pleasure?

The dark, uninvited thoughts caused him to pause. But a split second was all the time it took to push them aside and pull her into the tight circle of his arms.

"Yes. Together."

He whispered the words against her lips before he turned the contact into a fiery kiss that blocked everything from his mind, except her.

HIS MOUTH SLIDING over her skin, his hands touching the secret parts of her body was like a match setting fire to every cell in her body. All Stacy could think about was having him inside her, moving with her in that age-old dance of love.

When he finally rolled her onto her back and parted her thighs, she was desperate to have her body connected to his. And as soon as his hard shaft entered her, she arched her hips upward to take him deeper toward the ache that only he could ease.

The movement caused him to groan and she opened her eyes to see his jaw clamped as though he was in fierce pain.

Touching fingertips to his face, she gently whispered, "Win, is something wrong?"

His expression was a mixture of pleasure and pain as he looked down at her. "Oh, Stacy, I— Nothing is wrong. It's just that I want you so much it hurts."

"Let me take the hurt away."

Placing her hand at the back of his neck, she pulled his head down to hers and touched her lips to his. As she kissed him, she heard a needy growl deep in his throat and then his hips began moving in slow, steady thrusts that filled her with wave after wave of pleasure.

After that, everything became a blur as they strained to keep their lips together and their hands free to roam the other's heated flesh. Over and over, he plunged into her, his pace quickening with each passing moment, and she did her best to keep up with him.

But after a while, the need in her became so great she thought she would burst. As if he understood, he reached beneath her hips and pulled them tightly against his, and an explosion erupted inside her. Lights flashed behind her eyes and suddenly her whole body felt as if it were floating off the bed.

Crying out his name, she clutched his arms and then she heard him grunt with relief as he spilled himself inside her.

Stacy was still dragging in deep, ragged breaths when her senses finally gathered enough for her to become aware of her surroundings. And even then, she wasn't convinced the walls of the little bedroom had quit spinning. But the weight of Win's warm body draped over hers felt very real and very wonderful, and just so he wouldn't move away too soon, she wrapped her arms around him.

Against her breast, she could feel the heavy thud of his

heart and the rise and fall of his chest as he struggled to regain his breath. And in that moment, she knew without a doubt, that she loved him. He was the man she wanted to spend the rest of her life with. He was the only man she would ever invite into her heart. The certainty of her feelings filled her with a peace and joy she'd never felt before.

She turned her head and nuzzled her cheek to the side of his face. How nice it would be, she thought, to wake up in the morning and feel the shadow of his beard against her cheek.

"I hope you feel as good as I do right now," she murmured.

Shifting his weight off her, he propped his head on his hand and slowly studied her face. "Good? Stacy, you can't know..." Pausing, he drew in a deep breath before he continued. "You can't know what I'm feeling right now. I'm not even sure I know myself."

He didn't sound exactly euphoric or as blissful as she was feeling. But maybe sex was mundane for him, she thought. After all, he'd been married for eight years. Or maybe he'd just not felt the same incredible connection she'd felt to him while they'd been making love.

Making love. Yes. In her mind, she'd been making love to Win for weeks now. But did he view what they'd just shared as love? She wanted to think so. But not for anything would she try to pull that word from him; it had to come from his own free will. Because it was his true feelings and not just a way to appease her.

She gave him a tender smile. "Don't worry about it. I'm feeling enough for both of us."

His expression somber, he lifted a fingertip to her cheek and traced lazy circles upon her damp skin.

"Yes, I think you are. And—" With a helpless grunt, he

pressed his lips to her temple. "You're incredible, Stacy. You truly are. But I—think we should get dressed and be leaving."

Leaving! What was he thinking? That being this close to her wasn't right for him? That *she* wasn't right for him? The idea tore at her heart. "Get dressed and leave?" she asked hoarsely. "Why?"

Even as she asked the question, he was easing out of her arms and swinging his legs over the side of the bed. "I just—think it's best. For the both of us."

Maybe he thought it best to end their night together, but to her it was devastating. Could she have been so wrong in thinking he'd kissed her, made love to her with deep, genuine feelings? To think she might have misjudged him so badly caused a shaft of fear to shoot through her. She'd made mistakes in the past, but this time with Win, she'd instinctively trusted her heart to him. Had she made another terrible mistake?

"I don't understand. I thought—" Pausing, she shook her head. "What we had a few moments ago was special. You didn't think so?"

He cleared his throat and, without looking her way, reached for his clothing on the floor. "I told you a moment ago, Stacy, that I—don't understand what I'm thinking or feeling."

Obviously he was trying to tell her that any feelings he had for her weren't cut and dried. If there were any feelings at all, she thought grimly.

"So this has all been too fast for you?" she asked, unable to keep sarcasm from edging into her voice. "I wonder why you weren't concerned about the speed of things before we went to bed together?"

He slanted her an awkward glance. "I should've been. I wasn't thinking. I, uh, really wasn't planning on this—or staying all night. I imagine you knew that."

If he'd pulled a knife and stabbed her directly in the heart, she doubted she would've been more hurt or shocked than she was now. "No," she said in an incredulous voice. "I didn't know. Didn't you say the boys were staying over at your friend's place tonight?"

"Yes. But I need to, uh, check on some things at the ranch."

He stood and stepped into his jeans and Stacy had to fight the urge to yell at him.

"Lucky for you that you happened to suddenly remember these…things you need to do," she said, unable to keep a touch of bitterness from her voice.

"I'm sorry, Stacy. I hadn't planned on this happening."

Apparently not, she thought sickly. He'd had sex with her and now, for some reason she couldn't begin to fathom, he regretted it.

Drawing on all the patience she possessed, she said, "Sounds like you didn't plan on staying or leaving. Just what were you planning for this evening, Win?"

He zipped the fly on his jeans then stooped to pick up his shirt. "I don't know. I just have to go. Can't you leave it at that?"

He might as well have sloshed a bucket of ice water over her and, with her mouth set in a grim line, she climbed off the bed and began to dress.

So much for thinking she'd had a night full of bliss ahead of her. So much for getting the idea that Win actually felt something deep and real for her, she thought sickly.

Out in the living room, he hurriedly pulled on his jacket and hat while Stacy walked barefoot over to the fireplace and stood with her back to the flames.

"What are you doing?" he asked. "You can't go out without your shoes or coat."

"Not at this time of year," she replied then gestured to the bottle of wine he'd left sitting on the table. "Don't forget your wine. You might give it to Anthony as added payment for watching the boys for you."

He grunted. "Anthony only drinks beer. I'll leave the wine here. Maybe your parents will enjoy it."

"Okay." Her chest aching, she turned toward the fire to spare herself the sight of his miserable expression. "Drive safely going home. And thank you for dinner."

"I'm going to drive you home, Stacy. So get your coat and shoes."

She whirled around to stare at him. "Who do you think you are, Win Jackson? Just because you took me to bed doesn't mean you have the right to order me around. I have no intention of letting you drive me home. So leave. Go on and get back to the J Barb so you can get all those *things* done."

He walked over to where she stood. "I understand you're angry with me, Stacy. You're thinking I'm acting like a jerk. But I can't stay. Not now. And I'm not going to leave you here. Alone."

A curt laugh erupted from her. "I've stayed in this cabin *alone* many times. When I get ready to go home, I'll walk. The ranch house is no more than a hundred yards right through that stand of trees and there's a clear walking path the whole way. I don't need a ride."

He stared at her for a few seconds longer and Stacy didn't miss the anguish twisting his features, or the pain shadowing his eyes. It was hurting him to leave, she realized. So what was pushing him toward the door? If she only knew.

"Alright. Then I'll say good-bye."

"Good-bye, Win."

He left the cabin and moments later, Stacy heard the engine of his truck fire to life, but she didn't bother to glance out the window to see if he was leaving. He'd already left her before he'd ever climbed off the bed.

CHAPTER ELEVEN

"DAD, DO YOU think Joshua will ever make the basketball team?"

Win looked over at Oliver, who was sitting next to him on the gymnasium bleachers as they watched the after-school basketball practice.

"All the boys are on the team," Win explained. "Are you asking if Joshua will make the *main* team?"

Oliver nodded. "Yeah. That's what I mean. Some of the junior and senior boys are really tall. I don't think Joshua can take their place."

"You have to have more than height to be good at basketball. Joshua understands it takes time and lots of hard work to earn a spot on a team," Win told him. "Your brother might not ever be a starter."

Oliver grimaced. "Then why bother with all this practicing? We could be home riding horses instead," he grumbled.

"Being a main player isn't the important thing here, Oliver," Win said patiently. "Joshua wants to be a part of something with his friends. Someday, when you get older, you'll understand."

Oliver's head tilted from one shoulder to the other as he considered his father's remarks. "Why do I always need to be older? I'm smart right now."

Any other time, Oliver's response would've drawn a chuckle from Win, but at the moment he didn't have the energy or the inclination to laugh. Not when everything inside him felt half dead.

He glanced at Oliver then out to the court where Joshua was passing the ball to a teammate. Without his sons, his life wouldn't have any meaning. They were the only things that kept him moving forward these days.

"Yes, you're smart," he said to Oliver. "But in five more years, you're going to be a whole lot smarter."

"Gosh, Dad, by then I might be a genius."

Forcing his lips to form a smile, he patted his son's shoulder. "I hope you are, Oliver. Then you can teach me."

He needed someone to teach him a thing or two, Win thought dully, because these days he seemed to be doing everything wrong. Ever since he'd left Stacy in the guest cabin, he'd felt worse than a jerk. He felt like half a man. A man too timid to step out of the shadows and into the sunshine.

The scoreboard buzzed to announce the end of the practice and, as the players put away their gear and headed to the locker room, Win and Oliver descended the bleachers and walked out to the lobby of the gymnasium to wait for Joshua.

After ten minutes passed without any sign of the teenager, Win was about to head back inside the gym to see what was keeping him, when Joshua suddenly walked into the lobby with Anthony at his side.

"Before you start barking, it's my fault that Joshua is late," Anthony told Win. "I made him wait until I could join him."

Win refrained from rolling his eyes. "Why? Is he in trouble?" he questioned.

Anthony chuckled then, seeing Win wasn't laughing, he gave him a pat on the shoulder. "Lighten up, buddy. Joshua is one of my best kids. And I'm not saying that because you and I are friends. I wanted to walk out with him so I could catch you before you left. I thought the four of us might go out and grab some burgers, my treat. What do you say?"

Win glanced toward a window near the entrance doors. "It's cold and rainy and we have chores waiting. I think—"

Anthony quickly interrupted. "I think that's all the more reason you need to eat before you go home to the ranch. That way you won't have to fix supper after you do your chores."

"Yeah, Dad! Let's eat with Anthony!" Oliver exclaimed. "He eats good stuff like burgers and pizza!"

"I'd like burgers tonight, too, Dad." Joshua added his opinion.

Win leveled a somber look at his sons. "If it was left up to Anthony, you'd be eating burgers or pizza every night."

"Oh, come on, Win. I'm not that bad," Anthony told him. "Besides, one night this week won't hurt."

"And it might make you smile, Dad." Oliver spoke up. "That won't hurt, either."

From the corner of his eye, he saw Anthony flash him a meaningful look, but he didn't glance his way. He was too stunned by Oliver's remark to worry about what Anthony was thinking. Had he been acting like a crank with his sons? He'd not thought so, but apparently Oliver had picked up on his father's unhappiness. The idea bothered him greatly. He didn't want his boys suffering just because their father had made a mess of things with Stacy.

"Okay," he conceded. "We'll go, but we can't stay in town for very long. Remember, the animals at the ranch are hungry, too."

"Yay! Burgers! Can I have a milkshake, too?" Oliver asked Anthony.

Anthony chuckled as the four of them passed through

the double doors leading out of the building. "Why ask me? You'd better ask your dad," he told the boy.

"Well, I'm asking you because you're gonna be paying for everything," Oliver explained.

Anthony laughed again, but all Win could manage was a half-hearted grunt of amusement.

"As far as I'm concerned, you can have two milkshakes, Oliver. You're a growing boy," Anthony told him.

"Oliver, you always have to be a hog," Joshua goaded his brother.

"So what? Hogs are really smart," Oliver shot back at him. "And Dad just told me I was going to be a genius when I got older."

Joshua laughed at his little brother. "Now, you're fibbing, along with being a hog."

"I am not fibbing! Dad did say I might be a genius. Didn't you, Dad?"

"I did say you were going to get smarter. I think you put in the part about being a genius," Win answered.

Joshua snickered. "See. I knew you were fibbing."

"Oh yeah? Well, I'm the one who made straight A's on my report card! Not you!" Oliver boasted.

Win glanced over his shoulder at the bickering brothers. "It's raining. You two run on to the truck. And quit that darned arguing or we're going straight home."

As the boys trotted on to the truck parked at the far end of the parking lot, Anthony glanced over at him.

"They're just being typical brothers, Win."

"I know. It's just that I'm not in the mood to listen to it tonight. And if you think you're going to start lecturing me about Stacy, then you might as well forget it. I'm in no mood to listen to you, either."

Anthony merely chuckled at Win's sour warning. "This is going to be a fun meal for all."

"Who said anything about having fun? Is that what you think life is supposed to be? One big party?"

"All right. I've had enough," Anthony muttered.

He paused on the sidewalk and, before Win guessed what his friend was doing, he pulled out his cell phone.

"Joshua, this is Anthony. You and Oliver stay in the truck and wait. Your Dad and I will be there in a few minutes."

"What is this about?" Win asked.

With a hand on his shoulder, Anthony turned him in the direction of a red pickup parked several yards away from Win's.

"Since you don't want to talk over dinner, we'll talk right now in my truck," Anthony said flatly. "And I'm not in the *mood* to argue."

Win wanted to do more than argue. He wanted to walk away, but he knew the boys were most likely watching curiously out the window and he didn't want them to get the idea that something was amiss with their dad and his best friend.

Once both men were inside the dry confines of the truck cab, Win was the first to speak. "I've already told you, Anthony, I'm not going to have a discussion with you about Stacy."

"If you're not going to discuss the problem with me, then who are you going to discuss it with? Your brother?"

"No. I don't want him to know I've been a fool a second time."

Anthony gave him a hard look then nodded. "You know, you're absolutely right about being a fool. You're probably the biggest one I've ever known."

"Thanks for being such a good buddy," Win said sarcastically. "I can always count on you to make me feel better."

"Damn it, I don't want you to feel better. I want you to face up to what you're doing."

Staring out the windshield, Win muttered, "And what do you think I'm doing? Slacking off on my job? Being a bad father?"

"You'd never do either of those things. But you sure don't have any qualms about running away from a woman."

"Listen, Anthony, I told you that Stacy and I went out to dinner."

"That's been nearly a week ago. And you've not seen her since."

Win stared at him. "How do you know? Have you been talking to her?"

Anthony cursed under his breath. "You think I'd talk about you behind your back? To a woman?"

Did he? No. Anthony might be assertive at times, but he respected Win's privacy.

"If you must know, Joshua mentioned it to me," Anthony explained. "I think your sons are wondering about you and her."

"Oh. I didn't know," Win mumbled then shrugged. "I need to tell them that…well, nothing serious is going to happen with me and Stacy. That way they won't be confused and wondering."

"Won't be confused? Pardon me, but even your children can see you're daffy about Stacy. You think they'll understand why you're suddenly running backward? I'm an adult and I don't understand. How do you expect the boys to comprehend your behavior?"

Win wiped a hand over his face at the same time he tried to wipe the image of Stacy's beautiful face out of his mind. He'd had to call upon every ounce of strength he possessed to leave the cabin with her face a picture of wounded misery. And he hated himself a thousand times over for hurting her. He'd never intended to cause her pain. He'd only wanted to love her. But then fear had taken him over and he'd run like a coward.

"Look, Anthony, having a woman in my life just won't work. I came to that conclusion the night Stacy and I went out to dinner. I have too many memories, too many worries and doubts that I can't shed. I'd only end up making her miserable and then losing her."

Memories. Yeah, this past week he'd been assaulted with memories of holding Stacy in his arms, kissing her giving lips and loving her. He'd been totally stunned by the feelings she'd evoked in him. Making love to her had transported him to a far off beautiful place. One that he'd never wanted to leave. But as soon as his senses had returned to reality and he'd glanced around the cozy bedroom of the cabin, fear had seized him. All he could think was that he had to get away from the happiness and pleasure Stacy was giving him. He couldn't let himself love and lose again.

The sound of Anthony letting out a long breath, pulled Win out of his bleak thoughts and he glanced over at his friend.

"You know, buddy, everyone has memories and worries that we have to deal with and push aside," Anthony told him. "I think it's the losing her that's getting to you. Yes, you're afraid of losing her. Not because you'd make her miserable. No, you're frightened of losing her the way you lost your wife."

"Damn right. Wouldn't you be?"

"Yes, I'm fairly sure I would be frightened. Because you couldn't stop or prevent Yvette's death. I understand all that. But if you keep hanging on to your fear, you might as well go sit in a dark corner and let Stacy find some other man who'd be thrilled to give her the love she needs."

The image of Stacy making love to another man made him sick inside and, without even knowing it, a rueful groan slipped out of him. "How am I supposed to get rid of this fear, Anthony?"

"I can't offer you a magic cure. I only know that you can't let it continue to define the man you are, or how you live the rest of your life." He reached over and affectionately punched his fist against Win's upper arm. "Come on. The boys are hungry and so am I. And, Win, you're going to get this right. I have faith in you."

With a hopeless grin, he looked over at Anthony. "Thanks for putting up with me."

"I expect you to do the same for me—if I ever make a fool of myself over a woman."

"Ha! I can't wait to see that," Win joked and, as the two men left the truck and walked over to join the boys, he realized this was the first time since he'd left Stacy at the cabin that he felt like he was, at least, half human.

LATER THAT NIGHT, on the Bonnie B, Stacy was sitting at a small desk in her bedroom, going through a stack of artwork she'd assigned her students yesterday. She'd asked them to draw a picture of what the fall season meant to them and it was clear as she studied each paper that each child had their own special images. A pile of colorful leaves. A pumpkin. A cup of hot chocolate. A cat curled up on a rug. And then there was a red heart, so big that it nearly covered the whole sheet of paper. Obviously, the child was simply trying to say she loved everything about autumn.

She glanced at the girl's name at the bottom of the paper and even though Stacy wanted to smile, tears gathered in her eyes.

The evening Win had given her a ride home to the Bonnie B when her car had failed to start, she'd told him how fall was her favorite time of the year. As simple as that meeting between them had been that night, she'd felt a special connection to him. When she'd walked at his side, it had felt right and perfect. Had she been a fool then? Right from the very start?

"Knock, knock! Want some company?"

Robin's cheerful voice had her glancing around to see her sister's head peeping around the partially open door of her bedroom.

Hurriedly dashing away her tears with the back of her hand, Stacy stood and walked over to greet her. "I'm always happy to see my sister."

Robin kissed her cheek then stepped back to scrutinize her somber face.

"You taste salty."

Stacy avoided her sister's probing gaze. "It's the makeup I wore to school today. I've not cleaned my face yet."

"Is that what's making your eyes water, too?"

Grimacing, Stacy turned away from her, walked over to the bed and sat down on the side of the mattress. "I'm probably needing glasses. All the paperwork I go through puts a strain on my eyes."

"Strange that you're just now having a problem with eye strain." Robin walked over and sat next to her. "I think it's more of a heart strain problem."

Stacy stared at the floor as pain welled up in her chest. For the past week, since she and Win had said goodbye, she'd tried to appear normal and go on with her daily life as though nothing had happened. But Win's sudden rejection had shattered her and, not surprisingly, her family and friends were beginning to notice her despondent mood.

"I'm okay, Robin. Just disappointed, that's all."

"In Win, you mean?"

She looked at her sister. "Yes. But even more disappointed in myself. I should've known right from the start that Win wasn't ready for a serious relationship with me or any woman. I must've had my head in the clouds to think he could put the loss of his wife behind him and begin a new life with me. Anyway, it's over between us." She made a mocking grunt. "My romance didn't last long, did it?"

Robin scowled at her. "How do you know it's over? Have you talked to Win?"

"No. He hasn't reached out to me and I'm certainly not going to call him. He's the one who walked out after we—" She broke off as images of her and Win making love flashed through her mind. Shaking away the memory, she started again. "He's the one who walked out during our date. He came up with a lame excuse about needing to do things on the ranch, but we both knew he simply wanted to leave."

Robin's scowl turned into a confused frown. "Why do you think he wanted to put an end to the evening? Did you two have a disagreement?"

Stacy released a heavy sigh. "I only wish it was something that simple. We could've talked through a simple disagreement. But this—it goes much deeper, Robin. At least, I think it does. There are times when I'm feeling sorry for myself that I think Win just doesn't care enough about me to want to keep our relationship going. But other times, when I'm trying to look at things clearly, I think the problem is tied to him losing his wife so unexpectedly and at such a young age. I'm just not sure he's ready to get seriously involved with anyone again. You see, he told me how, before he'd left Whitehorn, he'd finally decided to try dating again, but things turned very ugly with the woman when he wanted to keep things casual."

"I suppose she was expecting a proposal or something close to it?"

Stacy nodded. "Right. And he didn't want to get that involved with her. But now...well, I can only wonder if his past is still haunting him. Either that or he just isn't interested in me anymore."

"Hmm. Well, it's not unusual for a man to run scared if he thinks he's falling in love," Robin said.

Falling in love? Could her sister be right? This past week she'd relived over and over their night at the cabin and the moments she'd spent in Win's arms. She'd carefully studied all the words he'd spoken to her and, as perfect as their lovemaking had been, she'd not heard anything from him about being in love with her. Did she dare even think he might love her?

We're kindred spirits. When Win had spoken those words to her, she'd been lying in his arms and his lips had been pressed to her forehead. Even now, after this week of not hearing from him, she wanted to believe the emotion she'd heard in his voice. She longed to believe he'd kissed her and made love to her with his heart.

"Robin, do you honestly think he could be falling in love with me?" she asked then shook her head. "Sorry, I shouldn't have asked you such a question. You don't really know Win all that well. And you've not seen the two of us together. You couldn't know how he feels about me. I don't even know myself. But I want to think——" Her throat was suddenly aching with hot tears, forcing her to swallow before she could finish. "Foolish or not, I want to think there's a chance he could be falling in love with me."

Wrapping her arm around Stacy's shoulders, Robin gave her sister an encouraging squeeze.

"I think I gave you this advice before, but I'm going to give it to you again anyway. Give the man a bit more time,

Stacy. He needs to come to terms with his past. And what he wants for his future."

Stacy gave her sister a lopsided grin. "In other words, call on my patience and wait."

Robin chuckled. "More or less. I happen to think Mr. Jackson is going to soon realize what a good thing he has in you."

"You're my sister. You're biased," Stacy said.

Robin rose and, grabbing both of Stacy's hands, pulled her to her feet. "I'm also dying for some of the hot chocolate Mom is making. Come on and have a cup with me. You need to get out of this room and put a smile on your face. Everything is going to work out, sissy. I'll make a wager that by the time Christmas arrives, you're going to be a very merry woman."

Doing her best to smile, Stacy planted a kiss on Robin's cheek. "Thank you, sweet sister. Now, let's go have that hot chocolate. I'm going to pile mine high with marshmallows and whipped cream."

Laughing, Robin ushered her toward the door. "Now you're talking."

THE NEXT AFTERNOON, after classes had been dismissed for the day, Win walked out of the school building to start across the parking lot to his truck when he noticed Julie standing at the designated pickup spot on the sidewalk. Since he'd noticed the girl boarding the bus before, he was surprised to see her waiting with a few of her classmates for their rides.

Pausing for a moment, he thought about walking over and quietly questioning her. Just to make sure her dad was in good enough condition to drive, but he didn't want to embarrass the girl, so he continued walking.

When someone tugged on his jacket from behind, he

was more than surprised to see Julie had chased him down the sidewalk.

"I apologize for interrupting you, Mr. Jackson, but I thought you might be wondering why I wasn't riding the bus."

"I was wondering," he said. "Is everything okay, Julie? Is your father coming to pick you up?"

The smile that suddenly spread across her face was so out of character for the withdrawn student, he could only stare at her in wonder.

"Oh no. Dad isn't coming. He's at work. He got a different job. One he likes a lot more than the last one. My mom is picking me up. She's moved back home now and…well, everything is just so much better. And you know something, Mr. Jackson? The next time you have a field trip, I just might get to go!"

"That's great, Julie. I'm glad you told me."

A car honked and the girl glanced over her shoulder. "There she is now! See you tomorrow, Mr. Jackson!"

She took off in a run to where a dark-haired woman was waving a hand out the window, and Win stood there watching as the girl happily joined her mother.

Wonder of wonder, Win thought. There were still good things happening in world and to people who deserved better in their lives.

As he continued on to his truck, he realized how much he'd like to call Stacy and share Julie's good news. Not that she knew the girl or that Win had ever mentioned her troubled home life to Stacy. She wanted *all* children to be loved and cared for, no matter where they went to school or who taught them. Hearing that Julie's situation had improved would definitely put a smile on her face.

The image of Stacy's smiling face floated through his

mind as he climbed into his truck and drove toward the elementary school to pick up Oliver.

Since Anthony had lectured him last night about Stacy, Win had been thinking about all his friend had said. Especially the part about Joshua and Oliver being confused about their father's behavior.

At school, Win had done his best to be his normal self and, as far as he knew, none of his students had noticed how miserable he was inside. But at home, it had been impossible to keep up the façade and he supposed his depression and grief had been fairly obvious to his sons.

He had to make a change, he thought. He couldn't keep living in this kind of misery. With his mind totally consumed by the woman he loved.

The woman he loved. Yes, he could finally admit that he loved Stacy. That was a start, at least. But what was he going to do about it? Where was he going to find the courage to face her and what his feelings meant to the both of them?

LATER THAT NIGHT, Win was sitting in a rocker in front of the fireplace when Joshua and Oliver surprised him with a mugful of coffee and a small plate of sugar cookies.

"Thanks, boys. This is really nice." He took a sip of the coffee and discovered the brew was really strong but sweetened just right. "So what have I done to deserve this special treatment? Or should I ask what have you done?"

Oliver was the first to speak. "We're not trying to make up for doing something bad, Dad. We just thought you looked tired tonight."

He eyed both boys as he picked up a cookie. Were they actually worried about him? The thought struck him hard.

"I am a little tired. But I'm okay."

They continued to stand a few steps away from his

chair, watching him as though they expected him to collapse, or yell. Win couldn't decide which.

"Don't you boys have homework to do? I know you do, Joshua. I gave your class two chapters to read for a test Friday."

Joshua nodded. "I'll have the chapters read, Dad. And Oliver will get his homework done, too. We, uh...we just wanted to talk to you."

He sipped more of the hot coffee. Between it and the heat from the flames in the fireplace, he was beginning to warm up from the hour he'd spent wrapping several water pipes with insulation. The weather had rapidly taken a turn toward winter and he'd needed to get everything prepared.

"Okay. Are you guys wanting to ask me for something? Like a new horse? Or saddles?"

"No! We don't want nothing," Oliver declared.

"Don't use double negatives, Oliver! Do you want to sound dumb?" Joshua scolded. Then, just as quickly, his expression softened and he patted his little brother on the shoulder. "It's okay. I know you forget. I do, too, sometimes."

Oliver gave his brother a grateful look, before he turned to his father. "We don't want to ask for stuff, Dad. We want to know why you don't smile anymore."

"Yeah. And why you don't see Ms. Abernathy anymore," Joshua added. "Don't you still like her?"

"We like her a lot," Oliver stated and then looked up to his brother. "Don't we, Joshua?"

Win was shocked at his sons' question and even more surprised to see his oldest son nod in agreement.

"We like Ms. Abernathy, Dad," Joshua said. "And we thought that—uh, you were going to start really liking her. And maybe make her our new mom."

Stunned, Win deliberately set the coffee and cookies

aside then studied the boys' earnest faces. Since they'd moved to Bronco, he'd never seen either of them look so concerned or serious about anything.

"Joshua, do you really mean what you're saying?"

The teenager moved closer to Win's chair. "Sure, Dad. Don't you believe me?"

"I'd like to think you wouldn't say something so important without really meaning it. But it hasn't been that long ago that you were making a point of trying to steer me away from her and all women."

Joshua scuffed the toe of his boot against the rock hearth of the fireplace. "Yeah, but that was before I met Katrina. She's made me see that not all women are bad. Like Monica back in Whitehorn. I believed she really cared about me, but she turned out to be a cheat. And Tara—she was downright mean. Stacy would never be like her. I understand that now."

"I'm glad you've figured these things out, Joshua. But if you have the idea that Stacy would be like your mother, you're mistaken. Stacy is nothing like her."

Win watched in wonder as Joshua and Oliver both sat on the floor at his feet.

"Oliver doesn't remember Mom," Joshua said, "so he can't compare. But I remember, and I can see that Ms. Abernathy isn't like Mom. But I don't care about that and neither does Oliver. Ms. Abernathy is really nice, and I think Mom would like her. I think she'd be happy if Ms. Abernathy became a part of our family."

Hearing Joshua's words and seeing the eager expressions on his sons' faces was suddenly wiping away the fog in front of Win's eyes. If his teenaged son was strong enough to put the tragedy of losing his mother behind him, then Win could surely find the courage and strength to move his life forward.

Reaching out, he rubbed the top of Joshua's head and then Oliver's. "You're right, boys, your mother would like Stacy. And I think she'd be happy to know her sons had another mother to love them."

Oliver's face lit up like a Christmas tree. "Does that mean you're going to see Ms. Abernathy and be happy?"

Win took a deep breath and let it out. "It means I'm going to call Stacy tomorrow."

"Tomorrow?" Groaning, Joshua rolled his eyes. "Why not call her tonight?"

"Yeah, Dad, why not tonight?" Oliver seconded his brother's suggestion.

"Because it's far too late. She's probably getting ready for bed. And I need to think about what I'm going to say to her. I'm certain she's upset with me."

She was probably more than upset, Win thought. By now, she might even be hating him. The idea hurt, but he realized the pain he'd been going through had all been self-inflicted. And knowing that made it all that much harder to bear.

"Okay, why don't you let me and Oliver call her on the way to school in the morning?" Joshua offered. "We'll invite her over here to the J Barb for dinner tomorrow night. She'll like that, Dad!"

"Yeah!" Oliver jumped to his feet and clapped his hands. "Me and Joshua can cook something good! That'll make her happy."

Joshua and Oliver had tried to make a few of their favorite dishes several times and Win had instructed them as much as possible with his limited knowledge of cooking, but preparing something edible for a guest would be a stretch for his sons.

"You boys believe you can cook something Stacy would like?"

Oliver straightened his shoulders as Joshua chucked his chin to a proud angle and said, "Dad, you know we make good spaghetti. It's easy."

"And we can have applesauce or pudding cups for dessert," Oliver added. "Ms. Abernathy will like those things, 'cause we have them at school for lunch."

Win was amazed by the excitement the boys were displaying. Not just over making a meal for Stacy, but also for planning to get her back on friendly terms with their father.

Wiping a hand over his eyes, he said, "Okay, you two, you have my permission to call Stacy and invite her to dinner. But I wouldn't get my hopes up that she'll agree to come. The last time I saw her, she wasn't very happy with me."

Stepping closer, Oliver lovingly patted his father's shoulder. "Don't worry, Dad. We'll talk her into it."

"Yeah, Dad. You just leave everything to me and Oliver," Joshua said then added, "Maybe you ought to get her some pretty flowers."

"Or buy her some fancy chocolate candy," Oliver was quick to suggest.

Flowers and candy? Win would do it. But he figured it would take more than those things to make Stacy forgive him.

CHAPTER TWELVE

THE NEXT EVENING Stacy informed her parents she was driving over to the J Barb for dinner with Win and his sons. Her father merely arched one brow at her while her mother's mouth formed a perfect *O*. Thankfully, neither parent had caught her before she'd left the house to give her a lecture about thinking with her head instead of her heart.

Yet now, as Stacy drove onto J Barb land, she wondered if she was asking to be hurt and rejected all over again. When Joshua and Oliver had phoned her early this morning, she'd been more than surprised. Oliver had been first to speak and he'd been full of his usual bubbly enthusiasm when he'd insisted he and Joshua needed her to come try out their spaghetti recipe. He'd even added that they had a new shaker of parmesan cheese for further persuasion. As charming as Oliver had sounded, she'd hesitated to give the boy an answer and then Joshua had quickly taken over the phone. The teenager had insisted they wanted to fix her dinner to pay her back for the great picnic food she'd fed them at the park. Which had sounded logical enough to Stacy, but she'd still had to ask the obvious, "Has your Dad agreed to you boys having me over for dinner?"

"Oh sure, Ms. Abernathy. He's fine with it," Joshua had insisted and then Oliver had snatched up the phone and added, "Dad says its okay to have you over as long as we don't give you burned food."

After that Stacy had to accept the boys invitation, but

she couldn't lie to herself. She'd been disappointed that Win hadn't called himself. But the fact that Joshua and Oliver had cared enough to invite her to dinner had filled her with a spark of hope that Win might possibly want to see her, too.

He probably wants this meeting so he can end things between you neatly and permanently, Stacy. He doesn't want to get into an ugly situation like the one he'd been in with Tara. That could be what this unexpected dinner invitation is all about.

The mocking voice in her head caused her foot to unwittingly slack off the accelerator. If that was Win's plan, she couldn't go through the humiliation. She'd rather go home and eat nails.

I happen to think Mr. Jackson is going to soon realize what a good thing he has in you.

Thankfully, Robin's remark suddenly pushed its way into doubts swirling around in her mind and she finished the last quarter mile to Win's house determined to face him with firm resolution.

The J Barb ranch house was a two-story structure surrounded by several tall evergreens. The outside walls consisted of a mixture of rough cedar siding and native rock, while the roof was galvanized tin. A large chimney of the same rock towered above the roof on the north end and the curl of wood smoke spiraling upward was a warming sight. Especially when she was trembling from the chill.

Or was the thought of seeing Win again making her shake? Either way, she had to get a grip. She wanted him to see she wasn't just a meek little second-grade teacher who couldn't hold her own with a rugged cowboy.

Tightening the rust-brown muffler around her neck, she left the car and began walking to a long porch with a roof supported by fat cedar post. Along the way, she was met by two friendly border collies and she paused long enough to greet them. The dogs yipped with excitement and followed her into the yard. As she and the pups headed for the porch, she noticed someone had thrown out wild birdseed beneath a tall cedar tree. Several red cardinals, along with a few sparrows, were pecking at the feed.

She was thinking how lovely the place looked when she heard a door open and close. The sound called her attention away from the birds and she went stock-still as she saw Win striding quickly toward her. He was holding one hand behind his back and she wondered if he'd injured his arm and made it immobile. However, as soon as he reached her, he pulled out a bouquet of white mums and red holly berries wrapped in green cellophane.

"Welcome to the J Barb, Stacy." He extended the bouquet toward her. "I hope you like chrysanthemums."

For a moment, she was so stunned, her tongue felt glued to the roof of her mouth and she swallowed twice in an effort to find her voice.

"I love chrysanthemums. Especially white ones." She looked down at the flowers nestled in the crook of her arm. "How did you know?"

"We're kindred spirits. Remember?"

Emotions pooled behind her breasts and rushed up to her throat. "I remember," she murmured then lifted her gaze to his face. "I don't understand, Win. Why—"

Before she could go on, his arm slipped around the back of her waist. "Let's go inside to talk. Where it's warm."

Her heart thumping with angst and hope, she said, "All right."

He guided her up the steps and across the porch. While he opened the door, Stacy glanced over her shoulder to see the dogs trotting toward the barn, which confirmed her assumption that the pair were working cattle dogs.

Inside the house, they walked from a short foyer and turned right into a large living room. She'd thought he would stop and seat her on the leather couch or one of the armchairs, but instead he guided her on to a door at the far end of the room.

Once they entered the small room, she realized the private space was an office, no doubt where he tended to schoolwork and the bookkeeping that went along with the ranch. There was a large desk equipped with a computer, and shelves built into one wall. The shelves were filled with books and other items that appeared to be souvenirs or mementos of special occasions. Along another wall was a couch covered in green tweed fabric.

Win led her over to the couch and waited for her to remove her coat. After she'd handed it to him, she took a seat on an end cushion. While she smoothed a hand over her blue-and-green-plaid skirt, he took his hat off and placed it and her coat on the corner of the desk.

With his head uncovered, her gaze went straight to his dark blond hair and suddenly she was remembering how the waves felt slipping through her fingers and how his skin had tasted as she'd pressed kisses over his face.

Clearing her throat, she looked past the desk to where a wide window looked out at a meadow dotted with evergreens and a herd of Black Baldy cattle gathered around a hay ring. She was still gazing at the peaceful scene when he walked over to where she sat.

"Here, let me put your flowers on the desk. We'll find a vase for them in a few minutes."

"Thank you."

She relinquished the bouquet to him and, after he'd placed it on the desk, he joined her on the couch.

When he reached for her hands, she very nearly pulled back from him, but quickly decided that avoiding his touch wouldn't accomplish anything. Especially when everything inside her was screaming to reach for him, to have him hold her tight in his arms.

"Win, what's going on? Where are the boys?" she asked.

"In the kitchen. Finishing making our dinner. I've told them I'd be bringing you in here to talk privately before we join them. So, they won't be barging through the door, if that's worrying you."

The soft laugh that erupted from her sounded like she was on the verge of hysteria. "Win, that's the least of my worries! I want to know why you let them invite me here to your ranch. After a week of hearing nothing from you, it's pretty darn obvious you've already quit on me and whatever we had between us. I honestly don't know why you bothered with flowers. I could've gotten the message without them."

His frown was almost comical. "Really? The boys seemed to think they'd send just the right message. And, by the way, you have a box of dark chocolates waiting for you in the kitchen. I think they want to give those to you personally."

"Flowers. Candy," she repeated dazedly. "I didn't realize Joshua and Oliver cared that much about me. Or that—"

Groaning helplessly, he gently pulled on her hands until her face was close to his. "The boys love you and so do I. That's why you're here. I can't say it any plainer than that."

She stared at him in stunned fascination. "You...love me? You're telling me that *now*? After the way you walked out on me in the cabin? I'm not a complete fool, Win. I don't believe everything a man tells me!"

His expression full of anguish, he shook his head. "Good thing you don't. Because I've said some things to you that weren't right. Like how I didn't want a woman in my life. That was the coward in me talking, Stacy. And it

was the coward in me that left you in the cabin. I thought...
I imagined you'd already figured out that I was running
away from you."

"Why?" The question came out in a hoarse whisper. "I
love you, Win. You don't need to run away from me. I'm
not going to try to back you into a corner, or expect you to
make some sort of lifelong commitment to me right now. I
understood then and I still understand that you need time."

His hands were suddenly on her shoulders, holding them
tightly as he gazed into her eyes. "You love me? Honestly?"

The sound that came out of her was something between
a laugh and a sob. "Oh, Win. I think I've been in love with
you from the first moment you said hello to me. That night
after we met, I went home and told myself there wasn't
such a thing as love at first sight. I told myself I was being
stupid. But all that talking to myself didn't work."

"Thank God, it didn't work," he said fervently. Then,
drawing her into his arms, he cradled her head against his
shoulder. "Oh, sweetheart, that night after we made love at
the cabin, I was rattled to the very core of my being. You
were so beautiful and giving and wonderful. And when
it struck me suddenly and deeply how very much I loved
you, it terrified me. All I could think was the unbearable
pain I'd go through if I ever lost you. And, to be honest, I
was feeling guilty, too."

She pulled her head back far enough to look at him.
"Guilty? Because you loved me?"

He nodded then groaned. "Yes, in a way. Because loving
you made me realize I was finally leaving my marriage to
Yvette. That was rough. I mean she'd been a part of my life
for so long. She'd borne me two sons. And even after she
died, she was still a part of my life—until now. Until you.
It's taken me this long miserable week to finally come to

terms with letting go and reaching for what I want in my life—and that is you and our children."

Her brows arched with surprise even as her heart was jumping with joy. "*Our* children?"

His forefingers tenderly touched her cheek. "Yes. *Our* children. You might be interested to know that Joshua and Oliver helped me see that Yvette would want them to have another mother. And they want you to be their new mom."

Stacy was so overcome with emotion that tears began to roll down her cheeks. "This is all so incredible, Win. These past days without any word from you have been worse than wretched. But I didn't want to give up on you. I wanted to believe that somehow you cared for me."

"Cared for you? Oh, darling, I want you to be my wife. And soon."

She realized she could finally smile, and it felt wonderful. "Soon?" she asked impishly. "You mean you don't want a long engagement?"

"No way! I want you right here in this house as my wife. As the mother of my sons, plus any brothers and sisters we'll give Joshua and Oliver. How does that sound?"

Laughing, now she asked, "Did you mean to say brother and sister in plural form?"

He chuckled. "I did. We need to keep the student population up so we can both have our teaching jobs," he joked and then his expression turned serious as his face drew close enough to kiss her cheek. "All kidding aside, I'd love to have two or three more kids. But only if you'd be happy to give them to me."

Her head was literally whirling with joy. "Oh, Win, I'd be more than happy. I can't wait for our life together to get started."

"Neither can I," he said.

With his hand at the back of her head, he pulled her

mouth to his and, for long, glorious moments, he kissed her in a way that told Stacy he loved her and would always love her.

When he finally raised his head, he rubbed his cheek against hers. "Ready to go try the boys' spaghetti?" he asked.

"I am. But before we go out to the kitchen, there's one thing I'd like to say." Wrapping her arms around his neck, she rested her cheek against his shoulder. "I'm thrilled that I'm going to become the boys' mother, but I—well, I hope that Yvette would approve of me. That I can be as good a mother to Joshua and Oliver as she was."

He eased her head off his shoulder and, cupping his hands around the sides of her face, he smiled at her. "I think you should know that Joshua believes Yvette would be happy to know you're going to be his and Oliver's mother."

Joy flooded through her. "Oh Win, I'm so happy he feels that way. I want the boys to love me just as much as I need and want you to love me."

His arms tightened around her. "This past week, I kept imagining how I would feel if something took your life and took you away from me. But I've decided, Stacy, that I can't go around living my life in fear. I have to have trust and faith that we'll be together for a long, long time."

"Oh yes, my darling. After all, we're kindred spirits." She plastered kisses on his cheeks and chin and, finally, on his lips. "And kindred spirits stay together no matter what."

Laughing, he pulled her to her feet and fetched the bouquet of mums from the desk. "Come on. Let's go give the boys our good news."

WHEN STACY AND Win entered the kitchen, the boys were sitting at a breakfast bar with their chins in their hands and looking worse than bored.

"Aren't you guys supposed to be cooking dinner?" Win asked.

As he and Stacy strolled to the middle of the room, Joshua and Oliver jumped off their barstools and stood anxiously eyeing them.

"The food is already done and the table in the dining room is set and ready. We're just waiting for you," Joshua said.

"Yeah. Just waiting to see if you two are happy now," Oliver said. "Are you?"

Win leveled a tender look at Stacy. "Are you happy?"

"Deliriously happy," she answered. "What about you?"

He chuckled. "I think my boots have sprouted wings. I'm pretty sure I flew here to the kitchen."

Loving the joy she saw on his face, she chuckled with him. "Maybe you did."

"Oh, Dad, you sound silly," Oliver said.

"Sometimes a person acts silly when he's really, really happy." He handed the bouquet of flowers to Joshua. "Put these in a vase of water for Stacy. Then you two join us in the living room. We want to talk to you before we eat."

Out in the living room, Stacy and Win sat on a couch that faced the fireplace while Joshua and Oliver sat on a braided rug at their feet.

"Is this going to be a long lecture?" Oliver asked. "'Cause we're really hungry."

Stacy looked at Win and burst out laughing. "We'd better make this fast."

"Right." Grinning from ear to ear, Win turned to his sons. "Stacy is going to become a part of our family. She's agreed to become my wife and your mother. How do you guys feel about that?"

A look of pure joy swept over Oliver's face while Joshua held his reaction to a little grin.

"Oooh, this is great. Really, really great!" Oliver practically shouted.

Joshua was doing his best to hold on to his fifteen-year-old coolness, but Stacy could see his eyes were twinkling with happiness.

"Yeah, Dad," Joshua said. "This is awesome. It's just what I—uh, that's just what me and Oliver want. To have Stacy make us a whole family again."

Stacy's heart was suddenly overflowing with love for Win and the two boys, who were soon going to be her sons, too.

"'A whole family,'" Stacy repeated. "Thank you, Joshua. You couldn't have said anything nicer. And you, too, Oliver. You guys are both very special to me, and I know we're going to be happy together as a family."

Looking as pleased as punch, Oliver looked from Stacy to his father. "When are you getting married? Tomorrow?"

Joshua gently elbowed his brother in the ribs. "Silly. It takes time to have a wedding! Like a week or so!"

Oliver looked crestfallen. "Oh. That's a long time."

Stacy and Win exchanged amused looks before he said, "A wedding takes longer than either of you think. And we'll need to have a few days away from our teaching jobs when we have the ceremony. That means we'll have to wait until the first long school break."

"Like Christmas!" Oliver burst out with excitement. "We get a lot of days off from school then!"

Stacy felt just as excited as Oliver and she looked eagerly at Win. "I would love to have a Christmas wedding, Win. What about you?"

He gently squeezed her hands. "Since it can't be tomorrow, I can't think of a more joyous time for a wedding. But I'm thinking we'll need more time for a honeymoon. What do you say we save it for summer break?"

"And take the boys with us on a family honeymoon?" Stacy quickly suggested while casting a coy grin at Win. "Since I'm marrying into a family of cowboys, you all might like to go watch the big rodeo in Cheyenne. From what I understand there's also a huge midway and plenty of fun things going on at the same time. That is, if you'd like it, Win. And the boys agree."

His gaze made a tender search of her face. "I'll be with you and the boys. Nothing could make me happier."

Clapping his hands, Oliver jumped excitedly to his feet while Joshua's grin spread from ear to ear.

"We like it," Joshua said.

"A whole lot!" Oliver added.

A thought suddenly struck Win as his look encompassed Stacy and his sons. "Well, speaking of rodeos, we don't have to wait until this summer to go to one. In a few weeks, the Golden Buckle Rodeo will be happening here in Bronco."

"I've been hearing some of the teachers talk about it," Stacy told him. "They're all excited about seeing Brooks Langtree. He's supposed to be a big rodeo star. In fact, he's the first Black rodeo rider to ever be awarded the Golden Buckle."

Win nodded. "Anthony has been talking about Brooks, too. He says it's been thirty years since Langtree's been to Bronco and he doesn't want to miss seeing him at the rodeo."

"Thirty years," Stacy said in amazement. "Then the man hasn't been here since I was born! Something important must be drawing him back here."

"Money, most likely," Win joked then said, "I'm only teasing. I'm guessing the man must have some sort of ties to Bronco."

Stacy shot him a knowing smile. "Like an old sweetheart?"

Win chuckled. "You would think in those terms."

"We don't want to forget the Bronco Harvest Festival, Dad." Joshua spoke up. "I've already promised Katrina I'll try to win her a teddy bear on the midway."

Oliver could hardly contain his joy as he hopped on one boot and then the other. "You know what's going to be the most fun? We're going to have a real mom to go with us."

Stacy wasn't going to spoil Oliver's happiness by pointing out she and Win would have to be married before she'd legally be his and Joshua's real mom. In her heart, she was already the boys' mother.

"A real mom is exactly right, son." Win stood and helped Stacy to her feet. "Now that we have everything settled, I think it's time we had dinner. And I have a surprise for you guys. We don't have to eat applesauce for dessert. I bought brownies from the deli and hid them in the pantry."

"Wow! Brownies! I'm gonna go find them and put them on the table!" Oliver shouted and took off in a run toward the kitchen.

"You better not drop them, Oliver!" Joshua called out as he trotted after his little brother.

As Win and Stacy followed the boys at a slower pace, he looked over at her. "We had brownies at the picnic, remember? I thought it might fit the occasion this evening—especially if you agreed to marry me. The only difference is, these brownies aren't homemade."

Slipping her arm through his, she smiled up at him. "Who cares if they're store bought or homemade? It's the thought that counts."

Pausing, he drew her into his arms and, as he kissed her, she knew for certain that Win had learned his lesson about love and trust and believing in always. And she'd learned that following her heart might've been a risky venture, but in the end, it had led her straight to the family she'd always wanted.

* * * * *

Don't miss the stories in this mini series!

MONTANA MAVERICKS: THE TRAIL TO TENACITY

Welcome to Big Sky Country, home to the Montana Mavericks! Where free-spirited men and women discover love on the range.

MILLS & BOON

The Heart Of A Rancher

Trish Milburn

MILLS & BOON

Trish Milburn is the author of more than fifty romance novels and novellas, set everywhere from quaint small towns in the American West to the bustling city of Seoul, South Korea. When she's not writing or brainstorming new stories, she enjoys reading, listening to K-pop music, watching Korean dramas and chatting about all these things on Twitter. Hop on over to trishmilburn.com to learn more about her books, find links to her various social media and sign up for her author newsletter.

Dear Reader,

Welcome back to the picturesque small town of Jade Valley, Wyoming, where you'll find gorgeous mountain views, delicious pies at Trudy's Café and opportunities to find happily-ever-after.

I've always loved stories of starting anew, both as a reader and a writer. I also enjoy thrift shopping (it's like a treasure hunt!) and seeing old buildings renovated and given new life. So the fact that all of those things play a part in Ivy Lake's life makes her a character near and dear to my heart.

It also takes a special person to make you believe in love again when your heart has been broken. For Ivy, that person is Austin Hathaway. And as fate would have it, Ivy is that person for him as well.

I hope you enjoy Ivy and Austin's journey to happily-ever-after.

Trish Milburn

CHAPTER ONE

IVY LAKE ENTERED the small ballroom and immediately spotted James on the other side talking to their boss and his wife. Ivy took a moment to appreciate the scene. Friends, family and colleagues were gathered at one of the company's hotels to celebrate her engagement to James. Since the hotel had an art deco design, they'd decided to have fun with their party and go with a 1920s theme. Black and gold Gatsby-esque decorations covered the white table-cloths, and lively jazz music filled the air. She was even wearing a flapper dress, a crystal-covered headband and Mary Jane pumps.

James looked dapper in his suit, and it hit her anew just how lucky she was to have a successful career, good friends and a handsome fiancé.

With a smile for the people she passed, she headed straight for him.

"Don't you look beautiful," Mrs. Sterling said as Ivy approached.

"Indeed she does." Mr. Sterling, who had built up an impressive collection of themed boutique hotels beginning here in Louisville and expanding to several other cities, gave James a friendly pat on the arm. "You're a lucky man."

"I am indeed."

"Is that right?"

They all turned to see a woman Ivy didn't recognize.

In fact, there were two unidentified women, and neither of them looked happy. Ivy started to ask if there was a problem, if perhaps they were disgruntled hotel customers, but she stopped when she saw the look on James's face. It had drained of anything remotely resembling color, and shock wasn't too strong a word to describe his expression.

"James? What's wrong?"

"I'll tell you what's wrong," the second woman said with a smirk. "We just ruined his plans."

Ivy shifted her gaze to the woman. "I don't understand."

"Of course you don't," she said. "He's pretty good at hiding all his girlfriends from each other."

"But not good enough," the other woman said.

Ivy wanted to push the two women out of the ballroom, to clear up whatever lies they were telling, away from the eyes and ears of Mr. and Mrs. Sterling and all the other guests, but that would likely draw even more attention.

"What's going on, James?" Ivy asked instead.

"I can explain."

Those three words sent a chill through her body. It was such a cliché coming from a man caught cheating that Ivy almost laughed.

No, this couldn't be happening. She refused to believe it.

"Why are you doing this?" she asked the women.

The sympathetic looks on their faces were almost worse than if they were hostile toward her, as if she was the one stealing their man. Instead, they pitied her. The woman who had spoken first, a cute blonde, extended her phone. On it was a photo of her and James at the Kentucky Derby, which had taken place only two weeks ago. She could tell it was recent because third-place finisher Sunrise on Sunday was clearly visible in the background.

Then the other woman, who was more voluptuous and had long, black hair, presented her Instagram feed filled with photos of her in a skimpy bikini and James in swim trunks. It was obvious they were vacationing in some tropical locale.

One photo stood out, and Ivy grabbed the phone to enlarge it. Sure enough, it was taken on Valentine's Day.

She slowly looked at James and pointed at the photo.

"You said you went to visit your mother that weekend because she'd fallen. This does not look like your mother or Wisconsin."

"I can explain," he said again, as if he had no other words.

White-hot shame washed over Ivy as she handed back the phone.

"Somehow, I don't think you can."

Feeling as if she might actually pass out or die of embarrassment, Ivy turned her back on James and headed toward the exit. Air, she needed air. The ballroom felt smaller with each step she took, as if the walls and ceiling were closing in around her. The murmur of voices was like the buzzing of bees in her head.

Suddenly, her sisters, Lily and Holly, were next to her.

"Ivy, what's wrong? You're as white as that tablecloth," Holly said, pointing at one of the tables set with beautiful china and crystal goblets.

"The engagement is off." Ivy could barely get the words out.

"Off? Why?"

"He cheated on me. With two different people." If not more. That idea horrified her, but if there were two, logically it could be more than that. She suddenly wondered how he had the time. And why he'd bother getting engaged and eventually married. It wasn't as if he was marrying into a fabulously wealthy family.

Without any further questions, her sisters ushered her out of the ballroom and then out of the hotel.

Right out of her engagement.

IVY SHOVED ANOTHER spoonful of chocolate ice cream into her mouth, not caring that she'd probably gained five pounds over the past couple of days. Why did it matter? She no longer had to fit into her wedding dress.

If there was one thing to be thankful for, it was that she'd accumulated a lot of days off and had decided to take them all at once. Maybe by the time she'd exhausted them she'd have enough courage to face her coworkers again.

But right now, the thought of having to see James made her physically ill. He hadn't called, hadn't even tried to keep her from leaving the hotel after the truth bomb had landed. Either he didn't care about her enough or he knew there was no way to talk himself out of the Grand Canyon–sized hole he'd dug for himself. The fact that it was likely both had led to her losing count of how many pints of ice cream she'd eaten.

A mirthless laugh escaped her. Not only had James's response been a cliché, but now she was living one. How many movies had she seen where the heartbroken woman drowned her sorrows in ice cream?

That thought propelled her to the kitchen, where she tossed what little was left of the ice cream in the sink and washed it down. Even when it was gone, she stared at the stream of water coming out of the faucet until she heard her mother's voice in her head telling her to stop wasting it. She shut off the tap and returned to the couch. Her apartment seemed quieter than ever now that she'd convinced her sisters and mom that she was fine and they should return home to Lexington. They'd tried arguing that they didn't want to leave her by herself, that she should come with them, but she'd declined.

In all honesty, she'd sent them on their way because she'd been on the verge of cracking. She'd needed to be alone to cry her heart out, to punch things, to send all the pictures of James through her paper shredder. She hadn't wanted an audience for any of that.

But with all those things done, now what? How in the world was she going to go to work every day and see the man who'd cheated on her and with everyone knowing it? She felt like the biggest of fools. If there was a major award for being an idiot, she'd have it on lock.

When nothing on TV caught her attention, she resorted to scrolling through social media. She'd already removed James and hidden his family members. It wasn't their fault he'd done what he had, but she also didn't want to see their posts. She'd probably end up removing them as well, but it felt wrong to do so now, as if she would be punishing them by association.

She watched kitty videos, read random posts about household cleaning hacks and urban gardening, got sucked into watching tours of tiny houses, colored a few pictures in her coloring app that appeared under the label "Zen." Unfortunately, she still didn't feel very Zen after she finished.

As she scrolled away from a video about a woman who lived in a converted grain silo, something caught her eye.

Click here for a chance to win a historic building in beautiful Wyoming.

With nothing better to do, she clicked.

The more she read, the more excited she got. The building was so cool. And the little town it was in looked charming. Her mind started racing with possibilities until it stopped on the perfect one. She could already imagine the building filled with handmade quilts, beautiful fabrics, endless baskets of yarn and sewing supplies. The dream her grandma Cecile had long had about opening her own quilt and fabric store settled in Ivy's brain as if it had been hers all along. Grandma Cecile had never realized her dream, but Ivy could do it for her.

Before she could talk herself out of it, she wrote the required paragraph about why she wanted to win and paid the fifty dollars to enter the contest. Maybe she was being a fool again, but she was pretty sure she'd already eaten that amount in ice cream and chips. At least if she was making another mistake, no one was around to witness it. But a chance at a fresh start far away from her cheating ex sounded way better for her peace of mind—and her waistline—than continuing to eat boatloads of self-pity food. If nothing else, it would be fun to daydream of the possible rather than remember what she'd lost.

IVY WOKE WITH a painful crick in her neck. She guessed that's what she got for falling asleep on the couch watching TV instead of actually dragging herself to bed. She rolled onto her back and grabbed her phone to check the time. A little number one next to her email icon drew her attention. She considered ignoring it, but what else did she have to do?

Congratulations! You have been chosen as the winner of the Stinson Historic Building Giveaway.

Ivy sat up so fast her head swam. She really should eat something remotely healthy. Protein would be good.

She scrolled through the message, then read it a second time. Alarm bells threatened to ring. Despite the research she'd done the night before, was this really just a scam? How had they chosen a winner so quickly? Was there something obvious she'd overlooked and, because of that, she was the only entrant? But the law firm handling the giveaway and transfer of the property was a real one in Casper. Jade Valley was a real town, and she'd found an article about the Stinson Building's past as the town's first grocery store. She'd tried finding a street view, but Jade Valley was one of those small towns that evidently hadn't received such a drive-through yet. Nothing in town had a street view online.

Still, she called the number in the email and paced as she talked to a woman at the law firm who told her that the owner had been reading the entries as they came in so that it didn't take long to pick a winner.

"He connected with your desire to start over, because that's what he's doing," the woman said.

Just to be sure, Ivy contacted the county government and found out that if she accepted the property, it would be hers free and clear of any debt or liens.

She stood in the middle of her living room, stunned at the turn of events. She'd seen that contest notice literally an hour before the deadline. And she'd encountered it right when the idea of a fresh start somewhere else seemed like the perfect solution to her current situation.

She squealed and did a little excited dance.

Her friends and family might think she'd lost it, but she was moving to Wyoming!

As soon as Austin Hathaway walked in the front door of his house, he heard his mother sneeze. He followed the sound to the kitchen and found her pulling a bowl of soup out of the microwave sitting on the rolling cart so she could reach it from her wheelchair.

"Are you sick?" he asked. "Do you need to go to the doctor?"

Sure, they had a stack of doctor bills that rivaled the tallest peaks in the Rockies, but he wasn't about to let his mother fall ill and not give her proper care either.

She shook her head as he took the bowl and placed it on the table for her.

"I'm fine. Just a bit of the cold since it's been damp."

Damp was an understatement. They'd had an abnormal amount of rain for May, more than twice the typical average. His muddy boots sitting on the front porch were proof of that. But ranch work didn't wait until it was sunny and dry. And there was always work.

"Are you sure? Because—"

"I said I'm fine." She sounded a mixture of tired and irritated.

It was strange how the irritation was actually a good sign. He knew his mother was depressed a lot, even if she did her best to hide it from him and his younger sister, Daisy. While it was understandable why she felt that way, he nevertheless felt helpless in the face of it. How did you help someone get over losing both her second husband and the use of her legs at the same time? It didn't matter that the loss of both had happened more than a year ago. They were still gone and always would be.

Deciding not to push her anymore, he didn't ask anything else.

"I'm going to take a shower." Between cleaning out a barn stall, replacing a couple of rotting fence posts and cutting up a tree that had fallen over the driveway when it uprooted from the wet soil, he'd gotten quite sweaty and dirty.

He was halfway down the hallway when he'd swear

he heard his mother murmur that she was sorry. It wasn't the first time he'd heard those words, but he always hated them. His mother used to be so active, first helping out on this ranch when she was married to his dad and later working with her second husband, Sam, in running his river rafting business. It didn't take a high IQ to figure out that she now felt like a burden, both physically and financially. And though the financial burden weighed him down like a stack of anvils on his shoulders, he would not let her or Daisy see that. They'd been through too much already. All he wanted to do was make their lives easier.

But that was difficult on what money ranching brought in, especially when it felt as if things kept breaking around the place. Fence posts, a tractor tire, the starter on his truck. Then there was the unexpected jump in the property taxes. That was why he took every extra job he could while still being able to keep the ranch afloat. He would keep this home for his family if it was the last thing he did.

He stayed in the shower longer than he should, but the hot water felt good and he was honestly too tired to move. But he finally did because he still had to go pick up Daisy from school. Her geography club, all three members, were meeting with their sponsor, Sunny Wheeler, to plan some projects for the summer and the next school year. Sunny had traveled the world with the job she had before moving back to Jade Valley, and Daisy loved hearing about all the places she'd been.

Daisy was typically a shy, quiet girl, but her eyes lit up and she talked more when she learned about a new place or bit of culture that she wanted to share. Even as a toddler, she was entranced any time there was a travel, history or nature documentary on TV. He knew she wanted to travel, and he hoped that whatever path she chose in life would allow her to do so. Yet something else he couldn't provide for her.

When he pulled up outside the school thirty minutes later, Daisy was waiting for him.

"Did you have a good meeting?" he asked.

"Yeah. We're going to focus on Antarctica over the summer and then cover various parts of Asia next year."

"Sounds interesting." Those places seemed like they existed in another universe to him. The farthest away he'd been was Seattle once to go to a baseball game with a group of friends. None of them had much money, so they'd pooled their resources and six of them had shared one hotel room. But it was still one of the most fun times he'd ever had.

"I also won the end-of-year prize for doing the most projects." She held up a certificate and an envelope. She tapped the latter. "I got fifty dollars. Can we stop at Trudy's?"

"Sure."

If she wanted a piece of pie or a milkshake to celebrate her hard work, she deserved it. But when they stepped up to Trudy's front counter, Daisy ordered not only one but two full meals then looked at him.

"Order whatever you want."

"I'm okay." She didn't need to be spending her money on him. It was supposed to work the other way around. She wasn't his child, but he was still in charge of keeping her safe, fed and clothed until she reached adulthood in four years.

"Please."

The tone of that plea, however, had him ordering a pork chop with sides. Daisy might be on the shy side, but she possessed that same stubborn determination to not be a burden that their mother did. He wished he could make them understand that he didn't see either of them as a burden. They were the only family he had, and he'd almost lost his mother.

"You're kidding." He glanced over and saw Jonathon Breckinridge, Sunny Wheeler's dad, chatting with a couple of his buddies. "I'm surprised anybody took that bait."

Trudy stepped up to the counter in front of Austin with the bag containing the desserts and bread that went with Daisy's order. She nodded toward the older men.

"You heard about what has everyone talking?"

"No. My cows aren't big on gossip."

Trudy chuckled. "They're probably smarter than we are. But this is actually interesting. There's a new owner of the Stinson Building."

"Really? Someone finally bought it?" John Young had been trying to unload that building for probably ten years.

"Not exactly. Seems John ran a contest online where people could enter for a chance to win it for fifty dollars."

Okay, so the building needed a lot of work, but a fifty-dollar price tag seemed like a steal. Whoever bought it could get enough salvage out of it to make that back and more. Or maybe they could afford to fix it up and flip it, sell it to someone with money to burn.

"Evidently there are a lot of people out there who want an old building," Trudy said, "because John made out like a bandit and is moving to one of those fancy retirement communities in Arizona."

"Maybe I should raffle off my barn," Austin said. "Then I could afford to build a new one."

Not to mention pay off all the debt, reminders of which arrived in his mailbox almost daily.

"You know," Trudy said, leaning in closer so others couldn't hear. "If whoever won that building wants to try fixing it up, they're going to need help. I can give them your name and number."

His heart skipped a beat at the idea of how much work that would be, how much income it might bring if the person didn't just hire a contractor to handle it.

"I would really appreciate that. You're the best."

Trudy waved away the compliment. "I'd be doing whoever the new owner is a favor. You're a good worker. I think I could tap dance on the new steps you built at the house and they wouldn't budge."

"You should have replaced those shaky steps ages ago."

"I know, I know. Just always too busy to think about stuff like that."

"You have to take care of yourself." He saw in her eyes that she knew he was thinking of his mom, so he decided to lighten the mood. "You don't want to give Alma an opportunity to snatch all your business."

The two older women, who had competing cafés directly across from each other on Main Street, had some sort of long-standing feud. The cause was a mystery that kept everyone in the county guessing. But neither Trudy nor Alma ever spilled the truth.

Trudy huffed. "Not darn likely."

Even Daisy laughed a little at that response.

Once he and Daisy were back in the truck that was now filled with the delicious smells of Trudy's cooking, he glanced over at his sister, who was sneaking a french fry.

"Go ahead and eat them while they're hot."

"I'll wait."

"I wish you had saved that money for something you wanted."

"This is what I wanted."

Just as he hadn't pressed his mother earlier, he let the topic go with Daisy. She had a few years before she was an adult, but she wasn't a little kid anymore either. And she was more mature than a lot of fourteen-year-olds, but then tragedy tended to make you grow up quick. He knew that from experience, having gone through losing his father as well.

He forced his thoughts away from the sadness of the past. It did no good to dwell. Instead, he allowed a little hope to flicker to life. If he could get a long-term renovation job and no more unexpected expenses popped up, he could start to chip away more significant chunks of debt. While Daisy dreamed of traveling the world, he had simpler dreams.

He wanted to make sure his mom and sister were always safe, had a roof over their heads and never had to go without necessities. He wanted to find a way to make them happy.

And he wanted to breathe that first breath of debt-free air so much he could taste it.

CHAPTER TWO

WHEN IVY SAW the sign for Jade Valley, she half expected
it to be a figment of her imagination. That would be on
par with how her cross-country trip had gone so far. First
had been a flat tire halfway across Missouri. Then her car
overheated in the middle of nowhere Kansas. It had been
so windy there, however, that if she'd had a sail to attach
to the car she could have coasted into Colorado on wind
power alone, if only it had been blowing the right direction. While she'd waited for a tow, she'd tried counting
how many times the blades of one of the nearby windmills
went around. After losing count, she looked up how long
those huge blades were. Half the length of a football field!

It took two days to have her car fixed in a little town
where the repair shop was one of exactly three businesses—the other two being a convenience store with a
single gas pump and a dingy little motel with half a dozen
rooms that had made her seriously consider sleeping outside on the grass instead. When she'd finally gotten back
on the road, she'd given considerable thought to retracing
her route right back to Louisville.

But no. She'd come too far, sold off too many of her
belongings and made too many life-altering decisions to
back out now. So she forged ahead, and when she'd made
it through Colorado without incident, she'd very nearly
stopped to kiss the Welcome to Wyoming sign. After one

last on-the-road night in Laramie, she'd driven the final three hundred or so miles to this, her new home.

Jade Valley was definitely a small town, but compared to where she'd stayed in Kansas it was a booming metropolis. Like so many Western towns, it was laid out on a simple grid. As she drove down Main Street, she glanced at the various businesses. She spotted the two restaurants—Trudy's Café and Alma's Diner—she'd seen advertised on her approach to Jade Valley and her empty stomach grumbled.

First things first, however. She made a right turn off Main onto Yarrow Street and drove another block.

And there it was on the corner, the building she had won. The historic building she now owned. Where she would live and hopefully be able to make a new start and an actual living.

But as she pulled over on the side of the street and stared at the building, panic threatened. The exterior looked more worn and abandoned than it had in the photos she'd seen. Even the windows appeared as if they hadn't been washed in several seasons, if not years. One had plywood covering what she assumed was a broken pane. How old had those photos with the contest listing been?

What had she done?

All the worried questions lobbed at her by her friends and family came rushing back in a jumble, but she shoved them away. Thinking positively was the key to her new future. Whatever it took, she would make a happy life for herself.

Surely the inside was better maintained. The outside was simply exposed to the elements and only needed some sprucing up. At least she hoped that was all.

Ivy took a slow, deep breath before getting out of her car. Then she stretched to rid herself of the kinks in her back and shoulders. One huge positive was that she was finally done with her days-long drive. She was well and truly tired of the driver's seat and staring at endless interstates. There sure weren't any interstates in or anywhere near Jade Valley.

She took a few moments to look at her surroundings. The street seemed to have a few other small businesses before it gave way to homes. She'd gradually get to know her neighbors, but first things first.

When a quick look in both directions revealed not a moving car in sight—that would take some getting used to—she crossed the street and retrieved the key to the front door from beneath a brick set next to the foundation on the side of the building. She'd thought it had been a joke when she'd been told that she wouldn't be picking up the key from the lawyer's office or even a realty company. This was the commercial equivalent of hiding a key in the flowerpot on the front porch of a house. She was genuinely surprised the key was actually there.

She wiped the dirt off the key and returned to the front, climbed the two stone stairs to the door. As she slid the key into the lock, she spotted the engraved stone square set into the exterior of the building.

Stinson Building, Built by E. M. Stinson, 1902.

The number of people who had walked through this historic structure lit a flame under Ivy's excitement again. She looked forward to learning more about the building's history. Maybe she'd even create an exhibit inside to appeal to history buffs. She'd spent some of those long hours driving from Kentucky brainstorming ways to get people through the front door with their wallets.

With renewed determination, she unlocked the door and tried not to wince at the resulting screech as she opened it. She stepped across the threshold and was greeted by the smell of dust and disuse. Her heart sank as she saw

how much dust coated the floor, some old store furnishings and several boxes that looked like they were on the
verge of actually collapsing and becoming dust. The floor
below the broken window appeared to have suffered some
water damage.

"No going back," she said, then put one foot in front
of the other, advancing slowly to make sure the floor was
sound.

When it felt spongey in spots, she couldn't help some
worry about the structural soundness of the building. Had
she given up everything for a money pit, even if it had only
cost fifty dollars to acquire?

Don't borrow trouble.

She heard those words in Grandma Cecile's voice and
took them to heart. Things didn't look awesome, but it
was to be expected for a building this old to need some
repairs and upgrades.

She felt as if her thoughts were attached to a yo-yo. One
moment she told herself that whatever needed tackling,
she'd tackle it. But then she discovered a disturbing stain
on the wall and thought she heard a decidedly rodent-like
scratching. A chill raced down her spine. She hated mice,
and the idea that it might be a rat truly freaked her out.

Trying to keep calm, Ivy crossed to the stairs at the
back of the main level and tested the first one by pressing
on it with the toe of her sneaker. It felt mostly solid, so she
eased her full weight onto it. When it didn't collapse, she
continued upward in the same manner. Her surroundings
didn't get any less dusty. If anything, it worsened as she
climbed. Plus she had to dodge thick cobwebs. The last
thing she wanted was to run into one of those, causing the
spitting, "I have ancient cobweb on my face" dance that
might send her tumbling back down the stairs.

She reached the top of the stairs and emerged into a

large, open room that mirrored the one below. Only this one was stuffed with the detritus of decades. The dim light filtering through the dirty windows allowed her to see a mishmash of furniture, more boxes, what seemed to be leftover construction supplies, a rack of flowerpots of all shapes and sizes, and—strangest of all—a random toilet.

This...this was supposed to be where she would live. It was a long way from livable. Where did she even start to make it so?

Again, careful in case the floor might send her falling through to the first level, she walked toward a small room in the corner that was obviously added later on. When she opened the door, it fell off the hinges and she had to jump out of the way to avoid getting hit. Dust erupted in a big whoosh when the door smacked the floor. Ivy coughed as she eyed the interior of the small room and saw where the toilet was supposed to have been installed.

The sudden urge to cry came over her, but she shoved it away. Crying wouldn't solve anything. What she needed was an action plan.

Her stomach growled so loudly she'd swear it echoed off the brick walls. Evidently, her first order of business should be getting some lunch. Maybe everything would look better once she wasn't hungry anymore. The growling happened again, as if her stomach was agreeing with her assessment of things.

She sneezed three times before she made it outside, and even though she hadn't been inside that long, she felt as if she needed a shower.

With a shake of her head, she began walking the block toward Main Street. She had to adjust her thinking. Her old apartment in Kentucky with an updated bathroom, her comfortable advertising job, easy access to anything she could possibly want—all those things were gone. They were the old Ivy. Today she was the new Ivy, and new Ivy could accomplish anything she set her mind to.

What she couldn't do was make money appear from thin air. She had some savings and earned a bit by selling off everything she couldn't fit in her car. Her reasoning had been that it would be easier to replace furnishings once she arrived and assessed the space rather than try to maneuver a moving truck across six states. But considering how much work her new home needed, her furnishings might be an inflatable mattress for the foreseeable future.

Since Trudy's Café was on the side of the street Ivy was already on, she headed there. The sooner she got food, the better. Because if her stomach kept growling as it had been the last few minutes, her new neighbors were going to think a bear had wandered into town. She wondered if that ever actually happened.

Trudy's was exactly how she'd imagined—quaint with a mixture of wildlife, scenery and local faces in frames on the walls. It was also busy, and many of the patrons looked up with curiosity at the unfamiliar person who'd just entered their familiar space. Ivy smiled then slid onto a chair at a two-seater table next to the wall.

A waitress arrived with a glass of water and a menu, then pulled out a pad and pen from her apron and stood waiting. Okay, not the friendliest person ever. Maybe... Katelyn, according to her crooked name tag, was having a bad day. Service work also came with verbal abuse that wasn't deserved from customers.

Ivy smiled and said, "Can I have a couple of minutes to look over the menu?"

Katelyn didn't eye roll, but she might as well have before she shoved the pad and pen back in her apron pocket and retraced her steps to the area behind the counter and then through the swinging door to the kitchen.

"It's not you," a middle-aged woman at the next table said. "Katie's just got a bad attitude. Chip on her shoulder."

Ivy didn't know quite how to respond to this unsolicited information, so she simply nodded and gave a quick smile before turning her attention to the laminated menu. Carbs, carbs, so many carbs. But then healthy offerings with low carbohydrates and fat content would have been more surprising than food meant to keep people fueled for ranch and other outdoor work.

Well, apparently she was going to be doing a lot of physical labor as well, so she could indulge without worrying too much.

She looked up to see an older woman approaching from the direction of the kitchen.

"Hello," the woman said as she reached the table. "You must be our new neighbor."

Surprise must have shown on Ivy's face because the other woman chuckled.

"I'm guessing you're not from a small town. You'll get used to everyone knowing everything soon enough. I'm Trudy, by the way."

Ivy glanced toward the front window where Trudy's name was painted.

"Yeah, that's me, the one and only Trudy in the whole county."

"It's nice to meet you. I'm Ivy Lake." Ivy extended her hand for a shake.

"Well, that's a pretty name if I've ever heard one."

"Thank you."

Trudy gestured toward the kitchen. "Sorry about Katelyn. Her parents made her get this job, and she's hated it from day one. Today's her last day, thank goodness. So I'm in need of a good waitress if you hear of anyone looking for a job."

"Well, considering I don't know anyone here, I'm afraid I can't help much."

Unless...

She hadn't waitressed since college, and she didn't yet know what kind of price tag she was looking at regarding getting her new building repaired, renovated and ready for business. Her head was suddenly filled with huge floating dollar signs. She knew from being in the hotel business that repairs and renovations always ended up costing more than anticipated. Always. She didn't know how much she was going to have to spend, but her gut told her it was more than she had in her savings.

"I'm interested." Sure, she'd been in town less than an hour, didn't have a place to sleep or shower and didn't know anyone, but she could be friendlier than Katelyn. "I have experience."

The surprise on Trudy's face almost made Ivy laugh.

"Let's just say the building I now own needs a bit more work than I was led to believe."

"Don't tell me John lied about it just so he could finally off-load it?"

"Was that the previous owner's name?"

Trudy parked herself in the chair across from Ivy.

"Yes. John Young has been trying to sell the building for close to a decade with no takers."

Ivy couldn't help the sinking feeling that she'd made another colossal mistake, that once again she was proving herself a fool. She sighed and ran a hand over her face. Trudy patted Ivy's other hand where it lay on the table.

"One thing at a time," Trudy said, sounding so much like Grandma Cecile that Ivy felt an immediate fondness for her. "I'm happy to give you the position, but maybe you want to get things assessed first, make a plan?"

"Trust me. Whatever my plan ends up entailing is going

to cost me more than I have saved. Right now, I'm feeling quite the idiot."

"Still, take a day or two to get settled then get back with me."

Ivy's stomach grumbled audibly.

"I have faith you'll figure it all out," Trudy said. "For now, let's start with satisfying your hunger. Do you know what you want yet?"

Forget calories and carbs, Ivy needed some comfort food. Some "I can't do this" food.

"I'll take fried chicken with mashed potatoes. And a salad so I feel remotely healthy."

Trudy chuckled as she patted Ivy's hand again. "Coming right up. And when you've eaten your fill, I've got a suggestion for a person to call about the building repairs."

As Trudy headed toward her kitchen, Ivy saw the woman at the next table smiling.

"You're going to be okay," the woman said. "Trudy has adopted you. That's like the Jade Valley official seal of approval."

Chalk one up in the "win" column for the day.

AUSTIN PARKED HIS truck on the side of the street behind a small, cranberry-colored crossover SUV with a blue-and-white Kentucky license plate. Judging by how much stuff was packed into the car, there was no mistaking who it belonged to. The new owner of the Stinson Building sure had traveled a long way. He wondered why someone would do that, pick up and move across the country to a place where they knew no one.

But her story didn't really matter to him beyond how it impacted what she wanted done to the building and whether she was willing to pay to have it done. He hoped that her not knowing anyone local would lead to her trusting Trudy's recommendation of him for the job.

He got out of the truck and waved to Gavin Olsen as he drove by. Gavin was going to hand over the title of newest transplant to Jade Valley, if Ivy Lake decided to stay in town.

Ivy Lake. Sounded more like a vacation spot than a person's name.

But her name also didn't matter. He knew how long the Stinson Building had sat empty and therefore how much work likely needed to be done to make it habitable. What he could earn from a job like this would take care of a lot of bill payments, and was why he'd hopped in his truck and practically sped to town after Trudy called to tell him the new owner had arrived.

"She's a sweet little thing," Trudy had said. "But she's going to need a lot of help based on what she found inside. John ought to be ashamed of himself."

"Well, she got it for only fifty bucks, so hopefully she can afford to fix what he neglected," he'd responded.

He hurried to the front door and knocked. He tried to see inside, but the windows were too grimy. However, he did think he heard the thud of footsteps on the wood floor.

"Oh, hey."

It took Austin a moment to realize the voice was coming from above him. When he looked up, a woman was roughly a third of the way out of the window. He shaded his eyes against the sun and could see that she was fairly young, maybe early thirties like him.

"Are you Austin Hathaway?"

"Yes, ma'am."

"Come on in. The door's unlocked. I'll be right down."

Her Southern accent wasn't something he heard often. Though it wasn't as pronounced as that of characters in movies set in the Deep South, she would definitely stand out in Jade Valley sounding like that.

The work that would need to be done struck him the moment he opened the door with a creak worthy of a haunted house. It became more evident as he stepped inside and his nostrils were assaulted by the stale, musty air—the odors of neglect and abandonment. As he scanned the interior, he noticed the lack of color. Everything was coated in a thick layer of dust, making the palette of the entire space range from shades of gray to a vague brown. As he walked to the middle of the room, he started estimating what would need to be done and how much it would cost.

He hoped Ivy Lake had a comfortable bank balance or credit card limit.

He supposed he'd soon find out as the woman in question appeared at the bottom of the stairs at the back of the room.

"You got here quick," she said as she approached and finally stepped into the light filtering in through the dirty windows.

Ivy Lake might be dressed in a T-shirt that said Thunder Over Louisville and loose workout pants with her reddish brown hair pulled back in a knot held by what looked like chopsticks, but there was no mistaking that she was pretty. He predicted it wouldn't be long before any eligible men within driving distance would be coming to make her acquaintance.

He might be one of those single men, but he wouldn't be in that line. The last thing he had any interest in or time for was dating.

"Trudy called me at the right time." The right time being any time he might pick up a well-paying job.

"Great."

"What exactly are you looking to do?"

She laughed a little and gestured at their surroundings. "Make this habitable for humans instead of spiders, mice and ghosts."

"You'll want to address safety first—foundation, supports, roof, electricity."

"And plumbing. I'm in serious need of usable plumbing and bathroom facilities. I'd like the commode in the middle of the floor upstairs to be more functional than a weird conceptual art piece."

"Sounds reasonable."

"So, what's next? You look around, see what needs to be fixed, then tell me a total that I hope doesn't make me stroke out?" The little laugh she tacked on the end held a hint of hysteria, like she was second-guessing all her life choices.

He needed to give her a reasonable enough quote that she wouldn't bolt immediately, because at some point the scope of this renovation project was probably going to overwhelm her and she'd go back to where she came from. At least he could do enough work that it would be easier for her to sell it than it had been for John. Still, he was curious about her intentions as they existed now.

"What do you plan to do with the place? Knowing that will help me quote the job properly."

"I intend to turn this into a quilt and fabric shop."

Making something like that profitable in a town as small as Jade Valley seemed like a flight of fancy to him. But there were other businesses in town that surprised him by making it from year to year, combining sales to locals and tourists alike, so what did he know? His business acumen didn't extend much past ranching and physical labor.

"Is that what you did before?"

She shook her head. "No, I was the advertising director for a chain of boutique hotels."

Yeah, she wasn't going to last here. He'd be lucky if she stuck around long enough for him to totally repair and renovate the place to sell it rather than abandoning the project midway or before.

He nodded once but didn't voice his thoughts about how ill-equipped she likely was for this undertaking.

"Well, I'll get started inspecting everything." Best to begin before she had second thoughts and that needed income slipped through his fingers like water.

Austin began with an examination of the exterior of the building. Coming from somewhere inside he heard music, not the country he was used to hearing but rather pop music. He thought he recognized a song that he'd heard coming from his younger sister's room. It amazed him sometimes just how much of a difference the seventeen years between their ages made. Often, he felt more like Daisy's father than her brother, even more so since her father's death.

Despite their age difference, however, that was the thing that really bound them together—the fact that they'd both lost their fathers and had witnessed their mother's sorrow in the wake of those losses.

Austin shook off those thoughts and focused on a careful examination of the building and writing down everything that absolutely had to be done in one column and things that should be done in another. Maybe if he gave her options, she would be more likely to hire him. It became evident that if she did, this would be the biggest job he'd ever undertaken. He tried not to get too excited about the potential income so that he wouldn't be as disappointed if it didn't work out.

Hours passed as he checked stone and brick, wood and glass, plumbing and a cursory look at the electrical. He wasn't certified to do the type of electrical work Ivy would likely need, but he intended to suggest Rich Tucker for that part of the job.

At one point, while measuring the square footage of the first-level floor, he caught himself humming along to Ivy's music. He stopped and listened, realizing it was an old bluegrass song. He supposed that made sense, considering where she had lived before. Her playlist seemed to be quite eclectic.

Once he'd examined everything on the lower level, he made his way up the stairs, announcing himself as he neared the top. What he saw when he stepped into the light of the upper floor, however, surprised him. Ivy had obviously swept and mopped the floor, and now was struggling to set up a tent.

"You do realize those are supposed to be used outside, right?" he asked.

She spun at the sound of his voice, making it obvious that she hadn't heard his approach despite him having called out as he climbed the stairs. Her sudden movement caused her to lose hold of the tent and the progress she'd made in setting it up. Her sigh of frustration made him feel bad.

"I've been battling with this thing for fifteen minutes, and so far it is winning." She glanced toward him, showing that she had several streaks of dirt on her face. "As for why I'm assembling a tent inside, as you can see I don't have a bed yet. Plus this will hopefully keep away any critters who have called this place home before today."

"You're staying here?" The idea would be comical if it wasn't ridiculous.

"Yes. It's my new home, after all."

Austin looked around. Though she'd made an attempt to clear away the worst of the dust and fresh air was flowing in the open windows, this still wasn't an ideal place to spend the night.

"There are some nice cabins outside of town a few miles, right on the river. Pretty place."

"I'm sure they have a nice rental rate too. As you have no doubt gathered, I need to save my money for other things."

Dread started to form in his stomach. No matter what he quoted her, was she not going to be able to pay? He'd have to require at least half the amount up front. He couldn't afford to devote the time to a job and then not get paid for the work.

Still, the idea of her sleeping in a tent in this old building didn't sit well with him.

"I'm not sure it's healthy to stay here yet."

"Don't worry. I plan to keep the windows open. It would be better if they had screens, but I'm willing to risk a bird flying inside if I can have fresh air. And I'll give you that, the air here is really fresh."

"You're going to get cold at night."

"I once walked three miles home in an ice storm when the roads weren't passable, so I think I'll be okay."

Some people had to learn the hard way.

CHAPTER THREE

AUSTIN HATHAWAY HADN'T been lying. Ivy woke up in the middle of the night shivering despite the thick comforter she'd excavated from her car earlier. As much as she hated to do so, she crawled out of the tent and went to close the windows. At least they were clean now. Once she'd wrestled them closed, she took a moment to stare up at the sky. Even with the lights of Jade Valley shining, she was amazed at how beautiful the starlit sky was. It was as if the number of stars she could see in Louisville had been multiplied a thousandfold.

Of course, it was just the lack of light pollution making it seem that way. She remembered accompanying her grandmother, mother and sisters to what Grandma Cecile called "the old home place" when Ivy was around ten years old. She, Lily and Holly had lain on a grassy hillside near a rickety old shell of a house where Grandma Cecile had grown up. Above them was a blanket of stars so expansive that the only way to describe it was "Wow."

She remembered thinking the stars twinkled like diamonds and that it had been the first time she'd seen the Milky Way.

When a shiver ran along her extremities, Ivy hurried back to the tent and tried in vain to get warm. Even thinking about her new handyman didn't help. Sure, she had sworn off men, but there was no denying the fact that Austin was really good-looking. Tall, lean, dark hair and eyes, with a bit of attractive facial scruff. She'd think of him like fine art in a museum—look but don't touch. And definitely don't try to take it home.

What she was most interested in was how high the estimate for his work was going to be. She'd made it clear that she wanted the building to be safe and solid; otherwise nothing else mattered. But she'd also told him that to shave off some of the cost she was willing to learn how to lend a hand. She'd seen the disbelief in his expression, the doubt that she would be able to do anything useful.

She'd spent her life defying expectations. It made her want to prove him wrong. Plus there was genuine desperation to make this work on her part. There was no plan B.

When it became obvious that she wasn't going to be able to go back to sleep, she exited the tent again. Using a jug of water she'd bought at the same time she'd gotten the tent the day before, she washed her hands and face. After brushing her hair, she headed to the convenience store. It wasn't of the twenty-four-hour kind, but they did open at four in the morning. People evidently started work early in this part of the country.

Though she didn't see anyone nearby and it was only a max of three blocks to the convenience store, she still drove. Small town Wyoming might not be the same as cities, but that didn't mean she felt safe walking alone at night.

"Good morning," the clerk said when Ivy stepped into the brightly lit store. "You're getting an early start."

Ivy had been in Jade Valley only a day, and already she wasn't surprised that someone she'd never met knew her identity. Trudy had told her the previous day that before Ivy arrived at the café, Trudy had already heard she was in town from three different people. Again, it reminded her of the stories Grandma Cecile told of her youth in a small town in the Kentucky part of Appalachia. Only now the speed of gossip was aided by the internet and smartphones.

"Lots to do," Ivy said simply as she walked straight for the restroom.

After she finished, she headed for the freshly brewed coffee. She grabbed some coffee cake to go with her strong brew as well as assorted snacks to get her through until lunch.

"I hear Austin is going to be working for you," the middle-aged woman at the cash register said as Ivy placed her items on the counter.

"Possibly. Depends on how much the bid ends up being."

"You won't find anyone who will do a better job or at a better price." The woman smiled before adding, "And there are worse things to look at."

While the last part was obviously true, Ivy really hoped the first part was as well.

"I've heard good things about his work." Before anything else was said about Austin Hathaway's level of attractiveness, Ivy grabbed her bag of purchases and headed back to her car.

Wanting to eat in a clean environment, she sat in her car in the lighted parking lot until she finished two squares of coffee cake and had consumed half of her large coffee. Once she was fortified with caffeine and sugar, she headed back home to get a jump on her massive to-do list.

By the time the sunrise lit the valley, she had hauled about half of the old boxes from upstairs down to the lower level. Most of the contents were either useless or so deteriorated she couldn't tell what it had once been. One box was full of flyers for a local church bazaar held in 1993. Another had a variety of mildewed matchboxes and half-used candles. It was a wonder some critter hadn't accidentally started a fire and burned down the building.

She started to open the windows on the bottom floor to get some fresh air only to discover they had all been nailed shut.

"Well, that doesn't seem safe," she said to herself.

"What doesn't?"

She yelped as she spun to see Austin standing in the open doorway.

"Sorry," he said, looking genuinely contrite. "I didn't mean to scare you. I seem to keep doing that."

Ivy waved off his apology. "It's okay."

He crossed to where she was standing, and she pointed toward the nails in the window frame.

"Probably to keep vandals and mischievous kids out," he said.

"Still, I'll be replacing those with some proper locks." She looked up at him, realized just how much taller he was than her—probably a full foot. "I'm guessing you have an estimate for me."

"I do." He held out a few sheets of paper folded in half.

She took it, preparing herself for the shock of many zeros.

"Well, here goes. Let's see if I need to sell some plasma."

"I kept things as reasonable as possible without cutting any safety corners."

Was it her imagination or did Austin look a bit nervous? He shifted from one foot to the other then back again.

She opened the paper and started scanning the list of repairs and estimated costs. Trying not to panic, she flipped to the second page, then the third. The final tally made her wish she had a chair to sit down on, but she also realized it could be worse. She'd seen some of the costs of renovating old buildings to turn them into hotels. While her building wouldn't require that kind of treatment, it still needed a lot of work. And good work wasn't free.

"While I didn't expect to have this big of an undertaking when I decided to come here, these numbers look reasonable."

It was quiet, but she still heard the sigh of relief that escaped Austin. Were jobs so hard to come by here that this was make-or-break for him? Worry that her shop wouldn't be able to recoup the cost of the repairs and renovations as well as allow her to pay her normal bills threatened to take up permanent residence in her thoughts. Once again, she refused to let it.

Only positive thoughts. Only positive thoughts. Only positive thoughts.

"When can you start?"

"Right now."

"Oh, well, you definitely come prepared."

"Yes, ma'am."

"Just Ivy."

He nodded. "As I noted on the estimate, I can't do the electrical, but I recommend Rich Tucker. He's very good with all things electrical."

"Considering I know exactly two people here now, I'll trust you on that."

"Okay, I'll get started on things I can do until he can come over."

Austin sounded so businesslike, almost as if he thought one wrong step and she'd fire him before he got started. Hopefully, he'd loosen up as the project got underway.

She left him to his work and returned upstairs. But before she could resume her own work, she had to sit down. With the floor or the closed commode the only options, she went with the latter and massaged her forehead to try to prevent the headache she felt forming. She'd just agreed to spend a sum of money that would drain all of her resources with any income from her store not yet visible on the horizon. She definitely needed to take Trudy up on that offer to waitress before someone else nabbed it.

Ivy grabbed her purse and hurried back downstairs. Austin was unloading a variety of tools and sawhorses in front of the building.

"I have some errands to run. You have my number on the card I gave you yesterday if you need to call me for any reason."

She jogged to her car with the aim of visiting a campground about ten miles out of town. For a modest fee, she could gain access to the bathhouse—a much cheaper option than renting a cabin or a motel room. Because she wasn't going to go apply for a job while grimy.

The campground attendant gave her a strange look when it was apparent Ivy was alone and didn't have an RV or even a pickup truck, but Ivy didn't offer any explanation. She just drove straight to the campsite directly across from the bathhouse. Thankfully, the campground was fully occupied with people sitting in the shade of their RV awnings drinking coffee, lying in hammocks reading books, or cooking over campfires. She tossed out a couple of smiles and waves to those she saw nearby but quickly grabbed her clean clothes and toiletries and went to wash away her hours of work.

It wasn't a fancy bathroom by any stretch of the imagination, but had a shower ever felt so good?

When she arrived at Trudy's Café, the place was packed. Ivy noticed that three tables hadn't been cleared after the diners left, so she started clearing them, depositing the dishes in the bus cart behind the front counter and the napkins and straw wrappers in the trash. Just as she finished clearing two of the three tables, new customers occupied them.

Ivy glanced at the waitress who was busy at the cash register, and the young woman nodded at her.

"What can I get you to drink?" Ivy asked the first couple.

Ivy and Stephanie, the harried waitress, fell into a rhythm of clearing and wiping down tables, taking orders and delivering food to the hungry lunch crowd. Trudy's brisk business renewed Ivy's hope that her own business would flourish too.

When the late morning to early afternoon rush dwindled to a few customers lingering over a late lunch, Trudy emerged from the kitchen and leaned one outstretched arm against the front counter as she looked at Ivy.

"Well, I guess you're hired."

"I haven't even interviewed yet."

"Sure you did, and you seem to know your way around."

"I waitressed to help pay my way through college."

"It shows."

"Thanks for your help," Stephanie said. "There are usually two of us working the midday shift."

"Happy to help. And happy to take the job. Renovations don't magically pay for themselves."

"Is it bad?" Trudy asked.

"It could be worse."

"Which means it also could be better. Well, I'll give you as many midday shifts as you can handle. I've got my early mornings covered by some longtime employees and the evenings by the younger set."

"You're a lifesaver."

Trudy chuckled. "So I've been told. Now, how about we all have some lunch?"

"Thank you, but now it's time for my other job—clearing my new home of years' worth of ick."

"Oh, sounds fun," Stephanie said.

"So much fun." Ivy laughed.

"At least you've got some company," Trudy said.

"Yeah?" Stephanie had obviously somehow managed to miss the gossip about Austin working on the building.

"Austin Hathaway is doing the repair and renovation work."

"He's a good guy. Good-looking too."

It seemed as if everyone thought Austin was the local heartthrob, and the way they referred to him made Ivy think he wasn't romantically attached. If people started to try to match-make, she was going to have to put a stop to it. Her heart and pride still hurt from the betrayal she'd suffered, so she wasn't open to exposing either to a repeat performance.

"If he can make the building habitable and inviting for customers, I'll be happy."

"Well, I'm not sending you off without a meal," Trudy said, and headed toward the kitchen door.

"Really, it's o—"

"Hush now," Trudy said.

"It's no use arguing with her when she wants to feed you," Stephanie said as Trudy disappeared beyond the swinging door.

"So I see. She reminds me of my grandmother."

Grandma Cecile used to send Ivy and her sisters home with enough food after a visit to feed an army platoon. Some people showed their affection with food. Grandma Cecile and Trudy were obviously two of those people.

Gifted with not one but two meals, Ivy drove the short distance home to find Austin sitting on the front stoop. As she approached him, it appeared he was having a simple peanut butter sandwich for lunch.

"Here," she said, extending one of the meals.

"I have lunch," he said, holding up the half-eaten sandwich.

"No offense, but I guarantee this is better."

"You don't have to feed me."

"I'm not. Trudy is. She sent me back with two meals, and I obviously don't have a refrigerator to keep the second one from spoiling."

He hesitated for a moment before he said, "Well, it would be a crime to have Trudy's work go to waste."

"Indeed."

As if they were lifelong friends, Ivy sat on the stoop next to Austin.

"So, how are things going? Please don't tell me you've found any additional problems."

"So far, so good. You'll be happy to know that at least the outside water spigot works out back. We'll have to check the plumbing inside though before it can be used."

"Well, that's a step in the right direction."

Austin opened his lunch container to reveal the roast pork inside.

"You're right. This is better than my sandwich."

"It smelled so good on the way back that I nearly didn't make it here before diving in. I'd already been salivating for the past two hours."

Austin looked over as he took a bite, the obvious question written on his handsome face.

"I might have taken a job waitressing at Trudy's to help pay for all this." She motioned to the building behind them. "To do this right, it's going to eat all of my savings."

Austin was quiet for a moment as he directed his attention across the street at a vacant lot.

"Are you sure you want to do this?"

There was a layer of hesitance in his question, and she could imagine him hoping that it didn't prompt her to back out and cost him some needed weeks of work. The fact he'd asked it anyway told her something about his character—that he didn't want to push her beyond her means. All the positive things she'd heard about him seemed to be true, at least so far, but sometimes people didn't show their true colors until you'd known them awhile.

She nodded and wiped her mouth with a napkin.

"When I saw the contest to win this place, it felt meant to be. Plus there's the fact that I quit my job and moved across the country with all my possessions."

"Not sure I believe in meant to be, but I'll do everything I can to make this place what you want it to be."

"Thank you. I appreciate that." She thought about what he'd said for a moment. "Maybe you're right about there being no meant to be, but there's definitely want to be."

They sat in silence for a couple of minutes while they both ate.

"So why a quilt shop?"

"It was time for a change, and this was something that my grandmother always dreamed of doing but she never got the chance."

"You're a quilter then?"

"I know how. She taught me and my sisters. But I haven't had time to really do much in recent years, what with work and…other things."

Things that would no longer take up her time.

"What about you?" she asked. "Have you been doing construction work since you were young?"

"Here and there. I also run my family's ranch."

"Look at us, a couple of two-jobbers."

Austin smiled a little, and it startled Ivy how much that small change in expression increased his already apparent attractiveness. If he wasn't already in a relationship, it was likely only a matter of time. Because with a small population, she guessed the depth of the dating pool measured on the kiddie end. Unless, of course, he had his own reasons for remaining single.

A newer red pickup pulled up to the curb and parked.

"That's Rich Tucker, the electrician," Austin said.

"Well, this looks like a very relaxed job site," Rich said as he stepped out of his truck.

He wasn't as tall as Austin, nor as good-looking, but it was obvious from his first word that he was more vocal and outgoing.

Ivy closed the take-out container on what was left of her lunch and stood.

"Mr. Tucker, nice to meet you," she said as she extended her hand.

"Please, call me Rich," he said with what was obviously a flirtatious smile.

"Okay, Rich." She retrieved her hand as quickly as possible without being rude and picked up the bag holding her leftovers.

Beside her, Austin stood as well. It gave her an odd sense of security, though she didn't think Rich presented any potential harm.

"I'll show you around," Austin said to Rich.

Ivy accompanied them inside and listened as Austin told Rich what he'd observed during his own visual inspection of the wiring.

"What are you going to do with the building?" Rich asked. "What kind of appliances and electrical needs?"

She told him how she wanted to outfit her living space and then what would be necessary for the business—lights, a few sewing machines for potential classes, heat and air so she could regulate both temperature and humidity levels.

"Okay. I'll get started checking the wear and tear. Any frayed or exposed wires, loose connections and outdated components will be the most obvious hazards."

As he went about his work, taking verbal notes on his phone about things like voltage levels, circuit load capacity and insulation, she continued to carry the musty boxes down from the upper level. Once she had several on the scraggly front lawn, she started examining the contents. As expected, most of it was total junk.

When she opened the box that had been ridiculously heavy, she half expected to find a cannonball inside. Instead, she was stunned to find a collection of old coins in individual plastic holders. What were the chances any of these were worth something substantial? She sank onto the ground and started looking up some of the coins on a valuation site. Several were worth a few dollars more than face value, which collectively was nice if she could find buyers. Yeah, with all the free time she had.

She pulled out another penny that appeared to be older than the ones she'd examined so far. When she checked the date, a jolt of surprise hit her. Wow, 1909. Maybe this one was worth a little more. She typed the description into the search bar and gasped.

"What's wrong?"

She looked up to see Austin looking at her with concern.

"Look at this," she said, extending the penny to him. "Then read this on my phone and tell me if I'm right in thinking these are the same."

He crouched beside her and first examined the penny, then the description, then the penny again.

"Looks like it's your lucky day." He glanced at the open box filled with coins. "You found this upstairs?"

A sinking realization came over her.

"I can't keep these."

"Why not?"

"It's obvious they were accidentally left behind."

"I don't think they were. John never used this building

for anything. He might have planned to at some point, but for years all he's wanted to do is sell it. So all that stuff upstairs was from the previous owners."

"Then this belongs to them."

"I don't think they'll have much use for coins or the money they might bring."

"Why? Are they already rich?"

"No. They're buried in the cemetery on the edge of town."

"Oh."

"When you became the owner of this building, you became the owner of everything in it." Austin tapped the edge of the box. "Including these."

"Well, now I'm going to fantasize that there's enough here to pay for all of your work."

"Maybe there's pirate treasure at the bottom."

Ivy laughed. "I like how you think."

She stood and dusted off the back of her pants, glanced at the box then at the building.

"Let me carry those back upstairs for you," Austin said as he picked up the box much more easily than she had. "I assume that's where you want it."

"Yes, please."

She followed him toward the stairs, thinking about how she hated the idea of leaving the coins here while she worked. But then her shifts at Trudy's would likely coincide with Austin's hours working on the building. And the fact that these coins had sat in that box for years without anyone finding them was a positive sign as well. Still, she'd like to research and catalog them as soon as she could so she could sell them.

But other tasks were more pressing.

She glanced up as they climbed the stairs, aiming to ask Austin when he thought she might have a working bathroom. But the words died in her throat as she caught sight of how nicely his jeans fit. Ivy sucked in a breath and started coughing. She barely averted her eyes before Austin turned and caught her looking.

"Are you okay?"

She waved her hand in front of her nose and mouth as she brought her coughing under control.

"All the dust. I feel like there's so much of it, I could plant a cornfield in it."

Heat swamped her, much more than her physical activity would create. She was not supposed to even be in an emotional place where such a thing was possible. What James had done to her still had the betrayal equivalent of new car smell. She came to Wyoming to focus on herself, on a new business venture, a new life. Not on a new man.

And yet the universe had seen fit to laugh in her face and give her a hot handyman.

Just great.

CHAPTER FOUR

AUSTIN TRIED TO focus on ripping up the floorboards with water damage below the broken window, but it was hard to tune out Rich's obvious flirting with Ivy. While she was nice, he noticed Ivy was not flirting back. Not that Rich noticed. The man was the best around for electrical work, but he was a bit oblivious to "I'm not interested" signals from women. To Austin's knowledge, Rich was just dense in that department and never crossed the line. If he did, Austin would be the first to drag him out by his collar. He didn't want Ivy to be uncomfortable or to question his judgment in his recommendation of Rich.

"Hey, Rich," he called out to give Ivy a way to exit the conversation.

Rich looked as if he was a smidge perturbed to be interrupted but was smiling by the time he reached Austin.

"You need something?"

"What's the estimate on how long it's going to take you to do the electrical?"

"Luckily it's not as bad as it could have been, so I should be able to wrap it up in about a week." He glanced toward the stairs, which Austin noticed Ivy had taken rather quickly after he'd called Rich over. "Plenty of time to determine what Ivy likes so I can make a good impression when I ask her out."

"You're going to want to abandon that plan."

Rich looked back at Austin. "Wait, are you already making a play?"

"No." The last thing he needed was another woman in his life, least of all one who more than likely would abandon this building and Jade Valley when neither lived up to her dreams.

Dreams too often gave way to reality, so it was best to live in reality to begin with.

"You sure? Seems like you're acting territorial."

"Because I need this job, and I don't want her feeling so uncomfortable that she decides to cancel it and leave."

"Uncomfortable? I didn't do or say anything I shouldn't have."

Rich sounded offended, and Austin didn't want that either.

"Listen, you are the best electrician anywhere near here, but what talent you have with electrical wiring you lack in picking up on women's social cues." Austin placed his hand on Rich's shoulder. "Sorry, buddy, but as they say, she's just not that into you."

"Really?"

Austin nodded.

"Well, that stinks."

"Look at it this way. You got a profitable job ahead of you."

Austin had to smother a laugh when Rich headed out to buy the supplies he needed to get started.

When Ivy didn't come downstairs for a long time, Austin thought perhaps she was hiding. He considered letting her know Rich had left, but right then he heard her descending the stairs again. He glanced over as she reached the bottom, another box in hand, and looked around.

"Rich left a while ago to buy some supplies."

"Oh, okay." She proceeded outside.

When he was finished removing the floorboards that needed to be replaced, he went outside to cut replacements.

"Any more hidden treasures?" he asked as he nodded toward the box in front of her.

"Not unless you count wrinkly flyers about the grand opening of JJ's Boot Shop."

"That place closed when I was in middle school, I think. Didn't last long. About as long as the print shop, the last business in this building."

"Well, that doesn't inspire hope that I'm going to become a successful business owner."

"A lot has changed since then," he said. "More tourists visit now. The fall festival has gotten an overhaul and brings in loads of people."

"That's a bit more hopeful."

The sound of a truck approaching caught Ivy's attention.

"I'm sorry about Rich earlier." Austin needed to clear the air, make sure she understood the situation and wouldn't feel the need to hide every time Rich was around or blame Austin because she had to.

"Was I that obvious?"

"Rich is great at his job, but picking up on subtleties not so much. I told him you weren't interested."

"Thank you. He seems like a nice guy, but I'm not interested in dating anyone."

That made two of them. Even though he didn't like talking about his own reasons, he couldn't help but be curious about hers. She was a very pretty woman, nice, from what he'd seen a hard worker. But she'd also entered a contest to win a building she'd never seen in a state on the other side of the country. She'd made comments about a fresh start. There could be a lot of reasons for that, but his gut told him at least part of it was romantic.

"Chances are others will try to ask you out," he said. "My advice is to make it clear you're not interested in dating."

"But carefully. It's a small town where I'm going to open a business. I don't want to offend people."

"True. But honesty is the best policy, as they say."

"If only everyone believed that."

That wasn't just a blanket statement, because there had been a slight edge to how she'd said it. Bitterness maybe. Perhaps something else, but he wasn't sure. Despite how he'd detected that Rich was making Ivy uncomfortable with his flirting, Austin wouldn't say he was an expert on reading emotions. His history had shown he wasn't. Otherwise, he would have picked up on clues that Grace had been more than frustrated with the situation in which they'd found themselves, that she was going to leave him.

His phone rang, making him realize he had been staring at Ivy. He jerked his gaze away and pulled the phone from the back pocket of his jeans. When he saw "Mom" on the screen, his heart rate accelerated. Was something wrong? That couldn't be how he answered the phone, however. Lately, she'd become more irritable if he hovered, if he offered to help her in any way.

"Hey, Mom." He did his best to keep any worry out of his greeting.

"I just got a call from Dr. Barton's office," she said. "They want to change my checkup to tomorrow morning. I told them I might not—"

"It's fine."

"But you just started this new job."

"Really, it's okay." At least he hoped it would be. Ivy didn't seem like the type of person who expected him to adhere to certain hours if he still got the job done in a timely fashion.

Even though it was now certain that his mother would

never regain the use of her legs, he insisted that she keep going to the regular checkups so that any postaccident problems could be addressed. And, honestly, the trips to the doctor at least got his mom out of the house and away from the ranch. They allowed her to socialize with other people. He always made sure they stopped at other places as well—the grocery, the post office, the library, Trudy's, wherever he could think of without raising her suspicions. Daisy knew instinctively what he was doing and aided him without saying so. His sister was more grown-up and intuitive than he could have imagined being at her age.

When the call ended, he turned to Ivy. "I'll need to get to work a bit later tomorrow, but I'll stay late." Which meant doing his ranch chores later than he liked, but there was no other option. Daisy could do some of them, but not all. Plus it was her summer vacation, and she deserved to have some time to herself after working hard in school all year in addition to helping him and their mother. She was already largely trapped at home so their mother wasn't alone, so he didn't want to add more to her burden. He didn't want her to grow up to resent him and their mom for robbing her of her youth.

"Everything okay?" Ivy asked.

"Yeah. I just need to take my mom to a medical checkup."

"Sure, take whatever time you need."

"Thanks."

When Rich returned, Ivy didn't disappear upstairs. And Rich had evidently taken what Austin said to heart because he kept exchanges with Ivy on a professionally friendly level. The three of them fell into what felt like a natural rhythm of attacking their own parts of the project. At one point, Ivy was carrying what appeared to be a bunch of old newspapers toward the exit when Rich said, "Come on, baby. You know you want to behave."

Ivy jerked her head in Rich's direction, but he wasn't looking at her.

"He's talking to the wiring," Austin said.

"Huh?"

Austin took a step closer to her and pointed the hammer he was holding toward Rich, who wasn't aware they were talking about him.

"He has the nickname the Electrical Whisperer because he talks to the wiring as he's working."

"Oookay, then."

Austin laughed. "I'm not one to believe in woowoo stuff, but he does have a gift. I've seen him make stuff work that any sane person would have tossed in the trash."

"If it takes woowoo to make this place safe at a price that doesn't force me into bankruptcy, bring on the woowoo."

"SO HOW IS IT? Are you ready to come home yet?"

Ivy heard the hopeful note in her older sister Holly's voice and experienced a moment of guilt. But that wasn't fair. This was her life and she should be able to live it how she wanted. Plus there might be close to eighty miles between Louisville and Lexington, but that still wasn't far enough away from her cheater ex. Any place with a Southern accent of any flavor wasn't far enough. Part of the appeal of moving to Wyoming was that it looked nothing like Kentucky. She'd never experienced waking up and being able to see snowcapped mountains out of her bedroom window.

"It's going great." Ivy deliberately didn't answer the second question because she figured her answer to the first did double duty. "It's like looking at a postcard from my bedroom window."

"Send me pictures. I want to see everything."

Oh no, that wasn't going to happen. Holly was in full protective big sister mode. The minute she saw the state of the Stinson Building, she would be on a plane to Wyoming to drag Ivy back to Kentucky even if she was a grown woman.

"I'm not where I can right now. Plus I'm having some renovations done, so it's a bit of a mess. I'll send you some when it's all done."

"What are you not telling me? Something's wrong, isn't it?"

"Holly, just stop. I appreciate that you care about me, but I can take care of myself. And this is something I want to do. I need to do it, okay?"

She'd told her family all that before she left, several times, but maybe it would sink in more now that she was here, fifteen hundred miles away.

"Fine."

Ivy heard the "But you can always come back home" even though Holly didn't say it out loud.

After a few more minutes of catching up, Holly had to go help a customer in the small floral shop she ran with their mother.

"I want at least one picture before the end of the day," Holly said.

"Yes, Miss Bossy."

As soon as Ivy hung up, she knew exactly what pictures she would send. But first, she needed to wash up so she didn't look like she'd forgotten how to bathe. She placed the small metal tub she'd bought at the discount store under the outdoor spigot and turned on the flow of water. Movement out of the corner of her eye caught her attention. There, sitting under one of the bushes that needed pruning, was a gray tabby cat. Its green eyes watched her with obvious wariness, its body poised to bolt if she moved in a way it didn't like.

"Hello, there. Are you one of my neighbors?"

She'd met several of the neighbors of the two-legged variety. Evangeline Taggert had a small pottery studio next door but not a lot of business, from what Ivy could tell. The lot behind the Stinson Building was residential, and an older gentleman named Reg lived there. Austin had told her to never call the man Reginald because he hated his full name with a fire to rival an erupting volcano.

She wondered if the kitty belonged to Reg or one of the other nearby residents. When she reached up to turn off the flow of water, however, the cat bolted. Either it was skittish by nature or feral. Whichever it was, she carried the water inside then brought a plastic bowl back out to fill with water for the cat. If it kept hanging around, she'd buy some cat food.

She heated some of the water on the camp stove she'd bought the previous evening along with a huge bag of trail mix and a warm sleeping bag. She told herself that when she had functional heating and air as well as an actual bed, she could use all these purchases to go camping. She imagined that's something a Wyomingite would do, and she was a Wyomingite now.

Once she was clean and had washed her hair, she walked over to the window, opened it and positioned herself for a selfie with the picturesque mountains in the background. She stuck her tongue out and snapped a photo, then sent it to Holly. Before she left for work, she decided to take another photo to post on Instagram. She considered what to say that wouldn't make it seem like she was trying too hard to not be the jilted bride-to-be.

You can't beat this morning view. #newadventures

She closed the camera app and finished getting ready

for her shift at Trudy's. Austin hadn't arrived yet, and Rich wasn't due to arrive until early afternoon. Austin had the copy of the building key she'd had made the day before, however, and she just had to hope that no one decided now was the time to see if there was anything worth stealing. She took some comfort from the fact that no one had broken into her obviously packed full car while it sat on the street.

With some time left before her shift started but not enough to do any substantial work, she went to sit on the front stoop and add some things to her online vision board for the quilt shop. She'd just bookmarked another fabric supplier's site when Austin pulled up to the curb, and he wasn't alone.

"Hey," she said when he got out of the truck.

"Hey. I just stopped by to drop off the new window before I take Mom and Daisy home."

Ivy eyed the two people still in the truck. The younger of the two looked too young to be a girlfriend or wife. Was she a much younger sister?

Austin moved to the back of the pickup to grab the window. Ivy got to her feet and walked over to the open truck window.

"Hello, I'm Ivy Lake. Would you like a little tour?"

"We can't—" Austin started right as the teenage girl said, "Yes, please."

Ivy glanced over at Austin in time to see the surprise on his face.

"Daisy, you know—"

"It's okay," his mother said. "Let her look around if Ivy doesn't mind."

Instead of getting out, however, the older woman sat where she was as Daisy scooted out via the driver's side.

That's when Ivy noticed the wheelchair in the bed of the truck. She hoped the surprise didn't show on her face.

"I don't mind at all. We'll be right back."

As she accompanied the girl across the street, Ivy noticed that Austin didn't come with them.

"So, your name is Daisy?" she asked as she opened the front door and gestured for the girl to go ahead of her.

"Yes, ma'am. I'm Austin's sister."

"Nice to meet you. And that's cool. We both are named after pretty plants. It's sort of a family thing with me though. My sisters are named Holly and Lily, my mom is Rose and my grandmother's first name was Lavender, even though she went by her middle name, Cecile."

"Those are all pretty names."

"And to add to the whole floral theme, Mom and Holly are florists." Ivy gestured around the lower level. "Pardon the mess. There's obviously still a lot of work to be done, but I think it's going to be awesome when it's finished."

"I've always wanted to see the inside of this building," Daisy said as she walked slowly ahead, looking at the pressed tin ceiling. "I love history."

"I do too. I'm hoping to eventually research the history of this place, maybe put up an exhibit in that corner." Ivy pointed at the front corner to the right of the door.

"I could do that for you. It'd be fun."

"I'm sure you have a lot more fun things to do on your summer break."

"Not really," Daisy said, seeming to deflate a bit. "I do have some Geography Club stuff and I'll do a lot of reading. And ranch chores to help out Mom and Austin."

She'd just met Daisy and already Ivy's heart went out to her. She felt an immediate affection for the girl, a kinship she couldn't yet explain. As she showed her around both floors of the building, an idea started percolating in her

head. When they returned to the bottom floor, she halted
Daisy before they stepped outside.

"I have a question for you. Before I ask, however, know
that your mother and brother will have to approve."

"Okay."

"I can't pay a lot, but what would you say about working here a couple of days a week researching the history of
the building, coming up with ideas for the exhibit? I also
have some old coins that I need researched and cataloged."

"Yes!"

The girl was so excited that Ivy suddenly wished she'd
asked Austin and his mother about the idea first. She would
hate it if they said no and crushed Daisy's excitement.

"They'll say yes."

Ivy certainly hoped so.

"DID YOU ASK Ivy for a job?" Austin asked Daisy when his
sister brought up the topic during dinner.

"No. All I said was that I liked history and that I could
research the building's history for her."

"She must have felt obligated to offer to pay you for
the work."

The way Daisy bit her lip told him that he was ruining
a potentially fun summer endeavor for her, but he knew
from what Ivy had said that she didn't have the money to
be hiring yet more people, even if it was for only a couple
days a week. Even so, he hated himself for extinguish-
ing his sister's excitement. She was typically so quiet and
shy. The way she had hopped out of the truck earlier and
chatted with Ivy as if they were the best of friends had
surprised him, and now here he was ensuring that Daisy
retreated back into her shell.

Hopefully it wouldn't last long, because his keeping the
renovation job and not making Ivy feel as if Daisy was tak-

ing advantage of her kindness were important. If not for the bills and how it was almost impossible to whittle them down, he wouldn't object to Daisy having a part-time job that she would no doubt love.

"I see no problem with it," their mom said. "Ivy is obviously a grown woman who can make her own decisions."

"Mom—"

"Daisy, can you go feed Pooch?" his mom said, cutting him off.

They all knew that she'd sent Daisy outside to feed their dog so that the adults could discuss the topic without her.

"She's doing this," his mom said as soon as Daisy's footsteps could no longer be heard on the porch.

Austin sighed. He didn't like disagreeing with his mother, but he was trying so hard to keep a roof over their heads and food on the table. But maybe this time, a compromise was the best solution.

"I will talk to Ivy tomorrow to make sure she didn't offer this simply out of kindness."

"So what if she did? You need to learn to let people make their own decisions. Stop trying to be everyone's parent. Daisy may have lost her father, but she still has me."

Austin winced. He didn't think he was overbearing. He loved his sister with his whole heart and wanted only the best for her. It wasn't fair that she'd lost her father like he had. It wasn't fair that he needed her to do more around the ranch and stay with their mom while he was working in town. But there was no one else to do those things, and he couldn't work twenty-four hours a day.

"You may disagree with me, but I need to talk to Ivy first. Even if she does truly want to have Daisy do the work, her first day doesn't have to be tomorrow."

His mom looked like she wanted to say something further, but she refrained.

After she wheeled herself away from the table and started loading the dishwasher, he stood and headed for the back door. He instinctively knew that his mom was not in the mood for a helping hand. It wasn't the first time he'd had to keep himself from offering to help her and remind himself that her doing normal tasks unaided was a good thing. He had to balance his urge to make things easier for her with not treating her like she was helpless. Often he didn't succeed.

Too many times, like now, he ended up feeling like the bad guy.

He started for the barn to take care of his horse, Merlin, when he spotted Daisy sitting on the ground with her legs crossed, scratching Pooch between his ears. Austin stopped and considered if it was better to talk to his sister or leave her to her thoughts. What more could he say that hadn't already been said? He'd be lucky if she didn't end up hating him before she reached adulthood.

"It's okay," she said, evidently realizing he was standing several feet away.

With a sad sigh, he walked over and sat beside her.

"I'm sorry if I always seem mean."

"You don't." She sounded as if she really meant that, which somehow made him feel worse than if she were angry and sulking like a normal teenager.

He rubbed Pooch's head when the tan mutt—one part shepherd and several parts other unknown breeds—placed his head on Austin's knee as if he detected Austin's inner exhaustion and was trying to offer comfort.

"I'm sorry I caused you and Mom to fight."

"Oh, Daisy. You didn't. I understand you wanting to have more freedom and do things you enjoy during your time off from school. And I understand Mom wanting to let you. I just…" How did he even put into words what he was feeling and have it make sense to someone not quite half his age? Sometimes he felt three times her fourteen years.

"Don't worry about me or Mom," Daisy said. "We'll be okay here while you're away from the ranch."

She sounded so grown-up and responsible that he wanted to cry. He wasn't totally responsible for the current situation, but he'd one hundred percent been the one to destroy her new spark of joy. He felt like the worst brother in the world, more like one of those mean parents who always said no.

The entire situation weighed so heavily on his mind that when he went to bed, he ended up tossing and turning more than sleeping. When he woke up a little after four in the morning, and it became obvious that he wasn't going to be able to go back to sleep, he got up and dressed. Might as well get his ranch work done and head to Ivy's early.

When he arrived not long after sunrise, he planned to sit in his truck while he drank his coffee until he made sure Ivy was awake. But to his surprise, she was already outside clearing overgrown shrubbery away from the front of the building.

"And here I thought I was getting an early start," he said as he crossed the street.

She made a circular motion toward her head. "Too many ideas floating around up here for me to sleep."

He could relate.

Ivy pointed at the area she'd already cleared, the pile of brush off to the side the result. "I'm going to add something to your to-do list, and I'd like to move it to the top of the list. Can you add a wheelchair ramp right here and make the entry into the store accessible?"

"Ivy—"

"I'm going to stop you right there. Yes, seeing your mother's wheelchair made me think of this, but it's a necessity anyway. Even without legal requirements, I want everyone to be able to access my store. And if your mom would like to come with Daisy, she should be able to."

Austin stared at Ivy and something moved in the area of his heart. When he realized what was happening, he looked away. She was simply a kind person temporarily in his life, nothing more. What he was feeling was just appreciation for that kindness.

"About Daisy—I talked with her last night and she understands that if you were just being kind to her in offering to let her work here, then you're not obligated. I know that you're being careful with the expenses of getting this place ready to live in and operate as a business."

He looked back at her to see her staring at him as if she couldn't believe the words coming out of his mouth.

"Did you tell Daisy she couldn't work for me?"

"Not exactly. I just told her that you might have seen her excitement and misinterpreted it as her asking for a job."

Ivy crossed her arms, and he'd swear her expression changed to one that made him feel as if he was about to get a scolding.

"Do I seem like a person who can't make rational decisions?"

"That's not what I meant." Why couldn't he stop saying the wrong things at the wrong times?

"Good to hear. I didn't offer Daisy the job because I felt obligated. They are tasks that right now I don't have time to do and ones she seemed genuinely interested in."

"If you're sure."

"I am. Now, on to the ramp." She motioned behind her. "Work up an estimate, and I'll go ahead and give you the money to get the supplies you need."

"Thank you."

"No need to thank me. What helps your mother will

help others. And what helps Daisy will help me. It's a win-win-win-win."

Ivy returned to clearing out the sad, forgotten shrubs as he started taking measurements and jotting down the supplies he'd need from the hardware store. He caught himself glancing toward Ivy more than he should. He noticed she was making a pile of small, flat stones she'd found once the bushes were cleared away.

"Planning on going rock skipping?" he asked.

"What?" She noticed he was pointing at the little mound of rocks. "Oh, no. I paint little pictures and sayings on them and leave them in random places for people to find."

"Okay." He drew out the word because he'd never heard of such a hobby.

"It's fun. When people find them, they post pictures. Sometimes they'll take them and put them somewhere else for someone else to find, or they paint their own and replace the original. You should try it sometime. It's relaxing and nice knowing it'll make someone smile."

He hadn't known Ivy long and didn't know her well, but already he was confident that she was genuinely one of the nicest people he'd ever met.

"I guess the world could always use more reasons to smile."

A flicker of something that looked like sadness passed over her expression for a moment before she smiled again. "Indeed."

Rich pulled up and parked, drawing their attention. The three of them once again fell into the rhythm of their own parts of the project. Rich did his talking to the wiring thing as he replaced what needed to be replaced. Ivy continued weeding and brush removal until it was time for her to get ready for her shift at Trudy's. And Austin headed to buy more lumber and concrete mix as well as order a handrail for the new ramp. Before he exited his truck outside the hardware store, however, he texted Daisy.

You can start work tomorrow.

He had just stepped into the store when she texted back. Thank you! This was followed by a huge smiling emoji.

It lifted some of the burden off his heart that he'd made his sister happy. Now if he could just figure out how to do the same for his mother. She'd lost so much, endured more than her share of heartache. He knew she needed to move on and she did her best, but grief still sat on her shoulders like an invisible weight. She had managed to start life anew after Austin's dad died, had been happy in her second marriage and had a daughter to join her son. But how could she move on from losing a second husband when her paralysis would remind her every day for the rest of her life?

"Hey, Austin." The sound of a familiar voice drew him out of his heavy thoughts.

"How's it going, Isaac?"

"Can't complain."

Isaac Lewis had been his dad's best friend, and he'd taken Austin fishing several times after his father's death. He also happened to be a good plumber.

"You have some time today?" Austin asked.

"Sure. This have to do with the job you're doing on the Stinson Building?"

"It does." He explained how Ivy needed operational indoor plumbing and restroom facilities.

"As luck would have it, I just had a job fall through. Instead of renovating their bathrooms, the Pilsons have decided to get divorced instead."

Sadly, disagreements about renovations and money had likely ended more marriages than that of the Pilsons.

"I met Ivy yesterday when I was in Trudy's. She's a little ray of sunshine, isn't she?"

"She's nice." Yes, a ray of sunshine was a good way to describe Ivy, but he wasn't going to give any potential matchmakers—and there were plenty in a town the size of Jade Valley—any ideas. Even if he admitted to himself that she was attractive and had he met her before he had met Grace, maybe he would even ask her out. But having your wife abandon you soured you on romantic relationships.

Isaac chuckled, but Austin chose to ignore the potential implication of that chuckle. Instead, he invited the older man to come over to the job site with him after Austin finished buying what he needed to build the ramp.

Twenty minutes later, Isaac was staring at the area that was supposed to be a bathroom on the upper floor of the Stinson Building.

"Well, nothing like starting from scratch," he said.

"How long do you think it'll take?"

"Miss Ivy will have a fine new bathroom by the end of the week. I can add plumbing for and install a kitchen sink too, if she wants."

"Really?" Even for Isaac, that seemed like a fast turn-around.

"Yes, I'm just that good."

Austin laughed.

"You've got the Electrical Whisperer downstairs, the plumbing genius upstairs, and you're the hardworking jack-of-all-trades. We'll turn this place around so fast, they'll write songs about us."

"I like the sound of that," Rich called out from the first floor.

Austin snorted then gestured dramatically toward the bathroom space. "By all means, work your toilet magic."

As Austin descended the stairs, he realized how much

his mood had lightened. Other than worrying about his mom, everything else seemed to be going well. But he was still hesitant to believe it would last, worried that if he let down his guard it would invite bad luck back into his life.

CHAPTER FIVE

TRUDY'S WAS HOPPING as if there was nowhere else in town to eat. But a quick look across the street showed that Alma's was equally as busy. Both places were full of the tourists who were temporarily stranded by their bus breaking down at the edge of town. Considering they'd had to walk about a quarter of a mile to get to the business area of Jade Valley, the group of women were in good spirits.

"So where are y'all from?" Ivy asked the ladies at the table where she was refilling water glasses.

"Oh, honey, I have to ask you that instead," one of the older ladies said. "I haven't heard a Southern accent live in a long time."

"I'm from Kentucky."

"Tennessee, though it's been forty years since I lived there. Everyone still tells me I have my accent though."

"I can hear it, though maybe it's softened a little bit."

"You, however, must be a recent transplant."

"I am. Less than a month."

"I came out to Denver for college and never went back. What brought you?" The woman leaned toward Ivy and lowered her voice a little. "A hot cowboy? That's what got me."

Ivy laughed a little and was startled when Austin appeared in her thoughts.

"Just ready for a change." She hurried away from the

table before the ladies could ask any further questions that she didn't want to answer.

As she and Fiona, another waitress who worked on the days when Stephanie was off, were kept running taking orders, delivering food to tables and making sure no one ran out of their chosen beverage, she learned the ladies had all been in a sorority together back in the early 1980s. Now they lived in all parts of the country and even in several international locales, but every two years they gathered back in Denver to embark on a week of adventures together. And this year's agenda was the Grand Teton and Yellowstone national parks. Now that their trip had experienced a setback, they were making plans to explore all the shops in Jade Valley and eat themselves silly.

"You will want to make sure to save room for dessert. Trudy is famous for her pies. We have five different flavors available today," she told the ladies at another table.

When one of the women expressed concern about gaining weight, another laughed and said, "You know calories don't count on vacation. I distinctly remember telling you that during our trip to Sedona last year."

This caused everyone at the table to laugh, and Ivy laughed right along with them. It felt good to do so, especially since the topic of conversation at another table was the upcoming marriage of a daughter.

Ivy had done a pretty good job of keeping thoughts of James and his betrayal at bay, so much so that she was proud of herself. Being so far away from Louisville, with surroundings that looked nothing like Kentucky, helped in that regard. So did working from the time she got up until she collapsed in her sleeping bag at night. She'd be glad to stop having to sleep on the floor, but at least she wasn't cold anymore and she'd cleared enough dust out of the top floor that she spent less time sneezing.

At the end of her shift, Ivy discovered that she'd done even better with tips than she'd thought. Fiona had as well.

"Buses full of generous ladies need to break down at the edge of town every day," Fiona said.

Even though she'd tried to push thoughts of James away, that conversation about the upcoming wedding stuck with her. If things had gone as planned, she'd be making her own wedding plans. She'd already been planning the honeymoon trip to Italy. His betrayal had robbed her of so much, including that dream vacation. Maybe someday her business would be so successful that she'd take a solo trip.

"You okay?" Fiona asked.

"Yeah, fine. Just remembered something I need to do for the renovation."

Find a way to excise all memories of James and the moment when he'd turned her world upside down.

Ivy tried to rid herself of the gloomy mood by buying a box of the little cherry and cream cheese tarts Trudy had made before she headed home. She imagined drowning her sorrows by stuffing her face with all of them, but in truth she'd probably share them with Austin and Rich. That would be a much better decision for her waistline.

When she reached her place, there was a third truck parked outside. Maybe it was someone Austin or Rich knew, perhaps someone delivering supplies they needed. But when she stepped inside, she noticed an older gentleman she'd met at Trudy's. What was his name? She'd met so many people that it was becoming difficult to keep all the names straight. She needed a flow chart to keep track of who was related to whom, who owned what businesses, who sided with Trudy and who sided with Alma in the mysterious feud she'd learned about from her coworkers.

"Hey," Austin said when he noticed her. "This is Isaac Lewis. He's helping out with the plumbing."

"We've met," Ivy said as she shook Isaac's hand.

"Good to see you again."

"Isaac said you should have a functioning bathroom sooner than if I do it myself," Austin said.

"That's the best thing I've heard all day, and I had a customer ask me if I'd been Miss Wyoming a couple of years ago."

Granted, the young man who might have been twenty was flirting, but still it had been nice to hear. Being cheated on didn't do wonders for a girl's self-esteem, even if she knew it wasn't her fault.

"In fact, indoor plumbing on the horizon is worthy of a celebration." She opened the box of tarts, and she had to laugh when Rich appeared from wherever he'd been as if answering a siren's call.

"Never get between Rich and sweets. You may lose an eye," Austin said.

Ivy didn't know why that struck her as hilarious, but she laughed so much she snorted. Maybe it was because she was normally a person who easily found humor, but the past few weeks had not offered much that was worthy of laughter. That a good-looking handyman, an electrical whisperer and a plumber would be what brought laughter back was unexpected but oddly on brand for her new hometown.

The four of them seemed to instinctively stay out of each other's way as they made progress toward their individual but interconnected goals. In her continued examination of deteriorating boxes, she found everything from old, musty hymnals to what looked to be some grandma's varied collection of vintage buttons. The washing and sorting of the latter, she added to Daisy's task list.

"It's amazing the amount of junk that's been stored up here," Isaac said after he hauled out the toilet, which he'd said wasn't going to work in the space allotted—probably the reason it had been sitting in the middle of the room.

"It does seem like Jade Valley's collective junk drawer." And yet it had sort of become fun to discover what all was left behind, like a treasure hunt.

As she carried a box of various and sundry useless items outside to the pile that Austin said he'd haul away for her, she noticed he'd made amazing progress with the ramp. He'd been building the wooden form for it when she returned from her shift at Trudy's. While she'd been upstairs working, he'd mixed and poured the concrete. Now he smoothed the surface.

"Looks great," she said after dropping the box beside the others. "How long before it's usable?"

"It should cure for about a week."

"That long?"

"Maybe a little less, but I'd rather go the full week to make sure."

She nodded. "After that, your mom can accompany Daisy if she wants to."

Austin straightened and wiped the sweat off his forehead. Ivy's heart skipped a little bit. A man who was that dirty and sweaty shouldn't look that good, but he did.

"I appreciate it. I don't know that she'll want to though."

"Well, it's a standing offer." She got the feeling there was tension surrounding the situation with his mother, but she didn't know him well enough to ask. There was a delicate balance between getting to know people and intruding.

"I'm glad Daisy is going to be helping me out though." She told him about the box of buttons and that she was considering how to incorporate them into the store. "Depending on what we find in that box, I might do some sort of display."

"I'm sure you'll think of something. Do you know what you're going to call the place yet?"

"Not one hundred percent. I've thought about Cecile's because it was my grandmother's dream to have a place like this, but that might also confuse people."

"Maybe just call it Quilters' Dream."

The rightness of that name lit up Ivy's brain like a college football stadium on game night.

"I love that. It fits perfectly." She looked up at the front of the building. "The quilt shop was Grandma Cecile's dream, and this building is my new dream."

"What was the old one?"

The question surprised Ivy, but when she looked at Austin, it appeared it had surprised him even more.

"Sorry, I don't know why I asked that," he said. "That's none of my business."

"It's okay. We all say things we don't mean to sometimes." She sighed. "But I'm not ready to talk about it."

The betrayal was too fresh, too raw, too embarrassing. She wanted to leave everything about it back in Louisville. This was her new start, the new stage of her life that was free of James. Ivy was determined to not let him taint it.

She noticed the look on Austin's face as he lowered his gaze to the concrete trowel in his hands. He looked as if a few more bricks had just been added to a load he always seemed to carry on his shoulders.

"Austin," she said, then waited for him to meet her gaze. "Don't beat yourself up over it. Just because I don't want to talk about it doesn't mean you have to feel bad. Curiosity is natural, especially when someone enters a contest to win a building, then picks up and moves across the country alone to start a new career. Heck, I'd be darn curious if it was someone else and found out someone who used to do advertising for a hotel chain was going to pivot and open a quilt shop. I mean, one of these things is not like the other."

Despite what she'd said, the oddest urge to just spill everything overcame her, along with the feeling that Austin would be a good listener. But she suspected he had enough going on in his own life without hearing about someone else's woes. As he was obviously curious about her reasons for coming to Jade Valley, she wondered about him as well. Why did he work so hard, barely taking a break? Did the fact his mother used a wheelchair have anything to do with the way he seemed as if he was always ready for the other shoe to drop?

It reminded her that she was far from the only person going through a difficult time. There were so many others navigating far worse. Maybe keeping things in perspective would help her heal, to be able to talk about what happened without feeling as if she might fall apart.

AUSTIN CAME BACK in from his early morning ride to check on the herd to find the kitchen table filled with a larger breakfast than normal. Daisy turned from the stove, wearing their mother's strawberry-patterned apron, a plate of crisp bacon in her hand.

"What's all this?" he asked.

"It's her first day of her first job," his mom said as she retrieved milk from the refrigerator. "We're celebrating."

Austin noticed that Daisy seemed a little nervous, but he had a gut feeling it had more to do with her thinking he might change his mind last minute rather than worrying about the actual job.

"That's a good idea, though this seems like enough for three meals."

"We can take some leftovers for lunch," Daisy said.

Again, he could tell there was more to what she said. He knew her well enough to figure she had said that to make sure he knew that he didn't have to worry about buying her lunch in town. Not for the first time, he hoped that when Daisy grew up, she got an incredible job that allowed her to do all the things she wanted to without having to worry about how much they cost. He was ashamed he couldn't give that to her, but if this job with Ivy set Daisy on that path, then it was a good thing.

As they ate, they talked about what he'd been doing on the building so far. He didn't mention the ramp because he was still trying to think about how he could convince his mom to come into town with him and Daisy on the days they were both working. He knew she could mostly take care of herself, but he worried about her mental state if she had too much time alone. Losses hurt the most when you were by yourself with nothing but time to think.

"It sounds like it'll be a nice place," his mom said.

"I bet Ivy would like to see the quilts Grandma Wilkes made," Daisy said while bringing a forkful of scrambled eggs to her mouth.

"I'm sure she's much more interested in those fancy art quilts."

"I don't know," Austin said, seeing a potential opening for getting his mom interested in something, maybe a reason for her to accompany them to town the next week. "Ivy seems to have an affinity for older stuff—the building, those old coins and buttons Daisy is going to be researching and organizing."

His mom made a noncommittal answer, and he and Daisy shared a conspiratorial glance. She was a smart kid, so she no doubt knew exactly what he was doing. But they both knew when enough had been said, when anything further would have the opposite of the desired effect.

Once he and Daisy were in the truck and on the way to town, he glanced over and saw she was reading a book, a common occurrence with his brainy little sister.

"What are you reading?"

She read out the title, about an expedition to the South Pole.

"That's not one of the places you want to go, is it?"

She shrugged. "I don't know, maybe. But my list has a lot of other places on it before Antarctica."

For him, it got plenty cold during a Wyoming winter. He couldn't imagine wanting to go to the literal ends of the earth where it was even more brutally cold. Though he worried about where she might travel someday and whether she'd be safe, he did his best to keep those worries to himself. After what she'd lost, she deserved to chase her dream unimpeded.

Thinking about dreams brought his thoughts back to Ivy. Though she'd been her usual kind self about his stupid question the day before, he still felt guilty for bringing up her reason for moving to Wyoming. It was even more obvious by her answer that she hadn't made the drastic change in her life simply because of a sense of adventure. Had she lost someone too?

Normally, he didn't bother wondering too much about other people's personal lives. He didn't have time for it, for one thing. But ever since he'd met Ivy, she'd sparked his curiosity. Surely he wasn't the only one though. It wasn't every day that someone up and moved across the country to Jade Valley, especially someone with no ties to the town or even the state.

When he parked in front of Ivy's place, Daisy was quick to set aside her book and hop out of the truck. He smiled at her enthusiasm for tasks that others would find tedious. But Daisy had always liked things that most of her classmates didn't, and for the most part she didn't seem to mind being different. She lived in her head most of the time.

At least that's what he assumed was going on with her. The unexpected excitement over this new job and how easily she seemed to talk with Ivy right from the moment they met made him wonder if he'd missed something. Was he so busy ranching and grabbing any other work he could get that he wasn't seeing things that were right in front of him? He made a promise to himself to set aside some brother-sister time so they could talk and do something together that was fun rather than work.

All he seemed to do was work. Part of it was necessity, but truthfully part of it was also so he didn't have time to think about Grace and how she really hadn't been in their marriage for better or worse.

Because he'd had a lot of practice doing so, he shoved those thoughts away again and got out of the truck to tackle another day of work.

As he got started scraping away the old paint around the windows, which thankfully and to his surprise was not lead-based, he caught himself looking in Ivy's direction more times than he cared to admit. He tried to tell himself it was to check on how Daisy was doing, but that was a lie. Then he'd tell his brain it was simply because she was nicer to look at than Rich or Isaac, which was both true and another lie.

He was actually glad when she headed to work at Trudy's, and he deliberately shifted to the other side of the building so he wouldn't be tempted to watch her walk up the street.

"Am I detecting a bit of interest?" Isaac asked, startling Austin with his nearness.

"No," he said simply.

Isaac chuckled. "Just so you know, that wasn't very convincing."

Austin looked over at Isaac. "You know what happened and why I have zero interest in another relationship."

Why did that statement, which had always felt absolutely true, feel as if it was a little shakier in the truth department now?

"Yes, you got a raw deal with Grace. But that doesn't mean you have to be alone the rest of your life."

"I'm not alone. I have Mom and Daisy and plenty of work to fill my days."

"Not the same thing, boy. Not the same thing at all."

As Isaac walked away, Austin felt like kicking himself again. Isaac had lost his wife, Birdie, two years before to a brain aneurysm. He'd suffered the type of sudden loss that didn't even allow for a goodbye, the same way Austin, Daisy and his mom had. Not that it was any less horrible, but at least Austin had the chance to say his goodbyes to his father as the cancer slowly took him away.

Isaac was such a jovial guy that it was easy to forget that he still grieved Birdie's loss.

Knowing nothing he could say would change that grief, Austin placed the paint scraper back on the windowsill. If only getting rid of sad memories was as easy as peeling off old paint.

When he later stopped to grab a cold bottle of water from the cooler at the front of the building, he noticed a look on Daisy's face that made him pause.

"What's wrong?"

"Am I seeing this correctly?"

He realized that she didn't look distressed but rather stunned. Stepping up beside her, he saw she'd pulled up details on an old penny she was holding in her hand. Austin leaned down so he could see what had surprised her so much.

No wonder she was stunned.

"Would someone really pay that?" she asked in disbelief.

"Maybe. People pay surprising amounts for collectibles."

Austin looked toward the open door and windows as if thieves might suddenly leap inside and make off with the valuable coin.

"Log it like the rest you've been doing. And when Ivy gets back, you're going to make her day."

Daisy's wide smile rivaled the sun. How long had it been since he'd seen her smile like that?

Even though she was excited, he could tell she was also nervous—so much so that when she needed to go to the convenience store to use the restroom, she made him promise to not leave the room where the coins were spread out on the old countertop left over from the Stinson Building's beginnings as a grocery.

When she returned, she held the orange soda she liked in one hand and his favorite grape in the other. Though it was not out of character for her, he still felt as if this was her once again thanking him for allowing her to take the job. Feeling a rush of affection for his sister, he put his arm around her shoulders and gave her a quick hug.

"That's enough," he said. "Keep your money for yourself."

When he spotted Ivy walking down the street a few hours later, he was glad that both Rich and Isaac were temporarily gone to buy more supplies. He trusted both men, but still the fewer people who knew about the value of what Ivy had lucked into the better.

"You ready to make someone's day?" he asked Daisy.

"Is she here?"

He nodded.

Daisy hopped up from where she'd been deep into her work of continuing to research the collection of coins, grabbing her phone and the miraculous penny.

By the time Ivy stepped into the building, Daisy was practically vibrating with excitement. Ivy noticed both of them staring at her and stopped in her tracks.

"Is something wrong?"

"The opposite," he said, then motioned toward Daisy, who rushed forward to show Ivy what she'd found.

Even more than when Ivy had found the previous valuable coin, she appeared shocked.

"I... I can't believe it." She looked between the coin and the listing on Daisy's phone several more times, then up at Austin, and finally at Daisy. And then she squealed and pulled Daisy into her arms.

As the two of them jumped up and down, moving in a circle, Austin laughed. Then, to his surprise, Ivy reached out and pulled him into a celebratory group hug. Her arm felt so tiny around his waist. She seemed even shorter while standing this close to her.

He realized just how long it had been since he'd been hugged. And how much he'd missed it.

CHAPTER SIX

TRYING TO FOCUS on clearing out the last of the upstairs junk after discovering she owned a penny potentially worth ten thousand dollars was like trying to sleep with a tornado siren blaring next to her ear. In other words, impossible. Hiding her excitement from Isaac and Rich when they returned from their errands proved difficult, and she kept checking the little zip-up pocket in her Capri pants to make sure the two really valuable coins were still there. She wasn't about to walk away from them until she could hopefully sell them.

"What do you plan to do?" Austin asked her as she dusted her hands after carrying a broken chair out to the front lawn.

"Get rid of them as soon as possible. The fear of losing them will make me a nervous wreck."

"Daisy looked up rare coin dealers, and there's one in Cheyenne. She's hurrying to get through the rest of the collection so you'll know everything you have."

Ivy glanced toward the open front door.

"She's a great kid, very hardworking."

"Yeah, she is."

"She reminds me of myself when I was her age. I wasn't as quiet, but I was bookish and loved history. It's part of what attracted me to my previous job."

"I thought you worked at a hotel."

"No, I worked for a hotel chain. We took old buildings

and renovated them into boutique hotels. One was an old textile mill. Another was a former distillery. A small college that closed. Even a former Thoroughbred racing stable. When I left, the owner was considering buying an old prison."

Austin shook his head. "Who would want to sleep in a prison?"

"You'd be surprised. People like unique experiences."

"I guess." He motioned toward the front door. "Daisy's reading a book about the South Pole for her geography club. When I asked if she'd ever want to go there, she said maybe."

"That's adventurous."

"A little too adventurous for my comfort, but when she grows up I want her to be able to go and live the life she wants, travel wherever she's drawn to. She's had a curiosity about the world since before she could even verbalize it. Mom has a picture of her sitting in front of the TV when she was two with this look of awe on her little face. Her dad was watching a documentary about the Zambezi River. I had to look it up because I had no clue where it was."

She hesitated asking the question that sprang to mind, but she'd been growing more and more curious about Austin. Even if she wasn't looking for romance, she couldn't seem to prevent her eyes from wandering to him when he was nearby. There was no denying he was an attractive man. His work ethic and how he took care of his family only added to that attractiveness.

"You said 'her dad,'" she ventured carefully.

"We had different fathers."

The fact that he used the past tense caused sadness in her heart. She didn't ask anything further, especially when Daisy stepped outside.

Austin shifted his attention to his sister. "Ready to go?"

"Yeah." But instead of heading toward the truck, she crossed the yard to Ivy and extended a notebook to her. "I should be able to finish with the coins in the morning."

"Wow, you're fast."

"It's interesting." She glanced around. "And exciting."

Ivy smiled. "So exciting. Thank you for your hard work."

As the two of them headed off down the street with Austin behind the wheel, Ivy realized that having Austin and Daisy around made her happy. Not long ago she couldn't even imagine being happy again. The life she'd planned for herself had been pulled out from under her. Maybe that was one of the reasons she felt so comfortable with Austin and Daisy. From what she'd gathered, they'd had their lives yanked in cruel directions too.

She heard a light chuckle and jerked her attention away from Austin's truck turning the corner onto Main Street. Isaac stood at the top of the steps leading into the building, an amused look on his face as if he was privy to a joke that no one else had heard. She suspected she knew the direction of his thoughts and had to figure out a way to change that direction.

"How goes the bathroom?"

He smiled, signaling that he knew very well what she was doing but didn't call her out on it.

"Good. Before you know it, you'll have such an awesome bathroom that you can charge for tours."

Ivy snorted a little at that.

"I'll settle for functional."

"There might be a slight delay in getting a couple of the items I ordered. I'll know for sure soon."

"Okay."

After everyone had left for the day, Ivy went out back to fetch a bucket of water from the spigot. She spotted the cat again, in almost the same spot. She'd asked both Reg and Evangeline about the cat, and both had said they suspected it was a stray.

"Well, hello there. Nice to see you again."

The cat just stared at her. Ivy wasn't sure if she was imagining it, but the cat seemed slightly less likely to bolt than the last time. Maybe it appreciated the water Ivy had set out for it.

"I've got a job for you too," she said. "You see any mice or rats, you take care of them. In exchange, I'll buy you the good cat food."

The cat responded by keeping its distance. But it didn't run away. Instead, it settled a bit more comfortably and began to lick its paws.

"I need a bath too." She had never looked so forward to a long, hot shower in her life.

Today's find in the coin box, however, made her breathe a bit more easily about the cost of her new bathrooms—the one in her home and the much smaller one for customers downstairs. She took the coin out of her pocket and turned it over and over, encased in its plastic holder. How was it possible that someone would pay thousands of dollars for a penny? She understood the concept of rarity equaling value, but it was still hard to wrap her mind around.

A sudden breeze cooled her skin. She wondered how she would fare during her first Wyoming winter. Even though she'd never been to the state before moving there, she knew that it would be a new type of cold. It was kind of funny she was the one who moved there when it was her younger sister, Lily, who was the fan of winter weather. Lily spent her days working in a hospital, where people often suffered and sometimes died. She said that seeing that made her really want to live, and so her vacations typically involved snowboarding or skiing in the winter, white-water rafting or hiking in the warmer months. The summer after she graduated from college, she had through-hiked the nearly twenty-two hundred miles of the Appalachian Trail with friends from her college hiking club.

With all that adventure in her personality, Lily had been the one to worry least about Ivy heading off across the country to start a new life. The two things her younger sister had said were that she simply hoped Ivy wasn't doing it too soon after her broken engagement and that she'd miss being able to just drive up to Louisville to see her.

Ivy missed her sisters and her mom too, as well as good friends she'd made while living in Louisville. But she needed the change at a soul-deep level. And if she had waited, she might have let common sense overrule taking a leap of faith.

She looked up at the impossibly blue sky. So far, she liked the leap of faith.

BY THE TIME another week of work passed, Austin was shocked at how much progress had been made, even though he'd taken part in it. True to his word, Isaac had completed the upstairs bathroom except for a couple of small items that were on back order. Austin and Daisy had laughed at the squeal of excitement when it had been revealed to Ivy.

"Sounds like she likes it," Austin had said.

"She's probably happy to not have to use public restrooms anymore. She said she's been to every business in town."

True. But based on things Ivy had said in passing, he knew she was most looking forward to having ready access to a shower.

He jerked his attention back to the sanding of the floorboards because he did not need to think about Ivy in the shower.

Rich hadn't arrived for the day, and Isaac left to do an emergency plumbing call. Since it was a day off work from Trudy's for Ivy, she joined Austin and Lily outside in the shade to have lunch. Instead of eating her sandwich, however, Ivy leaned back on her hands, lifted her face to the sky and closed her eyes.

"This weather is perfect," she said. "I know I'll likely be grumpy in the winter, but for now it's fabulous. It's ninety-three degrees back in Kentucky right now, with high humidity."

"That sounds miserable," he said, doing his best to not pay attention to how she looked beautiful even dressed in a worn T-shirt and shorts, with tendrils of her hair having escaped from her ponytail. He absolutely could not look at her legs. They were in danger of reminding him of how alone he'd been since Grace walked out on him without a word of warning.

It didn't help that he liked everything he'd observed about Ivy so far. He'd tossed aside his initial thought that maybe she wasn't that smart if she gave up a good job to move across the country into an old building that almost wasn't livable. She'd proven that she was actually smart as well as a hard worker and kind. Now he couldn't help but wonder what had driven her to make such a drastic change, which was the exact opposite of how he'd reacted in the wake of major upheaval in his life. He'd dug in his heels, put his head down and worked harder at the same things he'd always done.

The things that had driven Grace away.

"Now that the ramp is ready, you can bring your mom here," Ivy said, yanking his attention away from the past.

"Maybe." He sensed Ivy looking at him in the wake of his simple reply, but he pretended not to notice.

"Mom doesn't like to go places anymore," Daisy said.

"Daisy," he warned.

"It's not a secret," his sister said, surprising him by not immediately going quiet. She shifted her attention to Ivy. "Mom is still sad about what happened to Dad and her legs."

"Oh, I'm sorry to hear that. But it's understandable." She paused for a moment. "I don't mean to tell you how to handle your private family matters, but I'll share one thing. My mom said that the thing that saved her after my dad left was staying busy. My grandma Cecile, Mom's friends, they refused to let her stay alone too much. They made sure to provide her with things to do until Mom was ready to take those steps on her own."

"Mom has been through a lot, more than her share," Austin said.

"Which means she's in more danger of succumbing to depression." Ivy placed one of her hands on Daisy's knee and smiled. Then she met Austin's eyes. "I'm sorry if I'm stepping across a line, but I know from experience that being too alone with one's thoughts for too long isn't a good thing. It's not a path to healing."

Was she right? Had they given their mom enough time to grieve on her own? If they continued to do so, were they doing her more harm than good? He hated that there were no easy answers because everyone handled grief differently and healed at different paces. But what if his mom wasn't actually healing? What if she had suffered so much that there was no more healing in her?

"Tell me about your mom," Ivy suddenly said. "What things does she like?"

"She's always just worked being a mom, on the ranch, and then helping Daisy's dad run his river rafting business," he said.

"She likes art."

Austin looked at Daisy, wondering why she would say that. "Since when?"

"Since always. Didn't you notice how she used to doodle all the time?"

"Lots of people doodle."

"She's also the one who collected all that driftwood that was out in front of the office."

It took him a moment to remember what Daisy was talking about—a bunch of differently shaped pieces of driftwood that had been assembled to look like a white-water raft.

"I didn't know she did that. Why didn't she ever say anything about it?"

"She probably didn't think it was worth mentioning, but I thought it was cool."

Austin felt like a pitiful son. How had he lived three decades and never realized his mother had an artistic streak? He suspected that she never mentioned it because it wasn't practical and he, like his father, was of the practical mindset.

His appetite gone, he placed the rest of his sandwich in front of Daisy and got up.

"You're done?" Daisy asked.

"I'm still full from breakfast." He wasn't sure why he lied. Maybe it was so Daisy and Ivy didn't attribute his lack of appetite to the conversation they'd been having. "I want to finish sanding the bottom level floor today."

He turned and went back into the building, his mind trying to remember all the times his mother may have expressed a personal interest that he hadn't even noticed. In all his efforts to be a good son, had he been a bad one instead?

Ivy FELT TERRIBLE as she watched Austin walk back inside. Why had she pushed? Why had she asked such personal questions?

"It's not your fault," Daisy said.

"What?"

"I can tell from the look on your face that you think his mood shift was your fault. It's not."

"I shouldn't have offered my unsolicited opinion."

"It's…kind of good to actually talk about stuff." Daisy picked the edges of her bread off. It wasn't that she didn't like it because Ivy had seen her eat some a few minutes ago. It was a fidget as memories likely washed over her.

Ivy reached over and took one of Daisy's hands in hers but didn't say anything. It was silent support, telling Daisy she didn't have to say anything but that if she wanted to, Ivy would listen.

Daisy looked toward the front door of the building, as if checking whether her brother was within earshot.

"He's always so busy working, taking care of me and Mom. He's carrying the load of five people, two of them who aren't here anymore."

Ivy realized that Austin wasn't the only one carrying more than their share. From what she'd seen of the siblings, Daisy never complained. She seemed to keep everything inside. Was it so she didn't add to her brother's worries?

"You probably have figured this out already, but Mom was paralyzed in the accident that…" She trailed off, obviously finding it difficult to say the words. "My dad didn't make it."

"I'm so sorry, Daisy. No one should have to go through what you have. What your mother has. I can't imagine."

To lose not only one husband but two seemed cruel enough, but to be paralyzed as well was just too much. It was no wonder she suffered from at least some level of depression. Honestly, it would be more surprising if she didn't.

"She tries, I know she does, but she seems to just want to be alone a lot."

Ivy thought about how she'd hidden in her apartment eating seemingly endless amounts of junk food and ice cream after James's betrayal had been revealed. She'd felt dreadful and didn't want to see anyone or anyone to see her. How much worse must it be for Mrs. Chapman? At least that was what she assumed Daisy's mom went by, that she had taken her second husband's name.

"Do you think your mom will come with you two the next time you come to work?"

Daisy shrugged, her sandwich now totally abandoned. "I don't know, but I'll try."

"No pressure." Ivy considered if she should say anything else or let things be.

"Do you really think forcing her out of the house will help?"

Ivy didn't want to make a misstep that would hurt Daisy, Austin or their mother. But her gut instincts told her that the answer to Daisy's question was yes.

"At the very least, I don't think it will hurt."

Her instincts had failed her before, so she prayed that they didn't again. If they did, this time she wouldn't be the only person to get hurt.

AUSTIN'S NERVES VIBRATED just below the surface all the way into town two days later, afraid that at any moment his mom would change her mind and ask him to turn around and take her home. He could tell that Daisy's thoughts were running along the same lines. Instead of reading a book this morning, she kept chattering away about Ivy, the building, the coins, funny things that Rich or Isaac had said.

"Ivy certainly sounds like she has a lot of big plans," his mother said.

Austin could tell from her tone that she wasn't sure all

those lofty plans would materialize. He understood that line of thinking because he'd felt the same not that long ago, but gradually he'd started to believe that Ivy could accomplish anything. He still caught glimpses of sadness in her, and he guessed they had something to do with why she'd moved to Jade Valley. But they never lingered long as she thought of some new thing she wanted to add to her future store, as she stopped work to chat with any local resident who walked through the front door curious about the building's renovation and its new owner, as she laughed at Rich's recounting of a recent disastrous date he'd gone on.

During that last one, however, he'd noticed that her laughter wasn't as bright and full as usual. It led him to believe even more that whatever had driven her to Wyoming had indeed been romantic disappointment. He'd caught himself gripping his hammer more tightly as he worked on a simpler wooden ramp to give access to the back door of the building. He didn't like the idea of her being hurt. He knew what it felt like and wouldn't wish it on anyone.

Maybe she'd been the one to end things though, and her clean break had included a change in venue and career.

"She does," he said, bringing himself back to the present and what his mother had said. "She's a hard worker, so I won't be surprised if she accomplishes everything she sets out to do."

"I thought you said she probably wouldn't last."

He hadn't remembered saying that in front of her, but evidently he had.

"That's what I figured at first. But no matter how many things that Isaac, Rich and I have found that have to be fixed or replaced, she's asked about the best combination of quality, safety and price then let us do our work. Early on I suspected the next bump in the road would send her back to Kentucky, but she's still here."

Granted, finding two really valuable coins helped her financial outlook, if she could find a buyer. He hoped she could off-load those coins soon because he worried about her walking around with them—either that she would lose them or, unrealistically, that someone would figure out she had them and take them from her by force. He didn't even like the idea of her taking them to a coin shop by herself.

When they reached Ivy's, she was already outside power washing the exterior of the building now that he'd completed the exterior painting of the window frames and doors.

"Looks like she's an early riser," his mom said, a hint of respect in her voice.

"She said that she's lived in the Eastern Time Zone her entire life, so her body is still operating two hours ahead of the time here," Daisy said.

Ivy noticed them and turned off the sprayer.

"Welcome," she said to his mom as she approached the truck. "I hope you like doughnuts. I might have gone a little overboard at the bakery this morning."

"You didn't have to do that," Austin said.

"Does anyone ever *have* to buy doughnuts?"

He smiled a little at that. "No, I guess not."

"I've been known to enjoy a doughnut now and then," his mom said, surprising him with the slight lilt of amusement in her voice. "Especially if there's jelly filling involved."

"Then you're in luck," Ivy said as she led the way to the front of the building.

Austin pushed his mom's wheelchair up the newly constructed ramp and into the building.

"It still obviously needs a lot of work," Ivy said as she

gestured at their surroundings. "But at least it doesn't look like a dust storm just blew through anymore. And I've finally stopped sneezing."

Austin watched as his mom looked up at the ceiling, at every corner of the room.

"I haven't been inside here in probably twenty years. It was a used bookstore then, but that only lasted maybe six months."

"Sounds like this building has housed a lot of different businesses over the years."

"Yeah, always been one of those places where nothing lasts long."

Austin winced. Even though his mom didn't mean any offense, he hoped Ivy didn't take the comment as such.

"Well, I intend to end that trend."

His mom looked at Ivy, as if trying to read whether she really meant those words. He thought he saw Ivy fidget a bit under his mom's gaze.

"I hope you do," his mom finally said.

It said a lot about the dark place his mom had been since the accident that a simple comment like that, or the fact that she seemed to enjoy her powdered doughnut filled with raspberry jelly, brought him hope that she might be turning the corner.

"Are there any left for me?" Isaac asked as he stepped in the door a few minutes later.

"There's plenty for everyone," Ivy said, also pouring him a cup of coffee from her pump thermos.

Isaac took a cruller and pulled up an overturned five-gallon bucket to sit next to Austin's mom. "Good to see you, Melissa."

Austin hated that the two of them were in the same boat now, widowed and still grieving. At least his mom had him and Daisy at home. Isaac had to live in his house alone. Austin made a mental note to invite him over for dinner sometime soon. Maybe he could barbecue. It had been quite a while since he'd fired up the grill.

Daisy looked over at him and pointed at the box of doughnuts at the same time she wiped chocolate icing away from the edge of her mouth. She looked so much like she had as a little girl that he couldn't help but smile.

"You're not allowed to watch your figure if the rest of us are tossing ours to the wind for today," Ivy said.

His skin heated at her mentioning his figure, and he tried not to think about hers even though he'd definitely noticed it. Wanting to hurry and banish those types of thoughts, he practically inhaled his plain glazed doughnut then got to work applying grout to the places in the brick walls that had chipped away with time. He'd asked Ivy if she wanted the walls painted, but she said she liked the look of the bare, authentic brick.

"Covering it is like pretending the past didn't happen," she'd said.

There were times he wished the past hadn't happened, but that wasn't how the march of time worked. You had to make your way through the bad along with the good.

If only there hadn't been so much bad.

As he worked, he caught pieces of the conversation between Ivy, Daisy, his mom and Isaac. Even though his mom was the quietest, she did occasionally offer her thoughts on what items would sell best in the store, her memories of the Stinson Building and all the businesses she could remember being housed in it.

When he took a break to get a drink of water, Ivy came up to him, wrapped her hand around his upper arm and propelled him outside.

"What's wrong?" he asked once they were down the steps and around the edge of the building.

"What's wrong is that you are watching your mother like a hawk. She's not a child about to toddle into an open fireplace."

"Excuse me?"

Ivy looked toward the open windows before speaking again, her voice lowered. "You're hovering. I know she's your mom and you're worried about her—I totally get that. And I'm sorry, yet again, if I'm overstepping. But I think maybe you are too overprotective, and maybe you should work outside for a while."

Austin almost told Ivy that, yes, she was overstepping, that he knew how to take care of his mother. But something stopped him. Had he really been taking good care of his mom? Yes, he worked hard to provide for their family. He drove her to doctor appointments. Did all the things she no longer could around the ranch. But none of that had seemed to help bring her out of the depression that she sometimes tried to hide, tried to deny, but sometimes couldn't. Maybe he wasn't equipped with what it took to help his mom heal emotionally.

Unlike himself, he felt the urge to cry wash over him.

"Austin?" The concern in Ivy's voice caused his irritation at her to evaporate.

"Maybe you're right."

Ivy surprised him further by taking his hands in hers. "Look at me."

He exhaled then complied. The compassion he saw in her eyes moved something inside him, something that he was afraid to even attempt to name.

"I haven't known you long, but it's obvious you love your mother and Daisy. And that you'd do anything for them. But sometimes that leads to doing too much of one thing and not enough of another. That's not a criticism. It's just a fact of how humans operate." She hesitated, looked down at their joined hands as if them touching was nothing out of the ordinary. Maybe to her it wasn't, was just something she did when she was trying to be helpful.

He wanted to ask her if she was giving this advice because of personal experience, but he reminded himself that some things were private and should stay that way unless the affected party chose to share the details. He certainly didn't want to go around admitting that his wife had left him, that she'd forced him to make an impossible choice that had led to her leaving.

Austin didn't know what to say so just nodded. Then, wanting to rid himself of the twitchy feeling having her hold his hands caused, he retrieved them and turned toward the water sprayer.

"If you close the windows when you go inside, I'll take care of the sections you haven't washed yet."

He still hadn't moved when Ivy appeared at the window to close it. He looked up at her, and she gave him a reassuring smile before pushing the windows closed. As he set to spraying the dirt and debris of time off the exterior of the building, he couldn't get the sight of that smile or the feel of Ivy's small hands out of his mind.

CHAPTER SEVEN

IVY SAT DOWN beside Austin and Daisy's mom, who had told her to call her Melissa, and stared at the large space on the wall between the two sets of windows.

"I keep trying to think of something to eventually put there that would be eye-catching but fit the theme of the store," Ivy said. "I thought about a quilt, but that seems too obvious."

"Maybe a painting? Eileen Parker at the art gallery could probably put you in touch with someone. I heard that Maya Pine's husband is a painter. Maya runs the local news site since we don't have a newspaper anymore."

"Hmm, maybe." Ivy tilted her head sideways. "It would be cool to have something crafty, but I'm afraid that's not where my talent lies."

"I don't know. You seem to have a lot of ideas about how you want this place to look."

"I do, but you'll notice none of it involves me and a glue gun. I'd probably glue my fingers together."

There it was—a hint of a smile. Even though she was only getting to know Melissa, it felt monumental, like the sun peeking out from behind the clouds after two weeks of endless rain and flooding.

"Have you always liked old buildings?" Melissa asked.

"I have. I remember going to places like Fort Boonesborough, the Mary Todd Lincoln House and Federal Hill, which is better known as My Old Kentucky Home. That's the name of the song they sing before the Kentucky Derby."

"I guess you grew up around different types of horses than we have here."

"There are lots of Thoroughbred farms, true, but they weren't really part of my world."

"Rich people horses."

"Exactly."

They chatted some more about Ivy's growing-up years in Lexington, her time at the University of Kentucky, how her roommate had helped her land the job with the hotel chain after college.

"Daisy has talked a lot about the places that were turned into hotels. It sounds…interesting."

Ivy got the feeling Melissa hesitated on that last word because it surprised her. Maybe she hadn't been interested in anything for quite a while.

"I like seeing forgotten things given new life. Jade Valley reminds me a lot of some of the old downtown areas that have been refurbished and rejuvenated with new businesses. So many downtowns have died because of bypasses and box stores. I understand that times have changed, but just because something is old or has outlived its original use doesn't mean it should be abandoned."

Ivy considered her next words carefully, wanting to be subtle enough that it wasn't obvious what she was doing but not so subtle that the message she intended would be missed altogether.

"I guess life is like that too. My mom didn't know what to do with herself when my dad left. It was a kind of out-of-the-blue thing. But my grandma Cecile was a 'pick yourself up and dust yourself off' sort and gave Mom a bit of a kick in the pants. Grandma gave her the money to buy the florist business where she worked when the owner wanted to retire. She and my sister Holly still run it. I didn't figure out until I was an adult that Grandma had given Mom the money she'd saved for years to open a quilt shop." Ivy felt suddenly teary recounting the story, but she blinked several times to clear her vision. "That's why I'm going to make this shop work, to fulfill the dream she was never able to."

"That's a good way to honor her."

Figuring she'd said enough that she hoped would help Melissa, Ivy shifted the conversation a bit.

"I wish I had her creativeness though." She kicked the box of buttons that sat next to her foot. "Like she would know what to do with all these buttons. I can't stand the idea of throwing them away, but none of them match. I thought maybe displaying them in canning jars." She looked over at Melissa. "If you happen to get any ideas, I'm all ears."

Daisy returned from her trip to Little Italy to pick up the pizzas Ivy had ordered for lunch.

"Oh good, I'm starving," Isaac said as he appeared at the bottom of the stairs.

"Are you part bloodhound?" Ivy asked.

Beside her, Melissa actually huffed out a little laugh. Ivy noticed Daisy's shocked expression, one she quickly hid. The girl was easy to read. It was obvious that it had been a long time since she'd heard her mother laugh, but she'd hidden her shock so Melissa wouldn't realize that she'd just taken a big step in her healing process. Ivy wished Austin could have witnessed it. Maybe if he had, it would help lift some of the burden he so obviously bore.

Even though he surely had seen Daisy arrive with the pizzas, Austin didn't come inside. Did he honestly think she'd banished him even from lunch? Before she could get up to tell him to come inside, however, Isaac went to the window, opened it and yelled, "Get in here and eat, boy."

Ivy pressed her lips together to keep from laughing at the idea that Austin was a boy. Anyone with any sense could see he was a full-grown man and a handsome one at that. Chances were he'd meet an equally attractive woman at some point, get married and have at least a couple cute kids who would grow up on a ranch under the wide Wyoming sky, learning a strong work ethic from their father.

An uncomfortable tightness in her chest had her standing. She needed to be alone long enough to get rid of that feeling she knew all too well now. It visited her in the middle of the night as she lay in her sleeping bag, listening to the still surprising silence of the world around her. It caught her unaware when she saw a couple walking down Main Street hand in hand or when a customer in Trudy's was accompanied by an adorable baby.

She'd come to think of the tight feeling as the two Ls— loneliness and loss. Even though she was surrounded by people all day, every day, could even laugh and look forward, at night the reality of what had happened and the fact that she was really alone in her new journey would hit her full force. During the day she could mostly keep it at bay, but at night the truth would not be denied. Despite her determination to move past it and telling herself that James was not worth her tears, they sometimes came anyway. And now they threatened again.

"I'll be right back." She hurried up the stairs and walked straight to the windows at the front of the building. When she was feeling down, sometimes the incredible view of the mountains helped to lift her mood. She'd stare at them, marvel at the forces that made them, take deep breaths, and the tight knot in her chest would gradually ease.

This, however, was the first time the feeling had been this strong when she was around others. Did that mean that instead of getting past the pain of James's betrayal, it was getting worse? She'd thought she was doing remark-ably well in her first days in Jade Valley, but maybe it had been a temporary reprieve. Had running away from Kentucky been avoidance instead of a positive step in her own healing?

Who was she to try to guide others on a healing path when her own grief was so fresh?

No. You helped others even when you were hurting.

Maybe through helping others heal, she'd end up heal-ing herself. And if not, she'd still put some good out there into the world. Grandma Cecile had always told her that people should do something good every day, whether that was something as huge as hiding Jews from the Nazis in their attic or as simple as holding a door open for some-one at the store.

"Even if all you can do is smile at someone, you never know if that might be the thing that gets them through their tough day," she'd said.

Ivy had taken that mindset to heart. Some days were just more difficult than others. When she'd been struggling so much with an economics class in college that she'd been on the verge of tears all semester. When someone had sto-len her little car out of her apartment's parking lot and it had been found across the river in Indiana stripped to use-lessness. Definitely when her father had decided to leave.

And that moment in that hotel ballroom when it had be-come obvious that James was not the man she had thought him to be. That he did not love her like he had claimed.

Ivy deliberately thought of Grandma Cecile and how strong of a woman she'd been. She actually smiled when she thought of what her tiny grandma would have likely done to James if she'd been the one in Ivy's position. In-stead of running away, she imagined her grandmother climbing onto the top of one of those gorgeously appointed tables and announcing to everyone present that the engagement was off because James was a liar and a cheat, but that everyone should go ahead and drink and eat because James was footing the bill. Then she would have descended from the tabletop and kicked James in a certain place with such force that it would remain a memory for the rest of his days. Only then would she have turned and left the ballroom.

Grandma Cecile had been much cooler than Ivy.

Ivy realized she was sitting somewhere in between Grandma Cecile and Melissa—sad about what might have been, what she'd lost, and determined to not let it control her and keep her pressed down with that sadness.

She took a long, deep breath as she stared at one of the snowcapped mountains then let it out just as slowly. Determined to make the rest of the day positive, she turned and followed the smell of bread, pepperoni and sausage.

By the end of the day, her blue moment from earlier had drifted away like the puffy white pappus of a dandelion. Instead of dwelling on what might have been when she settled in for the night, she pulled out her phone and went to her favorite fabric site. She scrolled through the newest designs and bookmarked some really beautiful ones. A striking blue that reminded her of home caught her eye. When she magnified the design, she almost laughed because they were cute little dandelion puffs like the ones she'd just pictured in her mind. It felt like a sign that she was meant to have this fabric as a symbol of letting the past go. She wouldn't order it for quilts but rather for a dress to wear to the grand opening of the store.

Fearing it might be sold out before then, she went ahead and placed an order. That gave her another thought, and she searched for the perfect fabric to make Daisy a dress too. It didn't take long to find one that had compasses and maps, great for a girl who loved geography and wanted to travel the world.

Her shopping done for the night, she set her phone aside and curled into the sleeping bag. Not even a minute passed before a sound had her sitting up and her ears straining. When she realized it was someone trying to open the front door, her heart started hammering. She scurried out of the sleeping bag and crossed to the window. It was too dark to see much, but someone was definitely on her front stoop. She heard voices though she couldn't make out the words.

With her hands shaking so much that she almost dropped her phone, she called 911.

The good thing about living in a small town was that when you called 911, it didn't take the police long to arrive. But whoever had been trying to break in must have seen the patrol vehicle before she did because two figures went racing down the street. In the next moment, the night came alive with a siren and the bar lights atop the sheriff's department SUV. Whoever had responded to her call hit the accelerator and rocketed down the street after the prowlers.

Ivy turned on the light and looked around for anything she could use as a weapon. Her gaze landed on a length of pipe that Isaac had removed from the upstairs bathroom. She grabbed it and held it at the ready as she descended the stairs and flicked on the overhead lights to the main level.

Everything looked as it had when she went to bed. With her heart still thumping like a chased rabbit's, she crossed to the front door. She relaxed a fraction when she found it both still locked and the windows intact. Even so, she knew there was no way she was going to be able to sleep now.

She thought of the valuable coins upstairs and how she really needed to make plans to get rid of them.

Trying to get her nerves to calm down, she paced the floor that was due to receive the first coating of new polyurethane tomorrow. She glanced at the old wood and glass display cases that she'd cleaned and that Austin and Rich had pushed up against the wall after Rich had finished the last of his electrical work and declared her wiring updated and safe. She'd still have to pass an inspection, but she had confidence in Rich's work. What Austin had said about Rich being the absolute best electrician in the area, possibly the state, she now believed.

Thus why he was in high demand. He had a dozen jobs come his way while he was working on her building.

Isaac had just put the finishing touches on the upstairs bathroom too, and had moved on to finishing the downstairs bathroom.

Suddenly the idea of living alone in the building made her doubt the sanity of the move again.

The sound of a vehicle outside propelled her to the front window. She watched as an officer got out of his vehicle and approached her front door. She opened it before he even had to knock.

"Good evening, ma'am," the deputy said. A glance at his nameplate revealed his identity as J. Langston. "Can you tell me exactly what happened?"

She gave him the short rundown of events. "I take it this means you didn't catch them."

"No, ma'am. I'm going to sit outside for a while unless I get another call. If I have to leave, don't hesitate to call 911 again if they come back."

Despite her telling him that the door had still been locked, he requested to do a thorough search inside to make sure. Once he was satisfied that no one else was inside, he retreated to his vehicle. Even though she knew he was outside now, keeping an eye on her property, she still stayed up and made a list of the things she wanted to look for at the community rummage sale that weekend. She'd heard the proceeds were going to help fund various projects—the repainting of the Welcome to Jade Valley signs on both ends of town, stocking and running the local food bank, and a fund that helped pay the expenses of residents who had to go to Casper and Cheyenne for specialized medical care such as cancer treatments.

If she didn't forge ahead with her plans, the little voice in her head that liked to whisper that she'd made another mistake might grow louder. If she didn't continue working to make this building not only her business but also her home, she risked having the fear she'd experienced at the sound of someone trying to break in eclipse the joy she felt with each step made toward opening the store.

As the night dragged on, she shifted from planning for her living space to reading about all the legalities and tax filing requirements for the State of Wyoming. The latter was what finally started making her drowsy. She leaned back in the chair and focused on the splotchy ceiling that Austin would be painting soon. She loved the texture of the tin tiles, but since she was keeping the dark brick walls she wanted the ceiling to be what reflected the light from the windows. Customers were more likely to browse and buy in a bright, airy store than one that felt dark and gloomy.

She looked around the room, taking in everything Austin had done so far. Even though they had a good ways to go, it already looked like a completely different space. To be honest, part of her dreaded the day when all the work was done and Austin would no longer be a fixture in her life. And she had to admit that it was at least partially because he was so attractive. That admission had surprised her when she first realized the truth of it. Fresh off James's betrayal, she wasn't looking for someone to replace him. But like candy helped cover the bitter taste of medicine, eye candy helped ease the bitter pain of betrayal.

It was more than that though. Yes, Austin was handsome, seemed more so every day if she was being honest, but who he was as a person was also attractive. Ivy wanted to know more about him, but she was careful in what she asked—of him, Daisy or his mother. She didn't want any of them getting the wrong idea.

Getting to know all the layers of Austin felt like waiting for water and wind to erode away a rock. But maybe somewhere inside that rock was the surprise of an amethyst geode.

Ivy shook her head at her fanciful thinking. It was a sign her brain was overtired and needed rest, and there was no sleeping in tomorrow.

She dragged herself up out of the chair and went to glance out the window. Deputy Langston was still sitting outside, so she felt safe enough to turn out the light and head back upstairs. Once again she crawled into her sleeping bag, but despite her fatigue it still took a long time for the tension in her body to relax. She noticed every little sound, strained to hear if Deputy Langston drove away.

Ivy exhaled in frustration as she stared at the top of her tent. She forced herself to close her eyes and think of things that had nothing to do with prowlers. The types of treats she'd have at the grand opening of the store. How her mother had texted her to share a story of a ninety-seven-year-old man who had come into the floral shop to buy a dozen pink roses for his ninety-five-year-old wife for their seventieth anniversary. The fact that she'd given the stray cat the name Sprinkles and each day he seemed to become a bit more used to her and move a little closer.

Her thoughts started drifting as sleep inched up on her. An image of Austin, laughing at something Rich had said, made her smile. What a nice image to see before finally slipping into dreamland.

AUSTIN MADE IT a point to not watch his mom too closely when she came with him and Daisy, but even so he was seeing evidence that Ivy had been right about getting her out of the house. His mom chatted with locals who came by to meet Ivy—Sunny Wheeler, who was excited by the idea of having the quilt shop open in time for the fall festival; Maya Pine, who interviewed Ivy for the local news site about her plans; even Sheriff Angie Lee, who had chatted briefly with Ivy outside.

He overheard his mom sharing more details about all the businesses she could remember occupying the Stinson Building. He'd been startled to learn that she and his father had shared their first kiss out behind the building when they were supposed to be at the library studying for an English exam.

"Mom!"

"What?" she'd asked as she looked at him. "It's a perfectly normal thing for teenagers to do. As long as they don't go too far." This last bit she said with her gaze fixed on Daisy.

"Don't look at me," Daisy said. "There are exactly zero boys here I'm interested in."

Even though he thought Daisy a bit too young to date yet, let alone kiss anyone, her answer also made him a bit sad. Daisy would probably meet someone and fall in love during one of her future far-flung travels and make it less likely she'd ever live in Jade Valley after she graduated and went off to college. He wouldn't hold her back, wouldn't trap her somewhere she couldn't achieve her dreams, but it would still make him sad.

He placed the paint roller he'd been using on the ceiling back in the pan and rubbed his neck. A glance down revealed his mother was at the front door staring outside at something. Needing a break from having all the blood drain from his arm as he painted above his head, he descended the ladder to see what had drawn her attention. Ivy was at work and Daisy was at the library looking up old documents about the Stinson Building, so it wasn't either of them. And the last time he'd looked down, his mom had been sorting buttons into jars by color.

"What's so interesting out here?" he asked as he approached her.

She pointed toward the pile of junk he would be hauling off soon.

"Can you cut that piece of plywood into a square that will fit between those windows?" She pointed at the wall space between the two sets of windows on the left side of the building.

"Sure. What are you planning?" He thought about how Daisy had mentioned that their mother was artistic and crafty. Was she actually going to put that to use?

"Maybe nothing. Maybe something."

He latched on to that "maybe something" and retrieved the piece of thick plywood, cut it to her specifications and then gave it two coats of the white paint he was using on the ceiling.

"It should be dry by tomorrow." Even though Daisy and his mom didn't typically come to work with him every day, he wasn't going to remind her of that. If bringing his mom with him every day helped her become more like her old self, he would lift her and her wheelchair in and out of the truck however many times it took.

When Daisy returned from the library, she pulled him aside.

"I know why the sheriff came by earlier. Someone tried to break in here last night."

"What?" Fear shot through him, even though he knew Ivy was safe. "Where did you hear that?"

"At the library. Someone saw a sheriff's department vehicle sitting outside late last night, with all the lights in the building on. Well, you know how nothing is a secret in this town other than why Trudy and Alma don't like each other."

He knew he didn't like Ivy staying here alone. It would be the same for any woman living alone, he told himself.

Only that wasn't exactly true, was it? He didn't worry about Trudy all the time. Or Mrs. Miller, his former English teacher, whose husband was a patient in the nursing home. There were likely dozens of people who lived alone all over the county, ones who were even more in danger of a home invasion than someone who lived only four blocks away from the sheriff's department.

He tried not to assign too much meaning to his concern but wasn't entirely successful.

When Ivy returned from her shift at Trudy's, one look told him she didn't get enough rest the night before. She should probably go take a nap, but he knew her well enough by now to know she wouldn't.

He waited until she went outside to get something out of her car to ask her about what had happened the night before.

"How did you know…? Never mind, small town. Everything is fine. Sheriff Lee told me they caught the kids, two teenagers, not even from here. They'd evidently vandalized some older buildings in the next county over as part of some online trend. Unlucky for them, one of those buildings is owned by a big shot attorney in Portland who isn't inclined to go easy on them. With all the evidence they posted themselves, I think they are toast."

"Still, it could happen again. Aren't you scared here alone?"

"I won't lie and say I slept well after what happened, but I don't think Jade Valley has crime run amok."

He wanted to tell her to...he wasn't even sure what. Telling her to abandon her new home was a bridge too far. An alarm system maybe? He glanced toward the open front door and straight back through the first floor to the bottom of the stairs.

"I can enclose the top of the stairs with a wall and a door you can lock instead of your living space just being open to the bottom floor. It'd be an extra layer of protection."

Austin expected her to shoot down the idea, but she appeared to be considering it.

"I actually like that idea, even without the security concerns. Keep my work and home space more separate."

"Maybe you should get a safety-deposit box at the bank for the coins."

"I've already got an appointment to take them to a dealer in Cheyenne."

"I'll go with you."

She looked up at him. "Actually, I would appreciate that. It didn't bother me to drive cross-country, but having something worth that much with me makes me nervous. I'll pay for your time, of course."

"No, it's not work."

"I'm not going to take away from your work hours and not pay you."

"Fine." He wasn't going to accept pay for ensuring her safety, but she didn't have to know that until the trip was over. And he wasn't going to assign more meaning to his offer than was there.

"When is your appointment?"

"Not until next Monday, so plenty of time to finish that ceiling." Ivy smiled widely, and he found himself smiling back. It seemed the longer he was around her, the easier it was to smile. But, again, he told himself there were no romantic thoughts attached to that realization. She had that effect on everyone. Isaac and Rich had laughed at something she said on numerous occasions. Daisy seemed to come out of her introverted shell and shine brightly when around Ivy. It made him wonder if she was content with a brother who was so much older than she was, or if she had longed for a sister.

And then there was his mom. She was beginning to show an interest in life again beyond simply getting from one day to the next.

"What's that for?" Ivy asked as she pointed toward the piece of plywood he'd painted.

"I don't know. Mom seems to have something in mind. She wanted it cut to fit between the two sets of windows on the left wall."

"Oh. We were talking about what I should hang there. To be honest, I was hoping it might spark something in her. Daisy saying that your mom was crafty and artistic made me think it was worth a try."

"Why do you do that?"

Ivy looked up at him with a confused expression. "What?"

"You seem to try so hard to help everyone around you, people you barely even know."

"Don't you think there should be more of that in the world?"

"Well, yeah, probably."

"Both my grandma Cecile and my mom have always said that there are plenty of people in the world who don't care about others, but there can never be too many who do."

"And you've taken that to heart."

"I have. Also, it works wonders when you feel awful yourself."

"Do you feel awful?"

"Not in this moment, no."

Which seemed to say that at some point she had, and perhaps recently. Maybe it was even what drove her to Wyoming.

"Thank you," he said, nodding toward the building where his mom and sister had their heads bent over some task. "For caring about them."

"It's not just them, you know."

His heart gave an extra *ba-bump* against his rib cage, and he had to remind it that he was single and going to stay that way. Even so, he didn't know how to respond.

"Everyone has been kind to me, welcoming me to town, offering to help in any way they can," Ivy said.

Of course she meant the citizens of Jade Valley as a whole. He'd heard how nice she was and how well she fit into the community from Trudy to Maya Pine to the old guys who sat on the town square after they'd had their breakfast at Trudy's or Alma's each morning.

"She's a cute little thing," one of the men had said when a gaggle of them had wandered down to check out what was going on at the Stinson Building one morning.

"I bet someone snaps her up within a month," another had added.

"She's not a prize to be won," Austin had said, which had earned him a round of laughs and elbowing between the old guys, as if they were privy to information he was simply too young to know.

He'd managed to resist saying what he thought— that they were living in the past. No wonder their wives

kicked them out of the house each morning. They probably had to in order to have some peace and quiet or get
something done without their husbands underfoot. He
imagined the wives calling each other and saying in ex-
asperation, "You'll never guess what that old fool said
this morning."

The retirees were good people, would help anyone who
needed it, but they could benefit from some updating of
their views on women and relationships. If anyone ever
talked about Daisy that way in front of him, he'd drag
the guy by the ear to the river and toss him in for a nice,
cold swim.

"Do you think we can find a door that fits with the
age of the building?" Ivy asked, yanking him out of his
thoughts and back to the earlier part of their conversation.

"You're going to the rummage sale this weekend, right?"

She nodded.

"There's always the unexpected there, so I'd check there
first. If not, then we can check Fizzy's place."

"Fizzy?"

"He owns a junk and salvage place several miles outside of town. I've heard from Daisy that it would take days
to finish visiting the Smithsonian. Well, Fizzy's is kind of
like that. I wouldn't be surprised if there's a portal to another world in there somewhere."

Ivy laughed. "Well, this I've gotta see."

Why did Austin suddenly want to take her on a tour of
the bizarre landscape of Fizzy's, where seeing a Japanese
lantern, a chain saw carving of Bigfoot and a ten-foot-tall
pile of cigar boxes while standing in one spot wouldn't be
unheard-of?

Because she made him feel lighter inside. Like when

he was talking to and laughing with her he could set aside his burdens and simply enjoy life.

He suddenly dreaded when this renovation job would come to an end, and not just for monetary reasons.

CHAPTER EIGHT

THROUGHOUT HER LIFE, Ivy had been to yard sales, garage sales, estate sales and more than a few thrift stores. None of those compared to the Jade Valley Rummage Sale. Covering the yard of the Methodist church and the adjacent field, the offerings were a combination of items cleaned out of people's closets and garages, actual antiques, and a junker's paradise.

"Is Fizzy here?"

Austin actually laughed at her question. "That would require Fizzy to make more effort than he's accustomed to making. He's more of a 'stack it high and they will come' sort."

Even without Fizzy's contribution, Ivy was certain she would end the day with a lot of furnishings for her new home.

She was also probably going to be, as her grandma Cecile used to say, "fuller than a tick on a dog." Because the air was filled with the scents of grilling meat and deep-fried dough. Her mouth watered at the sight of fresh-squeezed lemonade being sold by the high school basketball team and a large variety of cookies made by the local garden club.

"This is like a yard sale on steroids meets the county fair," she said.

"Melissa!" one of the garden club ladies called out, all smiles and waves as she spotted Austin's mom.

Melissa had said she could stay back at Ivy's place, working on whatever she had up her sleeve for the wall, but Ivy had said, "I think the whole town turned out and we've all been working hard, so today we should go have some fun."

Ivy used her best "pretty please" face, and Melissa smiled and relented. After Melissa indicated it was okay for Ivy to take the handles of her wheelchair, Ivy called back for Austin and Daisy to lock up on their way out.

"It's so good to see you," the thin woman with hair dyed bright red said as she came out from behind the cookie table.

"You too, Suzanne."

Ivy was glad to see that despite her initial hesitance to come, Melissa seemed more open and willing to chat than when she'd first met her.

"Do you want to go around with us or stay to visit with your friends?" Ivy asked.

"You all go on." That she didn't appear to be saying that because she thought it was a burden for her to accompany them was another step in the right direction.

Ivy and Austin had only managed to get as far as the funnel cake truck before Daisy ran into her friend Candace and they were off as well.

"Looks like you're stuck with just me," Austin said.

"Oh, the horror," she said, with a dramatic back of her hand to her forehead.

Austin snorted at her display.

The truth was she didn't mind walking along the rows of offerings beside him, sharing fried dough covered in powdered sugar. She considered him a friend now, though there were no "Hey, let's be friends" statements like when you were a kid. As she'd tried to go to sleep the night before, her thoughts had kept drifting to him and how concerned he'd been about her safety following the attempted break-in. After how things had ended with James, it was nice to be around a guy who seemed as genuine as the first day of summer was long.

But she'd thought James was a stand-up and honest guy too, hadn't she?

She shoved thoughts of James aside, determined to enjoy this day and find the perfect items for her new home.

As if she'd summoned it, she spotted a metal bed frame two rows over. She practically leaped over people to get to it, trusting Austin to follow. By the time she reached the seller, however, she'd remembered to wear an only slightly interested expression.

"How much for this bed frame?" she asked.

When the man quoted a price, she winced. Not because it was a terrible price but because she knew it could be better. As she went back and forth with the guy, Austin stood beside her, saying nothing. Only when the owner of the bed frame stepped away to aid another customer did Austin lean close and say, "You do remember this is a charity event, right?"

For a moment his words didn't register, only the shivers that ran over her entire body at the sound of his lowered voice so close to her ear.

"I...yeah, I know."

The combination of his reminder of how the funds were going to be used and the need to move on had her agreeing on a price if the owner threw in a stained-glass lamp. The deal was struck, money paid and Ivy's name affixed to the items for later pickup.

She told herself that allowing such feelings for Austin to find a place to settle within her so soon after the end of her engagement was a very bad idea. This new life of hers was supposed to be forged alone.

When Austin was recruited to help a couple other guys load up a truck with heavy furniture, Ivy watched the shape of his biceps as he lifted. She caught herself smiling and shook her head, turning away to continue shopping.

"It's good to see Austin with someone again," a woman she didn't recognize said. She patted Ivy on the shoulder in the way of kindhearted strangers before moving along.

Ivy wanted to call her back and tell her that she and Austin were friends, nothing more, but it was too late. The middle-aged woman was swallowed by the increasing crowd. Ivy hoped erroneous rumors didn't start circulating. It was a widely known truth that gossip was the fuel on which small towns ran.

But as she moved from booth to booth, purchasing the items that would make her living space more like a home, she kept wondering about the person in Austin's past. She did her best to push away those thoughts and why she might be fixating on them by handing over money for some pretty teal curtains with rustic white rods, a couple of handmade quilts, an antique chest of drawers that matched the curtains remarkably well, a shower curtain with happy faces all over it, a folding chalkboard sign to use outside the store once it was open, and various other odds and ends.

Figuring she'd done enough shopping for the time being, she purchased a cold lemonade and went to sit on a circular bench that had been built around the base of an oak tree next to the church. That's where Trudy found her and parked herself next to her.

"I'm not used to seeing you outside of the café," Ivy said.

"I never miss this sale. Josephine can handle the kitchen just fine."

Josephine was a sweet woman who was even shorter than Ivy's five foot three. She'd come to the US twenty years ago from Mexico to do migrant farm work and had finally earned her US citizenship five years ago. And she made a marbled tres leches cake that was quite possibly the best dessert Ivy had ever tasted, not that she would say that in front of Trudy, who had quite the fine hand with desserts herself.

"One year I found a plate to replace one in a set I'd inherited from my mother," Trudy said. "I'd had that dinnerware set, minus the one broken plate, for thirty years. A couple of years ago, I was the first one to arrive and I got basically a new TV, a huge one, for ten dollars. Now I can pop some popcorn, sit in my recliner and feel like I'm at the movie theater."

Ivy laughed at that mental image. "I might be a little jealous."

"Since you're sitting down, I assume you've done a fair amount of shopping already."

"Enough that I hope I get good tips next week." And the potential buyer for the two valuable coins actually came through. She'd been careful not to sound desperate to get rid of them when talking to the dealer. When he'd said he thought he knew someone who would be interested, she'd told him that she didn't want to make the three-hundred-mile drive unless the buyer was serious, that she could arrange to sell it elsewhere.

She'd witnessed some expert bargaining tactics utilized by Mr. Sterling when he'd been trying to purchase properties to turn into hotels, and she put them to good use from time to time.

Ivy spotted the woman who had made the comment about Austin earlier.

"Who is that lady in the pink top looking at the bakeware?"

Trudy looked where Ivy indicated. "That's Ann Fleming. She's the principal at the elementary school. Why?"

Ivy knew she had to tread carefully, so as not to give Trudy the wrong idea.

"She came up to me and told me it was good to see Austin with someone again, but she moved away before I could correct her assumption."

Trudy made a sound that indicated she'd heard her but was uncharacteristically quiet. Ivy glanced over at her.

"So you don't know he was married before?"

That revelation startled Ivy, but she did her best not to show it. "No. Why would I?"

"I thought the two of you had gotten close."

"We're friends."

There was that "mmm" sound again, and it was enough that Ivy knew she had to reveal a bit about herself.

"I just got out of a long-term relationship, so the last thing I'm looking for is another one." Sure, she'd begun to appreciate the shape of Austin's body, the way her heart felt happy when he smiled, but that didn't mean she wanted to date him. The painful sting from James's betrayal still lingered. You didn't simply jump from an engagement to dating someone new. At least she didn't. The casual dater in her family was Lily.

"That's understandable. But you never know what life has in store for you."

"I hope it has a successful business in store for me."

"Of course. But a happy life isn't made up of just one thing."

"Right now, one thing is all I can handle." Sure, she was making friends, working at Trudy's and gradually getting more involved in the community, but those were not Big Things. Renovating an old building, starting a business with no guarantee it would succeed, rebuilding her life—those *were* Big Things. A romantic relationship fell into that category as well, and that space needed to stay vacant—at least until it wasn't battered and bruised and broken anymore.

Ivy deliberately engaged in conversation with everyone she knew, introduced herself to others, shopped a bit more, and ate a mouthwatering burger and delicious seasoned fries. She caught sight of Austin a few times and motioned that she wasn't ready to leave yet. When she made it back to the table where the ladies were selling the cookies, Melissa wasn't there.

"Austin took her to look around," Melissa's friend Suzanne said. "She said she had something she was looking for. It makes me happy to see her out and about, expressing interest in…anything. She used to be such a vibrant person, always busy doing something."

Even with how much she'd been around Austin, Daisy and Melissa, Ivy didn't know the details of what had happened. She knew it was a car accident that had caused Melissa to lose her second husband and the use of her legs, but that was all.

"She seems to enjoy coming to work with Austin and Daisy."

"I gathered that, though she didn't come right out and say it."

Even though she'd had plenty to eat while at the sale, Ivy still examined the cookie flavors.

"I don't need any of these, but I'm going to buy some anyway."

"Sweetheart, with your figure you could probably eat all these and not gain an ounce," one of the other ladies said.

Ivy laughed. "I assure you that that's not true."

She didn't buy them all, but she did buy two dozen—a variety of chocolate chip, sugar, oatmeal raisin, and cranberry orange. Between her, Austin, Daisy and Melissa, they probably wouldn't last long.

"Are you done shopping?"

Ivy looked over at the sound of Austin's voice and noticed he was alone. "Did you misplace your mom?"

He smiled. "No. She's with Daisy. Mom said she had a couple other places she wanted to go, so off they went."

He motioned toward downtown, and when Ivy looked she could see Daisy pushing her mom down the sidewalk.

"That's a good sign, right?"

He nodded. "I'm almost afraid to hope though. She's had ups and downs before, but it does feel different now."

Ivy hoped for the sake of everyone in his family that he was right.

With her list of purchases in hand so she didn't forget anything, she and Austin began to collect her new furnishings and load them into the bed of his truck. They proved to be a good team, and soon were headed back to her place. When she got out of the truck, she stared at her building. Sometimes it still didn't seem real that it was hers.

"You know, it just hit me we have to haul all this stuff upstairs," she said. "Good thing I bought those cookies. I'm going to need a reward after we're done."

They carried in the lighter items first, then the metal bed frame. When they finally came to the chest of drawers, Ivy groaned.

"You bought it," Austin said, his voice light with laughter.

"Oh, hush."

This caused him to smile fully. Her heart felt as if it had feet that it had just tripped over.

No, she could not let her feelings go down that road. It was too soon. She didn't know him well enough. He was evidently divorced, and there was at least the possibility that the dissolution of his marriage was his fault. He felt like an emotional land mine—one very tall, attractive land mine.

It was likely her feelings were simply a rebound reaction to what she'd gone through with James, some primal but unwanted need to feel as if she was enough—enough that a man didn't have to have two other women on the side, possibly more.

"It's not going to move itself," Austin said, intruding on her thoughts.

"Well, that's just annoying."

They took the five drawers out to make it lighter and easier to hold, leaving them in the bed of the truck. Then they each took an end, Austin the heavier top, and headed across the street. They got it inside and to the foot of the stairs before Ivy said she needed a break. Even without the drawers, the chest was heavier than it looked. It was obviously solid oak with not an inch of plywood to be found.

"Ready?" Austin asked after they'd caught their breath for a few seconds.

She nodded and they picked up their respective ends before heading up the stairs, which creaked slightly under the combined weight of two adults and a heavy piece of furniture that probably dated to the Taft administration.

Ivy's arms strained under the weight as she moved slowly backward, making sure to place her feet with care. Even Austin, who was no doubt used to dealing with cattle, horses and all manner of demanding physical labor on his ranch, grunted as they slowly made their way upward.

"Watch your step," Austin said.

Ivy nodded and made a sound that she'd heard him, but all her attention suddenly fixated on her nose and the powerful need to scratch the itch that had taken up residence there. Distracted, she felt her grip slip a little. On instinct she moved to adjust her hold on the chest, but she released it a bit too much. The next moment seemed to happen in slow motion and in a blur, both at the same time. She grabbed for the falling end of the chest. In the process, her foot turned sideways, slipping off the edge of the step. The weight of the falling chest landed on her fingers. Pain shot up her arm, followed by the feeling of needing to throw up. That had always been her body's response to intense pain—when she'd crashed her bike at age nine and broken her arm, the time in seventh grade when she'd been hit in the head by a spiked volleyball during PE, and when she'd slipped on a patch of ice while hurrying to class her freshman year at UK, which resulted in unintentional splits but luckily no broken bones.

She wasn't that lucky this time.

Austin cried out something, maybe her name or perhaps some other exclamation, but her pain receptors were too busy being overwhelmed for her to make out the actual words.

Miraculously when he set down his end of the chest of drawers, the whole thing didn't go careering back down the stairs. In a blink he was next to her, his eyes wide and his expression full of concern. Ivy was amazed she could even see his face through her tears.

"Can you stand?" he asked.

She tried, but the pain in her ankle joined that of the pulsing in her fingers.

"I need to take you to the hospital," Austin said, then eased her left arm around his strong shoulders and put his right arm around her waist.

Even with him practically carrying her entire weight down the stairs, easing past the still immobile piece of furniture, the pain radiating through her made her stomach heave.

"Bath...room," she said, her voice shaky.

He didn't ask why, simply steered her toward the downstairs bathroom that was thankfully close. Instead of leaving her though, he stayed by her side as she dry heaved a few times then as she splashed water on her face. She made the mistake of putting down her injured foot as she exited the bathroom, and a fresh wave of pain made her cry out.

Austin's arm tightened around her waist. "I'm sorry."

"Not...your fault."

"Ivy, I'm going to carry you to the truck."

"I can make it." She said the words, but even she didn't believe them. It felt as if they made her break out in a sweat instead.

Austin didn't even argue with her. With undeniable strength and ease, he swept her up into his arms and strode toward the open front door, a man with a purpose. Ivy relented and let her head rest against his shoulder, concentrating in a vain effort to contain her pain.

"What happened?" someone asked as he descended the front steps.

It took Ivy a moment to recognize the voice as Melissa's. She and Daisy were evidently back from their excursion.

"She crushed her hand and hurt her ankle," Austin answered, not slowing down. "I'm taking her to the hospital." Once he got her seated and buckled in, he hurried to his side of the truck. "I'll call when I know more."

Ivy knew it was only a short drive to the small local hospital because everything in town was a short drive. As she did her best not to throw up in Austin's truck, she experienced a moment of clarity that she was lucky Jade Valley even had a hospital. Lots of towns of its size didn't, necessitating a long drive to the nearest one.

Austin drove right up to the ER and hurriedly got a wheelchair. If she wasn't hurting so much, she would laugh at how he seemed to be trying to set a new land speed record for getting her into the hospital. Luck was with them as the ER wasn't busy and she was quickly assessed by a nurse. Austin managed to get a cool, wet cloth from somewhere and pressed it against her forehead as she lay on the hospital bed.

Another person appeared at her bedside, a woman who Ivy estimated to be in her late thirties or early forties. She asked about insurance, and Ivy had to explain that she was new to Wyoming and hadn't yet changed her insurance. And that her purse with all that information was not with her.

"I'll go get it and bring it back," Austin said, but didn't make any move to leave.

Maybe it being a small town helped again because the woman, who probably knew Austin, nodded and exited the examination area. Another random thought floated through Ivy's brain, that if this had happened in Louisville, at least one person would likely be looking askance at Austin, as if he might be the cause of the injury.

"I'm sorry," he said, as if on cue.

"It isn't your fault," she said again, more in command of her voice this time. "I had a klutz moment and am paying for it."

A doctor arrived then and performed an examination of both her hand and her ankle, then ordered X-rays of both. Though Ivy knew they were necessary to determine the extent of her injuries, she couldn't help thinking about how much the medical bills would cost because she hadn't yet met her deductible for the year.

The trip to radiology went fairly quickly, even if the movement required brought some fresh spikes of pain. Even though she hadn't been gone from the ER long, Austin had managed to retrieve her purse and get back before she returned to the exam area. One look at his face and she knew in her gut that he felt guilty for what had happened.

"You better not be blaming yourself," she said.

"I should have gotten someone else to help me."

"Don't. Do not act as if this was anything other than an accident. You want to know what caused this? My nose was itching and I got distracted."

Ivy found that despite his help, she was slightly irritated. Was this overprotectiveness and the taking on of guilt that wasn't his to bear at least part of why he got divorced?

Before she could examine that line of thought further, the doctor returned with her X-ray results.

"The good news is that your ankle is not broken, just sprained. You'll need to keep off of it for about a week. The bad news, however, is that your middle finger is broken. It won't require surgery, so that's a silver lining."

The not-so-silver lining was how much it hurt as the doctor set the finger and immobilized it with a splint. She barely kept her not-nice thoughts trapped inside her head. By the time she was dosed with some pain medication and sent on her way, she was ready to crawl into bed and sleep for about three days. The only problem was that her new bed didn't have a mattress and the chest of drawers was still stuck in her stairwell, if it hadn't given way to gravity and crashed into the floor at the bottom of the stairs.

When they arrived back in front of her building, Melissa and Daisy were sitting outside. Before Austin could help her out of the truck, Daisy hurried to push Melissa across the street.

"You're coming home with us," Melissa said.

If it was her own mother offering to take care of her, Ivy would relent without argument. But Melissa wasn't her mother, and Ivy did not want to be a burden the other woman didn't need.

"I'll be fine on my own."

"How are you going to do that?" Melissa asked, a stubborn streak showing that Ivy had never witnessed. "Austin said you have crutches."

"Very slowly," Ivy said, managing to smile.

"Don't be silly." Melissa motioned for Ivy to stay in the truck and for Austin to help her into one of the back seats.

"Trust my thirty-one years of experience, there is no use arguing with her."

"I always knew you were a smart boy," Melissa said as Austin lifted her into the truck.

Considering Ivy couldn't exactly make a run for it and was quite honestly too tired to put up much of an argument anyway, she found herself relenting. After Daisy quickly gathered a few personal items for Ivy, they all headed out of town in a direction she had not yet driven. She relaxed her head on the headrest and watched the landscape roll by, the pastures filled with cattle next to the road moving faster than the towering peaks in the distance. The combination of fatigue, pain medication and the hum of the truck's tires worked to make her drowsy. Her blinks grew slower and slower until her eyes remained closed and consciousness slipped away.

WHEN THEY ARRIVED at the ranch, the sun had slipped behind the mountains. As Austin turned off the truck's engine, Ivy didn't stir. Either the day had worn her out or the medicine she'd been given had knocked her out. By the time he got his mom into the house, Ivy still hadn't stirred. He hated to wake her, but he wasn't going to let her spend the night sleeping in his truck either.

He eased the passenger-side door open. Ivy moved a little, wincing in her sleep. Despite the abnormally strong command she'd given him to not feel guilty about her injuries, he couldn't help it. What-ifs kept going through his head. What if they'd left the chest of drawers on the first floor until Isaac came back to put the finishing touches on the downstairs bathroom? What if he'd been with her when she was considering buying the heavy oak piece and convinced her to choose something lighter?

Austin sighed. His middle name might as well be What-if considering how many times he'd asked himself that question over the past couple of years. He really didn't need to take on worrying about someone else when he had plenty to worry about already. But his mother had insisted on bringing Ivy here. And now he couldn't ignore that he'd found himself increasingly concerned about this unexpected person in his life.

Not wanting to startle Ivy, he tapped her shoulder. "Hey, we're here."

Her eyes opened a fraction, and she looked at him as if she'd never seen him before and was trying to ascertain his identity.

"I'm going to pick you up now."

Ivy opened her eyes a bit more and nodded. She looked as if she wanted to say something, but moved her mouth in a way that told him that it was dry as cotton.

Austin slid one arm below her knees and wrapped the other around Ivy's back, lifting her easily and pushing the truck door closed with his hip. Now that she'd been treated by a doctor and given medication and orders to take it easy, his earlier panic was replaced by a disconcerting awareness of how her small but feminine body felt next to his. It wasn't right to think of her in that way when she was so vulnerable, but he couldn't seem to stop the insistence of those thoughts. He needed to see her settled and then get out of the house as quickly as he could.

Daisy held open the front door for him and said she'd

retrieve Ivy's crutches. He still didn't know how she'd manage using them when she had a broken finger, but they'd deal with that later. Hopefully after he'd banished the thoughts that made him feel way too warm.

"Take her to Daisy's room," his mom said.

Austin didn't bother asking if Daisy had offered or his mom had made the decision, because his sister wouldn't mind either way. It was obvious that she was fond of Ivy and would gladly give up her room while Ivy recuperated.

After laying her on Daisy's bed and covering her with a quilt, he didn't linger.

When he stepped back into the living room, Daisy was coming through the front door with the crutches, the bag from the small hospital pharmacy and Ivy's personal belongings.

"Put them in there where she can reach them," he said, pointing to Daisy's room, "but don't wake her up."

He shifted his gaze and noticed his mother watching him with that observant mom expression he hadn't seen since before her accident. As much as he was happy to see more of her old self surfacing, now was not the time he wanted her to be able to read him like the front page of a newspaper.

"I'll be back later." He didn't explain where he was going or why, because he didn't enumerate the ranch tasks he was off to undertake each day unless it was something out of the ordinary. To do so now would draw more attention to the fact that he was, in fact, putting distance between him and Ivy as fast as he could.

CHAPTER NINE

WHY WERE HER eyelids so heavy? That was the first thought to amble through Ivy's brain when she woke up. The next question to bubble up from her gray matter was, what was that smell? As more of her brain emerged from sleep, she realized that whatever that aroma was it smelled delicious and that she was hungry.

She blinked at the dimness around her. Instead of the view of the inside of her tent, or even the ceiling of her building, she was in a small bedroom. She couldn't make out a lot of what she was seeing, but none of it looked familiar. Then there was the fact she was lying in an actual bed, something she hadn't done since her last night on the road before arriving in Jade Valley.

When she started to roll onto her side, her hand caught on a fold in the quilt covering her and pain shot up her arm, all the way to her eyeball, of all places. That's when everything came rushing back with blinding speed—the chest of drawers falling on her hand, the broken finger now secured with a splint and thick bandaging, the sprained ankle that had led Melissa to insisting she come home with them.

Ivy took a minute to let the worst of the pain recede then slowly sat up. She noticed the daisy pattern stitched onto the quilt she'd been lying under and surmised that she was in Daisy's room. Her gaze landed on her purse and the crutches. She dreaded trying to use them, but she couldn't have Austin carrying her everywhere.

She gasped as she suddenly remembered how she had leaned against his shoulder as he'd carried her into the house. Her face flushed at the memory. No, her whole body did. How was she going to go out there and face Austin?

Ivy pressed her uninjured hand against her face, finding the skin extra warm. She was overthinking the situation. As usual, Austin was just being kind and considerate, the protector that she'd observed him being almost from the moment she'd met him. That protection had simply extended to her in her time of need because her family wasn't nearby to lend her aid.

Her stomach rumbled, making her wonder how long she'd been asleep. She'd eaten enough at the rummage sale that she shouldn't be hungry until tomorrow, and yet here she sat wishing she didn't have a bum ankle so she could race toward whatever was cooking on the other side of the closed bedroom door.

Well, you can't stay hidden in this room forever. Go out there and get it over with. Don't act like Austin carrying you was any big deal.

She closed her eyes, took a few deep breaths, mentally did a couple of *omm*s worthy of a yoga session, then reached for the crutches. After a shaky start and a few bad words she uttered only in her head, she slowly made her way the short distance to the door and opened it. Right then, the door across from her opened, revealing Austin coming out of the bathroom.

"Oh, hey," she said.

She saw him start to reach toward her before catching himself and bringing his hands back down to his sides.

"Do you need help?"

"I can manage." She winced at the memory of how sharp she'd been with him in a bad moment at the hospital. "About earlier today, I'm sorry I was a bit too harsh."

"No worries. It was the pain talking."

That was true, but also not. But she wasn't going to get into all that now.

"Mom made beef stew." He said this in a way that made her deduce it had been quite some time since that had last happened.

"Another good sign?"

He nodded.

"Hmm, I wonder what I would have gotten if I'd actually tumbled down the stairs."

"A broken neck, most likely."

"You're probably right. I'll have beef stew and be happy about it."

Austin let her make her own way up the short hallway toward the combined living area and kitchen. Melissa and Daisy, who must have heard her clunking around, were setting the table and dishing up bowls of the wonderful-smelling stew.

"I hope you're hungry," Melissa said when she looked over her shoulder at Ivy.

"If I wasn't before, the smell of that stew would change that."

She pressed her lips together to keep from groaning as fresh pain rocketed through her finger and up her arm. Austin pulled out a chair for her then took her crutches as she sat.

"Thanks."

"Do you need more of your pain medication?"

She nodded as she slid more fully into her seat at the table. That's when she noticed that while her middle finger was the only one broken, the others were deeply bruised.

"Well, that's colorful," she said as she held up her hand to examine it.

"You're lucky you didn't break all of those fingers,"

Melissa said as she wheeled to the table, a plate of fresh corn bread on her lap.

"Thank you for inviting me to your home. I'm sorry to be a bother."

"You are absolutely no bother. Quite the opposite." Melissa didn't elaborate, but it was nice to see her in what Ivy instinctually knew was her element—fixing a delicious meal and taking care of others instead of having them take care of her.

The moment Ivy took the first bite of the stew, she knew it was the best she'd ever had. If she'd heard a choir of angels break out into song, she would have only been slightly surprised.

"This is delicious."

"I'm glad you like it." Melissa paused, ever so slightly. "I haven't made it in a long time."

Ivy saw Daisy and Austin glance at each other.

"Well, I think if you made this every day and put up a stand by the road, you'd be a millionaire within a week."

Melissa's sudden laughter, while not loud or lengthy, made Ivy smile. When she glanced at Austin, there was such naked gratitude in his eyes that Ivy felt the sting of tears. To hold them back, she blinked as she returned her attention to her food. She grabbed a piece of corn bread and crumbled it up in her stew.

"What are you doing?" Austin asked.

"What?"

He pointed at her bowl.

"Um, eating."

"No, the corn bread."

She looked at him as if to ask why he was asking a question to which the answer was obvious. "You've never done this?"

"No."

"You should try it then. I do this with white beans, pinto beans, stew."

Daisy was the first to give it a try, giving the combination a thumbs-up after taking the first bite.

"When I can, I'll have to make you all some burgoo." She explained that it was also a stew, native to Kentucky, made up of a variety of meats as well as lima beans, corn, okra, tomatoes, cabbage and potatoes. "Oh, I just had a great idea. When I open the store, I should have a bunch of Kentucky dishes available. Maybe some bluegrass musicians too."

Thinking ahead to how great finally opening her doors for business would be helped Ivy to not focus so much on her current state. At some point, the bad stuff had to stop happening.

"Did you notice the quilt on my bed?" Daisy asked a bit later, after they'd talked about what Daisy had learned about Antarctica for her summer geography club project and how the veterinarian was due to come by the ranch tomorrow to give the cattle a series of summer vaccinations.

"I did. Very pretty."

"Mom made it for me when I was little."

"Oh? You've never mentioned that you quilt."

"I haven't in a long time, even before the accident. I was just too busy."

It was the first time Ivy had heard Melissa mention her accident directly and the first time when there wasn't any hesitation in her speech when talking about the past. Ivy didn't want to give herself too much credit, but maybe her being here had given a little boost to the healing process that was likely already happening, albeit slowly. She certainly would have rather not sustained a broken appendage and a pair of crutches for it to happen, but life worked in sometimes painful ways.

After they finished eating, Ivy noticed that Austin helped Daisy clear away the dishes. It was nice to see that he wasn't one of those guys who didn't pitch in around the house just because he was a guy. In this smaller area, he seemed taller. And with less space around him, she found herself simply watching the way his body moved.

She suddenly remembered how she would catch herself watching James at the office and jerked her gaze away from Austin. Hopefully, Melissa hadn't noticed.

The combination of the filling meal and her medication began to make her drowsy again, but she needed to stay up until everyone else went to bed. She had no intention of ejecting Daisy from her room. She remembered being a teenage girl and how important her own space was to her.

"You should get some more sleep," Melissa said.

"I will later."

"I saw you eye the couch. I hope you're not thinking you'll sleep there."

"I'm sleeping on the couch," Daisy said. "I'm going to read for a while anyway."

"I don't want to take your room," Ivy said.

"You're not. I gave it to you. Big difference." Daisy's smile reminded Ivy of the flowers after which the girl had been named.

Feeling more tired by the moment, Ivy moved to get up. And suddenly Austin was there next to her, not touching or insisting she needed help but close in case she did.

"Does it hurt to use the crutches?" he asked.

"Not as much as I feared it would." She wouldn't claim it wasn't painful, though, because it was. But even if it hurt more than it did, she wouldn't admit it. Because having him carry her while she was fully conscious, and in front of his family, was out of the question.

As she thumped her way slowly back toward Daisy's

room, she tried to forget the fact that he'd carried her twice had happened at all. She hoped he did the same.

What truly annoyed her was that after she managed to get herself into bed and the throbbing pain subsided enough for her to relax, instead of quickly falling asleep, her thoughts fixed on what it had felt like to be carried in Austin's strong arms. Despite the fact she'd been in considerable pain the first time and almost completely out of it the second, certain memories were undeniable. Chief among them were his warmth and strength, how he had acted as if she weighed almost nothing, the way she'd felt protected. As if he was some jeans-wearing, suntanned, modern-day cowboy knight in shining armor.

She supposed he even had a horse somewhere on this ranch. Ivy giggled a little as sleep crept a bit closer and she pictured Austin riding across his ranch wearing a suit of armor and chain mail.

Ivy closed her eyes and gave in to sleep with that image still trotting through her mind and a smile on her lips.

AUSTIN REINED IN his horse, taking a moment to drink a swig of coffee from his thermos. The dawning of a new day was beginning to peek over the mountains that marked the eastern side of the valley, but he'd already been up more than an hour. He had a long day ahead of him, one that was probably going to include a lot more coffee considering how little he'd slept the night before. He hadn't been able to rid himself of the unsettled feeling caused by having Ivy sleeping under the same roof. No one other than his mom and Daisy had shared his space since Grace left.

Even though there was nothing romantic between him and Ivy, it still felt like too much to have her sleeping in a room only a few steps from his own. The way he had caught himself watching her while at work was already surprising and unsettling, but at least there he could leave at the end of the day. At home, he would see her each time he stepped into his own house. And yet he understood why his mother had insisted she stay here. He even agreed with her because Ivy shouldn't try to climb those stairs while on crutches, especially when no one was around in case she fell.

The long day of corralling the cattle, getting them vaccinated, and then returning them to the pasture was arriving right when he needed the distraction.

But as he herded cattle from where they were grazing into the corral near the barn, his thoughts kept straying to Ivy—the way she'd smiled at the rummage sale when she'd found salt and pepper shakers shaped like spools of thread, how she easily struck up conversations with anyone she met, the panic he'd felt when he saw the intense pain in her expression when the chest had slammed into her fingers.

It was a reminder of how quickly someone could be injured or worse. And that he didn't need more people in his life to worry about.

As he maneuvered the last few cattle into the corral, he spotted Dr. Parsons parking in front of the barn. Austin waved a greeting as he hopped off his horse and closed the gate behind the last steer.

"Perfect timing," Austin said as he approached the veterinarian, who had been taking care of the area's animals, big and small, since before Austin could remember.

"I hear you have some company," Dr. Parsons said.

"You'd think I'd stop being surprised how fast news travels around here."

Dr. Parsons laughed as he gathered everything he'd need to make sure Austin's herd was protected from a range of diseases. Austin got the herd circling in the corral and then a few on the outer edge of the group directed into the chute before closing a gate behind them. As he walked up to the head gate where Dr. Parsons was ready with the vaccines, he noticed Daisy walking toward them rubbing her eyes.

Austin experienced some sympathy for her. Not only did she not get to sleep in on her summer vacation, but she didn't even get to sleep in her own bed. But ranch kids didn't really get vacations. He wondered if, in addition to missing her dad, she also missed days spent on the river and spending time meeting people from all over who came to go rafting. Or maybe being around river rafting would be too difficult now, a sad reminder of what she and their mom had lost.

But Daisy wasn't one to complain. If she felt resentful or sad or angry, she kept it inside. He knew what that was like.

"You ready?" Dr. Parsons asked.

Austin nodded and got the first steer into position and closed the head gate, preventing the animal from escaping as the injections entered its hip. The process didn't take long, and when it was over Austin opened the gate to allow the steer to return to the pasture. The three of them worked in a familiar rhythm—Austin guiding the cattle into the chute and closing the gate behind them before moving to the head gate, Daisy urging the cattle in the chute to move forward, and Dr. Parsons administering the vaccines and entering the information in his records. Rinse and repeat, one steer after another.

About halfway through, one of the steers got nervous and put up an extra fuss, trying to back down the chute, which agitated the rest of the cattle behind him.

"Hey, now," Austin said, trying to calm the animal. He nodded at Daisy, who urged the ones in the back forward. As she did so, Austin opened the head gate and a pathway to freedom. But as the steer made a run for it, Austin used his years of practice to close the gate at the right moment.

Dr. Parsons made quick work of the vaccinations, and Austin quickly released the upset beast.

"If you spoke Cow, I don't think you'd like what that one is saying to you," the vet said.

"You're likely right about that."

The sun climbed in the sky, beating down on them and increasing the sweat running down Austin's neck. When they had about ten head of cattle to go, something caused him to glance toward the house. To his surprise, Ivy was standing at the edge of the yard watching what they were doing. Though it was likely just city girl curiosity, her eyes on him caused his skin to heat more than the sun did.

"I see what I've heard is right. She's a pretty girl," Dr. Parsons said.

Austin agreed but pretended as if he was focusing on his work and hadn't heard what the man had said. But it echoed in his brain. *Pretty girl, pretty girl, pretty girl.*

Of course, Austin didn't think of her as a girl. While she was young enough to be the vet's daughter, she and Austin were likely close in age. They'd never discussed the specifics, had no reason to.

But he didn't need for her to answer any questions about herself for him to know that she was indeed pretty. Even more beautiful than her long, wavy hair and petite figure was her wide smile. She'd be able to charm the sun into rising at midnight if she put her mind to it. If her store wasn't successful, it wouldn't be for her lack of trying.

He realized he didn't want to consider that possibility. If she failed, as he had thought she might when he first met her, the likelihood of her returning to Kentucky and him never seeing her again was high.

By the time Dr. Parsons finished with the last steer and

Austin released it back into the pasture, he felt as if he hadn't eaten for days. He'd nabbed a couple of the cookies that Ivy had bought the day before along with his coffee early that morning, and it was now midafternoon. Still, Austin thought he might take time to chat with the vet after their business was done. After all, Dr. Parsons was known as quite the talker. As luck would have it, however, he didn't have time to stick around and gab today.

"I've got a lead on a young vet who might want to give me a hand so I can retire one of these days," he said as he loaded his supplies back into his truck. "Cross your fingers."

As Austin waved goodbye to the vet, he noticed that Ivy was slowly making her way back across the yard to the house. Daisy had already disappeared inside. He resisted the urge to run to Ivy before she toppled over and injured herself further. Instead, he walked at a normal pace but was still able to quickly overtake her.

"You're not one to just sit back and take it easy, are you?" he asked as he came up beside her.

"Takes one to know one, as they say."

"Well, I have a ranch to run. It's sort of a never-done sort of job."

She stopped walking and looked back toward where he'd been working.

"I've driven past plenty of farms with cattle before, beef and dairy, but I've never actually visited one. I know this is a ranch, but still. Are all the vaccinations done?"

"Yeah. The last thing I need is sickness in the herd."

"Do you enjoy it?"

"Vaccinating cattle?"

"Ranching overall."

"I do. I mean, I've done it for as long as I can remember.

I'm third generation on this land. It's difficult sometimes, stressful, but I wouldn't want to lose it."

"Is there a danger of that?"

"There's always the danger of that."

The approach of another vehicle cut their conversation short. Austin was surprised to see Isaac coming up the driveway. Hopefully nothing was wrong at Ivy's place.

"I finished your downstairs bathroom and you can't even come see it," Isaac said as he stepped out of his truck, pointing at Ivy and her obvious injuries.

"I'll just have to heal quickly so that I can come praise your work properly."

"I'm going to hold you to that."

"What brings you out here?" Austin asked.

"Your mom called and wanted me to bring her a couple of things."

"I could have gotten whatever she needed."

"You can be in two places at once, can you?" Isaac pointed toward the corral and chute, the evidence of how Austin had spent his morning. "I was done for the day anyway. And your mom bribed me with pineapple cake. I was a little surprised, but I wasn't about to argue."

"You're not the only one. She made beef stew and corn bread last night too."

Isaac smiled. "I think having a patient to take care of has given her purpose."

For a moment, Austin resented the fact that his mother hadn't managed to find it in herself to emerge from her quiet and semi-seclusion for him or, more importantly, Daisy. But that wasn't fair to Ivy. She didn't deliberately get hurt. And it shouldn't matter what had helped his mother. What mattered was that she seemed to be turning a corner. Maybe it had taken something new, an outside force, instead of the things and people and situations she lived with every day.

He just hoped his mom's progress stuck after the newness of Ivy wore off, after she went back to her place in town, after his work there was done.

CHAPTER TEN

IVY HATED FEELING like an invalid. Sure, she was mobile and she knew it could be worse, but she had so much to do back at her place. Even while a guest of Austin and his family, she wished she could do more to help. But they insisted that she rest and recuperate, and her body seemed to agree. She couldn't remember the last time she'd taken so many naps. It occurred to her when she woke up in the middle of the afternoon the next day that maybe her fatigue wasn't all attributable to her injuries. Perhaps what James had done was really hitting home. Add to that her sudden decision to completely change her life followed by the upheaval of quitting her job, divesting herself of everything she couldn't fit in her car and driving cross-country to live in a place she'd never been—well, it was a lot of emotional up and down and sideways.

As her thoughts seemed determined to do, they drifted to Austin. Even though she knew she shouldn't even be thinking about another man yet, she couldn't prevent herself from doing so. A man shouldn't look attractive when dirty and sweaty after helping to vaccinate a herd of cattle, and yet he had the day before. It was a different kind of work than what he'd been doing for her in renovating her building, and yet he seemed to be skilled at both.

She heard the commode flush across the hall and wondered if it was him, Daisy or Melissa. Chances were it wasn't him because it was the middle of the workday. She was the only one drifting off to sleep every few hours. Lifting herself to a sitting position on the side of the bed, she was determined to do something productive today, something more than the online window-shopping she'd done the day before.

One thing she definitely needed to undertake was a shower, but that was going to require a couple of plastic bags to protect her bandages and a lot of care to make sure she didn't fall in the shower and injure herself further. The amount of mortification that resulted from something like that would be the end of her.

Her phone, sitting on Daisy's little white nightstand, rang.

"Hey, Lily," she said.

"What's wrong?" her younger sister asked.

"What do you mean?"

"You sound way too chipper."

"I'm always a delight."

Lily snort-laughed. "Spill it."

Ivy told her what happened. Suddenly, Lily's phone was commandeered by their mother.

"You broke what?"

"I'm okay, Mom. Seriously."

"But you're all alone, with no one to take care of you. See, you should have never left."

"Mom, stop. You're getting in a tizzy for no reason. It's not like I'm in traction or something. And I'm not alone. I'm staying at a friend's house until I can walk without the crutches."

"What friend?"

Ivy told her it was Melissa.

"Wait, that's the mom of the guy doing the work on your building, right?"

"Yes." She didn't elaborate because she wasn't a teenage

girl who needed to be kept away from spending the night under the same roof as members of the opposite sex. Ivy also was afraid her strange feelings toward Austin might actually be detectable in her voice if she said too much. She didn't need her mother dissecting what Ivy herself didn't fully understand.

"Do you need me to come?"

"No, Mom. I love you, but I'd like your first visit to be after I have everything ready and the store open."

"Okay." Her mom didn't sound happy about agreeing, but she did it anyway.

After a trip to the bathroom, Ivy made her way into the living area only to find it empty. Behind her, a door opened down the hallway. She looked back to see Melissa emerging from her room. Had she been napping too?

"Are you hungry?" Melissa asked.

"I'll just have a couple of cookies if there are any left."

"Would you like some milk with them?"

"Sounds good but I'll get it."

Melissa actually gave her a look that said to not be ridiculous. "I think I'll have better luck pouring it and getting it safely to the table, don't you?"

Ivy looked down at her splinted finger and crutches and said, "You're probably right about that."

At least the container of cookies was already sitting in the middle of the table. Ivy sat and opened the lid.

"It appears as if these have been popular."

"I'm pretty sure that's what Austin had for breakfast yesterday. He was up and gone before daylight."

"Ranch work seems to fill a lot of hours."

"It does. Of course, it's easier when there are multiple people to share the load. But now Austin has to shoulder most of it by himself."

"He said he enjoys it though." Ivy didn't want to risk

Melissa falling back into her well of sadness, not after the significant steps to pull herself out.

"He does. Still, it's nice to see him get out and do different things, like working on your building."

"It's been great having all three of you there. It makes me miss my own family a little less."

Melissa smiled as she placed the two glasses of milk on a tray that rested on the arms of her wheelchair then brought them to the table. Ivy got the feeling that Melissa could do more on her own than Austin thought she could. Ivy tried to put herself in his place though. Would she smother her mom with constant help if she'd been through what Melissa had?

As if it was the most natural thing in the world, they began talking about plans for the quilt shop that would be more than a quilt shop. Ivy told her about her ideas for carrying various types of yarn and hosting a knitting club. Melissa suggested a group quilt, housed in the shop but worked on by whoever had time to stop by and work on it, to be raffled off prior to Christmas.

"It could be an annual event," Melissa said. "Like the rummage sale, the proceeds could go to a different cause each year."

"I like that."

Time flew as they added one idea after another to Ivy's growing list of possibilities she kept on her phone—candle-making workshops, making a baby outfit for everyone in the county who had a new baby, monthly music on the lawn that would draw people off Main Street to Ivy's store.

"I've missed this," Melissa said after they'd been brainstorming for a couple of hours. "I used to come up with ideas of how to bring people to the river rafting business I ran with Daisy's dad." She hesitated for a moment, lost in her sad memories. "I was good at it."

"Do you mind me asking what happened?"

Melissa clasped her hands atop the table. "We were hauling the rafts back from the end of a group's float trip when we rounded a curve and a huge RV was half in our lane. My husband instinctually jerked to the right and we went rolling down a steep embankment. I was knocked out at some point before we hit the bottom and I didn't wake up until two days later." She stopped, took a deep breath, collecting herself. "When I did, I just wanted to go back to sleep. I couldn't believe fate had been so cruel to not only take a second husband from me, leaving both of my children fatherless, but I'd been robbed of my ability to fully take care of myself. In those early days, I thought it would have been better if I hadn't woken up. But then Daisy would curl up next to me in the hospital bed, her tears soaking my gown, and I knew I had to keep living."

"Not giving up is often the bravest thing we can do. It takes time to heal from a big blow like that, and no one else can dictate how you do it or how long it takes."

Ivy shared her own mother's struggle to raise three girls alone, how she remembered once overhearing her mother crying in her room late at night when she thought Ivy and her sisters were asleep.

"Loss finds all of us at some point, some more than others," Melissa said.

Ivy looked at her phone lying on the table without picking it up, thought about all the notes that she'd typed into it and how many of those ideas had been Melissa's.

"I have an idea I'd like to run by you," Ivy said.

"Okay."

"How would you like to work in the store once it opens?"

"Oh, you'll want someone more capable than me."

Ivy tapped her phone. "I think you just proved that you're plenty capable. There's no one else I've met who I think would be better suited. Access isn't a problem since there are ramps in the front and back. You said yourself that a lot of the ranch work isn't possible for you anymore, but this would be. I'll be there most of the time, but when I'm not I want to leave the store with someone I trust. You are that person."

Silence settled between them, and Ivy thought she could see the shine of unshed tears in Melissa's eyes.

"Let me think about it."

It wasn't a "no" and Ivy took that as a good sign.

Daisy came in from working in the garden and headed toward the shower. She gave them a quick wave but didn't stop whatever she was listening to on her phone. Ivy would guess it was the travel podcast she liked, one in which two best friends traveled the world off the beaten path. Instead of the typical tourist attractions, they took back roads, visited small towns and villages, and explored the lesser-known historical sites. When she had some time, Ivy aimed to give it a listen herself.

When Ivy glanced back at Melissa, there was a new type of sadness written on her face—the kind that said she knew her baby girl would leave the nest at some point for faraway adventures.

"She'll always come back." Ivy hadn't really meant to give voice to her thoughts, but it was the truth and maybe Melissa needed to hear it.

"I know. Just like I've always known that she'd be the one to leave Jade Valley while Austin would always be comfortable staying here. They're so different, those two."

"But they're also a lot alike. They're both kind, help-ful, a bit on the reserved side until you get to know them."

Melissa nodded. "It's good that they're as close as they are, considering the age difference. I thought it might not be that way. When I got pregnant with Daisy, I think it made Austin uncomfortable. But I can still see how he instantly loved her the moment we put her in his arms the first time. His eyes were huge."

Melissa laughed a little at the memory. Some unnamed yearning stirred inside Ivy. Maybe it was for what might have been, all the things she'd lost in that moment when what James had done became clear.

"If Austin ever becomes a father, I think he'll be a good one," Melissa said, a new sadness in her voice.

Ivy admitted to herself that she wanted to know what had happened with Austin's marriage. Whose fault was the divorce? Despite all his positive qualities, was he not a good husband? Had he done something to drive his wife away?

It was entirely possible, of course, that he was not the one at fault and that her trust in men had simply suffered a seismic shaking.

As if he'd sensed that they were venturing close to discussing his most personal information, Austin came into the house through the back door. When she caught sight of him, Ivy had to press her lips tightly together to keep from laughing. Because Austin was covered nearly head to toe in mud.

"Well, I haven't seen that look in a while," Melissa said, as if this wasn't the first time she'd seen her son looking as if he'd wallowed with hogs.

"What happened?" Ivy asked. "I doubt you set up a mud-wrestling ring as a side hustle."

"Let's just say one of the four-legged residents of this ranch was feeling a bit irritated today and took advantage of where I was standing."

A snort of laughter made it past Ivy's best efforts to keep it in check. In the next moment, Melissa joined her.

Daisy, who'd just emerged from the bathroom after her shower, joined the chorus of laughter.

"If someone had caught my head in a metal contraption and given me two shots in the rear, I might hold a grudge for a while and push them into the nearest mudhole the first chance I got too," Ivy said, then laughed some more.

"I don't like any of you very much right now."

Austin's words as he headed toward his room only caused them to laugh harder.

DESPITE WHAT HE'D just said, Austin felt exactly the opposite as he stood behind the closed door of his bedroom. He didn't often cry, but he felt the sting of tears at the sound of his mother's laughter. Real, deep-down laughter. And he knew in his soul that it was because of Ivy. Even if he had walked into the house looking exactly as he did now, without her presence he doubted his mother would react in the same way. She might have laughed, but it would have been…what was that word he'd heard Daisy use recently? Ephemeral.

Again he experienced that confusing intertwining of feelings—gratefulness that his mother seemed to finally be emerging from the dark, but admittedly a bit resentful that it had taken an outsider to bring that change about.

He shook his head. This was no time to be selfish or petty. The only thing he needed to feel was thankful.

He definitely didn't need to think about how attractive Ivy was with her hair pulled back into a ponytail and her whole body shaking with laughter.

Grabbing clean clothes, he headed to the shower. When he was finally free of all the mud and dressed again, he walked into the living area to find the kitchen as active as a hive of agitated bees. Daisy was pulling bags of chips out of the cabinet. Ivy, balancing a bit shakily on her crutches, was mixing something in a bowl. His mom saw him and extended her arm. In her hand was a package of hot dogs.

"Fire up the grill."

He took the package. "Did I miss something?"

"We decided it's a junk food and movie marathon night," Daisy said, sounding as if she thought this was the best idea ever.

He headed out back and got the grill going. Usually when he grilled, it was burgers or steaks. He didn't even remember buying hot dogs. Daisy must have gotten them at some point.

They also weren't one of those families that ate in front of the TV, so when they all parked themselves there with their hot dogs and chips with box brownies baking in the oven, it felt like a special occasion.

Daisy commandeered the recliner, she and his mom sharing a foldable TV tray between them. That left him and Ivy to share the couch.

"Daisy, let Ivy have the recliner so she can put her foot up."

"No, I'm fine here," Ivy said.

So much for putting some distance between them. He split the difference between sitting as far from her on the couch as he could and sitting too close. Either option had the potential to cause questions he didn't want forming in his mom's or sister's head.

They ended up playing rock, paper, scissors to decide who got to pick the first movie. He won and picked a newer sci-fi film.

"That surprises me," Ivy said before she stuffed a potato chip in her mouth.

"What? Did you think I'd only watch Westerns?"

"No. I'm not sure what I thought you might like."

He was beginning to think he liked her a little too much,

but he wasn't about to say that. It felt a bit too much like walking along the edge of a steep cliff while blindfolded to even admit it to himself.

They stuffed themselves with hot dogs, chips and brownies, and even popped bags of popcorn halfway through Daisy's choice, unsurprisingly a film about a woman traveling through Europe while trying to figure out what she wanted to do with her life.

"Must be nice to be wealthy enough to do that," he said.

"She actually wrote articles about her travels along the way and sold them," Ivy said. "She also would take on daily jobs here and there to make enough to keep traveling."

He'd never had the travel bug like his sister, but even he thought that sounded interesting.

By the time the second movie was over, his mom said she didn't have another one in her and went to bed. Daisy had fallen asleep in the recliner.

Even though he suddenly felt awkward and as if he wanted to follow his mom down the hall, Austin stayed seated. He picked up the remote and extended it to Ivy.

"Another?"

She shook her head. "I think I'm done, though I'm not sleepy. My sleep schedule is all off-kilter."

"Do you want to go sit outside?" What was he doing? If sitting here next to her with the lights on and his sister in the same room was awkward, what would it be like out under the stars, just the two of them?

"Sure. I could use some fresh air."

He escorted her out the front door, stayed beside her in case she slipped as they made their way slowly toward a bench beneath a large oak tree. When they reached the bench, Ivy sat and stretched the leg with the sprained ankle out in front of her.

"How are you feeling? Still in pain?"

"It's there but manageable. Better than the first day though."

"That's good."

He looked up at the sky, and as his eyes adjusted he picked out a couple of constellations.

"You can sit," Ivy said. "I promise I don't bite."

Though it would be wiser to remain standing, he settled himself next to her. He immediately wished he hadn't because there was way less space between them now than there had been on the couch. Thankfully, he didn't have to navigate pointless conversation. Ivy seemed content to sit quietly and look up at the night sky.

Austin took inspiration from that and did the same. He realized that despite living somewhere with excellent stargazing opportunities, he didn't actually do it often. He was either focused on the task in front of him or in bed so he could get up early the next morning. It was nice to simply sit and be, to enjoy the nighttime beauty he took for granted.

"I liked living in cities," Ivy said. "But every time I've been away from them at night, someplace where I can see the sky like this, I'm always in awe."

"Yeah. I admit I don't take advantage of this view enough."

"I'd tell you not to work so much that life passes you by, but I'd be saying that from a place of privilege. I know you work as much as you do out of necessity. But hopefully you won't forget to do this from time to time."

He looked over at Ivy, and his heart thumped a bit harder when he saw her smiling at him. If he hadn't been through what he had, would he lean forward and kiss her? But abandonment tended to damage your ability to trust.

"You seem to be deep in thought."

He averted his gaze, once again staring up at the sky. "Just trying to remember when I sat out beneath the stars with anyone."

It had to have been with Grace, before the accident, before she had left him to face one of the hardest periods of his life alone.

Ivy grew quiet again, and he got the feeling that this time she was the one thinking about the past. She let out a sigh that was loaded with meaning. He wasn't sure what kind of meaning, but it felt heavy.

"I remember exactly the last time I watched the stars like this. It was when my ex proposed to me."

Austin's gaze went immediately back to Ivy's profile. He certainly hadn't expected that.

"You were married?"

She shook her head. Had her ex broken off the engagement? He didn't pry even though his mind was crackling with questions.

"I know everyone wonders about why someone like me would quit her job and move cross-country to a place she's never been. They probably speculate all kinds of reasons, all of them some version of me running away from something or someone, and they'd be right."

Oh no, had the ex been abusive? His muscles tensed at the very thought that someone had hurt her like that.

"I ran away from the embarrassment of being a fool. I couldn't face going back to work and having to see the man who betrayed me every day."

She told him about how she'd worked with her ex, about how during their engagement party two women had shown up with proof that he had been cheating on her with both of them. No wonder she had wanted to start over somewhere no one knew her, though she shouldn't have had to.

"He's the fool, not you."

A hint of a smile tugged at the edge of her lips. "I appreciate you saying that."

"They aren't empty words. I mean them. A man who would cheat on you isn't worth thinking about."

She looked over at him, held his gaze for several seconds before lowering hers.

"While I agree with you, it's easier said than done. I loved him, was going to marry him. You can't just turn off feelings, even if they betray you."

He knew that all too well.

"I will say that the move has helped, as I'd hoped it would. Being in a new place, around new people, putting everything into a new path has sped up getting over it way more than those days I laid around in my apartment eating self-pity ice cream."

He wasn't sure if that reaction was better or worse than how he'd worked himself to exhaustion after Grace left. He'd told himself at the time that he hadn't had a choice. Someone had to take care of his mom and Daisy, the ranch, the animals. Someone had to pay the bills and hold together what was left of his family.

"I'm going to say something once, and you can either take me up on my offer or forget you ever heard me make it," Ivy said. "I've gathered that you see yourself as your family's protector, their rock. I doubt you ever unburden yourself to them, to anyone. Maybe you're one of those guys who isn't into sharing feelings and keeps everything inside, but if you ever need someone to talk to, I'll listen."

It took him several seconds, but he finally managed a thank-you. But he didn't share his story. He didn't see any good coming from reliving how his wife had gone on a trip to Denver and never come back.

A coyote howled in the distance, and he used that as a flimsy excuse to say they should go back inside. As she had promised, Ivy didn't say anything else about him spilling the beans about his own unhappy past. But the simple fact that she'd offered, right after confessing how she was still healing from a betrayal of her own, meant a lot to him.

Maybe too much.

WHY HAD SHE told Austin about James? That was the first coherent thought Ivy had the next morning. As she lay in Daisy's bed with the early morning light illuminating the collection of maps, posters and teenage mementos, she wondered why it had felt so easy to confess what had prompted her change in life trajectory.

One thing seemed certain though. She had found herself feeling closer to him, more able to open up, than he was with her. Of course, it wasn't a requirement that he tell her about his past in response, but she could now admit that she'd hoped he might. She was curious, yes, but it was more than that. What she'd said to him about how he seemed to keep everything bottled up, so as not to be a further burden to those already carrying a lot of burdens, was true. She had offered to be a willing ear not only as a way to repay him for all of his help but because she really did consider him a friend now. Sometimes she flirted with the idea that if she allowed it, maybe he could be more. But the fact that he'd divulged nothing the night before told her that he didn't feel the same. She reminded herself that he didn't have to. Just because one person felt a certain way didn't mean someone else was required to return those feelings. It was better to know early, before words that ended up being lies were exchanged.

Needing to get back to her new home and to work as soon as she could, she tested putting weight on her ankle. She winced against the pain and sank back onto the side of the bed in frustration. The pain was less than when she'd first twisted the ankle, but it definitely wasn't waitress-worthy. She would have to be satisfied with doing more planning for the eventual opening of her store.

As she left the bedroom several minutes later, wearing an indie band T-shirt and a pair of loose lounge pants, Ivy made her way first to the bathroom and then the living area, which once again she found empty. She glanced back down the hall and saw that Melissa's bedroom door was closed. Not wanting to disturb her, Ivy eased out the front door to sit on the porch. She noticed Austin's truck wasn't in the driveway. Either he was somewhere else on the ranch or had gone into town.

She sighed, wishing she was more mobile so she could explore a bit. Before being brought here, she'd never set foot on a ranch before. Though she could tell it wasn't a huge operation, since Austin largely ran it by himself, it was larger than most farms she was used to seeing back in Kentucky. But the last thing she needed to do was fall and hurt herself further. She couldn't afford that, and it would be a terrible way to pay back Melissa, Austin and Daisy for temporarily housing and feeding her.

Being limited in what she could do made her think about how much harder it must be for Melissa, who was so used to being active and able to go wherever she wanted. Ivy couldn't imagine what it had been like to wake up grateful to have survived such a horrible accident only to discover she'd lost another husband and would never walk again. Some people had to endure more than their share of bad luck. Considering everything Melissa had been through, it made Ivy's recent heartbreak seem small by comparison.

She heard the approach of Melissa's wheelchair before the door opened.

"Ivy?"

"Yeah, I'm here." She pushed up out of the chair where she was sitting and took two steps with the crutches. "Do you need something?"

"Follow me."

Ivy did so, back to Melissa's bedroom. Melissa tapped something under a sheet on her bed.

"I hope you like this, but if it's not what you're looking for, you don't have to use it."

Curious, Ivy crutched her way to the side of the bed as Melissa pulled away the sheet.

"Oh, wow." Ivy let her gaze roam over what Melissa had done with the wood she'd had Austin paint and the old buttons. She'd created a wall hanging depicting a vintage treadle sewing machine using the black and gold buttons, a pin cushion with red ones, and seemingly every color imaginable for spools of thread and a patchwork quilt draped over a ladder-back chair. "This is gorgeous."

"Well, that seems like an overstatement."

"No, it's not. I love everything about this. And it is absolutely going to be hanging in the store where everyone can see it."

Ivy's heart filled with happiness when she glanced at Melissa and saw the pride there.

"I thought about your offer," Melissa said. "If you truly think I could be of use, I'd like to take you up on it."

"This day just keeps getting better and better."

Austin, it seemed, was not as thrilled by his mother's news as Ivy was. Not that he told Melissa this. But after dinner when Daisy went to call one of her friends and his mom was busy in the bathroom, Ivy asked him what was bothering him. He'd been quiet and tense all throughout the meal.

"I wish you had asked me about offering Mom a job before doing it."

"Excuse me? Last I checked she's a grown woman able to make her own decisions."

This was his overprotectiveness speaking, she knew that, but it hit her as a bit patronizing as well.

"Yes, she is, but I don't want her getting hurt again."

"Do you honestly think I'd do anything to put her in danger?"

"You wouldn't mean to, but what if the store doesn't work out? She will have something else taken away from her."

Ivy stared at him. Although a part of her could understand him wanting to protect his mother, it also hurt that he thought all Ivy's efforts would be for naught. The truth was a lot of new businesses didn't make it, but she was determined to not be one of those failures.

"I wouldn't have offered her a job if I didn't think my business would be successful or if I didn't think she could handle it."

Before she said something she would regret, she got up and started for the front door.

"Ivy," Austin said as he followed then blocked the door.

"You had better think twice before you say something like I might get hurt if I go outside. Remember, I'm a woman armed with two metal crutches."

"I'm sorry. I didn't mean—"

Ivy held up her injured hand. "Don't. You did mean it. But I'm going to prove your doubts—about me and about your mom—are wrong."

CHAPTER ELEVEN

IT TOOK EVERY bit of willpower Austin had not to follow Ivy. He hated the idea of her falling out there in the dark and breaking something else because he'd let his concerns tumble out of his mouth. Ivy was right, of course. His mother was indeed a grown woman, and he should be thankful she was showing enough interest in life again to accept a future job. He *was* thankful. But at some point over the past few days, his positive view of how Ivy's friendship was bringing both his mom and Daisy out of their different kinds of shells had turned to worry. And he didn't think that worry was unfounded. If Ivy's business failed, if she gave up on the wild-hair move to Wyoming and went back to Kentucky, Daisy and his mom would lose yet something else meaningful.

He waited five minutes then stepped outside. Expecting to see her sitting on the bench they had shared when she revealed what her ex-fiancé had done to her, his anxiety spiked when he saw the bench was empty, as was the porch. Holding down the need to call out to her, he stepped off the porch and scanned the fencing along the driveway. No sign of her. Telling himself not to panic, he made his way toward the barn. He noticed the door was ajar and relaxed a little.

Should he go inside or return to the house, trusting Ivy to be okay and to get herself back inside?

"I know you're out there."

He guessed that answered his question. Stepping forward, he slipped into the barn and found Ivy sitting on an overturned bucket. Pooch had his head on her lap, enjoying a good scratch between the ears.

Austin walked past her and leaned his arms on the edge of the stall where Merlin stood. He had so much he wanted to say and yet couldn't find the words.

"I'm sorry if I overstepped," Ivy said, not looking at him. "I shouldn't tell someone else how to handle their family situation, especially when they didn't ask."

He turned to face her. "Part of me knows you're right, but there's also a big part that's afraid. If Mom loses one more thing, she might not be able to recover next time. Daisy and I might lose her too."

Ivy looked as if she wanted to respond but kept her thoughts to herself.

"What is it you want to say?"

She looked up at him then. "Are you sure you want to hear it?"

He nodded once.

"I think you need to trust your mother to find her own pace of healing, to find her own path to whatever comes next."

Maybe Ivy was right. Very likely she was because he thought perhaps she could see the picture more clearly than he could because he was part of the picture.

"I'll try."

Again, he got the feeling that she was holding something she wanted to say in check. Instead, she simply said, "Okay," and shifted her focus back to Pooch.

"Looks like you've made another new friend."

"I've always liked dogs. What's his name?"

"Pooch."

Ivy looked up at him as if he was pulling her leg. "Seriously?"

"Yep."

"That's only one step away from just calling him Dog."

"When he was a pup, he got more than his fair share of the milk so his belly was all pooched out. Daisy thought the word was funny, and since it had a double meaning it stuck."

"Well, no matter your name, you're a good boy, aren't you?"

Austin smiled at how Ivy baby-talked to Pooch and rubbed her nose against his. She had such an easy way with people and animals. If he was being truthful, he envied it a little. If he was being really truthful, he envied Pooch a little.

That admission should startle him, but it didn't. Not really. The change in how he looked at her and felt about her had been gradual, and he realized that he'd been aware of the change on some level despite trying to ignore it. But even if he admitted it to himself, he didn't know if he'd ever admit it to her. Perhaps his ill-advised words earlier had been as much about how he'd feel if she left as it was about his concerns about his mom and Daisy. If he admitted he was beginning to have feelings for her and then she left, it would be that much worse.

Plus, wasn't it too soon to even be considering another relationship? His divorce had only been final for a year. Despite the passage of those twelve months, the wound left by Grace's abandonment still felt raw sometimes. It made him sad and angry by turns.

"Is there a day next week when you would be able to go

to Cheyenne with me?" Ivy asked. "I told the coin dealer I had to reschedule, though I didn't tell him why."

"I can go any day."

And hope that spending that many hours alone with Ivy didn't tempt him to give in to his new feelings.

THE MORNING AFTER their talk in the barn, Ivy awoke to find Austin gone from the ranch.

"He said he was going to do some work in your building while you weren't there," Daisy said when Ivy had come into the kitchen.

It had been the first of three days during which she hadn't seen him at all. He left the house early and came back late. She spent the time doing more planning with Melissa, delving into the history of the Stinson Building as well as Jade Valley as a whole with Daisy, and gradually working to put more weight on her ankle for longer periods of time. As the ER doctor had predicted, at the one-week mark she could walk without the aid of the crutches, though she was still careful not to overtax it or make any sudden movements.

Feeling as if she had worn out her welcome, at least with Austin based on how he was staying away from the house during all the waking hours, she got up even earlier than him on the day she'd decided to go home. She eased her way out the front door so she didn't wake up Daisy, who was snoozing away on the couch. Ivy noticed that the girl slept how she did, in the fetal position. An unexpected pang settled in Ivy's middle. She'd miss sharing meals with Daisy and Melissa, laughing with them, planning the store with them.

She'd still see them, of course, but it wouldn't be like this little pseudofamily she'd enjoyed the past week.

She reminded herself that part of the reason she'd moved

to Jade Valley on a whim was to prove to herself that she was just fine on her own. And maybe once she returned to her new home and had a few days away from sharing a living space with Austin, the very bad idea of being increasingly attracted to him would fade. Hopefully, his work on her building would be done soon and she'd see him even less, causing the feelings to disappear entirely.

In the meantime, there was something magical about being awake and outside as a new day awoke from its slumber. She heard the first tittering of birds, felt a slight breeze drift across her skin and inhaled the cool freshness of the beautiful mountain valley. Leaning against the wooden fencing that started at the barn and stretched parallel to the length of the driveway, she watched as the peaks of the mountain range to the east became silhouetted by the rising sun. Taking out her phone, she snapped several pictures as the horizon shifted from indigo to yellow then orange.

Right as the top edge of the sun was becoming visible, the front door of the house opened. Austin was actually getting a later start today. Ivy watched as he headed toward his truck and as his step faltered when he spotted her. For a moment, he seemed to not know whether to continue on his way or cross to where she was standing. Was he concerned he would invade her moment of solitude? Or did he think she was still upset about how he'd reacted to her offering Melissa a job? She'd thought they'd come to an understanding about that, but maybe it still bothered him.

Had he stayed away from her these past few days so they wouldn't argue about it? Or maybe he was using his own alone time to figure out how to balance wanting to protect his family with allowing them to do things where they might get hurt.

"You're up early," he said when he got close.

"Had to get up early to catch my ride to town."

"You're leaving?" He scanned the area around her, evidently only then realizing that her crutches were lying against her bag and not under her arms.

"Yes. I've imposed on your family long enough, though I really appreciate you-all letting me stay here while my ankle healed."

"Are you sure you're ready?"

She lifted her leg and rotated the ankle as a demonstration. There was still some tenderness, but she didn't tell him that.

"Did you tell Mom and Daisy?"

"No, but I can call them later. And I'll see them soon."

"We'll stay for breakfast."

He wasn't asking, but she also didn't mind. She liked the idea of saying goodbye and expressing her thanks in person, but Austin had been leaving so early and she'd made her decision to go home after they were both asleep the previous night.

"Okay, but I'm cooking."

"I'll help."

"Can you cook?"

"I've lived alone before."

Ivy laughed a little. "That doesn't mean you know how to cook. And a cup of ramen, popcorn and frozen dinners don't count."

"I'll have you know I only had one of those things."

"Popcorn?" It was a logical guess since they'd had some a few nights ago while watching movies.

He nodded. "I don't like spicy food and frozen dinners don't even taste like food."

"I'll agree about frozen dinners, but I love a good hot bowl of spicy noodles. It's great for clearing out your sinuses."

Austin snorted. "I don't consider a food's ability to clear my sinuses a selling point."

He moved to lean back against the fence beside her, watching the sunrise.

"Bet you didn't see anything like this in Louisville."

"You're right about that, though the city has its positives too—lots of museums, concerts and festivals on the river, loads of great restaurants and cool neighborhoods. I've never been one to believe that the small town versus city debate is as cut-and-dried as some people do. I can like the vibrancy and choice available in cities as well as the slower pace and neighbors-helping-neighbors aspect of small towns simultaneously. By the same token, I can dislike the traffic and air pollution in cities while also not being a fan of the lack of choices and the negative side of having everyone know your business in small towns. Life is complicated and so is where you live."

"That's a very enlightened outlook on the world."

"Thank you. I try." The smile she gave Austin came easily. When he smiled back, Ivy felt a tension she hadn't been aware of release in her chest.

When they stepped back inside, Daisy was no longer in the fetal position on the couch. She had kicked off her quilt and was now lying on her stomach, one leg and one arm hanging off the edge. Ivy smothered a laugh while Austin just shook his head.

"How she's comfortable like that, I have no idea," he whispered as the two of them headed to the kitchen.

The girl also managed to sleep through all the unintended noise Ivy and Austin made in their efforts to prepare breakfast.

"I bet she was up late reading," Austin said. "She's been that way even before she could read. Mom used to catch her up past her bedtime flipping through books over and over, as if she knew there was more to them than her little mind could comprehend."

"It's good to have a curious mind. I wish more people did, to be honest."

"You're probably right."

"I usually am."

Austin laughed a little under his breath and tossed a bit of scrambled egg at her. Adept at dodging flying food courtesy of the food fights she'd had with her sisters over the years, she batted the egg away and it hit Austin right between the eyes.

"Oh, it's on." He broke off a bit of biscuit and took aim.

Ivy, in turn, picked up a spatula and assumed the pose of a baseball player at bat. That caused Austin to pause, and then he burst out laughing. Realizing how ridiculous they must look, she started laughing too. She laughed so much that she had to hold her stomach and wipe away tears. Austin was in a similar state. It was as if he hadn't laughed in so long that it was all bursting forth at once. For her, it felt good to see him laughing and to be able to really do so herself. Laughing was so much better than crying.

As she finally started to calm down, she noticed that they had an audience. Melissa appeared to be amused, and Daisy…well, Daisy, with her hair looking like a female version of Edward Scissorhands's, seemed to think they'd taken leave of their senses.

Maybe they had. And maybe that's exactly what they both needed.

"You ready?" Austin asked three days later as he and Ivy sat in his truck a couple of blocks from the coin shop.

She smoothed her hands down the front of her dark brown slacks. Today was the first time he'd ever seen her in her professional attire, and he could easily imagine her working as an advertising executive. She'd said she hoped that dressing this way and assuming a professional demeanor in the negotiations would prevent the potential buyer from underestimating her and thinking he could get away with a lowball offer.

"Ready as I'm going to be. I stayed up until a ridiculous hour last night reading everything I could about these coins."

She had decided to only bring the two most valuable coins. The rest she could sell gradually. And she'd been concerned that bringing in a lot of lesser-valued coins would lessen the impact of the two top-dollar ones or possibly make her seem more desperate for money. She knew the value of what she had, and she said she was prepared to walk away if she felt she wasn't being offered what they were worth. He didn't know if he could walk away from thousands of dollars for two coins, even if offered half of what all the sources were saying they were valued at.

He accompanied her into the shop, which appeared to deal in more than coins. At a glance, he saw an array of pocketknives, cigarette lighters, arrowheads and postage stamps.

"Hello," Ivy said to the older man standing behind one of the display cases as she strode forward with a business professional's confidence. "I'm Ivy Lake and I have an appointment to meet with a potential buyer."

"Well, hello. We've been expecting you." The man motioned her toward a room with the door standing open, part of a round table visible.

Austin saw a slight stiffening of Ivy's spine, but he doubted the other man noticed. But she'd detected something off.

"Great," she said. "I've always liked people who arrive early for appointments."

So that was it. They were trying to knock her off her stride from the moment she entered by claiming she was the one who was late. He smiled to himself at how she wasn't having it. These guys didn't know what they were up against.

Introductions were made once they entered the meeting room, and Austin noticed how Mr. Tifton, the potential buyer, took note of his presence next to Ivy. He'd been right to come with her, and not just so she didn't have to make the long trip alone.

"Where did you get these?" Tifton asked.

"I inherited them."

Not in the traditional sense, but he didn't need to know that and Ivy didn't elaborate.

Tifton took out a magnifying glass to examine the coins, consulted something on his phone. As he did so, Ivy pulled up something on her own phone. When Austin realized she was online shopping for new bedding, he had to bite his bottom lip. Was she playing mind games with Tifton, making him think she was communicating with other potential buyers?

After several minutes, Tifton made an offer for both coins—one that was substantially lower than what all her research had told Ivy they were worth.

"Is that your final offer?"

Tifton nodded, looking confident.

Ivy picked up the coins and slipped them back into her purse. "Thank you for your time."

She pushed back her chair and stood, and Austin followed suit as if he'd been expecting her reaction all along.

To the shop owner, she said, "I appreciate you setting up this meeting."

"Wait," Tifton said. "You're not even going to negotiate?"

Ivy offered up a smile, but it wasn't one of the ones that she wore when she was happy. This one was cool and professional without being frosty.

"I'm not a haggler, especially when I know the worth of something. Have a good day, gentlemen."

Austin held the front door open for Ivy as she walked through with a confident stride. Once the door shut behind them, she said, "Don't look back."

"Are you sure about this?"

"It's a gamble and I'm mentally crossing my fingers, but I think I read him correctly. He wants the coins."

They walked up the sidewalk, back toward his truck. When they reached the crosswalk at the end of the first block, Austin was questioning whether Ivy had read Tifton correctly. Right before they started to cross the street, however, he heard hurried footsteps behind them.

"Here we go," Ivy said so only Austin could hear her.

"Miss Lake." It was the owner of the shop.

Ivy looked back. "Yes?"

"Mr. Tifton would like to make another offer."

"I'm listening." Ivy was making it clear by not taking a step back toward the shop that she was waiting to see if the offer was worth the effort.

The owner looked around, likely to make sure no one was within earshot, then revealed the amount of the new offer, a total of fifteen thousand dollars. Ivy, to her credit, did not squeal or jump or otherwise express the joy he had no doubt she was feeling inside.

"That sounds acceptable."

When they returned to the shop, the transaction happened fairly quickly. Once Ivy was certain the money had been transferred to her bank account, she thanked both men again and headed for the exit. For a second time, Austin followed her. He was amazed at how she kept her cool as they retraced their steps down the street. As they reached the crosswalk, however, instead of continuing ahead, Ivy suddenly grabbed his wrist and pulled him to the left.

The moment they were out of sight of the coin shop, her unaffected facade fell away. She emitted a restrained squeal and performed a little dance that had him laughing. Her smile was the widest he'd ever seen it. In the next moment, she pulled him into a hug that surprised him so much that he almost lost his footing. But she was so happy it was infectious, and he found his arms wrapping around her.

As if she suddenly realized what she was doing, Ivy let go and stepped back.

"Sorry. I just thought I was going to burst if I didn't let out my excitement. I can't believe that just happened."

He knew she was talking about the coin sale, but it was also true of the hug. His body felt abnormally warm, abnormally tingly. He wouldn't have minded if the hug lasted longer, but it was a good thing it hadn't.

"We have to go out to celebrate, someplace nice."

"Nothing too nice because I don't have fancy clothes."

"I'm sure we can find something."

After they checked into the hotel Ivy had booked for the night, they both went to their respective rooms to relax before dinner. He took the opportunity to call his mom.

"Is everything okay there?" he asked when she answered.

"We're fine. Isaac is here. He brought dinner from Alma's."

"That was nice of him." Austin hadn't asked Isaac to check on his mom and Daisy, so did that mean his mom had called him to come over? There couldn't possibly be something percolating between them, could there? That would be...odd. Maybe it was just two longtime friends, both of whom had lost their partners, looking out for each other.

"How did the meeting go?"

"Really well. We're going out to eat to celebrate in a few minutes."

"Have a good time, and don't worry about us. Focus on enjoying yourself while you're there."

He felt as if there was some extra layer of meaning in his mother's words, but he wasn't sure what they were. Did she simply want him to have an evening where he wasn't responsible for anyone? When he might be able to set aside his concerns? Could he do that?

When he left his room a few minutes later, he was determined to try. The feeling of that hug from Ivy still lingered, but he had to remind himself that this night was simply two friends enjoying a night away from their ever-present work. But the moment Ivy stepped out of her room two doors down, the whole only-friends thing flew right out of his head. She had changed into a cute pink skirt and white top. His heart started beating as fast as it had the time he'd almost been trampled by a bull.

The powerful urge to leap back into his room and lock the door, putting a barrier between them, nearly overwhelmed him. How could he feel this way after what Grace had done to him? How could he even consider being with another woman so soon after his divorce, one he hadn't seen coming?

Yet the pull toward Ivy was becoming stronger each day. And today, it had grown stronger by the hour.

"I don't know about you, but I'm ready to do some damage to a plate full of food," she said.

"I could eat."

Ivy smiled, and it made his heart flutter.

They ended up at a place that was nice but not too nice, but the menu looked awesome.

"I don't want you being cost-conscious tonight," Ivy

said as they perused the menu. "And no arguments against me buying dinner."

The thought of letting her pay for him didn't sit particularly well, but he was also aware that feeling that way wasn't exactly a modern mindset either.

"Then maybe I'll buy the most expensive thing on the menu," he teased.

"Go right ahead. Except perhaps not the top-shelf drinks," she said, pointing at the liquor behind the bar.

"You don't have to worry about that. I'm not really a drinker."

Leaning into the whole Wyoming cattle rancher thing, he ordered a thick, juicy steak, while Ivy ordered lobster.

"Want to share?" she asked when their huge entrées arrived. "You're not allergic to shellfish, are you? I should have asked before I ordered."

"No, but I've never had lobster."

"Well, you're in for a treat."

"So are you," he said. "Because just the smell of this steak is making my mouth water."

They each cut off a section of their main dish and placed it on the other's plate.

"Oh my, this is good lobster," she said as soon as she took a bite. "Not as good as Maine lobster, but really good."

He had to agree, though the steak was still better in his opinion.

"I have to ask," he said. "How did you know what those guys were doing earlier when they made it sound like you were late for the appointment?"

"I've seen that tactic before, several times. Sometimes it's about the time of appointments, but others it's trying to make you believe you already agreed to some term you know you didn't or pretending that they aren't as interested as they really are. My former boss walked away from buying an old flour mill once when the owner said he couldn't possibly let it go for a lower price. My boss knew he was full of it because that place had at least a decade's worth of vegetation growing all over it. You could barely see the building beneath all the kudzu vines."

"You were impressive today."

"Thanks. Good to know my skills are still useful despite my change in career."

"Speaking of, when do you think you'll be able to open?"

"I'm hoping end of August, right before the weather starts to cool off and people want cozy quilts and yarn to knit."

"And in time to work out any kinks before the fall festival."

"Exactly."

Ivy grew more animated and excited as they continued to talk about her extensive list of plans for the store, ones his mom had helped to create.

"Did you see the wall hanging she created for the store?" Ivy asked.

"Wall hanging?"

"Remember the wood she had you cut and paint? And that box of buttons?"

He nodded.

Ivy looked up something on her phone then handed it to him. He couldn't believe what he was seeing.

"Mom made this?"

"Yes. Isn't it awesome?"

It really was. How had he not known that his mom had this type of creativity in her?

"I know you have concerns about your mom working, but I honestly think it will be great for her. And for me too, because I'll need help, your mom is a local and knows a lot of people, and she has experience in running a business and dealing with retail customers. Plus I really like her. And Daisy." Ivy looked at him and grinned. "I guess you're not half bad either."

"Wow, high praise."

Ivy laughed before taking a bite of her garlic mashed potatoes.

Their conversation flowed from her business to his. Austin was surprised by all the questions Ivy had about ranching. She seemed genuinely interested, and he liked the newness of the experience in having someone be that interested. He was used to being around people who were already familiar with the ins and outs of the cattle business.

"You really do like it, don't you?"

"I do," he said.

"You've never thought about doing something different?"

"Not really. I like doing the renovation work, but it's always secondary and a means of making sure the ranch isn't at risk. I will do whatever I have to in order to ensure Mom and Daisy don't lose anything else, including their home."

The waiter appeared and asked if they'd like to order dessert.

Ivy placed her hand on her stomach. "While I love dessert, I'm afraid I have no room."

"None for me either."

"I think I need to walk this meal off," Ivy said after she'd paid the bill.

"Sounds good to me."

As they walked along the street, they checked out what was in the various shop windows—Western artwork, Western wear, Western jewelry, books about the West.

"No mistaking where we are," Ivy said, looking amused.

"I'm sure there are places in Kentucky where everything has to do with horses."

"True. Horses, bourbon and basketball."

Though she was now a resident of Wyoming, albeit a new one, Ivy acted like a tourist, snapping photos and buying little Wyoming-themed gifts to send back home to her mom and sisters. When they reached one of the tall cowboy boot public art pieces, Ivy had him take a series of photos of her with it while she struck funny poses—hugging it, pretending to ride a horse like the Pony Express rider painted on the boot, pointing at her pursed lips while kicking up one foot like an old-style pinup model.

He couldn't help laughing at her antics.

"Come on, let's take a picture together." She grabbed his hand and pulled him next to her in front of the boot. "Oh, come on, smile." She elbowed him gently in the ribs, and in response he unthinkingly grabbed her around the waist and pulled her close to his side as he smiled.

After a moment of having a startled expression, Ivy smiled too. He held out her phone with his other hand and took a few pictures of them. They were acting like a couple, and an even larger part of him than earlier liked the sound of that.

As he started to hand the phone back to her, they fumbled the exchange and nearly dropped it on the concrete. Somehow, in the process, he ended up with her hand that was holding the phone clasped between both of his hands. And then their gazes met…and held. Ivy seemed as at a loss for words as he felt.

"Am I imagining…something between us?" He felt as nervous as if he was skydiving for the first time.

Ivy continued to stare up at him, as if her brain was slowly processing an appropriate answer to his question.

"I don't think so, though I also keep questioning if I'm imagining it."

He understood why she likely felt that way. Not so long ago she'd thought she'd be marrying someone else.

"I know that feeling."

Over the top of her head, he noticed a family approaching the boot, probably wanting to take their own vacation photos. As he shifted his hand to entwine his fingers with hers and guide her away from the boot, it felt natural and nerve-racking at the same time. Was he making a mistake? What exactly did he want to happen?

"Is this okay?" he asked, lifting their joined hands without looking over at her.

"I...think so. Though, to be honest, I feel a bit weird. Like it's too soon or I'm not really feeling what I think I am."

She slowed then stopped next to a bronze statue.

"Are you okay?" He turned to face her but didn't let go of her hand, so small compared to his.

"If I...feel something, does that mean that I didn't really love James? Do feelings change that quickly? I mean, I wasn't just dating him. I was engaged."

"I think as a general rule, feelings are complicated. I've been asking myself some of the same questions, trying to convince myself that I wasn't really growing to like you more and more because I've only been divorced for a year."

"But I was in a relationship much more recently, a serious one."

"Serious for you. Maybe the fact that he betrayed you eroded those old feelings at a faster rate than normal."

"That sounds sensible, but it still feels a bit confusing."

Not wanting to push if she wasn't ready, he started to slip his hand out of hers. But Ivy suddenly tightened her grip.

"Don't." She looked up at him. "I like the feel of you holding my hand. Maybe if you keep doing it, things will become clearer and less confusing."

And so they walked around some more with their hands linked, switching their serious concerns for lighter conversation. Across the plaza, a band struck up a song and they gravitated toward the music. When other couples began to dance, Austin took a leap and pulled Ivy into the flow of dancers.

"I'm not used to dancing to country music," she said.

"Just let me lead."

She did, and the sound of her laughter as she occasionally tripped over her own feet filled his heart with a brightness that he wasn't sure he'd ever felt before. He'd been happy with Grace for most of their marriage. He remembered happy times when he was a kid, before his father died. There was lots of laughter when Daisy was a baby with impossibly tiny fingers and toes, a toddler who held his hand as she started her first adventures in the world, a little girl who managed to convince him to splash in her kiddie pool with her.

But this, what he was feeling in this moment, was different. He wasn't sure he even had the vocabulary to describe it. Maybe like warmth spreading outward from the deepest part of him, overtaking spaces that had been cold since Grace left him, even before that. The rate at which the intensity was increasing made him wonder if it was visible to those around them.

They danced to a couple of songs before he saw the slightest wince on Ivy's otherwise joyful face.

"We've overdone it with your ankle." It wasn't a question because he already knew the answer. "I'm sorry."

"Don't you dare apologize. I'm having a great time."

"So am I, but we should call it a night. Long day tomorrow." They had a couple places Ivy wanted to go to buy some items she couldn't get in Jade Valley before they made the long drive back.

Ivy sighed as if she hated cutting the evening short. "You're right."

Austin looked back across the plaza and realized how far they'd wandered from his truck.

"Would you like a piggyback ride?"

Ivy laughed. "I am not doing that. We're not in a K-drama."

"A what?"

"Korean TV dramas. Someone is always giving someone a piggyback ride."

They made the walk back to the truck slowly. Austin told himself it was out of consideration for her ankle, but that was only partially true. He was holding her hand again and didn't want to let it go, even though he knew he'd have to.

Ivy didn't seem to be in any hurry either, and he wondered how much of that he could attribute to her ankle and how much to the same hesitance for the evening to end.

By the time they reached his truck, the sky was fully dark, the sun coming up somewhere on the other side of the world. Daisy would likely be able to rattle off those locations.

Austin opened the passenger-side door but still didn't immediately release Ivy's hand. He felt as if he had become a different person from the one who had left Jade Valley early that morning. But that made him wonder if this new version of himself, with all the electric feelings crackling along his nerves, would disappear as soon as they returned to Jade Valley. Would all his memories of what had happened over the past two years rear up like a grizzly with his long, sharp claws ready to rake deep gashes into him?

Was this time in Cheyenne just a momentary departure from his constant fixation of taking care of his family, working from dawn till late to make sure they were all safe and wanted for none of life's essentials?

Was his giving in to his feelings for Ivy, even a little, setting himself—as well as his mom and Daisy—up for more heartbreak? He couldn't fully make that question disappear. And yet the pull toward Ivy kept building, so much so that he leaned forward slowly. Part of him wanted her to stop him, to put her hand against his chest to halt his advance, to say it was too soon for both of them. But when she did none of those things, he felt as if he was jumping off a cliff toward an impossibly blue ocean below.

Despite that one voice telling him he was making a mistake, his lips finally touched Ivy's lightly. She didn't pull away but there was a moment of hesitance, perhaps in which her own mind was telling her something similar, before she kissed him back.

The kiss didn't last long, but it left him feeling as if his feet weren't quite touching the ground. He gave her hand a light squeeze before releasing her and walking around to the driver's side. He didn't hold her hand while driving to the hotel either. It was partly because he wanted to keep both hands safely on the steering wheel. Cheyenne wasn't a big city, but it was way bigger than he was used to navigating on a regular day. He also wanted to give them both time to process the kiss they'd just shared, how they had held hands a lot of the evening. He needed time to figure out if he really wanted to go down this road, and he suspected Ivy was examining similar questions. Her earlier one about how she could feel something for him so soon after having been engaged was proof of that.

Honestly, he should ponder the answer to that particular question as well. What if what she was feeling now was just her latching on to someone who made her feel good after her ex had made her feel so bad? What if Austin was only a potential rebound relationship?

When they reached the hotel, they walked through the lobby side by side but still without touching. On their floor, they reached her room first.

"Good night," he said, hesitating only a moment before taking a step toward his room.

Ivy caught his hand, halting him.

"I had a really good time tonight," she said. "And no matter how much I think about it, this feels real."

Tension released all throughout this body. His smile showed outwardly the growing happiness he felt inside.

"For me too."

Ivy smiled in an oddly shy way that made him fall for her a little more. Austin lifted Ivy's hand to his lips and kissed the back of it.

"Get some good sleep. I'll see you at breakfast."

Ivy nodded and slipped into her room. Austin stood staring at her door until he heard the click of her dead bolt locking into place. When he turned toward his own room, he had to resist the urge to whoop and skip down the corridor like a kid who'd just won a year's supply of candy.

CHAPTER TWELVE

DESPITE BEING TIRED from a day that started really early, Ivy could not calm her mind enough to sleep. Instead, she sat in the dark of her room and stared out the window at the lights of Cheyenne. It wasn't as big and busy as Louisville, but she liked the vibe of the small city. It felt like a different world from Louisville or Lexington the same way she felt like a different person here. She wondered whether her mind would be grasping so much for answers if more time had passed since her breakup with James. Would she still question if her feelings for Austin were real or reactionary?

She tried to remember precisely the progression of her feelings as she'd first been attracted to James, as they had begun to talk, their first date, as they'd grown closer, and eventually his proposal. Were those early stages the same as what she was feeling toward Austin now? Why couldn't she remember the finer details?

As she watched the lessening number of cars pass by on the streets, fewer numbers of pedestrians on the sidewalks, the gradual shutting off of lights in various businesses, she thought about all the moments spent with Austin. From the early days when she'd explained to him what kind of work she wanted done and she could see how he wasn't quite sure she was serious but also wanted the work, to how they'd laughed over dinner tonight and then walked hand in hand and danced together.

And then there was the kiss. She wouldn't describe it

as hesitant, but there had been a restraint to it. Compared to how James had kissed her the first time, full of a passion that had sent her head spinning, Austin's kiss had felt tender and like he was gauging if it was something they both wanted to happen. When she'd seen what he intended to do, she honestly hadn't been sure. But when his lips had touched hers, it had felt so nice, as if it was beginning to erase all those heavy feelings of betrayal that had trailed her across the country and kept sitting in a corner of her heart waiting to pounce when she was most vulnerable.

But it had been over quickly, too quickly. And yet, at the same time, she appreciated the briefness. Much more and she might have been overwhelmed, unable to dissect her feelings in the aftermath. As it was, it felt as if her mind was deep in the throes of a boxing match. In this corner, common sense. In the opposite corner, trusting her feelings.

Was she placing too much emphasis on the amount of time that had passed since her breakup with James? Was there some unwritten rule about how long you had to wait before starting a new relationship? About how long was necessary between relationships to know the second one was real and not just a desperate search for someone to make you feel loved again?

After almost all the outside activity had come to a halt, Ivy finally crossed to the comfortable bed and crawled under the covers. As she began to feel herself drift, she came to a conclusion. Despite the seeming swiftness of her attraction to Austin, it hadn't been immediate. That seemed to indicate that he wasn't a rebound guy but rather someone she truly liked, more so every day. She would let her feelings lead her where they wanted and see what happened.

ALL THE LATE-NIGHT ponderings and worries seemed to evaporate with the rising of the sun the next morning. Ivy carried her bag downstairs to meet Austin, who was already up and drinking coffee like the super early riser he was. Austin drove them a short distance to a restaurant known for their generous breakfasts.

"I need fuel if I'm going to be forced to go shopping," Austin said.

Ivy shook her head. "You'd think I was going to force you to march across a desert."

"Is that an option?"

They continued to joke over what was, indeed, a large breakfast about which was better—pancakes or waffles—with each enumerating the reasons why the other was wrong. Ivy believed firmly that the answer was pancakes, and nothing would sway that belief. Texture, taste and shape were all superior to waffles, in her opinion.

Despite his comments about hating shopping, Austin was a good sport about traipsing through furniture stores and a couple of antique shops. By the time the truck was loaded with an antique treadle-style sewing machine, some vintage light fixtures, and a fluffy chair and ottoman for her living space, there was only one stop left on her list.

"Do we have enough room for a mattress set?" she asked, hands on hips, as she looked at the back of the truck.

"Yeah, we'll make them fit."

She supposed they'd have to because she couldn't just pop back over to Cheyenne easily. The other option would be either a closer store, which would likely be more expensive, or going the mail-order mattress route. She didn't like the latter idea because she couldn't test it first and, most importantly, she wanted an actual bed to sleep on tonight. She had exhausted her willingness to sleep on the floor in a sleeping bag. If her two old coins had only brought enough to buy a mattress set, that was one hundred percent what she would have bought.

After they had been in the mattress store for a while, her trying out one mattress after another, she sat up on the side of one and said, "I feel like Goldilocks trying out the beds in the three bears' house."

"We get that a lot," a salesman said as he approached them, passing a younger female employee. Then the guy pointed at the mattress where she sat as he looked at Austin. "You should try it out too."

Right as Austin opened his mouth to respond, a baby squalled across the showroom, accompanied by a flurry of exclamations from his parents. The salesman muttered something unflattering as he rushed toward the family. Even though she was still startled by the man's comment, Ivy quickly gathered that the toddler had spilled a sippy cup full of milk on a new mattress.

When her eyes met Austin's, heat raced up her neck into her cheeks.

"I feel like we just saw karma in action, don't you?" Austin said.

Ivy snort-laughed, belatedly hiding her mouth behind her hand. That he'd just dispersed the awkwardness between them in the wake of the encounter with the salesman made her like Austin even more.

"Can I help you with anything?" This question came from the young woman the salesman had jetted past.

"I have a question," Ivy said, still sitting on the edge of the quite comfortable mattress. "If I buy this right now, do you get the commission or does he?" She nodded toward the salesman, who seemed to be in a bit of a heated discussion with the parents of the milk-spilling toddler, who was still making his displeasure known.

"If I process the sale, I get the commission."

"Let's do that."

The young woman, whose name tag read Becca, smiled. "Gladly."

Ivy and Austin followed Becca to the cash register, where she ran Ivy's credit card.

"Thank you for your business," Becca said as she handed back the card and the receipt. "This is only my second day here, and this is my first sale."

Across the room, the salesman handed off the ruined mattress situation to another man Ivy assumed was the store manager and hurried toward them.

"Thank you, Becca," Ivy said when the other guy was within a few feet. "It was nice to meet you, and I think you have a good future in sales. You have a pleasant way with customers."

There was a twinkle in Becca's eyes as she thanked Ivy for her kind words. She knew exactly what Ivy was doing.

"You're bad," Austin said, obviously amused, as they left the building to move the truck around to the side loading dock.

"Who, me?" Ivy asked as she walked backward in front of him, holding her palms to her cheeks and batting her eyelashes in faux innocence.

"Austin?"

At the sound of his name, spoken by a woman with short blond hair, Austin froze. Every speck of humor disappeared from his expression in one blink of Ivy's eyes. He turned his head toward the woman slowly, as if afraid the Grim Reaper might be standing there ready to drag him away to the afterlife. Ivy noticed that he didn't speak.

The woman glanced at Ivy, as if trying to figure out who she was and how she fit into Austin's life, before returning her gaze to him.

"It's good to see you again." Her smile looked shaky, as if she wasn't sure whether she should smile at all.

Instead of responding, Austin turned away from her and said to Ivy, "Let's go."

The blonde reached out and grabbed Austin's arm. "Wait. Can we talk?"

Austin looked at her fingers gripping his biceps in a way that sent a chill down Ivy's spine and made the woman remove her hand.

"I don't have anything to say to you. That time has passed." He strode past Ivy toward his truck. She gave the woman one more quick look before she hurried after him.

The tight set of Austin's jaw told Ivy that now was not the time to ask questions. Instead, she stayed quiet as he drove around to the side of the building, as he helped the workers load her mattress set and secure it for the long drive back to Jade Valley. She worried that all the fun they'd had on their trip had just been obliterated by the appearance of that woman. If she had to guess the blonde's identity, she'd put money on her being his ex-wife.

The way the woman acted, and how Austin had reacted in turn, made Ivy wonder if she'd been wrong about him. He'd seemed so cold, so distant, so angry at the woman's request to have a conversation.

Possible reasons the two of them had reached that point spun in Ivy's head as Austin drove away from the mattress store and headed toward I-80. She noticed how tightly Austin held the steering wheel and that he looked straight ahead. It felt very much as if he was doing everything in his power to keep his anger reined in.

Half an hour passed before he finally spoke. "I think we should remain friends."

Confused by his statement, she nevertheless replied, "I do too."

"Just friends."

"Oh." That "oh" was one part shock and one part a sudden pain in her chest. The tears pooling in her eyes surprised her too, and she turned to look out the window as she blinked them away.

"I had a nice time the last two days, but I shouldn't have let it go further."

Ivy pressed her lips together as her eyes stung and *not again, not again, not again* echoed in her head.

"That night you told me about what James had done to you, I didn't reciprocate."

"You didn't have to," she said, doing her best to not let her voice betray how hurt she felt. "I didn't share my story expecting you to do the same."

"Still." He went quiet for several long moments. "You've probably guessed that was my ex-wife, Grace."

"I thought it might be." Ivy cleared the lump in her throat and shifted her gaze to the road ahead, her mind already scolding her for allowing herself to be vulnerable again.

"After Mom's accident, I made plans to bring Mom and Daisy to live with us," he said. "Grace didn't have anything against my family, but she was against the plan. She said we could help out, but that they had their own home. They could sell the rafting business and use the money to hire help. When I told her that there would be no money left after Mom paid off the business mortgage and that Mom wouldn't be able to work to pay the house mortgage, Grace dug in her heels."

Despite her own aching heart, Ivy felt her dislike of his ex-wife growing with each word he spoke.

"She said that she'd spent the latter part of her teens and half her twenties helping to raise her younger siblings when her mother passed, and that she hadn't signed up for more long-term caregiving when she married me. A part of me understood. She had to give up a lot at a young age, but she told me I was going to have to choose—her or my mother and sister."

"That's not a fair choice. It's a cruel one."

"Yeah." He sounded tired, the kind of tired that came from dredging up old memories of things you didn't want to think about anymore. Ivy tried to set aside her own feelings to understand his.

"So...she filed for divorce?"

"Eventually. She went on a trip to visit a friend in Denver, and she never came back. When she was past due to come home, I called to make sure she was okay. I thought maybe she'd been in an accident. Despite how we'd been fighting, the idea of her being hurt in a car wreck so soon after Mom scared me half to death. When she told me she was still in Denver and that, while she was sorry, I was on my own, I lost my temper and said some not nice things."

"That's understandable." After all, she had done the same to James, even if he hadn't been where he could hear those words.

"Some time later, I'm not even sure how long it was because everything was a blur during those weeks, I was served divorce papers. I was so angry I signed them five minutes after I got them."

His hesitance to start another relationship made even more sense now. So did his understanding of her when she shared what James had done. They'd both been betrayed, both unsure if being in another relationship was worth the potential heartache.

Still, that didn't erase the sting of him saying he didn't want to go any further with her. Maybe he just needed some time to process seeing his ex again. Maybe his call-

ing it quits with Ivy romantically was just a knee-jerk reaction and tomorrow he'd change his mind again.

But that wasn't fair to her. She wasn't the one who'd
betrayed him.

"Why do you think she wanted to talk to you today?"

"No idea. Don't care." His words were clipped, and Ivy
took it as evidence that he didn't want to talk about Grace
anymore. Fine. She didn't exactly have warm, fuzzy feelings about the woman or this entire situation either.

They slipped into silence, and Ivy stared out the passenger-side window at the short green and brown grass
of the High Plains. Any other vegetation was sparse on
the flat to gently rolling landscape, so different from the
western part of the state. Montana might be known as
the Big Sky State, but the vastness of the blue sky dotted
with puffy white clouds outside her window would give
it a run for its money.

Ivy let Austin be alone with his thoughts while she sat
with hers, but the longer the quiet stretched, the more antsy
and irritated she became. She began to stew because even
though she totally understood the hesitance to start a new
relationship after being betrayed, she'd opened herself to
one with him—and he knew what she'd gone through, how
difficult it had to be for her to do so. But she was undecided
as to whether she should tell him that. After hearing what
Grace had done, would Ivy be showing a different kind of
self-centeredness by telling him how she felt? Would it just
help verify to him that he was making the right decision in
ending things barely after they'd started? Should she take
this out to protect herself from further hurt?

As the quiet stretched, the hum of the truck's tires on
the road, combined with her limited sleep the night before, made her eyelids drift closed. She forced her eyes

open, thinking she should stay awake to make sure Austin did as well.

"You can take a nap," he said, as if he'd heard her thoughts. "I'm wide awake."

She looked over at him. Though she doubted his thoughts about his ex had been left behind them as the miles passed, he didn't seem as tense as when they'd left the mattress store. His grip on the steering wheel was more relaxed, and his jaw wasn't clenched. Maybe the farther they traveled away from Cheyenne, the better he felt.

And that thought made her mad because what if ending things with her was part of what had helped him relax?

She didn't ask him if he was sure it was okay for her to sleep, because he didn't even take his gaze off the highway to glance at her. The invisible barrier between them was growing thicker with each mile he drove.

Instead, she leaned as much as she could to her right, turning her head so that she faced the passenger window. But despite her fatigue, Austin's dismissal made her feel more awake. She watched as the flatter land gave way to more hills as they climbed in elevation. She couldn't help wondering what his ex-wife had wanted to talk to him about. Did she now believe she'd made a mistake and wanted to get back together? From Austin's response to Grace, Ivy didn't see that happening.

But it wasn't totally certain, was it? Despite his obvious anger about what Grace had done, what if they did work things out? They'd loved each other enough to get married before, and stranger things had happened. A larger lump formed in Ivy's throat. Maybe those tentative first steps in her own romantic relationship with Austin had simply been a product of being far away from home, just the two of them. Even without Grace's appearance, would it have disappeared as soon as they returned to Jade Valley? Would being back in his normal environs make Austin think he'd made a mistake, and things would have turned out the same way—with him ending any further development of their romance?

Yes, she was getting good and mad at Austin. But a part of her still understood on some level why he was acting as he was, and that made her even madder at Grace. She'd like to give the woman a substantial piece of her mind. Despite how she'd unfairly had to shoulder a lot of family responsibility early, it was still an incredibly hurtful decision to abandon Austin when he needed her most. As if having lost his stepfather and nearly losing his mother wasn't enough of a blow, he'd had to find out that his wanting to take care of his mother and sister was the bridge too far for his wife. His caretaker heart was the thing that made Grace bail on their wedding vows.

"I wouldn't do the same thing to you," she said.

"I can't take that chance."

The finality of that statement, how quickly he'd made it and the resulting painful stab in her heart made Ivy glad she wasn't facing him.

It took a long time, but fatigue finally won out over anger and hurt, forcing her to fall asleep. It surprised her when she woke up to discover they'd not only passed through Laramie but were already approaching Rock Springs. They'd be back in Jade Valley in less than two hours.

She glanced over at Austin and he looked pretty much the same as when she'd fallen asleep. Then the anger and hurt came back full force. In the next moment, she made a decision. She wouldn't fight for a relationship the other person didn't want. Back to professional distance.

"Would you like me to drive and give you a break?" she asked.

"No, I'm good."

Once again, he didn't look at her. And his succinct response told her that he wasn't in any more of a mood to talk than when she'd slipped off to sleep. She, however, didn't think she could stand the silence for the rest of the trip. They didn't have to talk about their pasts, but she needed to talk about something.

"How much longer do you think it will take to finish the renovation work?"

"Probably only a week."

"That soon?" She experienced a pang of loss and he wasn't even gone yet. But the way he was acting now, it would be best to get the job finished and both of them back to their separate lives. She wondered if he'd even convince Melissa that working for her wouldn't be worth the time and gas it cost for him to take her to and from work.

"Yeah, if not sooner."

Did he sound like a man who couldn't wait to be rid of having to be around her?

So much for talking to help alleviate the uncomfortable air between them. She pulled out her phone and saw she had a text from Lily.

Who is the hot cowboy?

Ugh. Ivy realized she'd accidentally sent one of the pictures of her and Austin next to that big boot art piece along with some of her solo selfies and scenery shots from around Cheyenne.

That's Austin, the guy who is doing the renovations on the building.

Why do you look like a couple on a date?

We don't. We were goofing off because we had time to kill between yesterday's errands and today's.

Why did he go with you?

He has a truck. I don't. Did you notice any of the other photos I sent you?

Yeah, yeah, all very nice.

Ivy rolled her eyes.

"What's wrong?" The sound of Austin's voice surprised her, coming after such a long period of him not speaking.

"Nothing." He wasn't the only one who could offer short, emotionless responses.

Plus, after what had happened earlier, there was no way she was going to reveal that Lily was teasing her about him. And she wasn't going to tell Lily that she'd kissed the "hot cowboy" either, because it looked as if that was a onetime thing.

Ivy chatted with Lily for a while longer, asking about her and Holly, about their mom, all of their jobs. Yes, she was letting the conversation distract her from the man sitting across from her. Ivy started counting down the minutes until she could escape the suffocating feeling of being trapped in a confined space with a man who'd done a one-eighty where she was concerned.

Good to know now before she was any more invested.

Except that she felt the sting in her heart every time she allowed herself to think about how much she'd enjoyed her time with him yesterday and that morning before Grace had appeared and ruined everything.

When Lily said she had to go, Ivy wanted to reach through the phone and prevent it. Instead, she simply said she'd talk to her sister again soon. She also promised to send pictures of the renovations because they were all dying of curiosity. Now that it looked a lot better than when she'd taken possession of the building, her family would hopefully not freak out as much.

About an hour from Jade Valley, Austin pulled over at a convenience store to fill his truck up with gas. She hurried inside to use the restroom and to get away from Austin for a few minutes. After taking her time to buy a couple of drinks and some snacks, she went back outside to see Austin looking at his phone. When he noticed her approach, he slipped it back into his pocket and resumed his spot in the driver's seat.

"You didn't need to get me anything," he said. "We're not far from home."

"It's okay. I had the munchies."

Anything to occupy their remaining time together. And to make it seem as if he hadn't hurt her as much as he had. Admitting that she'd allowed herself to feel too much too fast was embarrassing and made her feel too raw and pitiful.

When they finally pulled up in front of her building, Rich was there waiting. Had that been who Austin was texting earlier and not his ex-wife? Of course, Ivy had spent so much time in the store that he could have texted both. Back in Cheyenne, he'd been abundantly clear that he had nothing to say to Grace. But what if during all those quiet hours since then he'd changed his mind? Had his anger given way to curiosity about what Grace wanted to say to him? Was it possible they could move past her betrayal and try again?

Ivy hated the idea of that after what Grace had done, hated the idea of anyone returning to someone who'd betrayed them. That feeling stemmed partly from her expe-

rience with James, but not all of it. She still remembered
how mad she'd been when one of her college friends kept
getting back with her boyfriend, even after he'd cheated on
her multiple times. She may have yelled something about
leopards not changing their spots and stormed off, and
their friendship had never been the same until it gradually faded away altogether.

Was that what was happening between her and Austin now, the beginning of fading away despite the fact
he'd claimed he wanted to remain friends? Right now, she
wasn't sure she even wanted that.

While the two men made quick work of carrying the
mattress set upstairs and the old sewing machine to the
bottom level, she busied herself taking in the smaller items.
It was all done within a few minutes. Rich gave her a curious look before departing for another appointment. That
left her with Austin, awkwardness still lying between them
like a thick morning fog but at least not trapped in the truck
together with miles to go.

"Thanks for all your help," she said, trying to act as if
nothing had changed between them since they'd set off
from Jade Valley yesterday.

"No problem. I'll be back in the morning to work out
back."

She nodded, glad that he would be working to clean up
the small courtyard area behind the building and mostly
out of her sight.

Without saying anything else, he got in his truck and
drove away. Her heart sank way more than it should have,
proving that she hadn't learned her lesson. She'd come to
Wyoming with the mission of forging an independent life
for herself, and she'd instead allowed herself to start to fall
way too easily for another man.

If he wanted to go back to a purely boss/contractor relationship, well, that was fine with her.

At least that's what she told herself.

AUSTIN WALKED STRAIGHT to the barn when he got home, bypassing the house because he needed time to get his sour mood hidden away before he encountered his mother and sister. Both of them were too observant for him to get away with some flimsy excuse like he was tired.

He was as upset with himself as he was with Grace. He hated that he'd allowed her to get in his head so much that he'd been twisted in tight knots all the way back to Jade Valley. Worse, he'd shut out Ivy, ended things with her. Having Grace show up out of the blue had felt like a sign from the universe that he was making a mistake starting a new relationship.

Even if it hadn't felt like a mistake as it was happening. While he'd held Ivy's hand, danced and laughed with her, he'd felt better than he had since before his mom's accident. If it was only him he had to worry about, maybe he'd be okay by morning and he could go apologize, tell Ivy that he hadn't meant it and hope they could pick up where they left off. But his own feelings were not his only concern. And after the way he'd told Ivy he only wanted to be friends, how he'd let her know that he couldn't take a chance on more, he figured she was done with him anyway. He certainly would be.

He knew sometimes people had whirlwind vacation romances, but one limited to twenty-four hours seemed ridiculous. If he'd hurt Ivy, especially after what she'd been through in her last relationship, kicking himself repeatedly sounded like a just punishment.

He'd been in the barn about an hour when the sound of

approaching footsteps told him that his mom had likely sent Daisy out to see why he wasn't coming into the house.

"Hey, kiddo," he said as Daisy entered the barn.

"Mom said to come in and eat."

"I'm not hungry. I had a lot to eat today."

"What's wrong?"

"Nothing."

"You're lying." She didn't say it harshly, but rather using a matter-of-fact tone.

Instead of denying it, he said, "You should have seen the size of the breakfast I had. It was enough for a basketball team."

"Fine, don't tell me. But I've got five dollars on Mom not letting you off with that flimsy excuse. Wouldn't you rather talk to me instead?"

Austin stopped sharpening the lawn mower blade but kept staring at it.

"I ran into Grace in Cheyenne this morning."

"Seriously?"

He nodded.

"What did she say? Not that I care."

"That's pretty much what I told her, that I wasn't interested, and walked away. Didn't look back."

"Good."

This was the most fire he'd seen out of his little sister in a long time. It took a lot to make her mad, so when it was apparent that she had been angered it was best to stay far away until she cooled down. Daisy might be on the quiet side most of the time, but she was like him—protective of her family.

"Don't tell Mom. I don't want to upset her," he said.

Daisy agreed to keep his secret.

"How did it go at the coin shop?"

"Really well. Watching how Ivy handled the situation, it's easy to assume she was very good at her previous job."

And that if anyone could make a quilt shop in the Stinson Building into a success, it was her.

"I'm glad Mom is going to be working in her store. I think it'll be good for both of them."

"Both?"

"Yeah. Mom will be out and around people, and she'll feel useful. And Ivy won't be alone all the time. She tries not to show it, but I think she gets lonely. She probably misses her family."

All because James had been the biggest of fools, cheating on a beautiful, funny, talented woman. The man really was an idiot.

But Austin probably was as well, because he'd gone from kissing Ivy to almost completely ignoring her on the long drive back home, telling her that being with her wasn't worth taking a chance. If he could rewind time, even by only a day, he wouldn't have given in to his growing feelings. Everything was now much more complicated. What was she thinking at that moment? Did she think that he'd taken advantage of her vulnerability after she'd told him how she'd been betrayed by James?

"Hello?"

He pulled himself out of his thoughts when Daisy waved her hand in front of him.

"You have on your thinking-too-much face," she said. "She doesn't deserve you hurting your brain over her."

"I'm not." At least not the *her* Daisy was referring to.

His sister didn't look convinced.

"I promise."

He knew she still didn't believe him as she turned to head back inside, but she didn't press him further. Once she was gone, he finished sharpening the lawn mower blade, put it back on the mower, then sank onto a wooden bench. His thoughts drifted to the night before, to how nice it had felt to give in to the feelings he'd tried to deny and kiss Ivy. He pressed his hand to his chest, still able to feel how it had seemed as if his heart had expanded and floated within him like a heart-shaped balloon. And then Grace had appeared and popped it with a huge pin.

Deflated. That's exactly how he felt now, and he didn't know what to do about it. Should he find a way to reinflate that balloon or toss it away altogether?

CHAPTER THIRTEEN

WHEN FIONA CALLED IVY to see if she could cover her early morning shifts at Trudy's because she was sick with some respiratory virus that had her coughing like a seal's bark, Ivy accepted. Her ankle might protest some, but she figured she could wrap it to give it extra support. She'd have to be careful with her healing finger, but the extra hours at work would serve a dual purpose—earning more money that she could invest in her store and staying away from Austin.

She did her best to understand how seeing his ex-wife would rattle him, but she still couldn't help feeling hurt. When she did see him, she could almost believe their romantic twenty-four hours hadn't even happened. He avoided eye contact, was all business. Maybe she should be thankful for that because it would make moving on again easier. But the truth was, her heart felt badly bruised.

When her extended shift was over for the day, she ran a few errands before finally heading home. As she turned the corner at Main and Yarrow, her heart did a weird combination of sinking and speeding up when she saw Austin's truck was still there. Of course it was. He wasn't one to cut a workday short. Plus he seemed in a hurry to put the renovation project behind him. Today, he'd been working on light fixtures inside plus moving the old wood-and-glass display cases that she had sanded and stained to the spots she'd indicated.

If her brief romance with Austin was over, she could at least be excited about how soon she could start the process of stocking her store.

When she stepped into the building, the first thing she noticed was that Austin was not inside. The next was that not only were the antique display cases and the new light fixtures in the appropriate spots, but the button wall hanging Melissa had made was now hung on the wall.

"That looks awesome," she said as she approached Melissa, who was busy on Ivy's laptop computer.

"I'm glad you like it."

"I love it, so much so that I think you should make some more pieces like it and we'll sell them in the store."

"Funny you should mention that. I just bought a cheap collection of old buttons online, and they'll be here by the end of the week. I already have several ideas if Austin can stop being grumpy long enough to cut some boards for me."

Ivy fixed her gaze on the wall hanging so that Melissa didn't see how the sound of her son's name affected Ivy.

Once again telling herself to only focus on the positives, she thought about how much having a purpose and a creative outlet had breathed new life into Melissa. Even if Ivy and Austin weren't going to be a couple, she was happy with the friendships she'd made with his family. Sure, it would take a while to get past things not working out with him, but hopefully they could return to being easy friends again at some point.

"Are you okay?" Melissa asked. "You look like you have a lot on your mind."

"I do. It's not every day that a girl starts a brand-new business." Ivy infused her answer with excitement, which wasn't entirely fake. The closer she got to actually ordering products and setting up the store, the more it seemed as if it was really going to happen.

As she climbed the stairs to her home, however, she couldn't maintain the smile she'd offered Melissa. Though she knew she shouldn't, she looked out the back window. Austin and Daisy were behind the building, cleaning the old stones that made a sort of patio area. Most of them had been covered with years of dirt and vegetation, but enough were visible to know they existed. She'd found a couple of outdoor chairs during her culling of the building's contents. Some cleaning and a new coat of paint would make them perfect for the patio area. Who would sit with her, she didn't know. Maybe it would just be her and Sprinkles.

Though she knew she should move away from the window, stop watching Austin, she couldn't quite make herself do so. As she watched him use a shovel to remove some of the accumulated years of disuse, she noticed how his T-shirt stretched across his back, how his strength made the work look easy. She remembered how she liked seeing him smile and hearing him laugh. She'd gotten a glimpse of the man he could be if he didn't have so much weighing on his shoulders. Mixed with her anger at him for not believing in her enough to give them a chance was the realization of how much she was going to miss seeing him every day. She'd swear she could hear the ticking of the minutes until he was gone getting louder and louder.

AUSTIN SHOULD HAVE known something was up by how quiet his mom was on their way home after work, but he'd been so caught up in his own thoughts that he hadn't really noticed. It had started to dawn on him that something serious was on her mind as he watched the way she cut her chicken breast during dinner. Warning lights started blinking red and Daisy headed to her room after loading the dishwasher, leaving him alone with his mom.

"I'll go feed Pooch," he said as he started to get up from the table.

"Sit." It wasn't a request. The way she said that single word took him back to when he was a kid and had made a decision that got him into trouble. Now, as then, he complied.

"Is something wrong?"

"That's what I want to ask you," she said. "Why have you and Ivy been avoiding each other ever since you got back from Cheyenne?"

"We're not. We see each other every day."

"My legs may not work any longer, but my eyes are perfectly fine. And I know what I've been seeing. Something happened between you two while you were gone, didn't it?"

He sighed. "It's nothing for you to worry about."

"So you're the only person in this family who gets to worry about anyone?"

Now his mom sounded irritated, bordering on angry.

"I didn't say that."

"You didn't have to. It's been abundantly clear for some time now." She took a slow, deep breath, seeming to gather herself so she didn't outright explode. "I appreciate everything you've done for me and Daisy, everything you continue to do, but you're holding on too tight and your focus is too narrow."

He must have looked confused because his mom's expression softened a bit.

"You and Ivy like each other. I'm fairly certain the cattle could see that if she spent time in the pasture with you. Even if you don't tell me what happened on your trip, I know something did. When you left, the two of you talked and joked easily with each other. Now you can barely meet each other's eyes when you're not avoiding each other entirely. And I can't tell if Ivy is sad or mad. Maybe it's both."

So he hadn't been imagining it. But he had been trying to ignore it, telling himself over and over that ending things before they went any further would protect them both.

Austin considered how to handle the conversation so that after it was over he didn't have to address the topic of Ivy and him again.

"We thought maybe there could be something, but there isn't."

"You mean that you won't let there be anything." She made this accusation so quickly that it showed she had it at the ready, that she'd been dissecting his actions well before tonight.

"Don't you think I'm old enough to make my own decisions?"

"Yes, but I also have the right as your mother to tell you when you're being stupid."

He jerked a little at that jab.

"I don't have to have a crystal ball or be able to read minds to know what is going on," she said. "You are refusing to allow yourself to find happiness again because of what Grace did. That's giving her too much power over your life."

Amazing how similar his mom and Daisy sounded sometimes.

"Mom, I have my reasons."

"If one of those reasons has anything to do with me, I'm going to be really angry."

"Why? Because I don't want you and Daisy hurt again? Because I don't want to be hurt again?"

"So you're going to just be alone the rest of your life?"

"I'm not. I have you and Daisy."

"Do not use us as an excuse. You know someday Daisy

will go off to college and then to see the world. And I won't live forever."

"Don't say that." The idea of losing either of them ripped him apart inside.

"It's a fact. I'm twenty-two years older than you. And even if I live to be a hundred, it is not the same as having a life partner and you know it."

"Well, I don't have a very good track record with that, do I?"

"Austin, I remember distinctly when you were a little boy and you fell off your pony. You didn't even cry. You got up, dusted off your little jeans and climbed back on. You've done that about everything your entire life—except trying to find love again."

"It hasn't been that long, and I have plenty else on my plate."

"And I'm sorry for that."

"It's not your fault."

"Part of it is. I know I've not been much help since the accident."

"You've been grieving."

"And I will continue to do so, but I'm also still here and I have to keep on living. You and Daisy deserve a mother who is fully here, not one who might at any moment sink into depression. I loved Sam and I miss him with my whole heart. Same as with your father. But I am tired of living in a fog. I'm going back to work, and I'm going to contribute to the family finances so everything isn't on you."

He started to interrupt her, to say he was fine, but she held up her hand to stop him.

"I'm excited about the opportunity to work in Ivy's store. If what you're worried about is the store not making it and Ivy leaving Jade Valley, you can put those worries to rest. That girl has a great head for business. She's ambitious and determined but isn't overstretching."

"But even good businesses fail. People you think would never leave do. And then you're left to pick up the pieces. I don't want to go through that again. I can't put you and Daisy through that again either, because I know how close you both have gotten to Ivy."

"So you think that by not allowing yourself to like her, to date her, we magically wouldn't be sad if Ivy decided to go back to Kentucky? Do you realize how foolish that sounds? You've gotten so good at self-sacrifice that you've forgotten who you used to be."

Those words felt like a bomb going off, one he hadn't known was approaching. Had he really gone too far in his protectiveness of his mother and sister? Of himself? Had he used protecting them as a convenient excuse to not open himself up to being hurt again?

He realized he'd used seeing Grace again as another convenient excuse.

If he really thought about it, Ivy didn't seem like a person who would deliberately hurt someone else—especially considering how she had suffered because of her previous relationship. But he'd already pushed her away. The fact that she had been avoiding him to the fullest extent possible, coupled with his mom's observation about Ivy's mood, told him that he'd likely already blown his chance.

He looked across the table and saw his mom watching him, likely interpreting every small change in his expression the way she had his entire life.

"What if I've already messed up my chance?"

"What if you haven't?"

Not able to wait until tomorrow to find out the answer, he grabbed his keys, gave his mom a kiss on the forehead and ran to his truck.

Please don't let me be too late.

IVY KNEW SHE had to get past thinking about Austin every time she looked at her refurbished floors, her freshly painted ceiling and the new pane in the window that had been broken when she first arrived in Jade Valley. This was her home and would soon be her business, so she would be spending a lot of time in the building. Maybe once it was filled with patterned fabrics, colorful yarn and various sewing notions the memories of Austin standing in a certain spot and moving in a certain attractive way would fade.

Until then, memories of him seemed to be everywhere. She would get past her hard-and-fast fall for him—because, no matter that she'd so recently been engaged to someone else she loved, she had fallen for Austin. Maybe this was her cosmic punishment for opening her heart too easily.

Feeling antsy, she decided to try out the new firepit she had constructed out of some old leftover bricks that had been hidden under weeds and grass next to the back of the building and some fast-drying cement. Tonight felt like a night for s'mores. After a quick trip to the grocery and locating an appropriate stick, she lit a fire and watched as it grew to a useful size.

The first bite of gooey marshmallow and chocolate squeezed between graham crackers burned her tongue a little, but she didn't care too much. It was delicious and just what she needed. It didn't escape her notice that the s'mores were serving the same self-pity purpose the copious amounts of ice cream had after her disastrous engagement party. But sometimes you just needed an infusion of sugar to make you feel a little bit better.

Tomorrow she would be better. She would shift the part of her thoughts stuck on Austin over to join the ones focused on the work that lay ahead of her. Each day after deciding to move, it had gotten a bit easier to not think about James and his betrayal. Throwing herself into work had helped her heal faster than if she'd stayed in Louisville, having to see him every day. She could do it again, even if Jade Valley's size and the fact Melissa would be working for her meant Ivy would inevitably see Austin from time to time.

But tonight she would allow herself to remember all the fun and lovely moments she'd spent with Austin, particularly during their trip to Cheyenne. The laughter, the hand-holding, the shared excitement over how much she'd gotten for the coins. And the kiss. Her heart ached at the knowledge that they would never share another.

Trying to not sink too far into sadness, she focused on the fire. She followed the sparks as they floated up toward the twilit sky. It was a beautiful, peaceful evening despite her new heartache.

As she was finishing off her second s'more and about to assemble a third, her phone rang. Not in the mood to chat with her sisters or mother because they would immediately be able to tell something was wrong, she almost ignored it. But she glanced over in time to see the call was from Austin. Her heart leaped in surprise and hope, but immediately on the heels of that was worry. Had something happened to Melissa? Or even Daisy?

"Hello?"

"Where are you?" Austin sounded breathless, which made her worry even more.

"At home."

"I just knocked on your front door. I guess you didn't hear it."

"I'm out back."

Why was he here?

She'd just set the makings of the next s'more on the

paper plate sitting on the little metal table between the two old metal chairs when Austin rounded the corner of the building in front of her. Somehow he looked even taller than normal. He stopped suddenly, as if he'd forgotten why he was there or perhaps because he was telling himself that he shouldn't be.

"Did something happen?"

Still, he didn't say anything. Worried, she took a step toward him. "Austin?"

"Did I ruin everything?"

"What?" She glanced toward the building, wondering if he was talking about something he'd worked on earlier.

This time, he moved toward her. His steps were slow, hesitant.

"Us," he said. "I was wrong when I pushed you away. I know I don't deserve it, but I want to ask for another chance."

Ivy's heart started beating faster. Was he really asking her that?

"You made it clear you weren't interested in anything beyond what happened in Cheyenne. I got the distinct impression you even regretted that."

"I know. I'm sorry. I..." He looked up at the darkening sky for a couple of beats before fixing his gaze on her again. "Running into Grace less than twenty-four hours after we admitted we had some feelings for each other felt like an ominous sign." He shook his head. "This sounds out there, but it felt like the universe was reminding me of what happened the last time I trusted someone, cared about someone. I was bombarded with all these thoughts that I had to protect Mom, Daisy and myself from having to go through that again."

"I told you I wouldn't do that to you. I know what it's like to be betrayed, hurt by the person you care deeply about."

"I know. I also know I'm an idiot and may have ruined everything. I can't blame you if that's the case, but I hope you give me another chance."

Only minutes ago she'd been sitting by the fire sad that things hadn't worked out, but now that Austin was here and saying he was actually still interested she grew wary. She'd had enough of the ups and downs of romance, the never knowing what drop was right around the next corner.

"I don't think you'd ever deliberately hurt any of us," he said. "I knew that deep down, but I let the fear take over. I can't stand the thought of Mom or Daisy losing anything or anyone else."

"Life is filled with losses. We can't avoid all of them, no matter how hard we try. And some of us suffer more than our share. It's not fair, but that's life. You know what else life is filled with, though? Good moments. Great moments. Wonderful people."

"You're right. I know you are."

"But you've been in protective crisis mode for so long that it's hard to stop. And it causes you to hurt others rather than be hurt."

He looked at her for several heartbeats, as if wondering how she had figured it out, before nodding.

"But I want to stop. And start with you for real."

She stared at him for a few seconds, trying to decide how she wanted to respond. "Are you sure?"

"Yes. But if it's too soon for you, I'll wait. It hasn't been long since your breakup."

"Trust me, I've asked myself countless times if what I feel for you makes any sense, how much it hurt when you called things off, whether it means that I didn't love James. But then I wondered who set the time limits—how long we have to wait after we lose someone to think about being with someone else, how long is too short and why.

And you know what I think? We have to go with our instincts, and it's no one else's business but the people directly involved."

After a moment's hesitation, Austin took a slow step forward.

"You have such a healthy way of looking at things. I'm not sure I'm smart enough to date you."

The word "date" made Ivy feel giddy, more so than even when James had first asked her out.

"Don't underestimate yourself. A person has to have a good head on their shoulders to juggle all the balls you have been."

The light in the sky was growing dimmer, but the orange glow of the fire illuminated Austin's smile.

"I'm really sorry I hurt you," he said. "I'll do my best to never do that again."

"See that you don't."

"Does that mean we can give us a second try?"

"Yes." She refused to think about how the last time she'd said yes to a man, it had been a proposal for a marriage that never happened. That was the past. James was the past. The present was about her reclaiming her happiness in all its forms, and one of those definitely included Austin.

CHAPTER FOURTEEN

AUSTIN PAUSED IN assembling a set of display easels he'd built for the history exhibits Ivy had ordered based on Daisy's research about the Stinson Building. He glanced out the window that faced Main Street.

"It's only been about thirty seconds since the last time you looked," his mom said.

Though it was good to hear amusement in her voice, he still blushed a little at her teasing. He hadn't felt that way since he'd first started seeing Grace, which seemed ages ago.

Daisy snickered beside him, and he acted as if he was going to grab her. She squealed and ran to hide behind their mom.

"Don't use me as a shield."

Daisy acted affronted. "You started it."

"Technically, your brother started it by looking out the window so often, as if that will make Ivy appear faster."

"I should have left the two of you at home."

Daisy and his mom looked at each other for a moment then laughed in unison. Austin would be irritated if seeing them happy didn't make his heart feel full. Still, he quickly finished his task and headed outside. A few days ago he'd wanted to hurry to complete all the tasks this job had required, but now that he was basically finished he dreaded reaching the end of the day.

He scanned the front yard of the building. It could really use some landscaping, but Ivy said she'd tackle that later. Now that the building was livable and usable for her store, her focus had shifted to ordering stock and finalizing how she wanted to display it. That was definitely more in his mother's wheelhouse than his. Soon he'd be back to full-time ranch work, only able to see Ivy when they made plans to spend time together or when picking up his mother after work. They hadn't gone on an official date yet, but it had only been two days since their decision to make a go of it, followed by sitting next to the fire and eating s'mores until all the marshmallows were gone.

He looked up the street, and there she was. His smile was instantaneous when she waved from a block away. He resisted the smitten teenager urge to run to her, but only barely.

"Are you waiting for me?" she asked when she got close.

"Maybe."

Her smile would light up the deepest cave.

"So, you want to go on a date?" she asked.

"Sure. What do you have in mind?"

"How about a hand-in-hand walk through… Fizzy's?"

That was not at all what he'd been expecting. "Fizzy's?"

"Well, you did talk the place up and I haven't been yet. What's better for a first date than a treasure hunt?"

Dinner, a movie, a nice walk along the river.

But when he thought about it, it made a sort of sense. So much of their time together had revolved around the way she was rebuilding her life here in Jade Valley. It had been nice watching not only the building come back to life, but also his family. And when he thought about it, Ivy fit that description too. While she'd been nice and friendly right from the start, there was a new brightness in her eyes now, the proverbial bounce in her step that hadn't been there when they'd first met. If she wanted to go picking at Fizzy's, a-picking they would go.

He hadn't counted on his first date with Ivy including his mom and sister tagging along, but Ivy said the more the merrier. And an hour after arriving at Fizzy's, he had to agree. While Daisy went off in search of books and things that appealed to her sense of adventure, his mom and Fizzy sat on Fizzy's front porch drinking cold sodas in glass bottles and laughing at something or another.

"They sound like they're having a good time. Aren't you glad they came with us?" Ivy gently poked him in the ribs to tease him.

"Yes, though at some point we're going to go on a proper, 'just us' date."

"I like the sound of that." Ivy slipped her fingers through his as they moved from one of Fizzy's buildings full of stuff to the next.

"What about these?" Austin pointed toward several large cubby shelves.

Ivy's eyes lit up like it was the best Christmas morning ever. "Those are perfect for yarn skeins. I wonder how much they are."

When she started to step forward, he gently tugged her back.

"You won't find prices on anything here. You make an offer and Fizzy either takes it or he doesn't. If he likes you, he'll be willing to haggle."

"I can do it, as you saw at the rummage sale, but I don't especially like to haggle." She stared at the shelves. "But I have an offer in mind. Let's keep looking though."

Austin was surprised by how much he enjoyed shopping with Ivy. He'd never enjoyed shopping with Grace, but to be fair this was an entirely different type. This was shopping to make a dream come true.

As he watched Ivy looking through an old cigar box full of thimbles, he couldn't help smiling.

She glanced up at him and stopped riffling. "What?"

"You look so happy right now."

She smiled as she let the box lid close.

"That's because I am." She walked toward him, gripped the front of his shirt and pulled him down to where she could plant a quick kiss on his cheek.

It was over so quickly that for a moment Austin was left a bit wobbly on his feet.

"What was that for?"

"I just felt like it." And with a mischievous smile she turned back to her personal treasure hunt.

When they finally returned to Fizzy's front porch, the older man and his mother were laughing so hard that they were wiping away tears. Austin stopped in his tracks and stared. Though she'd begun to laugh more easily lately, he literally could not remember the last time he saw his mother laughing with her entire body and soul. Next to him, Ivy squeezed his hand. When he looked down at her, he felt such a wave of gratitude that it almost felled him right there in the middle of Fizzy's years of accumulation.

After a few moments of simply appreciating how much his mother's outlook on life had changed since Ivy's arrival in Jade Valley, he and Ivy continued toward the porch.

"What is so funny?" he asked.

His mom waved off his question. "You don't need to know."

"Well, now I'm really curious."

"A tale from the past that is going to stay there."

Austin decided his unsatisfied curiosity was a price he was willing to pay for his mom's happiness.

After Fizzy got his laughter and resulting coughing under control, Ivy made her offer for the cubby shelves.

"I've had so much fun this afternoon that I'm going to let you have them for half that."

"Wow, thank you."

"Mom, do you have something on Fizzy?"

That question caused his mom and Fizzy to look at each other and start howling with laughter again.

"That must be some story," Ivy said to him as the two older adults laughed themselves silly.

By the time they loaded up Ivy's purchases and Daisy had paid for a book of world maps from the early 1900s, Austin helped his mom back into the truck and they all headed back into town. As they got closer, it started to rain. Austin wanted to hurry so that Ivy's items didn't get wet, but he wasn't about to endanger her or his family. When they arrived in front of Ivy's building, his mom said that she'd sit in the truck so the rest of them could hurry to get the truck unloaded.

When everything was safely inside and thankfully only a bit damp, Daisy went back to the truck. Left alone with Ivy, he tugged her gently out of sight of his mom and sister.

"I had fun today," he said.

"I'm glad."

"That said, I get to choose what we do on our next date."

She looked up at him and grinned. "Deal."

Feeling his heart fill with happiness, he pulled her close and kissed her. It was more than a quick peck this time, but he didn't let himself get carried away either. They'd agreed to take things slowly to make sure they did things right and that they both really were ready to move on.

He didn't feel any doubt anymore. He was falling in love with Ivy, and it took a lot of restraint not to tell her that. But she'd been in a relationship more recently than him, and it wasn't fair to her to go back on his word that they'd take things one day at a time. She had a lot on her plate right now, and he didn't want to add any stress to her life.

"I know today was my official last day of work, but you can still call me any time you need help. I'm your…" He trailed off, not sure how Ivy would define their relationship.

"Boyfriend?"

"Are you okay with that term?"

"Absolutely."

The way she said that with her whole being made Austin feel as if he was floating all the way home.

"ARE WE ALMOST THERE?"

Across the truck from Ivy, Austin laughed at her question. Though her eyes were closed, she could picture him so clearly. Over the past couple of weeks, they'd spent as much time together as work allowed. He'd picked up another job rebuilding a porch and adding a wheelchair ramp for an elderly couple after word got around about the work he'd done on her building, including the addition of the ramps.

"You sound like Daisy when she was a kid asking, 'Are we there yet?'"

"All kids ask that at some point or another. I remember me and my sisters asking Mom that every time we went anywhere outside of Lexington."

"In answer to your question, yes, we're almost there. But don't you dare peek."

"This better be good."

After he finally parked the truck, assisted her out of it, then led her forward for a couple of minutes, she was allowed to open her eyes.

The view that greeted her wasn't merely good. It was magical.

"Oh, it's gorgeous here." She walked a few steps to the top of a hill overlooking an expanse of the valley through which the river meandered. The sun glinted off the water, the sky was an impossible blue and the surrounding mountains seemed straight out of a fantasy realm.

"I'm glad you like it."

"How could anyone not like it?" She turned to look at him and noticed the picnic basket in his hand. "Oh, and food too? I think you might be a keeper."

Ivy hoped Austin didn't read too much into that last statement, even though she believed it with her whole heart. She hadn't told her family about him yet because she knew they'd think she was moving on to another relationship too fast. Lily had teased her about the "hot cowboy," but if she knew that Ivy was now seriously falling for him, she would sound the family alarm. It wouldn't surprise Ivy if both sisters and their mother showed up on her doorstep to try to talk some sense into her.

She relaxed when Austin didn't seem to mind her allusion to a long-term relationship. In fact, his smile gave her hope that he was feeling the same way. She needed that boost after the dream she'd had the night before, one in which Grace had shown up in Jade Valley with an apology that swayed Austin. That scene had drifted away to be replaced with one of Austin and Grace getting married a second time on the front steps of Ivy's building. But somehow she didn't own the building anymore. Austin had managed to take it away from her and give it to his new bride.

Ivy had woken up with her heart racing and her jaw clenched so tightly that it hurt.

"Are you okay?"

"Yeah, more than okay." She stepped away from memories of the nightmare and toward Austin. "Did you get a picnic lunch from Trudy?"

With the summer weather so nice now, they had been making lots of picnic meals for tourists to take with them on their outings. Trudy always slipped in a flyer about how to stay safe in bear country with respect to food.

"I'll have you know I made all of this myself."

Ivy grinned. "Is it sandwiches and chips?"

Austin gave her an affronted look. "No, it's *premium* sandwiches and chips."

Ivy laughed. "Oh, I stand corrected."

But he hadn't lied. The thick roast beef sandwiches were delicious, and he had paid attention to what she liked and brought her favorite sour cream and onion chips. His thoughtfulness, the postcard view and sharing it all with the man who meant so much to her made it no less than a perfect day.

"What's in the storage container?" she asked as she pointed inside the basket.

"You'll find out when you finish your sandwich and chips."

"Okay, Mom."

Austin made a *pffft* sound before taking a big bite of his sandwich.

Ivy was happy to just sit in the incredible quiet, a type of quiet that it was hard to believe still existed in the modern world. Other than the sounds of their eating, all she heard was the breeze in the pines and the tittering of some bird in a nearby tree.

"It's so peaceful it makes me not want to leave," she said.

"I know that feeling. I happened upon this spot several months ago when I felt like the stress was going to crush me. Most of the time I dealt with it fine, because there was no other option. But there was something about that day where I couldn't breathe all of a sudden and I just started driving. Somehow I ended up here. I think I sat here for like two hours, but by the time I left I felt lighter and able to handle everything again. Like you said, it felt peaceful. When I was trying to think of someplace special to bring you, I thought of this." He pointed toward the valley spread out before them. "Being with you makes me feel the way this place does, lighter and able to handle anything."

Ivy was so touched that she couldn't find the right words to respond. Instead, she placed her hands on his cheeks and kissed him. When she pulled away, Austin smiled at her.

"Well, that's better than the dessert I brought."

"Hmm, I'll reserve judgment. I do like dessert."

"If you like the dessert better than kissing, I might have to leave you here."

"There are worse places to be left." As soon as the words left her mouth, she realized how he might take them. "I'm sorry."

He shook his head. "It's okay. We don't need to tiptoe around each other anymore, don't you think?"

She considered that for a moment. "I agree."

Still, she didn't immediately ask the question that had been sitting in her mind unanswered since that day in Cheyenne. But they were moving forward, getting closer every day. Best to get it out there in the open.

"Are you curious about what Grace wanted to talk to you about that day?"

"No." His answer was immediate and sounded decisive. "I suspect she wanted to say she was sorry, even ask how Mom was doing. Maybe part of her would have even meant it, but it doesn't matter to me anymore. Someone who just wants to stick around when times are good isn't someone I want to be with."

Ivy entwined her hand with Austin's. It was amazing when she thought about how they'd both been betrayed, both thought they didn't want to be in a relationship again, and then they'd found each other. Louisville and Jade Valley were almost like two different worlds. If not for her seeing that contest to win the Stinson Building at nearly the last minute, she and Austin would have never met.

"You ever think about what the odds must have been for us to ever even cross paths, let alone get together?"

"More than once," he said.

"It's weird how life works. When I was standing in that hotel and those women showed me proof of what James had done, it felt as if the world fell out from under me. I didn't know how I was going to go back to work and not be angry every time I saw him. I sat in my apartment eating buckets of ice cream and wondering how I could avoid dying of mortification every time I saw someone who was there that day. When I won the building, it felt like a lifeline and I took it."

"I'm glad you did."

Ivy looked up at Austin and felt happiness suffuse every cell in her body. "I am too. I really am."

Hopefully someday the little voice inside her head would stop telling her to be careful how happy she was or she might tempt fate to snatch it away again.

She leaned her head on his shoulder and they sat like that for a long time, simply enjoying the beauty of Wyoming and the comfort of each other's company. Eventually, however, curiosity had her lifting her head and tapping the picnic basket.

"Where did you get this?"

"My mom bought it when she decided my dad was the one for her. She made him a big lunch and brought it to the ranch. Unfortunately for her, Dad was at the back of the ranch working with my grandfather when she delivered it, and my grandmother wasn't keen on her being so forward."

"Did your dad get it eventually?"

"Grandma grudgingly gave it to him that evening. He

didn't know how to respond and didn't want to disappoint his mother, so he ended up not saying anything to my mom for a long time. She was heartbroken and thought he didn't like her. It took overhearing another boy saying he was going to ask Mom to a school dance to kick Dad into action. They went to that dance and were a couple from that night until he passed."

"My heart breaks when I think about everything your mom has been through, more than any of us."

"Which is why I'm so thankful that she's doing better now. Even if you and I had never started dating, I would be eternally grateful for how you've helped her and Daisy. And me." He laughed a little. "Even the stray cat, who I swear is going to let you pet him one of these days. I think you're just a fixer of broken things."

"That's a nice compliment but gives me too much credit."

"You don't give yourself enough credit. There's something about you, like…an inner light or something. People feel good just being around you."

"That's the nicest thing anyone has ever said about me."

"It's the truth."

Ivy blinked against sudden tears. In that moment, she knew that she loved Austin. But some instinct told her that it was still too soon to say so. The timing, despite being in this stunningly beautiful place he'd chosen to share with her, still wasn't right. But she knew it, and it filled her heart with a joy that was hard to contain.

"So, now for the most important question of the day…"

"What I made for dessert?"

"Bingo."

Austin reached inside the picnic basket and retrieved the plastic storage container.

"Prepare to be amazed," he said as he gripped the edge of the lid. "This is some of my finest work."

"I'm overcome with anticipation."

He slowly pulled back the lid to reveal…

"Are those bourbon balls?" Gone was her teasing, replaced by genuine shock.

"They are."

"You really made these?"

"With the help of online videos."

Ivy picked up one of the round candy balls made of bourbon, chocolate, wafer crumbs, pecans and butter, originally created in Kentucky.

"Austin, this is so good," she said after taking the first bite.

"Thank goodness. I had to throw out two batches before this."

Ivy's immediate laughter almost had her snorting bourbon ball bits out of her nose. It was so good to laugh with her entire soul and have someone with whom to share that laughter.

After they were full, they took a few minutes to snap pictures of the valley and some selfies together. Austin surprised Ivy by planting a kiss on her cheek when he took one of them with the valley in the background. Even before looking at it, she knew it was going to be her favorite. She might even make it her lockscreen since there was no hiding their relationship anyway. She was fairly certain half the town somehow knew about them within twenty-four hours of Austin arriving at her s'mores-filled pity party.

A bit of thunder rolled in the distance right as the wind picked up a bit.

"Seems Mother Nature is putting the kibosh on our perfect outing," Ivy said.

Austin pulled her into his arms and said, "We'll come here again."

"I'll hold you to that."

THE PHONE RINGING woke Austin. He glanced at the clock and his heart started thudding harder. No call that came at nearly one thirty in the morning was a good one. He didn't recognize the number but he answered anyway.

"Austin, this is Angie Lee."

Waves of panic threatened to drown him when he remembered the last time Sheriff Lee had called, to tell him about his mom's accident. But now his mom and sister were safe in their own bedrooms. What could...

Please no.

"Is Ivy okay?"

"She's safe but distraught. Lightning struck her building and it's on fire. She's wet and cold from the rain, but she refuses to even sit in my car."

"I'll be right there."

More thunder rumbled as he quickly got dressed and grabbed his keys.

"What's wrong?" Daisy asked as soon as he stepped out of his bedroom.

He noticed his mom had already gotten up and was wheeling herself out of her room. Quickly he shared with them everything Angie had told him.

"Go," his mom said. "But be careful."

He knew what her fear was, and he promised that he would take care.

"And bring Ivy back here. We'll have things ready for her."

Even though he was in a hurry, he took a moment to kiss both his sister and his mom on the tops of their heads then raced for his truck. As he drove toward town, the sky was almost continually lit with lightning. Chances were high that the fire at Ivy's wouldn't be the only one caused by the weather tonight. By the time he hit Main Street, the rain was gone even if the lightning and wind weren't. His heart was beating fast as he made the turn onto Ivy's street. The fire department was still there, but the fire was either out or at least under control.

His heart sank when even in the darkness he could see that a large part of the roof was damaged or gone. When he spotted Ivy standing on the sidewalk on the opposite side of the street, she looked even smaller than her normal petite stature. He quickly parked, already opening his door as he turned off the ignition.

When Ivy spotted him, her face crumpled and the tears started to flow. He erased the distance between them and pulled her into his arms. He hugged her close, placing his hand against the back of her head.

"Thank God you're safe," he said.

Her only response was to cry harder. Austin let her and had difficulty not crying himself. Over the top of Ivy's head, he made eye contact with Angie. She gave him a sympathetic look then went back to her conversation with the fire chief.

Austin didn't know how long he stood there holding Ivy, but her sobs gradually lessened in intensity then faded into an occasional sniffle.

"It's ruined," she said against his chest.

He knew she meant more than the actual building. Her dream, her new beginning had a literal and figurative jagged hole in them.

"You don't know that. Wait until daylight to assess how bad it is."

She sneezed and that's when he noticed that she was barefoot, though she'd managed to grab her purse and phone. Without asking, he picked her up and carried her to his truck and set her inside. He used a flannel shirt that he kept in the truck to wrap her cold, wet feet. He wanted to scold her for putting herself in danger of getting sick, but he was so thankful that she wasn't hurt or worse that he held his tongue. He would bring her home with him where they would take good care of her while she worked with the insurance company to make things right again.

They sat in the truck with Austin holding Ivy's hand until the fire department left. But when he put his hand on the key to start the truck, Ivy suddenly said, "No, wait."

"We'll come back in the morning." Right now she needed to get dry and warm. If he knew his mother, she would have some hot food waiting when they arrived, no matter that it was the middle of the night.

Ivy pointed out the window toward where Angie was pulling something out of the back of her sheriff's department SUV. When he realized that it was the wall hanging his mom had made, he had to blink rapidly. Ivy had paused in the midst of escaping to rescue the piece his mom had put hours into.

"You should have just left it," he said, his voice cracking a bit at the thought that her taking the time to get the wall hanging could have cost her life. "It's replaceable. You aren't."

"I had to save it."

He didn't argue with her because she was already upset, had already lost so much. Even if the damage wasn't total, it was still a huge setback after they had all worked so hard to enable her to be ready to open before the fall festival rolled around.

He got out of the truck to retrieve the wall hanging. Angie sent a sympathetic look in Ivy's direction.

"Go ahead and take her home," Angie said. "I'll wrap up things here."

Behind her, a couple of deputies were already stretching caution tape around Ivy's building. It wasn't a preventive barrier, but he knew that Angie would make sure that no one went prowling around to see if they could scavenge anything inside.

"We'll come back when it's daylight, but call me if you need anything."

"Don't rush. Make sure she gets some sleep. I'll be surprised if she doesn't end up with at least a cold."

After he settled the wall hanging on the floor behind his seat, Austin drove out of town toward the ranch. Even though he needed to be careful on such a dark, wet night, he held Ivy's hand the entire way because he wanted to remind her that she hadn't lost everything. He was still there. So were Melissa and Daisy, Trudy, all the people Ivy had befriended since her arrival in Jade Valley.

By the time they arrived at the ranch, the storm system had moved out. The moon was even peeking out from behind the dark clouds. Again, he lifted Ivy in his arms and carried her inside.

"Oh my," he heard his mom say when she saw Ivy's bare feet.

He set Ivy down and framed her face with his hands. "Why don't you go take a warm shower? We'll have some dry clothes and hot food for you when you're done."

"I'm sorry," she said.

He smoothed some of her damp hair away from her cheek, tucking it behind her ear.

"There's no reason for you to be sorry."

Daisy gave him a look that said she would take over now. She hurried to her room to gather the things that Ivy would need. When they'd both left the living room, his mom motioned him into the kitchen.

"How bad is it?" she asked softly.

"It was too dark to tell for sure, but it's not good. At least part of the roof is…" His voice broke, thinking about how Ivy may have been asleep right under that roof when the fire started. What if she had fallen down the stairs in her panic to get out? "It's gone."

His mom took his hand and squeezed it. "She's safe. We'll take care of her. She's family now."

He and Ivy were a long way from that type of relationship. They hadn't even said they loved each other, though he knew without a doubt now that he did love her. But even without the words, she felt like part of their family. For the first time he believed he might be able to make that type of commitment again. He just had to wait to see if she felt the same way.

CHAPTER FIFTEEN

IF THE DAMAGE to her new home had been frightening during a dark, rainy night, seeing it in the light of day was devastating. If Austin hadn't been standing next to her with his arm around her shoulders, Ivy was certain that her legs would have buckled beneath her. As she walked carefully across her living space, the bright blue sky she saw when she looked up through the giant hole in her roof felt incredibly out of place.

Sadness settled in her heart as she examined the damage to the original floors that Austin had revived with hours upon hours of repairing, sanding, sweeping and refinishing. The chest of drawers that had led her to the ER and the mattress she had purchased in Cheyenne were no more than soggy trash now. Shoes, clothing and mementos she had hauled all the way from Kentucky were completely lost as well.

Ivy felt like weeping all over again, but she'd already cried so much the night before—first in Austin's arms outside as the firefighters fought the fire and again when she'd finally curled up in Daisy's bed. All that crying resulted in the pounding headache she'd had all morning. The fact she might have slept only an hour didn't help. Neither did the question that kept banging against the sides of her skull like a mallet.

What now?

Needing something proactive to do, she gathered what

few things had survived the combination of fire and water, including the coins she hadn't yet sold. It was sad when all of your worldly possessions were a car and what fit in a two-by-two-by-three-foot plastic tote. She sighed so deeply that it felt as if it fell all the way to the center of the earth.

"It'll be okay," Austin said as he came up behind her and placed his strong, supportive hands on her shoulders.

She appreciated his words of comfort, but she wasn't at all sure things would be okay after this. She'd already sunk everything she had into revitalizing a building that had been in worse shape than she'd anticipated. But at least then the roof had been intact and a rainstorm hadn't found its way inside.

She nearly laughed as she remembered finding the box of matches and candles and marveling that the building hadn't burned down before. The building had sat vacant but whole for years, but right when it was going to realize a new purpose it had sustained what was likely life-ending damage. Her business hadn't even been able to open before it had gone belly-up. Maybe the building was cursed and that's why nothing ever lasted there.

"Let's go," she said. "I don't want to look at this anymore."

As she turned to leave, she caught a glimpse of what had been the lovely bathroom Isaac had built for her. Odd that a bathroom could make her teary again. She swiped at her eyes and headed for the stairs.

"I can carry that for you," Austin said.

"I'm good." It was strangely important for her to hang on to her possessions with her own hands.

"Are you okay to drive?" Austin asked after she put the tote in the back seat of her car.

She nodded, and they got into the driver's seats of their separate vehicles. Ivy would never tell Austin that as they reached Main Street and Austin turned right, she almost turned left and took the same road out of town that she had taken in when she'd arrived in Jade Valley. But she felt as if wherever she landed, the dark cloud of failure would simply follow and start planning its next attack.

When they reached the ranch, she didn't get out of her car. The energy it would take to do so seemed impossible to muster.

Austin noticed that she wasn't moving so he came toward her car. She rolled down the window as he reached her door. Thankfully, he didn't ask inane questions like "Is something wrong?" or "Are you okay?" The answers were obviously yes and no.

"I'm going to call my family before I go in," she said.

"Okay."

The fact that he knew she needed some time alone made her love Austin all the more. That's when she started to panic. What was she going to do now that she didn't have a home or a place for her business anymore? How was she going to make a living? Working at Trudy's was nice for getting to know people and bringing in a bit of money, but it wasn't what she'd moved across the country to do. Why did her happiness keep getting snatched away?

She tried to work up the nerve to call her mother to tell her what had happened. She rehearsed how she would launch into the topic for the least possible freak-out on the other end of the call, but she knew that no matter what she said and how she said it her mom and sisters were going to...well, freak out. And to be fair, if she found out any of them had escaped a house fire in the middle of the night, she'd be quite freaked out too.

To put it off a little longer, she first called her newly acquired insurance agent. Of course, Shelly Deneen already knew all about the fire. Something like that didn't happen in the middle of Jade Valley without everyone knowing about it. When she was finished with that call, however, it was time to get the dreaded call over with.

"Hi, Mom," she said when her mom answered on the second ring.

"What's wrong?"

Why were her mother and sisters so dang good at detecting when something was wrong based on no more than two words?

"What makes you think something's wrong? I can't call my mother?"

"I can hear it in your voice."

Ivy sighed. So much for easing into the news.

"I'm totally fine, but I can't say the same for my building." She swallowed hard, determined to get through the next few minutes without crying again. Her head already felt as if it was going to crack open.

"Come home," her mom said when Ivy finished telling her about the fire.

"Mom, it's too soon to make that type of decision. I haven't even met with the insurance adjuster yet."

"At least for a visit. We miss you, and having some distance might help you decide what you want to do next."

Maybe her mom was right. After what had happened with James, putting a lot of distance between her and him had really helped. But she couldn't keep moving across the country every time something went wrong. She looked up at the house, and her heart ached. Should she have allowed herself to get so close to Melissa and Daisy? To fall for Austin? Had he been right to worry that she would end up hurting all of them? She certainly hadn't planned to, but she hadn't planned for literal lightning to strike her new home either.

"I'll think about it and let you know."

They talked for a few more minutes, but only about a quarter of her mind was paying attention to the conversation. The rest was being bombarded with questions for which she had no answers.

After they ended the call, Ivy continued sitting in her car for a couple more minutes. She wasn't ready to go inside where she wouldn't be the only one with questions. Needing more time to sort out her thoughts, she got out of the car and started walking along the path she'd seen Austin take to access his back pastures. She hadn't seen any of the ranch land beyond the areas where the house and barn sat.

A couple of minutes later, she crested a hill and saw a small, curving flow of water. She knew here they would likely call it a creek though it wouldn't even merit that title back in Kentucky. Wyoming was way more arid than her home state, so she suspected what lay before her was often just a dry creek bed but now had flow because of the previous night's storm.

Even with Wyoming's vastly different landscape, Ivy had grown to love that difference. It, as well as the people she'd met and the work she'd done, had helped her to jumpstart the healing process necessary after her breakup. She didn't want to leave here for many reasons, not just her feelings for Austin. But would she really have a choice? Her winning the building at just the right time had been a fluke, one that wouldn't be repeated. Even though she had insurance, she had a horrible feeling in the pit of her stomach that the payout wasn't going to be enough.

The longer she was out walking, the more she expected Austin to come looking for her. But he continued to give her space. By the time she was ready to retrace her steps, she still didn't know what she was going to do regarding her future but had decided that she did want to visit her family. She'd grown to care about Melissa a lot, but nothing compared to being enveloped in the arms of your own mother.

The distance she'd covered came as a surprise to Ivy as she made her way back to the house. She stopped a couple of times to take photos because she'd thankfully been able to save her phone if not her laptop. If she was going back to Kentucky for a visit, she wanted lots of beautiful shots to show her mom and sisters. Towering mountain peaks, a hawk in flight, colorful wildflowers for which she hadn't learned the names yet, even Austin's herd of cattle.

When she finally reached the house, she found Austin replacing the roof on Pooch's doghouse.

"Did you have a good walk?" Austin asked as he paused in his work.

Ivy gave Pooch a rub on his head, which he seemed to greatly enjoy.

"It was nice. I don't think I'll ever stop being amazed at how pretty it is here."

"You won't. I've lived here my whole life and it still catches me unaware sometimes."

Ivy crouched and gave Pooch a hug. Something about the action almost made her cry again. The tears were constantly right there ready to spill. She noticed Austin glancing her way, and the fact that he was holding back questions of his own was painfully obvious.

"My mom told me to come home for a visit, and I'm going to take her up on that. I can't do anything with the building until all the insurance stuff is settled anyway. I... I need some time to think about how I want to proceed."

Austin didn't reply beyond a simple "Mmm."

Was he worrying that she wouldn't come back the same way Grace hadn't?

She stood and walked up to him, wrapping her arms

around his waist. Now was not the right time to tell him she loved him, but maybe she could show him.

He hugged her back and placed a gentle kiss on her head. "Do what you have to do."

Those words were still echoing in her mind and her heart as she took off from the Denver airport the next day, bound for Lexington. The problem was she still had no idea how to proceed with her life, but she knew she hated the idea of not having Austin in it.

AUSTIN FINISHED BUILDING the porch and ramp for Mr. and Mrs. Harbin in record time. Then he attacked his normal ranch chores and every task he'd put off for lack of time. He had to keep busy so that he didn't give his mind the opportunity to worry that he'd never see Ivy again. It didn't work, but he kept trying. She'd only been gone for four days but it felt like four years.

After clearing and cutting up some limbs that had fallen in the storm that led to Ivy leaving Jade Valley, he headed toward the house for a cold soda. Even thirsty, he still didn't want to go inside. He'd seen the looks his mom and Daisy had been giving him, ones filled with concern, but they hadn't commented on his long hours and the reason for them. To put off encountering them for a little while longer, he headed for the garden.

"Okay, now I know you're avoiding us," Daisy said as she exited the house via the back door. "You hate weeding the garden."

"Thought I'd give you a break from it."

"Yeah, right."

He looked up at his sister's uncharacteristically disbelieving tone. There was an edge of annoyance in her words too.

Daisy crossed her arms, and the way she looked at him made her seem way older than her actual age.

"You're worried Ivy won't come back, aren't you?"

Austin jerked out a weed with more force than necessary and pitched it aside.

"When did you get so smart?"

"You know I've always been smart. And observant."

"The attitude is new."

"I'm tired of all the adults in my life doing frustrating things."

"What exactly did I do?"

"It's what you haven't done. You're moping around worried that Ivy won't come back to Jade Valley, but you haven't done anything to make sure she does."

"I talk to her every day, ask how she's doing, how she's enjoying seeing her family despite the circumstances."

"Have you told her you love her yet?"

That question startled him.

"How do you know I do?"

Daisy tilted her head a smidge. "Are you serious right now?"

He continued staring at his sister, wondering why she suddenly seemed more mature than him.

Daisy came to crouch in front of him.

"If it was any more obvious how the two of you feel about each other, it would literally smack everyone nearby on the face."

"You think she loves me?"

Daisy rolled her eyes. "Why are men so dumb?"

A moment passed but then Austin laughed. "You sure got sassy. I'm not sure I like it."

"People grow up. At least some of us do."

"Okay, that's enough." He pulled his little sister into a gentle headlock and messed up her hair.

"Hey!"

He released her and let himself fall back to sit on the grass at the edge of the garden.

"I don't want to tell her how I feel on the phone, and I can't go flying across the country."

"Then show her instead."

"How?"

"You'll have to figure that out."

"Well, you're no help."

Daisy smiled then surprised him by planting a quick kiss on his cheek before shooing him away from the garden so she could finish the weeding he'd started.

He stepped into the house to grab a soda from the fridge. His gaze landed on the wall hanging made of buttons and knew that whatever he did to convince Ivy that Jade Valley was still her home, it had to center around making sure her dream could still come true here. Hoping that a drive would knock some usable ideas loose, he got in his truck and headed toward town. He first went to the grocery and bought some cat food. Ivy had been feeding the stray she'd named Sprinkles, and he could at least do that for her.

The cat was nowhere to be seen when he filled the bowl at the back of the little patio area, but that wasn't surprising. While the cat had gradually been coming closer to Ivy, the same could not be said for him.

After he finished, he walked slowly around the outside of the building. Then he did the same inside, assessing how much damage there was and how much it would take to make the building usable again. Was it possible? Could he somehow make it happen?

"Austin?"

He turned and saw Trudy standing at the top of the

front steps. Not wanting her to come inside, he hurried back to the entrance.

"Did Ivy get home safely?"

A pang hit him that Trudy referred to Kentucky as Ivy's home rather than Jade Valley. He knew what she meant, but it still stung.

"She did."

"Any idea how long she's going to stay there?"

He looked behind him at the mess Ivy had left behind. He wouldn't blame her if she never wanted to see this place again...at least not in its current state.

"I don't know, but I have an idea and I need someone to tell me whether it's crazy or not."

"That sounds intriguing."

He didn't know if it was really intriguing or even feasible, but he told her anyway.

"You know, that's the best idea I've heard in a long time."

Austin found his smile again. He was going to make this work, no matter what it took.

Ivy HANDED THE credit card back to the man who'd just bought two dozen red roses.

"Good luck with your proposal," she said.

"Thanks. If only these roses would make my nerves go away."

"That would be nice, wouldn't it?"

As soon as the man exited the floral shop, the smile dropped off her face. Though it was nice to spend time with her family, even kind of fun to work in the shop again, her life still felt as if it was drifting untethered. As had expected, the insurance payout wasn't going to give her the funds she needed to get her own store up and running. With each day she spent back in Lexington, she felt that dream moving farther and farther away. Though she talked to Austin every day, either by phone or text, she wondered whether he was moving farther away as well. Sometimes he seemed distracted, as if he was already forgetting her.

Had she fallen for someone else who didn't care as much for her as she did for him? Did she have some fatal flaw that made her pick the wrong men over and over?

She shook her head. Austin wasn't like James. She knew that deep in her heart.

Didn't she?

The fact that she hadn't seen James's betrayal coming kept haunting her, making her doubt what she believed. Suddenly, the smell of fresh flowers and the hopeful expression of the man about to propose to his sweetheart overwhelmed her.

"Mom, are you okay if I leave?"

Her mom looked worried, as she had since she'd picked Ivy up from the airport.

"It's such a nice day I think I want to go for a walk."

"I'll go with you," Holly said as she came out from the back storage room.

Ivy wanted to be alone, but her family seemed to have made a pact before her arrival that they were not about to let that happen. But if she went back to Jade Valley, she wouldn't see her mom and sisters for a long time so she agreed to let Holly tag along.

They ended up at the UK Arboretum and fell into step beside each other on the loop trail. After some throwaway comments about the nice weather and the pretty flowers and plants, Holly got to the point of her tagging along.

"Have you made any decisions yet?"

"No. What I want to do and what I can do may be two different things."

"But you want to go back?"

Ivy stopped and looked at her sister. "I do. I just don't know how, or whether I'm making yet another in a string of mistakes."

"If it wasn't for Austin, would you be as conflicted?"

She'd told her family about Austin on her second day home when they'd grown suspicious of how much she was looking at her phone. To her surprise, they hadn't warned her to be careful about moving too fast. In fact, they'd seemed happier for her than she'd imagined they could be. Lily had commented about how Ivy's face lit up way more when she talked about Austin than it ever had whenever she mentioned James. That had surprised Ivy because she had loved James, even though now she hoped she never crossed paths with him again.

"I'm not sure," she finally said in answer to Holly's question. "He's a big part of the reason, but I also really like the town and the people. I just don't know how to make it work."

Which was why she'd been home for a month already. With each day that went by, she worried more that Austin was moving on without her—either because his feelings weren't as strong or because he was protecting himself from being hurt yet again.

Her phone buzzed with a text. When she saw it was from Austin, she experienced a wave of the conflicted feelings she'd started having the last few days. Was he texting to say he missed her or that he wanted to call it quits yet again, and for real this time? If it was the latter, could she really blame him? She knew what Grace had done to him, and yet Ivy had stayed away longer than she'd intended. But with each day that passed, one thing led to another, one doubt to another. She told herself she wanted to have everything figured out before she returned to Jade Valley so that she wasn't a burden on Austin, Melissa and Daisy.

But the truth was she was scared that her new dream and new romance were both over and that if she returned to Jade Valley she'd have to face those truths in person.

Can I video call you now?

Ivy was surprised by Austin's question, and panic ensued. He was a decent guy, so maybe he was calling to break up with her as close to face-to-face as he could manage under the current circumstances. Her hands shook as she responded with a simple affirmative.

When she saw his smiling face on her screen, hope replaced fear. He wouldn't be smiling if he was about to break up with her.

"Where are you?" he asked.

"On a walk at the arboretum with Holly." She turned her phone so that Austin could see her sister, who smiled and waved.

"Nice to sort of meet you," Holly said.

"You too."

"I'll let you two talk now. I need to walk off the strawberry shortcake I had for lunch."

After Holly set off down the path, Ivy found a shady spot to sit.

"I have a surprise for you," Austin said.

"Yeah? What's that?"

Instead of replying, he lifted his phone so that she could see behind him.

"Surprise!" The chorus of voices startled her.

Those voices belonged to a lot of familiar faces—Melissa and Daisy, Trudy, Stephanie and Fiona, her neighbors Evangeline and even Reg, Angie Lee, Eric Novak, Sunny and Dean Wheeler, Maya Pine and Gavin Olsen, Isaac and Rich, Fizzy, Melissa's garden club friends, several of the business owners from around Jade Valley. She wondered what was going on that had brought them all together. And then she realized where they were and her breath caught. It was her building, but it had somehow acquired a new roof while she'd been gone.

"What is happening?"

"I told you, it's a surprise."

He turned the camera and she saw Daisy pull a cloth away from a new wooden sign in the front yard, one that said Quilters' Dream. The sign and building were surrounded by landscaping that hadn't been there before. Scattered among the new shrubs and flowers was a collection of painted stones. She wondered if they were the ones she'd collected while cleaning away the overgrowth.

The bigger question, however, was why would they put up a sign and do landscaping for a business that wasn't likely to ever open?

"Austin, I appreciate all this, but I think—"

"Before you finish that sentence, let me take you on a tour."

"A tour?" Had he cleaned up some of the mess in the hope it would weigh the scales in favor of her returning to Jade Valley?

She watched as he walked toward the front door of her building with everyone he passed smiling and waving. When he stepped into the building and panned the camera around, she couldn't believe what she was seeing. The vintage display cases looked much like they had before the fire. The floors appeared to be replaced. Melissa's wall hanging was back in its spot.

"Daisy did this," Austin said as he focused on the corner Ivy had dedicated to the history of the building and Jade Valley, which now held an impressive collection of historic photos and text to explain them.

Ivy was speechless as Austin climbed the stairs to the second level. Yet another surprise awaited her at the top. The door that had gotten damaged during the fire had been replaced by a beautiful wooden door painted dark blue. In white script, someone had painted "There's no place like home."

Austin opened the door and emerged into a room that no longer had a hole to the sky above it.

As he panned the camera, she had to blink back more tears. Her living space was fully outfitted with items that hadn't been there when she left.

"I don't understand. How did this happen?"

"Community effort. Almost everyone in town donated time, supplies or money to make this reality. By the way, Fizzy was extra generous. I think he has a little crush on you. I had to remind him that you have a boyfriend already." Austin turned the camera back toward him. "You've made an impression on a lot of people since you arrived here. We all want you to come back."

Ivy swiped at the tear that escaped, but at least this time it was born of happiness instead of loss.

All her questions about the future became answers. She was going back home.

Back to Jade Valley.

Back to the man she loved.

AUSTIN TOOK OFF his hat and wiped the sweat off his forehead. The temperature had shot up the past couple of days, but ranching required outdoor work no matter the weather. Thankfully, however, his herd was looking good.

He'd been so busy with organizing, overseeing and contributing to the community's overhaul of Ivy's building that he now had to focus on his ranching duties, especially since he'd been hired to build a shed for a couple who had a vacation home several miles north after Trudy had recommended him. He'd found out that any time she heard of those types of jobs, she had a rotation of people she suggested to do the work and he was on the list. As a thankyou, he'd given her a package of steaks from his freezer and bought two of her pies.

He looked out across the pasture toward the mountains and remembered what Ivy had said about constantly being amazed by how beautiful it was here. He couldn't wait to see her again. Not knowing when she might return was difficult, but her reaction to the video tour led him to believe she was in fact coming back. She'd been so overcome with what he, her friends and new neighbors had done for her that it had been difficult for her to speak. He'd finally told her that they could talk again when she was ready.

An out-of-place sound drew his attention, and he turned quickly in case a predator was nearby. When instead he saw Ivy running toward him, he thought maybe he'd been out in the heat too long and she was a mirage.

But then she nearly crashed into him and pulled him down into a kiss that made him stumble. He wrapped his arms around her and kissed her back, putting into it all the words he hadn't yet said.

"How are you here?"

"Plane, car, my two feet," she said. "I needed to get here as fast as I could."

Austin smiled. "There was no rush. I'm not going anywhere. Although I'm really glad to see you."

"I needed to tell you something in person."

His heart thumped hard against his rib cage. Was she—

"I love you. No pressure if you're not ready to say—"

He halted her words with another kiss, not holding anything back. "I love you too. So much."

"Really?"

"Really." He picked Ivy up off her feet and swung her in a circle, whooping his unbelievable happiness.

Ivy laughed as if joy filled her entire body.

He knew exactly how she felt.

EPILOGUE

FALL HAD ALWAYS been Ivy's favorite season. Turning leaves, cooler temperatures, harvest festivals, Halloween—she loved it all. So it felt perfect that the grand opening of her quilt shop coincided with the Jade Valley Autumn Extravaganza. If she had thought the rummage sale crowd had been big, it was nothing compared to how full Jade Valley was for the festival. It felt as if all of Wyoming was filling the sidewalks and shops, including her own. In fact, people had been waiting outside when she unlocked the front door that morning, and there had been a steady stream since.

Locals were stocking up on sewing and knitting supplies. Tourists were buying everything from hand-dipped candles to expensive quilts to boxes of the quilt-themed Christmas ornaments Melissa had suggested might be big movers. She'd been right.

Ivy glanced across the room to where Melissa was talking with a group of women from Provo, Utah. Bits of their conversation floated over to Ivy, and it sounded as if the ladies were part of a quilting club back home. They were loading up on the unique fabric patterns that Ivy and Melissa had spent hours together selecting.

When the Pinecone Pickers, the bluegrass band she'd hired for the day, struck up "Blue Moon of Kentucky" outside, Ivy smiled. The day's "Kentucky Meets Wyoming" theme had been Austin's idea. He, Isaac and some other guys were busy manning the food booth that featured both pulled pork barbecue made with sauce that she had ordered from a famous restaurant in Kentucky, and prime rib sandwiches. Daisy and her geography club were selling chips and drinks, as well as handling the payment transactions for all the food concessions. The garden club ladies were once again selling their impressive array of cookies.

Trudy, who was busy at the restaurant, had nonetheless managed to get her church to donate the use of all their folding chairs for the day. The last time Ivy had a moment to glance outside the open front door, most of them were filled with people eating and tapping their toes to the music.

"Are you ready?" Ivy asked the older lady who stepped up to the cash register.

"I better be or my credit card is going to literally start crying."

Ivy and the woman both laughed.

"Your mother was telling me how you moved out here by yourself to start this store," the woman said, pointing to where Ivy's mom was chatting up another customer. "I like that kind of adventurous spirit."

"Thank you. It's a great place to live. Wonderful people and you can't beat the view."

"You're right about that."

As the woman left, Ivy noticed Lily bringing another large box of yarn out of the storage room Austin had built during the second renovation of the building. With no one currently in line, Ivy moved to help her refill the cubby shelves that had miraculously survived the fire and subsequent dousing.

"Where's Holly?"

"She went to buy some more bags of ice for the drink

coolers outside. I also ordered us all some fountain drinks with the good ice."

"Bless you."

It was beyond wonderful to have her family here for her grand opening. Despite her telling them to go enjoy the festival, they had insisted on lending a hand.

"I think your hot cowboy has sold the equivalent of a dozen cows and several pigs outside. It's as if people haven't eaten for days."

Ivy laughed. "Maybe they have been eating light so they can gorge themselves this weekend."

"Sounds like a solid plan."

As the hours passed, Ivy kept expecting the flow of customers to dwindle. The fact that they didn't gave her hope that her venture was really going to be a success. Several customers, both local residents and those who had traveled hours to attend the festival, had assured her that they would be back.

After she finished another transaction, her mom joined her behind the counter and wrapped her arm around Ivy's shoulders in a quick hug.

"I'm so proud of you."

"Thanks, Mom. That means a lot to me."

Her mom pointed toward the exit. When Ivy looked that way, she could see Austin outside laughing with an older gentleman she'd seen a couple of times at Trudy's but whose name she couldn't remember. Now that she was in Jade Valley for good, however, there was plenty of time to get to know people better.

"I also approve of him," her mom said of Austin. "He is perfect for you."

Her mom had never said anything so complimentary about James, although she'd gotten along with him fine.

"You think so?"

"Any man whose eyes light up the way his do when he looks at you or even when he talks about you when you're not around is a keeper."

"I'm glad you think so because I plan on keeping him."

When things finally slowed down enough in the store to allow Ivy to go outside, the band was playing "Orange Blossom Special." She hummed along as she headed for the barbecue booth.

"What can I get you, ma'am?" Austin asked, his mouth spreading into a wide grin.

It struck her how much easier his smiles came now than when she'd first met him.

"Pulled pork sandwich, please."

He handed over a sandwich. "What else can I get for you?"

"How about a dining companion?"

"Go on," Isaac said. "We can handle this."

Austin grabbed a bag of chips for her as he left his post. She still had her huge soda with the good ice from the convenience store. They sat in two chairs in the back row, and when she sat down she realized how much her feet ached. It would have been more comfortable to wear her broken-in sneakers, but she'd chosen some cute white sandals instead because she'd been determined to wear her new dress. It seemed almost a lifetime ago when she'd chosen the blue fabric with the dandelion design.

"Oh, it feels good to sit down."

"I'd say your grand opening has been a success."

Ivy looked over at him. "It wouldn't have been possible without you."

"And a lot of other people."

"And a lot of other people." She leaned toward him and whispered, "But you're still special."

"So are you." He planted a kiss on her forehead then draped his arm along the back of her chair. "Now eat."

She smiled. Austin may have changed in some ways, but the man was always going to take care of the people he loved. Her mom was right.

He was a keeper.

* * * * *

WESTERN

Rugged men looking for love...

Available Next Month

That Maverick Of Mine Kathy Douglass
Courting The Cowgirl Cheryl Harper

··

Fortune's Faux Engagement Carrie Nichols
The Rodeo Cowboy's Return Cathy McDavid

··

 LOVE INSPIRED

A K-9 Christmas Reunion Lisa Carter
Bonding With The Cowboy's Daughter Lisa Jordan

Keep reading for an excerpt of a new title
from the Intrigue series,
BOUNTY HUNTED by Barb Han

Chapter One

Crystal Remington repositioned her black Stetson, lowering the rim, after she opened the door of the Dime a Dozen Café off I-45. She scanned the small restaurant for Wade Brewer. At six feet, four inches of solid muscle, the thirty-three-year-old former Army sergeant shouldn't be too difficult to locate against the backdrop of truckers and road-tripping families.

In the back left corner, Mr. Brewer sat with his back against the wall. His position gave him an open view of the room. As a US marshal and someone who was used to memorizing exits, Crystal appreciated the move. At his vantage point, no one would have an opportunity to sneak up on him from the side or behind.

He glanced up and then locked onto her, not bothering to motion for her to come sit down. In fact, he looked downright put out by her presence. What the hell?

Tight chestnut-brown-colored hair clipped close to a near-perfect head and a serious face with hard angles and planes, she didn't need to look at a picture to verify her witness's identity. This was the man she was scheduled to meet. After deciding she wasn't a threat, he leaned forward over the table and nursed a cup of coffee as she walked over to join him.

He picked up a sugar packet and twisted it around his

fingers. "Marshal Remington, I'm guessing." Most would consider him physically intimidating, but she'd grown up around a brother and a pair of cousins similar in size, so it didn't faze her.

"That would make you Wade Brewer." Crystal sat down, then signaled for the waitress before refocusing on Brewer. Even with facial scars from an explosion during his time in the service, the man was still beautiful. "Ready for the check so we can get out of this fishbowl and I can get you to a safe place?"

"Do I look like I need your help?" he shot back with daggers coming from his eyes. She wasn't touching that question. "Remind me why I agreed to this when I'm fully capable of taking care of myself?"

Crystal waved off the smiling waitress who was unaware of the tension at the table. And then she turned all her attention to her witness. "First of all, two of the people I love most in this world are lying in hospital beds fighting for their lives while I'm sitting here with you, so have a little respect."

Brewer didn't flinch. Instead, the most intense pair of steel-gray eyes studied her. The unexplained fear that he might pull something like this had been eating at her since she'd learned about his background. Tough guys like him generally didn't go around asking others for help. They handled life on their own terms and, generally speaking, did a bang-up job of it. She'd dismissed her worry as paranoia. Then there was the fact of her grandparents' serious car accident that had been weighing heavily on her mind. Didn't bad events usually occur in threes? If that was the case and her witness decided to bolt, she had one more to go. Lucky her. "Now that we have that fact out of the way, you are the key to locking away a major criminal who—"

"Is currently in jail," he interrupted without looking away from the rim of his cup.

From here on out, Wade was Brewer to Crystal just like everyone else she referred to. Using last names was a way to keep a distance from people. First names were too personal.

"And has a very long reach on the outside with two lieutenants and more foot soldiers ready to kill on command than you can count on both hands." She needed to get him out of this café and on the road to Dallas if they were going to get there in time to pick up the key to the town house tonight. "Why are we talking about this? I thought this issue had already been decided. It was my understanding that you agreed to enter into my protective custody. Has something changed that I haven't been informed of since six a.m.?"

"I've had time to sit here and think." Brewer took a sip of black coffee, unfazed by the emotions building inside her and emanating from her in palpable waves. "Maybe it's time to change my mind."

"Why is that, Mr. Brewer? What possible thought could you have had that would cause you to do an about-face right now?" If he said the reason had to do with her being a woman, she might scream. She'd come across perps who'd believed they could outrun or outshoot her due to her having two X chromosomes. They'd been wrong. If that was the case with Brewer, she could assure him that she was just as capable as any man to do the job or she wouldn't be here in the first place. Brewer didn't give her an indication this was the issue, but she'd come up against this particular prejudice a few too many times in the past and it always set her off.

To his credit, Brewer didn't look her up and down. Instead, he stared into his cup. "It's simple. I'll be able to stay on the move a lot easier if I'm alone. Being on the move doesn't make me a sitting duck."

"I can offer a stable safe house, Mr. Brewer."

The look he gave said he wasn't buying it. "You have no guarantees." Didn't he really mean to say she wasn't strong enough to cover him if push came to shove?

"Not one witness to date has died while following the guidelines under the protection of a US marshal," she pointed out. "I can't say the same for folks who decided they could do it themselves." She folded her arms across her chest and sat back in her chair. "Our track record speaks for itself."

Brewer didn't seem one bit impressed. The terms *dark* and *brooding* came to mind when describing him.

She needed to take another tack, offer a softer approach. "First of all, I want to thank you for your service to this country." She meant every word. "And I realize your training provides a unique skill set that most who come under my protection don't possess." Pausing for effect would give him a few seconds to process the compliment and, maybe, soften him up a little. "I have no doubt you were very good at your job, Sergeant. But make no mistake about it—my training is suited to this task. And I'm damn good at my job. If you have any doubts, feel free to contact my supervisor or any of the other marshals I've worked with over the years. This isn't my first rodeo."

He dismissed her with a wave of his hand, which infuriated her.

Taking a calming breath, she started again. "If the fact

I'm a woman bothers you, say so upfront and let's get it out of the way."

His face twisted in disgust. "I've served alongside a few of the most talented soldiers in the Army, who happened to wear bras. The fact you do has no bearing on my decision whether or not to strike out on my own."

Embarrassed, heat crawled up her neck, pooling at her cheeks. She cleared her throat, determined not to let this assignment go south. "You have no reason to trust me other than the badge I wear. You don't know me from Adam. I get that. Not to mention your military record is impeccable. If we were at war, you'd be the first person I turned to. This situation is stateside, and you have no authority here."

"I have a right to defend myself," he countered.

"Same as every citizen," she pointed out. No doubt he packed his own weapons, not that he needed a license to carry any longer. Scooting her chair closer to the table, she leaned in and lowered her voice. "Did you take care of your aunt?"

"Yes, ma'am. She has been relocated to a secure location," he said. Taking care of his elderly aunt had been his first priority after Victor Crane had been taken into custody and was the reason they were meeting north of Houston, his home city. "Without your help, by the way."

"Fair enough." Crystal could see she was losing him. Was it time to cut bait? Leave him on his own? The way she saw it, there wasn't much choice. His mind seemed made up. Then again, there was no harm in trying. She'd throw out a Hail Mary anyway and see if it worked. "At least make the drive to Dallas with me. Consider changing your mind about protective custody. What's the worst that can happen?"

He flashed eyes at her.

She put a hand up to stop him from commenting. "How about we get inside my vehicle and you can consider your options on the highway heading north?" she said. "You change your mind, I'll personally drop you off anywhere you request. No questions asked."

Brewer gave her a dressing down with his steel gaze. If he was testing her, she had no intention of backing down.

With the casual effort of a Sunday-morning stroll, he shifted gears, picked up his mug and drained the contents. After reaching into his front pocket and peeling off a twenty, he slapped it onto the table, shouldered his military-issue backpack, then stood. "Let's go."

A celebration was premature. Crystal stood up, turned around, and walked out of the diner, keeping an eye out to make sure no one seemed interested in what they were doing. She didn't like meeting this close to Galveston, Brewer's childhood home, or Houston, where he currently resided. Victor Crane would no doubt have someone on his or her way down to make certain Brewer couldn't testify. With a pair of loyal lieutenants, Crane wouldn't even have to make the call himself if Brewer's name got out as a witness. He'd been Crane's driver, so the odds of that happening were high now that Brewer had disappeared.

He followed her to her government-issue white sedan parked closest to the door without taking up an accessible parking spot. She half expected him to keep walking right on past and was pleasantly surprised when he stopped at the passenger door.

It was too early to be excited. She'd given him the out to change his mind anytime during the ride to Dallas in order to convince him to get into the car.

"I should probably hit the men's room before we continue north," he said, breaking into her small moment of victory like rain on parade day.

"All right." On a sharp sigh, Crystal took the driver's seat, figuring it was a toss-up at this point as to whether or not he would return. She tapped her thumb on the steering wheel after turning on the engine as Brewer headed inside the restaurant. What was he going to do? Sneak out the bathroom window to throw her off the trail for a few minutes? Were negotiations over? His mind made up?

She'd give him five minutes before she gave up and called it in.

BREWER CONTEMPLATED DITCHING the marshal for two seconds in the bathroom. Getting far away from Galveston and Houston was a good idea. Dallas? Was it his best move? He'd only been out of the military for six months now and hadn't come home to a warm welcome in his former hometown other than his aunt despite his service to his country.

In all honesty, he'd brought the town's reaction on himself. He'd barely graduated high school due to the number of fistfights he'd been in. He'd worked two jobs to help provide for his elderly aunt, who was technically his great-aunt, which had tanked his grades. He could have been more focused in school, except that he'd hated every minute of sitting in class. Before he'd shot up in height, he'd been bullied. And then, he'd gotten angry. The football coach, in an attempt to court him, had given Brewer permission to use the weight room before school, which he'd done religiously to bulk up and then use his newfound muscles to punish. By junior year, he'd taken issue with anyone who'd looked sideways at him and had the power to back it up.

And he'd done just that a few too many times for the principal's liking and pretty much everyone else in town whose kid he'd beaten up.

The military had given him a purpose and an outlet for all his anger, not to mention a target to focus on. He'd gone from hating the world and blaming everyone for his hard-luck upbringing to being able to set it all aside and compartmentalize his emotions. His childhood had had all the usual trappings that came with a drunk for a father who apparently couldn't stand the sight of his own child. As for his mother, she'd been a saint to him until she'd up and disappeared. The Houdini act had made Daniel Brewer hate his son even more. The man could rot in hell for all Brewer cared after what he'd ultimately done. As far as his mother went…what kind of person left a five-year-old behind to live with a drunk? Her sainthood had been short-lived as far as he was concerned. It had died along with all his love for her.

Brewer fished his burner cell out of his pocket. He fired off a text to his buddy to say this was him on a new number and to pick up. Then, Brewer put the phone to his left ear and made a call. The burner phone was new since he'd turned his old one over to the US Marshals Service for safekeeping. It was too late to regret the move now.

His buddy picked up on the second ring. "Trent, hey, it's me."

"Dude, I tried to call you." Trent Thomas breathed heavy like he was in the middle of a run. "What happened to your phone?"

"I borrowed this one." He hoped Trent wouldn't ask any more questions. They'd been military buddies early on in Brewer's career, Trent having been the closest thing to a friend in basic training when they'd both had their backsides handed to them.

A disgruntled grunt came through the line. "I had no idea what that bastard was really up to, Brew."

"Figured you didn't," Brewer reassured his buddy. The two had gone to the same middle school, high school, and boot camp. They hadn't really gotten to know each other until the latter. They forked in different directions after basic.

Then Trent had been a godsend when Brewer had medically boarded out of the Army. He'd been the first to make calls to find work for Brewer, work that had given him a reason to keep going after his life-changing injury. And now the job put his life in jeopardy. There was no way Trent could have known Crane wasn't the head of a legitimate company as they'd been told. Brewer's buddy would never do that to him.

"I feel like a real jerk for putting you in that position, dude. Especially after what you've been through and all."

"Don't sweat it," Brewer reassured. "Besides, this'll all be over in two shakes, and I'll be on the hunt for a new job."

"What can I do to help?"

He knew Trent would come through. "I need a place to hide out for a few days until I can figure out my next move. Somewhere off the grid, if you know what I mean."

The line went quiet for a few seconds that felt like minutes as Brewer turned on the spigot to wash his hands.

"I can help with that, Brew. No problem." He rattled off coordinates that Brewer entered into his cell after telling his friend to hold so he could dry his hands.

"I'll owe you big-time for this, Trent."

"Consider it payback for the position I put you in," Trent

said with a voice heavy with remorse. He wasn't normally an emotional guy, so the intensity registered as odd.

After what he'd been through in the past twenty-four hours that had led him to standing in front of a bathroom mirror in a roadside café made him more than ready to get off the grid, where he could catch his meals and cook his own food. Civilization wasn't as civilized as he'd wanted it to be.

"I'll be in touch when I can." He ended the call on the off chance someone was listening. Freedom was near. All he had to do was ditch the marshal sitting in the parking lot and get on the road.

After entering the coordinates into his map feature, he smiled. This place was so remote, all that showed on the screen was a patch of trees. Near the Texas-Louisiana border close to Tyler, he could easily see himself getting lost and finally finding some peace until time to go to trial.

So why was his first thought that he didn't want to disappoint the blue-eyed, ponytail-wearing marshal sitting out front?

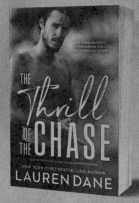
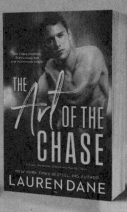

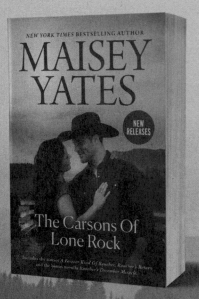